Advance Praise for *The Midwife*

"Jolina Petersheim's lyrical storytelling absolutely sings— but it's her quick-paced plot, complex characters, and insights into the Plain world that made it impossible for me to put *The Midwife* down."

LESLIE GOULD
Bestselling author of *The Amish Midwife*

"Masterfully told . . . riveting . . . with enough twists and turns to surprise any reader. I promise this story will make you think, pull at your heartstrings, and keep you turning pages until the end."

SALOMA MILLER FURLONG
Author of *Bonnet Strings: An Amish Woman's Ties to Two Worlds*

"The bonds of motherhood and choices made ripple across generations in this powerful story that challenges the reader to examine modern-day ethics in light of eternal truths. A story of hope and restoration, *The Midwife* is a tale to be savored."

CARLA STEWART
Award-winning author of *The Hatmaker's Heart*

"*The Midwife* is a stunning narrative that explores maternal attachment in all its forms and God's all-encompassing care and plan. Ms. Petersheim colors outside the lines with her unique writing style, and I have once again fallen in love with her work."

KELLIE COATES GILBERT
Author of *A Woman of Fortune*

"In *The Midwife*, Jolina Petersheim's thoughtful storytelling illustrates how God's love can woo us from pain and hiding into the abundant life He has created."

DENISE HILDRETH JONES
Author of *Secrets Over Sweet Tea*

P9-CSE-557

"*The Midwife* reads like a story that's been unearthed instead of imagined. Decades of pain and rejection are peeled away slowly, deftly. Jolina Petersheim weaves a brilliant story that lets us absorb the years and grow with her characters. By the time they're ready to consider the risk of holding out and the cost of letting go, so are we."

SHELLIE RUSHING TOMLINSON
Belle of All Things Southern and author of *Heart Wide Open*

"Englisch and Mennonite worlds collide in this poetically written story, layered with intrigue, mystery, and redemption. With a large cast of characters, readers are sure to find a version of themselves and the gift of hope in the pages of *The Midwife*."

ELIZABETH BYLER YOUNTS
Author of *Promise to Return*

Praise for *The Outcast*

"Petersheim makes an outstanding debut with this fresh and inspirational retelling of Nathaniel Hawthorne's *The Scarlet Letter*. Well-drawn characters and good, old-fashioned storytelling combine in an excellent choice for Nancy Mehl's readers."

LIBRARY JOURNAL, STARRED REVIEW

"Petersheim's emotional story leaves readers intrigued by the purity of Rachel's strong will, resilience, and loyalty."

PUBLISHERS WEEKLY

"Like Hawthorne, Petersheim clearly dramatizes the weight of sin, but she deviates from the original by leaving room for repentance."

WORLD MAGAZINE, CHOSEN AS A "NOTABLE BOOK"

"Surprising and satisfying, this epic first novel of love and betrayal, forgiveness and redemption will resonate with people from every corner of life."

RIVER JORDAN
National bestselling author of *Praying for Strangers*

"From the first word until the last, *The Outcast* captivates and charms, reminding us that forgiveness and love are two of life's greatest gifts. A brilliant must-read debut novel."

RENEA WINCHESTER
Author of *In the Garden with Billy: Lessons about Life, Love & Tomatoes*

"*The Outcast* is an insightful look at the complexities of living in community while living out one's faith."

KAREN SPEARS ZACHARIAS
Author of *Will Jesus Buy Me a Doublewide? 'cause I need more room for my plasma TV*

"[This] riveting portrait of life behind this curious and ofttimes mysterious world captivated me from the first word and left me breathless for more."

LISA PATTON
Bestselling author of *Whistlin' Dixie in a Nor'easter*

"I have to say I've never been a fan of the Amish fiction genre. I'm still not. But Jolina Petersheim's *The Outcast* was the only Amish fiction book I've ever read from cover to cover."

IRA WAGLER
USA Today & *New York Times* bestselling author of *Growing Up Amish*

"A story of hypocrisy and redemption in a secretive community that will keep the reader turning the pages."

MICHAEL MORRIS
Award-winning author of *Man in the Blue Moon*

the
MIDWIFE

JOLINA PETERSHEIM

Tyndale House Publishers, Inc.
Carol Stream, Illinois

Visit Tyndale online at www.tyndale.com.

Visit Jolina Petersheim online at www.jolinapetersheim.com.

TYNDALE and Tyndale's quill logo are registered trademarks of Tyndale House Publishers, Inc.

The Midwife

Designed by Dean H. Renninger

Edited by Kathryn S. Olson

Published in association with Ambassador Literary Agency, Nashville, TN.

Some Scripture taken from the Holy Bible, *New International Version*, *NIV.*®
Copyright © 1973, 1978, 1984, 2011 by Biblica, Inc.® Used by permission of Zondervan. All rights reserved worldwide. www.zondervan.com.

Some Scripture quotations are taken from the *Holy Bible*, King James Version.

The Midwife is a work of fiction. Where real people, events, establishments, organizations, or locales appear, they are used fictitiously. All other elements of the novel are drawn from the author's imagination.

Library of Congress Cataloging-in-Publication Data
Petersheim, Jolina.
 The midwife / Jolina Petersheim.
  pages ; cm
 ISBN 978-1-4143-7935-7 (sc)
1. Midwives—Fiction. 2. Mennonites—Fiction. 3. Single women—Fiction. 4. Christian fiction. I. Title.
 PS3616.E84264M53 2014
 813'.6—dc23   2014005592

Printed in the United States of America

20   19   18   17   16   15   14
7   6   5   4   3   2   1

In memory of our unborn child, whom we will hold again,
and to all those who have lost. May you receive beauty for ashes.

ACKNOWLEDGMENTS

How do you even begin to thank all those who have helped you put ink to paper?

Firstly, to my Tyndale team, composed of Karen Watson, Stephanie Broene, Kathy Olson, Maggie Rowe, Julie Dumler, Shaina Turner, and all those whom I might not interact with on a regular basis, but who make things run so smoothly behind the scenes: Thank you for believing in my rough-cut stories and for providing the tools to make them shine.

To my agent, Wes Yoder: Again, it's been a privilege to work with you. Thank you for your wisdom and dependability during every step of the publishing and life journey. You have been such a blessing to me.

To my wordsmith-partners-in-crime, many of whom I have never even met but whom I still count as cherished friends: You all have gone above and beyond the call of duty to help my writing find its way into readers' hands. Thank you, thank you; I want to be sure to offer that same helping hand when your books are birthed. We need this community more than ever before.

To my readers: Well, I could not be writing this if not for you. Thanks for giving a fledgling writer a chance and for offering your support through word-of-mouth, messages, and reviews. Each of you has become so very dear to me. I hope our paths cross in person soon.

To my midwife, Robin: From that winter night two years ago when I sprinted the fire-escape stairs of the birthing center to increase my contractions so I wouldn't have to go to the hospital, to this recent fall morning I called you, sobbing, to tell you of the loss of our unborn child, you have been there for me. Thank you for your steadfast maternal love for those of us who are in the process of becoming mothers ourselves. You are a gift to womanhood, and I am honored to call you friend.

To my best friend, Misty: No acknowledgements would be complete without letting you know how dear you are to me. Though miles may separate us, we will forever remain neighbors and sisters in my heart.

To my parents and siblings, from both maiden Miller and married Petersheim sides: As the years pass, I no longer see a division between law and love. We have truly become one family. Thank you for the prayers, the laughter, and—yes—even the tears. We are so blessed to have you in our lives.

To my daughter, my Balm of Gilead, who is right now waking up in her crib: I pray that you will know in your heart that you have been cherished since conception. Rest assured in the fact that you are loved to the heights and to the depths, and that your father and I would go to both measures to protect you. Yet we know that before you were ours, you were his—your Creator's. And so we daily entrust him with your precious life.

I would like to thank my gem of a husband, who—through hardship and triumph—has truly become my other, sometimes better, half. God sure knew what he was doing when he put your logical self into my zany life. Thanks for always being my first reader, and for being patient with me until I heed your thoughtful advice. I could not do any of this without you, nor would I want to try. I'll love you forever.

Lastly, I thank my Creator for giving me the idea for *The Midwife* shortly after my own daughter's birth, and for orchestrating the timing, so that I would begin the editorial process after the loss of our unborn child, when I needed to find healing through this panacea of story. Thank you for giving me strength to offer others hope. May they see your light reflected on every page.

PROLOGUE

I saw you that day we came to Tennessee to take your
daughter—and their daughter—back. The Fitzpatricks
carried the child out to the rental car and placed her like
a bundled heirloom in my arms. She was half-asleep and
fragrant from her nap, and she yawned and cuddled right
against my chest as if she had always been there. Thom and
Meredith went back inside to gather the rest of her things,
and that's when you crossed the yard and looked at the
car—and it seemed that you were looking right at me.

I could feel your eyes boring through the tinted glass
and seeing the woman who had abandoned you holding
tight to your child. I wanted to go to you. I hope you
know this. I wanted to ask your forgiveness, but I was still
too afraid. I could barely recognize you beneath your Plain
clothes, and I could see in your bearing that you were
stronger than before.

What if you hated me? You had every right. It was
better not to know.

So I remained silent. I remained a coward. I locked the doors and kissed the child's warm forehead. I pressed my back against the seat and breathed. I watched you walk up those porch steps like a lamb to the slaughter. Inside the house, I knew, you would learn that you would never see your daughter again. . . .

part
ONE

1

Beth, 1995

Nine minutes after the chapel bells heralded the first academic session, Dr. Thomas Fitzpatrick came into the department. His glasses were snow-spotted and the toggles of his peacoat off by one. Keeping my fingertips on the keyboard, I watched him walk the length of carpet down to his office. Then I looked at the computer screen. *Winslow, Beth (1995)*, it read. *Solomon's Choice: Finding an Ethical Solution for Remorseful Surrogates. Master's Thesis, Simms University.* My heart beat double-time with the computer cursor's pulse. From the cabinet, I took Thom's favorite cup and saucer, poured water from the kettle on the hot plate, dolloped the PG Tips with cream, and carried it down the hall.

I pushed the door open farther and stood in the entrance, waiting. Located near the radiator, Thom's office was humid. It smelled of thawing wool and frostbitten winter. Gold-embossed collector's editions from Gray's well-known *Anatomy of the Human Body* to the rare *A Discourse upon Some Late Improvements of the Means for Preserving the Health of Mariners* were stacked in teetering heaps throughout the room. From experience, I knew they were organized in a labyrinth only Thom could traverse.

Wall-to-wall shelves were bookended with souvenirs from Meredith's and his trips overseas: an urn filled with pottery shards gathered from shores whose waters harbored a flooded Grecian city; a child-sized drum, its top stretched taut with buckskin; an aboriginal mask whose mouth gaped into a yawn. Despite these variegated treasures, the books were the only things Thom was particular about. The only things he did not want touched.

Thom had shed his coat. Beneath it, he wore the tweed blazer with the stamped brown buttons and worn leather patches on the elbows that always made him too hot during his animated lectures. His yellow scarf hung from the back of his swivel chair and coiled up on the floor. A cup and saucer with cream skimming the surface of yesterday's tea sat like a paperweight on the notes scattered across his desk. Thom's desk, the rolltop slid back, was centered beneath a rectangle window that was flush with the ground outside the basement offices and whose ledge was piled almost to the top with snow. This allowed just enough natural light to reveal the floating dust that permeated the air in the ancient brick building.

"Dr. Fitzpatrick?"

Thom's head came up. His fountain pen paused on a note that, even after a year as his graduate assistant, I still could not decipher. Swiveling his chair to face me, he blinked, his great mind awakening from some cerebral dream. "Hello, Miss Beth," he said. His British accent was distinct, even after twenty years in the States.

Crossing the room, I set the saucer beside the one I had brought yesterday and took one step back. Then I looked at the pennies glinting in my polished loafers and said, "I just came to tell you that . . ." I paused. "The second beta test doubled to 437. We still need an ultrasound to confirm the heartbeat. But it looks like you and Meredith . . ." The words faltered behind my smile. "You and Meredith are going to have a baby."

"A baby?" Thom stared at me a moment—apparently captivated by the news we had so long anticipated—and then squinted at the calendar above his desk. I could see the date, circled in red, when my twenty-two-year-old uterus had received one grade A and two grade B fertilized embryos belonging to Thom and Meredith. "That's wonderful. What are you—" he calculated the days by tapping his fingertips on his thumb—"fifteen days post transfer?"

I nodded.

"It will be around September, then?"

"Yes." I swallowed. "Mid-September."

He said, "Meredith and I were married in September."
I had a hard time envisioning the woman, who had participated in the IVF with an air of martyrdom, as a younger,
blushing bride. He continued, "You have any idea what it is?"

Even after the procedures that let me stand in my professor's office with his child tucked inside my womb, the
intimacy of our conversation felt wrong. He needed to be
having this discussion with his wife, Meredith, who was
already back at work, despite the surgery that had reset the
reproductive schedule of the affluent Fitzpatrick lives.

"No idea," I lied, when I already sensed a girl. "How're
you going to tell Meredith?"

"Not sure." He sighed. "Take her out for dinner?" Thom
was silent, contemplating this. Then he picked his glasses up
and hooked them behind his ears. "A baby," he repeated with
that same whispered awe. The tortoiseshell frames pushed up
on his cheeks as he smiled. "How're you feeling?"

I ducked my head. "Really, Dr. Fitzpat—" My cheeks
flushed. "Thom, I mean." I dared to look up now that
his glasses were in place; a barrier between us, transparent
though it was. "I'm fine. I've done this before."

"I forget sometimes," he admitted. "But promise you'll
let me know if you're feeling any nausea, and we'll cut back
on your hours or divide your work load with Suzanne."

I nodded and broke eye contact. I did not want Thom to
see my confusion surrounding the dynamics of our relationship, which was quickly becoming so hard to define. I
pointed to the fresh cup of tea I'd set beside his desk.

He took an obligatory sip and dabbed the side of

his mouth with the back of his hand. "Perfect," he said. "Thank you."

Tears needled my eyes. Hair brushing hot cheeks, I collected yesterday's cup and saucer and left his office without letting the painted knob catch. Taking a seat at my desk, I stared at the computer screen and typed:

This year, over four hundred babies were born to surrogate mothers within the United States, and many of these children will never be held by those who carried them. Although many options exist for the creation of a family, such as foster care and adoption—

Breathing hard, I held Delete until the page went blank, turned off the computer, and cradled my face in my hands.

This is a business transaction, I told myself.

That is all.

As I sat across from Thom and Meredith Fitzpatrick, I had to wonder how they had come to this place. Not to the restaurant with its mahogany tables and menu whose only entry I could pronounce was *hors d'oeuvres,* but how they'd come to be married that fall day a few years after my birth. Albeit unversed in the psychology of marital relationships, as I'd never been married myself, I at least knew the rule that opposites attract. Perhaps Thom had once been as drawn to Meredith's domineering personality as she'd been to his passive one. Yet I had never seen a couple who seemed so far apart, and here I was six weeks pregnant with a child who would make them a family.

"You won't drink, will you?" asked Meredith, watching me over her glass of wine that probably cost more than I spent on a week's worth of groceries.

I shook my head, clearing my throat to reply, "No, ma'am," as anything else would sound rude to someone accustomed to subservience.

Thom's laughter was too brittle to cover his frustration. "Come on, Meredith. She's already been through the screening process."

"You're exercising? Eating properly?" she continued, ignoring him.

Beneath the table, I placed a hand against my unsettled stomach. "Yes," I replied.

Meredith leaned back as the waiter slid onto the table salmon ribboned across a bed of lettuce. "And you're able to juggle pregnancy and graduate school?" She flicked open a napkin and draped it over her lap.

I said, "Yes," and smiled at the waiter, who set before me a long wooden paddle with a browned artisan loaf and a small bowl of walnut pesto. Though it was meant as an appetizer, it was the only meal my stipend could afford. The Fitzpatricks had offered to pay for my meal, but I declined their offer out of pride. I didn't want the division line between us to become nebulous with favors. "I haven't had any morning sickness," I continued. "And I didn't with my previous pregnancy. So . . . I should be fine." I hated how inadequate I felt. Not like someone capable of safely bearing the Fitzpatrick's child.

"Yes. About that . . ." Meredith set down her fork. "Why didn't you want to keep the child?"

The ease with which she asked me, a complete stranger who happened to be incubating her offspring, such a personal question sucked the breath from my lungs. Closing my eyes, my mind reeled with the image of that precious baby in my arms, who had looked around the delivery room with the same remarkable, two-toned irises as his father. I recalled the blue cap I'd knitted during freshman biology peeking above the striped blanket. The petals of his tiny pink hand reaching out to twine the stem of my smallest finger. How the Mennonite midwife, Deborah Brubaker, had allowed me to nurse him as a wrenchingly beautiful gift to me.

After I'd signed the release forms that allowed the adoptive parents to pick my child up and take him away, Deborah had come into my hospital room and switched off the television. I had turned it to a morning talk show discussing the second anniversary of *In re Baby M*—the infamous custody battle that resulted in America's first court ruling in favor of surrogacy. Surrogate mother Mary Beth Whitehead had been granted visitation rights to the child she had carried for William and Elizabeth Stern, known as "Baby M." Whitehead had birthed the child and relinquished her as contracted, but twenty-four hours later, Whitehead demanded that she be given back by threatening suicide. Once the Sterns returned the child, Whitehead had fled New Jersey, taking the newborn with her. The Sterns had tied up the Whiteheads' bank accounts and issued a warrant to arrest Mary Beth and her husband.

From my rapt expression while watching the talk show, Deborah must have sensed the case was giving my eighteen-year-old heart foolish hope that, though my son's adoption was closed, if I simply demanded he be given back as Whitehead had done, one day I could hold him again. Deborah had silenced my protests when the television screen faded to black and dropped the remote into the pocket of her scrubs. Then she'd crossed the room and held my forehead with one cool hand. At this foreign, maternal touch, I'd recoiled and buried my face in the hospital pillow. Deborah, as if sensing the deeper hurt beneath my loss, began to sing Pennsylvania Dutch lullabies until my angry sobbing and the contractions shrinking my vacant womb had ceased.

Thom's steak knife clattered to his plate. I opened my eyes, drawn back to the present. "My word, Meredith," he said from between his teeth. "This dinner's to celebrate the pregnancy, not spring an interrogation."

Meredith faced her husband. He stared back, unflinching beneath the wielded scalpel of her gaze. I then realized that Thomas Fitzpatrick might not be as passive as I thought. I wondered what else about him might not be as I'd thought. Wearing a black suit coat accented with brass cuff links and his unruly hair slicked with gel, he looked as refined and wealthy as his wife, not the prototypical absent-minded professor with perpetually smudged spectacles and tea-splotched notes layering his desk.

"I just want her to understand how serious this is," said Meredith.

I sat there stunned, wondering how she could say that—how she could ask me these things—when we had both endured the clinical and psychological screenings. When we had both received injections for the synchronization of our cycles, gone through the ovarian and endometrial stimulation, the monitoring, the egg retrieval and transfer. The entirety of the in vitro fertilization procedure had been invasive if not painful, and I was just at the beginning with thirty-four more weeks to go.

Thom said, "Her name's Beth."

"Okay, then. I want *Beth* to understand how serious this is."

The harsh undertones in the way Meredith said my name drew me up short. I shivered, although she had reserved a table for us near the fire. I said, "I'll take good care of your child."

Her blue eyes ricocheted away from her husband and back to me. In them I read uncertainty, doubt, jealousy, and I found myself questioning what kind of mother she would make. But I wouldn't let myself stop to think any further. I couldn't. This was a business transaction, I reminded myself; that was all. With the money from their check, I could pursue my PhD in bioethics and say good-bye to Thomas Fitzpatrick and to the child of his that I had birthed.

Meredith picked her fork up and set it down again. Leaving her napkin draped across the seat, she stood and picked up her purse. "Excuse me," she said.

Thom and I watched his wife stride across the restaurant in a pair of heels that glinted beneath her dress pants. He said, still watching her, "It's not your fault, Beth."

I looked down at the table. "Your wife's protective. I think—I think that would be normal in a situation like this."

Across the restaurant, crystal rang in a toast.

"Hey—" Thom reached across the table to touch the radial artery on the inside of my wrist. It thrummed to life. I could picture the warm blood rushing up through the vessels in my arm and pouring into my heart. "I hope you know what this means to me. To us."

A year and a half since my graduate assistantship had assigned me to Thomas Fitzpatrick—the quiet, unobtrusive man with an Opie Taylor cowlick and a surprisingly boyish grin. A year and a half since I had become the grader of his multiple-choice tests. The one who rinsed his delicate teacups and located his slides on the Law of the Three Ps and refilled his Montblanc fountain pens with fresh ink. And this—*this*—was the first time he showed me any affection.

For the length of time it took another ember to fall, I sat motionless and savored the feel of his fingertips grazing my skin. I withdrew my hand, curling it in my lap as if it had been struck. "You're welcome," I said. I had never been one for words.

Thom's wife returned, her lips pinched and her purse tucked beneath her arm. His smile faded. He slid out of the seat to stand beside her. In heels, Meredith Fitzpatrick was a head taller than he was. It was amazing that after all the time I'd sat in Boswell Auditorium and watched him give lectures on Nigel Cameron's article "Embryos and Ethics" and Kenneth Alpern's *The Ethics of Reproductive Technology*, I'd never once realized that Thomas Fitzpatrick was not larger than life, but a rather short, middle-aged man.

"It was nice to see you," Meredith said.

I said, "You too." Her smile made me question the sincerity of her words.

"I'll see you on Tuesday, then?" Thom asked me.

"Something for . . . ?" said Meredith.

"Not for the baby," Thom replied. "For her thesis."

Meredith said nothing else. Thom retrieved her coat from the maître d' and held it by the shoulders while she slid it over her arms, the silk lining slipping easily over her white cashmere sweater. Thom leaned over to give me a rather awkward side hug. Meredith shook my hand. By the lines bracketing the bright slash of her mouth, I knew she would despise me for prolonging an unbearable evening if I asked them to drive me to my car.

So I sat on one of the velvet benches flanking the restaurant's entrance, as if I were simply waiting for the valet to bring my car around. I smiled as Thom opened the front door for Meredith. The foyer filled with a blast of cold. Outside, the balding valet with the earmuffs reached into the pocket of his parka and dangled car keys in front of Thom. Loneliness and sadness engulfed me. I watched the Fitzpatricks drive away, their headlights barely penetrating the sleet propelled by gale-force winds.

Sure that they'd gone, I exited the restaurant. The

huddled valets in their black dress slacks, black shoes, and downy parkas reminded me of emperor penguins awaiting the passage of winter. The valet with earmuffs nodded; the others barely glanced my way. I hunched my shoulders around my neck and, in my thin loafers, retraced the two blocks to La Trattoria. The checkered awning was bent with the weight of snow. An unlit neon sign claimed that twenty-four hours a day pizza was sold by pie or slice. The sign on the door said *Closed*.

With numb fingers, I pried open the frozen driver's-side door of my car. As the windows defrosted, I grabbed a cassette tape, got out, and scraped a circle in the icy windshield. Clambering back into the driver's seat, I sat on my hands and then blew on them. I'd just started to grow warm when the personal risk of this business transaction hit me. I began to shake so hard, my teeth clattered. I held my knees together to keep my legs from trembling. Out of all the mistakes I had made, signing on as the Fitzpatricks' gestational surrogate could turn out to be the worst.

Rhoda, 2014

Perching the basket on my hip, I scale the porch steps and enter the kitchen, letting the screen door slam. I dump the pole beans in the sink and set the basket on the countertop. Keeping my back to Alice, I start snapping.

Her hands, which have been slicing flattened dough

into squares, grow still. "People need to know we're out here, Rhoda."

"They already do, or they wouldn't have sent that journalist."

"They don't give real journalists these kinds of stories."

"If she's not a real journalist," I say, "then why'd you bother talking to her?"

"I had to. Something's gotta change."

The beans are so dehydrated from the sun, I have to score my thumbnail into the flesh to sever the ends. But nothing can be wasted. Not anymore. "We're fine."

"You keep saying that, but pregnant girls can't live on pot pie and green beans alone."

I toss a bean into the bowl and grip the edge of the countertop. Stress coils around me until every ligament in my body feels like a bowstring. "I *know* what they need."

"Of course you do." Alice walks over and places a hot, floured hand on my arm. It is all I can do not to swat it away. "The Lord knows you took good care of me and Uriah," she says. "But times—they were different then. We had more food. We had more help. And your job was just to take care of us girls, not manage a farm at the same time."

I stare down at the old stone bowl I've painstakingly filled with shriveled beans and resist the impulse to knock it to the floor.

Almost eighteen years ago, while helping maneuver a posterior baby down the birth canal, former head midwife Fannie Graber suffered a slipped disk, a painful graze

of nerves against bone that forced her into early retire-
ment and forced me into her position at the tender age of
twenty-four. Ever since that night when I found myself
doing what I never thought I would, I've been caught
between my desire to make Hopen Haus a success—by
begging the Old Order Mennonite church to let us have
electricity and state-of-the-art equipment—and my desire
to keep Hopen Haus as archaic as possible so that my previous life and the secrets pervading it can remain sheltered
from the outside world.

But now that a majority of the Dry Hollow Community
has left—seeking promises of better jobs and more land—I
still find myself crouching behind a list of rules no bishop
is here to enforce. Perhaps we should have gone with the
community as they wished, yet I couldn't. And although
the invitation remains open, I still can't. Hopen Haus,
which translates to Hope House in English, is not my life.
It is the place where my life ended. And so, haunted by
memories made stronger by the location where they were
formed, I cannot leave.

Alice does not understand this. She does not understand
why we did not leave when most of the community did.
She does not understand why I demand that our lives and
the lives of the girls who come here remain Plain—though
we enforce no dress code beyond modesty—nor does she
understand my hesitance to ask the townspeople for help.

I should not expect her to.

Two months after my daughter's birth, I helped birth
Alice Rippentoe's illegitimate son, Uriah, a long-limbed

creature whose dark complexion and stormy disposition contrast the Hebrew meaning of his name—"my light is Jehovah."

If Hopen Haus draws publicity and a real journalist digs deeply enough that the skeletons in my life are revealed, it will not dramatically affect Uriah's life. But me? This life, ushering other mothers' children into the world while never having a child to call my own . . . this is the only life I've got.

Returning to her pubic bone tattooed with Aquarius, I inch my way back up the center of Star's stomach a centimeter at a time. My three fingers dip in the hollow where her uterus drops off and her abdominal cavity begins. This is the fourth time I've measured twenty-two weeks. According to her chart, she's supposed to be twenty-five.

"Everything okay?"

I nod, as I am unable to trust my tongue. If Star wants somebody to hold her hand through the next fifteen weeks, she needs to get Alice or Charlotte to do her checkups, not me. Each time I've examined Star, she's reeked of cigarettes. Yet when I informed her about the effects of nicotine on an unborn child—increased risk of stillbirth, premature delivery, calcified placenta, low birth weight—she's stared right into my eyes and denied having an addiction.

The ocher stains on her teeth contradict her words.

Star dusts off the seat of her jeans and, as she leaves the room, pats five-year-old Luca Cullum's head, who's been outside the door, whining like a puppy. Though I've spoken to his mother, Terese, about his frequent interruptions, Luca still comes in without asking and hops up on the sanded slab serving as our examination table. Swinging his legs back and forth, he reaches over and slips the silver top off the largest glass jar. He shakes his dirty-blond mop to the side and attempts to use what he must believe is a giant Q-tip to clean out his ears.

I roll my eyes at his lack of manners and file Star's folder under *S*, since she won't tell us her last name. "Need something, Luca? I've got some work to do."

"Yeah'um." Luca claps the lid back on the glass cylinder. I wince, sure that he's cracked it. "There's news people outside," he says.

"News people?" Sliding hands beneath Luca's armpits, I lower him to the floor and unfurl a sheet over the table in preparation for the next appointment. "Luca. Really."

"I ain't lying." He whips out his cotton swab and points it to the window. "Go look."

I raise an eyebrow but walk over to the window and peel back the curtain Charlotte sewed to ensure the girls' privacy. My jaw drops. A long black van scrawled with the silver words "Channel 2 News" is parked at a cockeyed angle in front of the east steps. A man in a collared shirt and khakis holds a microphone before Charlotte's quivering mouth. Another man dressed in a T-shirt and jeans snaps pictures of Alice.

Dropping the curtain, I turn to Luca, who just smiles.

"See," he says. "Told ya there was."

2

Rhoda, 2014

Supper at Hopen Haus is a family affair. Everyone is
required to attend, even if battling late-afternoon nausea
that redefines morning sickness. I take my seat at the head
of the two tables made uniform with mismatched cloths
and watch the four girls clamber over the benches at speeds
proportional to their bellies' sizes. Everyone quiets as I lower
my head to signal the silent grace. Afterward, the girls begin
to talk and greedily consume the meal: sautéed kale doused
with vinegar, *grummbeere supp*, and radish sandwiches stuffed
with crumbling portions of the goat cheese Uriah made
before he went to Canada with Wilbur Byler.

My appetite has vanished. I have a difficult time being grateful for such meager fare. Hopen Haus is at its lowest capacity since Fannie Graber founded it twenty-five years ago, yet we cannot take many more boarders without someone going hungry. I look down the table again—imagining where these girls would live if we were forced to close our doors.

Our youngest boarder, Desiree Jones, is fifteen weeks pregnant and fifteen years old. She has slick pigtails that poof out behind her ears, and a mocha baby face contrasted by a chip on her shoulder as large and scathing as her mouth. Desiree's social worker brought her to us from the projects in Knoxville, and here Desiree will remain until her mother's child-abuse allegation goes to court.

Terese Cullum is in her late twenties. She has pale blonde dreadlocks bound in a kerchief and wears peasant skirts and chunky turquoise rings, the latter of which she refuses to take off regardless of her body's rising water retention. At twenty-eight-weeks pregnant, she shows signs of early-onset preeclampsia. She and her five-year-old son, Luca, hitchhiked here from southern Tennessee. Her boyfriend—who fathered her unborn baby, but not Luca—abandoned Terese at a rest stop without so much as a dime.

Our driver, Wilbur Byler, brought sixteen-year-old Lydie Risser to us four months ago. Wilbur said Lydie was from the Split Rock Community in Kentucky, and that though Lydie's parents had hired him to drive her to Hopen Haus, they hadn't told him that she was even with child. But as she clambered out of the van in her cape dress and long twin braids, the humiliation singeing Lydie's cheeks explained it all.

I know how Star arrived, but I am not sure who dropped her off. One morning, just after dawn, I heard the crackle of tires on the lane and crawled from beneath the quilts on my bed to look out the window. A heavyset girl was leaning against the open passenger door of a small white truck. She wore baggy jeans and a sweatshirt, as it was March and cold. Her hair was the only circumspect thing about her; it was short and twisted into stiff purple spikes. The girl suddenly flung out her arms, arguing. A backpack sailed out of the interior of the vehicle—hitting her stomach.

She staggered backward, clutching the burden. The truck then bounced down the washed-out lane. The girl kept watching until the taillights had winked out around the bend near the old cattle chute. And then she dropped her backpack, clutched her hair with both hands, and cried. Even after I sent Charlotte outside to welcome the girl in, she refused to tell us anything beyond what would soon become obvious: she was newly pregnant and alone.

Charlotte now mistakes the reason for my sullen demeanor and reaches over to pat my hand. "Maybe they didn't air the story," she soothes, a natural *grossmammi*, even though she's neither been married nor had a child. "It's been a week, and we've not heard anything yet."

She goes back to spooning her soup. I pull both hands below the table and curl them into fists. To my right, Alice's gaze brands my skin. When I meet it, she shifts away. Her guilty silence speaks volumes.

"Oh, they've used it," I say, watching as below her white *kapp*, the tips of Alice's ears slowly turn red.

Alice Rippentoe was baptized into Dry Hollow Community's Old Order Mennonite church one year after I was. But differences of opinion, such as her wanting publicity for Hopen Haus and my despising it, have cropped up countless times since we became midwifery peers. I am grateful for that night, six months before Alice joined the church, when a slipped disk christened my position as reluctant head midwife and gave my opinion more weight than hers.

She cuts her eyes over at me again, the color of them like a thundercloud. "I didn't know the news would pick the story up. Okay, Rhoda? I just thought that journalist—"

"Well, they did," I interrupt. "They picked the story up, and now they've got our pictures, too." When I went outside to send the Channel 2 News team away, an attentive cameraman had taken my photo before I could turn away.

Charlotte shakes her head, heavily buttering a piece of salt-rising *brot* and layering it with red-veined radishes. "*Ach*, such a shame," she murmurs.

Unlike orthodox Charlotte, who's never once stepped foot outside Old Order Mennonite parameters in her fifty-seven years, I am upset not because I believe any captured image is idolatry, but because I've been using this cloistered lifestyle to conceal my past. Now, with that one brilliant flash, everything I have worked so hard to keep in darkness may be revealed.

"Can't we just talk to them?" Alice asks. "Ask them to retract the story due to our religious beliefs?"

I take one fist out from beneath the table and hammer it on top. *"No!"* Panic makes my voice louder than I intend. Star bristles and looks over in alarm. Smiling to reassure her, I lower my voice and lean toward Alice.

"Telling them we want the story retracted will make it seem like we've got something to hide, and they'll come back here to find out what it is." I shake my head. "No, all we can do now is wait and hope it blows over."

<hr />

"Get back here!" The baritone command is still resonating when it is chased by two German shepherds with tawny coats and silvered muzzles. The dogs trot up to the entrance of the dining room and pause while thwacking their plumed tails against the doorframe and smiling.

Hopen Haus's range of boarders is matched only by their family members, who sometimes visit without warning, as if to make sure we are indeed taking care of their kin. Therefore, I am only slightly perplexed by the sound of a stranger's voice and the appearance of his dogs in our dining room. But as the dogs' owner comes to stand in the doorway and I ready my simulated hostess smile in greeting, I look beneath the grizzled beard of the man and see a smooth-faced boy I knew a lifetime ago.

A *life* ago. My smile falters. The room pulses with my sporadic breath.

Seeing my struggle, Alice rises to her feet. Looper lowers his head, and I can spot the slight thinning at the cowlick's curl. He hooks his fingers beneath his dogs' collars. "Sorry," he mutters. "For intruding." And I wonder if Looper is apologizing for intruding on our meal or for intruding on the life that I have built apart from him.

"No need to be sorry," says Alice. I watch her move toward him. My tear-glazed eyes make their bodies waver like a mirage. Cradling his elbow—a habit from her *Englisch* life that she has yet to break—Alice guides Looper over to the high-back chair at the head of the two tables; a position that is the counter-opposite of mine.

He smiles while taking the seat. The matching dimples that I remember comb the graying strands of his beard. "I don't mean to put y'all out," he says. I am caught off guard by his words that are so slow, they sound poured from a jar.

"You're not," Alice says. "We're used to visitors." She pinches off pieces of *brot* and drops them before the old dogs that have padded over and curled in half circles behind Looper's chair. She motions to Lydie to bring another place setting. "Where've you traveled from?"

Looper's eyes slice through the confusion crowding the table and cut me in half. "Wisconsin," he says. He smiles his thanks at Lydie, who sets a bowl steaming with *supp* and clatters silverware beside it. "Originally, I mean. Now . . ." He leans down and runs his hand over the head of the dog closest to him. "Now I live wherever my dogs are allowed to stay too."

"What do you do for a living, Mr. . . . ?" asks Charlotte.

"Just call me Looper." He scoops a spoonful of new *grummbeere* and dumps them into his mouth, gingerly

24

mulching the food and blowing out their trapped heat. "Mainly drywalling," he says. "But I can do excavation, finish carpentry, electricity, plumbing. . . . Guess handyman would be the better title." He drains his Mason jar in one long gulp.

Alice nods at Terese, and she brings the pitcher over from the sideboard and refills his glass with sassafras tea. "And that's why I'm here." Looper wipes his mouth with the cotton napkin, but beads of moisture still cling to his beard.

"Why?" asks Charlotte.

"From what I saw on the news, it looks like this place could use a little sprucing up, and I wondered if you'd allow me to do the job."

The story has aired and Pandora's box has opened.

He looks at me. I swallow hard and unhook my tongue from the dry roof of my mouth. "Perhaps we . . . we can discuss this after the meal?" I ask.

"Of course." Looper smiles, dropping the balled napkin beside his plate.

With my fork, I puncture a red *grummbeere* flecked with parsley. Buttered broth seeps from the holes, but I do not have the strength or the appetite to bring the vegetable to my mouth. I know Looper looks at me for an answer, as do Alice and Charlotte. But with the secrets of our past, I don't know what answer to give.

───※───

Constellations pin themselves to the velveteen night when Looper finally interlaces his hands and rests them on the worn knee of his jeans. "How long you been like this?" he asks.

Though the question's vague, there is no need for him to clarify. I can't imagine how ridiculous he must think I am—wearing the costume of my Plain dress and scraped bun as if I thought that, by assuming a different leading role, I could forget our story. "Eighteen years," I whisper.

"Eighteen years!" He pulls one of my *kapp* strings and barks out a laugh that causes his dogs to lift their heads and look around the yard before seeing nothing of interest and returning to the pillow of their paws. "You were barely eighteen when you left."

"I *know* how old I was." I am grateful the only light comes from the fireflies that lie like a glittering blanket over the field. I am fraught with his disbelief at how young I was then, when I know these intervening years have not been kind.

"It's pretty brilliant," he says. "Dropping off the face of the earth by joining a Mennonite commune." Leaning forward, he digs into the back pocket of his jeans, takes out his wallet, and tosses something onto my lap.

I look down and see a piece of paper folded into a square. Opening it, I can make out a column of words beside a large black-and-white image. The ink is spotty, and the woman featured has her hand up in an attempt to shield her face, as any respectable Mennonite woman would. But even with my *kapp* and altered features, there is no doubt Looper—surfing the Internet—would've instantly recognized me. The bold title reads, "Abandoned

Mennonite Community Becomes Home For Unwed Mothers." I am sure that journalist made me sound like a saint, which only adds to the plethora of lies.

I fold the article—the edges softened with handling—and pass it back. "This is called a community, Looper. Not a commune. And I had no choice."

He snorts. "Beth, you don't know the choices you had."

His use of my real name strips off my costume and shuts off the stage lights. I clench my teeth against the desire to shield my nakedness, when revealing who I am—even for a moment—is the very least this long-suffering man deserves.

"I might not have," I say, "but I know going home wasn't one of them."

"You don't know that."

"And neither do you."

Even the bullfrogs ringing the goat pond grow silent, as if the unspoken words between us have clotted their ballooning throats. Still, Looper says nothing, just clicks his tongue. The dogs heave up arthritic hips and stumble over, panting from the mild exertion and the heat. Easing down onto their haunches, they lean their bodies toward his. Their tails thump an unsteady tempo on the porch boards. Looper gently tugs on their pointed ears and ruffles calloused fingers through their shiny coats. As he does, I do not see the golden gleam of a wedding band. I despise myself for noticing.

"So . . . you're willing to work for room and board?" I ask, pulling us both to safer ground.

"Yeah, Laura Ingalls, I am. Got no bills to pay and nowhere to be, so I'm a free man." Looper leans toward me with his hands still stroking the dogs and knocks his shoulder against mine.

I flinch at his touch and glance over my shoulder at the windows. In the darkness, I can't tell if anyone's watching. "This isn't high school, Looper."

The smile melts off his face like a veneer. "Don't you think I know that?"

"And if you're going to work at Hopen Haus, you need to treat me like your employer."

"But you're not paying me."

"Fine, then. Your peer."

The screen door squeaks as someone pushes it open. I turn and see Star scrounging in the floppy pocket of her bathrobe for the cigarettes that, whenever I search her room, I am never able to find. But then she lifts her head with its smashed razorback of purple hair and sees us sitting on the steps. Dropping the cigarette pack into her pocket, she shuffles back inside and lets the screen door slam.

I emit a disheartened sigh.

Looper brushes a hand in my direction and gets to his feet. "You know, you might look different, but some things about you are the same as they were twenty-four years ago."

I know my indifference makes him angry. But I have shut my heart down for so long, I cannot let myself care— or at least not let him think I do. "And what's that?" I ask.

"You still think you're too smart to let anyone near you, including me."

I stand and fold my arms, bracing myself against the truth of his words. "That's not fair."

"Not fair?" He steps closer. "I'll tell you what's not fair—" His voice hitches. He looks down at the fog filling the enclave of the valley, swirling around the foundations of the homes built in one day by a community now struggling to exist. He looks back at me. When Looper speaks, his voice is calm, though his eyes glow like the fireflies in the field. "Beth . . . Rhoda—or whoever you are—your family and I've spent years trying to find you, so let me tell you: not fair's letting everybody think you're dead."

Beth, 1996

Ned Truitt from Reproductive Endocrinology waved as Thom and I came out of the academic president's office. We waved back. Adjusting his earphones, Ned strolled past us with his heavy backpack bobbing over his white lab coat. Thom and I moved away from the office, but we did not glance at each other or speak. I pushed up my sleeve to check my watch. It was all for show. Throughout that meeting, I'd known just how much time we had left. That's why I had so blithely signed more forms releasing the university from liability concerning their professor's hiring a graduate student to bear his child.

"Want to grab lunch?" I pointed to The Grill, located across from the Student Services Center.

Thom said, "No," and glanced behind him. I looked, too, at the opened white blinds hanging over the glass door centered with the university seal. I could just imagine the president and the dean hunkered over that lacquered table while their eyes peered out at us by the light of the titled green lamp. I knew Thom was thinking this as he said, barely meeting my eyes, "We can't, Beth. Things . . . they must be different now."

My heart contracted. I moved down the steps toward the student post office. Again, it was all for show. Six years had passed since I left my father and younger brother behind. In all that time, I had made little effort to stay connected with my family—inadvertently abandoning them to the same extent my mother had abandoned us. But even if I had stayed in touch, I doubted they would have sent me mail.

My right loafer had just touched the third step when Thom reached down and brushed the edge of my sleeve, that simple gesture girding my threadbare hope. Without looking at him, I climbed back to the landing. Thom took my elbow and led me away from that peering office glass and out the double door. We stood on the covered porch next to the cigarette receptacle that had freshly ground ashes clotting the air.

"You understand. Don't you, Miss Beth?" he said. "Even if we both keep quiet like we've agreed, if students saw us together, they'd assume the worst. And rumors . . . would start."

I looked around the campus, buying time to gather my thoughts. The wind had whipped the snow and salt into meringue. It clung to black branches of the trees marching past the brick buildings with their white columns, towering cupolas, and gilded clocks. Students pressed around us on all sides—scarfing down sandwiches peeking above tinfoil, poring over index cards jammed with notes, chatting with fellow classmates about weekend plans.

Even though it had gotten easier, as many of my graduate school classmates were married and therefore not preoccupied with the frivolity of my undergraduate years, I still felt I was trapped beneath a globe depicting only one season. All around me life transpired, seasons changed, people lived and died, yet I remained the same—stagnant, barren . . . alone.

"But aren't we together now?" I whispered. "Aren't we being seen together now? At the restaurant, you said how much this all meant to you. I thought . . ."

I knew exactly what I had thought, but I could not voice it. Months had passed since that brisk afternoon Dr. Fitzpatrick led me from the office down to the viaduct overlooking the river swollen with crumpled red-and-brown leaves. We had stood side by side, staring straight ahead in silence, until Thom's hesitant voice asked if I'd be willing to carry his and Meredith's child without explaining why Meredith could not carry their child on her own.

That day I first formed Thom's name on my lips within his hearing. I had agreed to gestational surrogacy not because I wanted the money, nor because I had overcome the pain of bearing my child only to give him away. I had agreed because I had never imagined that what I thought would bring Thom Fitzpatrick and me together would actually tear us apart.

Thom now said, "I'm sorry, Beth." He let his outstretched hand fall down to his side, as if it were a physical extension of the futility he felt. "I should never have asked you."

I tried peering through his spectacles to read the meaning behind his words. By the slant of the winter sun, I instead kept seeing my own reflection that was morphed gaunt and featureless by my desperate, watery gaze. "You can't say that." My voice trembled with anger, with fear. Pressing a hand to my stomach, I stared up at him. "You can't. We're too far in to think of taking words back."

Thom nodded sadly and touched my sleeve. Turning, he converged with the throng of students whose white coats and bright scarves fluttered behind them like kites. But even after Thomas Fitzpatrick had crossed the viaduct to the other side of campus, I could still see him. My chest ached watching his ruddy hair and peacoat getting pummeled by the wind. I stood there until my face lost feeling. The belfry chimed the half hour. I remained focused on the hollow sound until I was sure my professor had disappeared from view. I knew then that the phantom promise of love had far stronger coercion than money.

3

Crossing the parking lot, I heard Thom's car door slam.
I moved faster. I could feel his eyes scanning me until my
walk felt ungainly; my head, odd.

"Hold on," he called, jogging to catch up. I heard the
jangle of keys in his hand.

Since the afternoon two weeks before, when we'd met
with the president of academics and the dean, Thom and I
had not talked beyond the standard exchanges my research
project required. I had made sure these exchanges were
as curt and as professional as possible. Thom would not
get the chance to tell me that things had to be different
again. They were different already. This time, however, *I*
was going to be the one who initiated the change. This

was the very reason I had refused Thom's carpool offer and demanded we each drive from the university to the clinic.

Tidbits of asphalt crunched beneath my heel as I reeled to face Thom. I shaded my eyes against the afternoon sun pricking through scattered felt-gray clouds. But more than shielding myself from the sun, I wanted to shield Thom from seeing the pain in my eyes.

"Aren't you worried someone's going to see us?" My voice sounded hostile.

Thom's smile vanished. Taking my elbow, he said, "No, Miss Beth. I'm not worried."

"Where's Meredith?"

His grip on my arm tightened. "Work."

A lean, dark-haired man held the clinic door open for a shuffling pregnant woman who I assumed was his wife. As we passed, they nodded with the familiarity established through common ground. I realized we must look like another quintessential American couple: two kids and a cookie-cutter house guarded by a white picket fence and a dog.

In the clinic, Thom stood beside the fountain until I finished signing in. We both took a seat on one of the faux leather sofas lining the left-hand wall. The corners of my eyelids began to jerk. Thom drummed his knee. *What does he have to be nervous about,* I wondered. If things got out of hand, despite all the legal measures taken to ensure they wouldn't, Thom's wife could simply withhold university donations until her husband's job was reinstated.

At forty-five, Meredith Fitzpatrick was the head

financial adviser for the Catholic hospitals throughout
the nation and had used the university as a convenient,
tax-free catchall for her surfeit of dollars. By accepting her
donations, the university had become a puppet manipulated by Meredith's French-manicured hands. Thus Thom
had become the university's youngest tenured professor
the same year Meredith wrote a check earmarked for the
remodeling of Ridgeview Apartments, where I lived. And
thus, when Thom and Meredith's lawyer sent the university
a confidential memo regarding the commercial surrogacy,
they turned a blind eye to the fact that one of their largest donors was hiring her husband's graduate assistant as
a surrogate.

My graduate assistantship and stipend, on the other
hand, were insured only by my silence. If in a moment
of weakness I failed, I would lose everything.

Thom stopped drumming his knees. He picked up
a magazine about proper prenatal and postpartum care,
which I found ironic. He taught reproductive science,
but I doubted he knew how to care for a child after birth.
Flipping through the pages, he said, "There are things
about this situation you cannot understand."

I looked over at him. "About the pregnancy?"

He nodded. "I should've told you that day I asked you
to become our surrogate." He paused. "But I didn't want
to scare you away. I didn't want you to say no. We had no
other choice, you see. Not on such short notice. When
Meredith went in for her yearly physical, the doctor discovered a benign fibroid in her uterus that had grown to such

an extent, the only way to remove it was to do a complete, radical hysterectomy. Not even her ovaries were allowed to remain. Nothing." Thom paused to flip through the magazine. I knew he was not reading a word.

"She and I'd always planned on having children," he continued. "We talked about it even when she was putting me through medical school. We just wanted to wait until we had traveled some. Until our careers were more established, until we were more financially stable." He laughed. Behind his glasses, his eyes remained somber. "But the years passed, and that 'one day when' never came. Meredith's surgery was our wake-up call. We thought our dream of having children was over. Then I started thinking: Meredith was already on a low-dose contraceptive, so if she started taking Lupron to regulate her pituitary gland and shut down her ovaries, she could begin intramuscular injections to stimulate the growth of follicles on her ovaries."

"Controlled ovarian hyperstimulation," I said.

Thom nodded. "Within two months, the doctor could still give Meredith the complete hysterectomy needed. But while removing her ovaries, he could simply harvest her eggs."

"You just needed a recipient," I said, and then glanced over at the fountain, embarrassed by my candor. This was his wife's reproductive system we were discussing, not a case study in a book.

"Yes," Thom said. "We could harvest the eggs, but after Meredith's hysterectomy, we'd have no womb to plant them in. That's when the truth came out: All these years later,

Meredith still wanted to focus on her career. Still wanted to travel more. She still wanted to focus on her life and not on a child who would have to *become* her life." Thom flipped another page. I wished he would stop the pretense. I wished he would look at me. A woman with a pin-striped skirt and glossy claret heels was called back. Thom draped the magazine across his lap. He did not look at me. "I am the one who made it all happen," he said. "*I* am the one who contacted you . . . the doctors, the lawyers, as I knew that if it did not happen now, it never would."

"Bethany Winslow?"

I glanced up, and the nurse's scanning dark eyes met mine. She smiled and I nodded; Thom and I stood. She asked my birth date at the door and led us through the narrow peach corridor over to a small carpeted room with a scale and a chair. It felt both uncomfortable and intimate to have Thom watching me stand in my stocking feet on the scale. He must have felt as strange as I, for though there was not much to be seen, he kept peering around the room. Every once in a while, his eyes would flick back to my stomach, and then up at my face. I wondered if he hadn't let himself believe what was happening until now. I hadn't let myself believe it either.

"First-time parents?" the nurse asked, pulling the Velcro cuff apart with a dry rasp.

Thom nodded, and I shook my head. There was no easy way to define our relationship. This being a fertility clinic, the nurse must have seen other complicated scenarios. She did not ask any more questions. She just took my blood pressure, then led us to a room that was pale-blue and square with one oblong window facing the west side. Cutaway diagrams of the female anatomy in the three trimesters of gestation were the only art gracing the walls. A model of the reproductive system sat on a Formica countertop next to a deep, stainless steel sink.

"Dr. Hancock will be right with you," the nurse said before pulling the door.

The room echoed with quiet; it felt like the two of us were trapped inside a tomb. I leaned back against the examination table, and the paper covering it crackled. Thom strode the tiled space in between the table and the wall.

"Would you like to take the chair?" I asked. His frenetic movements were making me more nervous than I already was.

Shaking his head, he laced his arms behind his back. "You're sure you don't mind me being here?"

"Thom, it's your child."

He stopped moving, then came back to face me—mere inches away. Behind his glasses, I could see the blue starbursts in his green eyes, the brown freckle dotting the left. "It *is* my child, isn't it?" he said.

I feared he was going to cry. I did not know how I could comfort Thom when I had promised myself that I would not reach out to him again.

Dr. Hancock, the reproductive endocrinologist, came in five minutes after Thom had reined in his emotions and resumed pacing. Crossing the room to shake Thom's hand, she asked how I was feeling and then asked me to lie back on the examination table. My long brown hair spread across the table like a sheet. My mind flashed between past and present, as if confused to which it belonged.

Every movement, every gesture, every sound was a reminder of my previous pregnancy. The fact that I had carried a child to full term, followed by a natural birth, made me a perfect candidate for surrogacy.

The fluorescent lighting bathing the room in a maritime glow faded. I closed my eyes. It was as if I were sitting back at my desk on that late-winter day after the entire bioethics department had gone home. I could almost hear Dr. Fitzpatrick's shuffling gait due to his loose-fitting Birkenstocks.

Then he'd stopped moving so abruptly, I knew that he had seen me. I didn't turn, so he would be unable to perceive my tear-stained face. I heard him shift the strap of the leather satchel crisscrossing his shoulder. "Need a ride?" he'd asked.

I knew he was uneasy, seeing me staring at my computer screen that I had already shut down. But I was too blindsided by grief to offer him reassurance that I was all right. I didn't even know if I was.

When I did not reply, he came and knelt in front of my swivel chair. "Miss Beth?" He reached out as if to touch my hand. He withdrew it and instead searched my eyes. "Are you hurt? Did . . ." He lowered his voice. "Did someone hurt you?"

Alarmed he would think my catatonic state from an

attack on campus, I shook my head and unclenched my fist. I held the crumpled paper out to him. He smoothed it on the thigh of his pant leg before holding it up. His eyes met mine. I could read his bewilderment as easily as I could read the words and numbers on the 4×6 page. It was today's date that I had unthinkingly torn off my small desk calendar in preparation for tomorrow, when I realized what that day was—what that day *meant*. I was shocked to find that so many pages of days had passed since the day that had changed my life forever had come and gone.

"February third," I'd whispered. I stared at Thom's silhouette that was bathed red by the emergency lighting of the basement office. "The day my son was born."

Thom had replied, "Your son?"

A year ago, we were not as close as those weeks leading up to the signing of the contract for the IVF. But I knew it seemed strange to him that I had never revealed this information before now. What Thom did not know was that, besides the staff present during the twenty-four-hour labor and the parents who adopted my child after his birth, I had not revealed this information to anyone. Not even to the child's father, with whom a single dance beneath a starlit Wisconsin sky had blurred the lines between friend and lover.

Perhaps it was the cocoon of the darkened office warmed by the emergency lighting's glow. Perhaps it was having Dr. Thomas Fitzpatrick kneeling down, staring up at me with such empathy that in his glinting spectacles I could see reflected the pain I felt. I don't know what it was about him or about that moment, but before another cathartic tear could fall, I began to peel back the layers of self-protection that had accumulated during my years alone.

I began to tell Thom what nobody knew, what nobody had guessed or asked in all these years. I told him that that day—the third of February—was the birth date of the four-year-old son whom I had given up for adoption. The son I had given away as if he were unwanted, when I had never wanted to keep, to cherish, to hold anyone more. I don't know how long I talked. The words flowed out of me as if a dam had given way. The only way I could keep afloat was by hanging on to the truth, hoping that it was enough to keep me from drowning.

Throughout it all, I cried. I cried the gut-wrenching sobs that, for four years, had caused me to clench my jaw in my sleep and wake with my head trapped in a throbbing fog whose vestiges clung all day. Thom let me cry at my desk, in the darkness, without touching me; without even offering a handkerchief, as I would expect from a man who wore tweed blazers and drank Earl Grey tea from antique cups. But his eyes never left my face until the tears had dried. I found that quality to be more gentlemanly than all the rest.

"You all right?" he'd asked. I heard the worry in his voice.

I found the strength to nod. It was a lie. I had known since that day my signature relinquished my son that a part of me would never be all right again.

"Good." Thom smiled. I saw traces of boyhood still lingering around his mouth. Rocking back on his Birkenstocks, he got to his feet. He went and fetched my boiled wool coat from the rack in the corner of the room near the line of chairs where undergrads came to sit, trying to get an inroad with the professors. I remember how surprised I was that, without asking, Thom had known exactly which coat was mine. Thom held it by the padded shoulders while my arms slipped into it. He kept the door open until I had passed beneath his elbow into the hallway that opened into the wintry night beyond.

I had thought that on the sidewalk, Dr. Fitzpatrick might reach out to me in some way. He didn't. It was as if that darkened office had enveloped us in an intimacy that was lost outside. Instead, we walked in watchful silence until I reached my bike. Thom held the handlebars steady as I worked my right leg over the seat and kicked up the stand. Then he pushed my back gently as I pedaled down the icy sidewalk that would lead me to Ridgeview Apartments, which his wife's money had renovated ten years ago. . . .

Dr. Hancock brought me back to the examining room by squirting warm gel onto my stomach and rolling the sonogram wand above my pubic bone. She was older than I was but younger than Thom. Perhaps thirty-five, forty. She had chin-length black hair sweeping high cheekbones and almond-shaped eyes accented with liner. She wore no jewelry besides chocolate pearl studs. Her hands, as she deftly kneaded my stomach, were warm. On the other side of the room, Thom cleared his throat and averted his eyes as my khakis were unzipped and peeled down below my hip bones.

My vision shifted back to Dr. Hancock as she guided the wand back and forth, harder and harder. The dimples around her mouth deepened. I knew for what she was searching, and my own frenzied heartbeat began to pound throughout the room. Thom moved closer and met my eyes. I saw the fear in them that something was wrong; something that, with our medical knowledge, we still had not foreseen.

"Let me get Dr. Chun," Dr. Hancock said. "He can always find them in a heartbeat."

Thom and I had long crossed the point of lightening tension with humor. We did not smile in return. Thom resumed pacing as we waited; he hadn't made one return trip when he asked, "You haven't spotted, have you?"

My mouth was too dry to speak. I shook my head.

"I'm sure it's nothing," he said after four lengths of pacing. Thom nodded at his own reassurance. Walking over to the window, he split the blinds to peer down at the parking lot. Dr. Chun came in and smiled at me, then saw Thom near the window. Thom turned to face him. I saw that, despite his words of comfort, Thom's skin was as white as the doctor's coat.

"Nervous, Dad?" Dr. Chun quipped, coming over to the examining table. He kneaded my womb, then rolled the sonogram wand to the left and waited a moment to distinguish my rapid heartbeat from that of the heartbeat of someone beyond me. "There it is," he whispered. My eyes were focused on Thom. The doctor glanced over his shoulder.

"Hey, Dad," Dr. Chun said, "I think she wants you closer for this."

Thom left the window and walked over to me without lifting his eyes to my face.

"It's okay," I said, looking at the sweat rimming his hairline and his fingers tugging at the cuffs of his oxford sleeves. "Your baby's going to be okay, Thom. I'll make sure of it."

Taking off his glasses, he wiped his eyes and reached across the examining table to take my hand. I closed my eyes and turned my head toward the wall. Tears saturated the hair at my temples and leaked to pool in the whorl of my ears. And all the while, the room flooded with the sound of my heartbeat mingled with the heartbeat of the child who was Thom and Meredith Fitzpatrick's.

But who could never be mine.

Rhoda, 2014

A lone cricket chirps in a darkened corner of Hopen Haus, and even *he* sounds stifled—parched. The log-and-chink walls push in close. I cannot breathe around the aroma of cedar chips lining my dresser drawers and the mildewed rafters crisscrossing overhead. I know this panic attack is due to more than just temperature. It's because of Ernest Looper's disquieting presence.

I pad barefoot down the stairs and go out to the east porch, expecting to find him. But it is almost midnight. The steps are empty; the swing, still. And then I hear music coming from the barn. The few dandelions that have escaped the goats' insatiable mouths rub their feathered heads against my legs as I cross the yard. Loosening some bobby pins shackling my *kapp* over my bun, I tug out a few face-framing strands. But my hair is burlap-brown needled with silver—nothing like Alice Rippentoe's halo of curls.

I used to be relieved that these cape dresses and *kapps* buried every hint of femininity as if beneath a shroud. I had never cared for my appearance, and now it no longer mattered what I looked like. What was important was how well I could care for others. Yet walking down the hill toward this man whose presence once filled up my days but who now only consumes my past, I find that the shapeless dress reminds me that I am indeed a woman. And that when I lost my daughter, I let my dreams go with her.

Looper's headlights pierce through the barn slats, illuminating the bats swooping after prey. His truck radio is playing "Hotel California." His dogs must smell me because they begin to bark. My pulse quickens. After our altercation on the porch three hours ago, I am not sure how Looper is going to receive me—or if he is going to receive me at all. I tell myself that I am being foolish—a woman on the cusp of menopause acting as infatuated with Looper as sixteen-year-old Lydie Risser is with Alice's eighteen-year-old son. And though Looper and I are far removed from the summer that both united and tore us apart, I cannot help remembering how it felt to be not just his carpooling friend who proofread his love letters but the girl he finally saw.

The tinny rasp of metal upon metal boomerangs across the night as Looper wrenches bolts free and then tightens them again. I come around the corner of the barn. The dogs stop barking and amble over with wagging tails and eager grins. Peering around the worn brown hood of the Chevy, Looper smiles and points to the exposed engine.

"A beaut, huh?" His casual manner puts me at ease. But I should have known; Looper's never been the type to rehash old wrongs.

I pick my way around scattered lug nuts and coated blue cords peeled down to shredded copper. Recalling the interior of his Firebird, I remember that Looper's never been the cleanliest of men.

"Wouldn't know much about trucks," I say, "seeing as I haven't driven a car in the past eighteen years."

Looper tosses the wrench into a worn metal box and uses both hands to slam the truck hood. I step back as dust rises from the vehicle in a plume. "Forgot about you being Mennonite." He grins, grime filling in the crow's-feet framing his green-gold eyes. His nails are ragged and filled with dirt; his T-shirt, grease splattered and torn, revealing a patch of skin far paler than his arms. His hair is thinner. He even seems shorter, somehow—not like the six-foot-two, chiseled quarterback with the string of high school girls who were my archenemies and his pep team.

"What happened to you, Looper?" I ask and then wince at my implication that who he has become is not enough.

Looper bends to gather up the scattered tools and chucks them with a clang into the box. Snapping the lid, he hefts the toolbox onto his truck bed and looks at me. "You."

"What?"

"You," he repeats. "*You* happened to me."

"You mean, when I left?"

Looper climbs up into the driver's side of his truck. He uses the shoulder of his T-shirt to wipe his neck and hands. "The first time, when you left for college? Or the second time, when you left for good?"

"I didn't leave a second time, Looper. I just never came back home."

"You know what I mean."

Wanting to sprint out of the barn, I walk on flat, dirty feet over to the buggy we should have sold two years ago when Hopen Haus auctioned off the horses we couldn't afford to keep. But somehow the buggy has remained: a mannequin for a gossamer gown embroidered with spider sacs and dust. Picking up a horse brush rusting red on the barn floor, I swipe the seat of the buggy and climb inside.

"So," I ask, now that I can't see him answer, "what did I do to turn you into a drifter who trades family for dogs?"

"Hey," says Looper. "Keep my dogs outta this." But his words lilt with a smile.

The Eagles sing the longest refrain. The dogs pant.

Looper makes a noise in his throat that is half clearing, half groan. "Guess after you left," he says, "I thought I'd just wait 'round for you to come back. But then years passed with me just waiting, and you never did come home. I got married, then divorced. No kids, just the dogs. Worked at Winningham's for a while, and every couple months or so, your dad would come in there needing a trowel or a plumb line."

Stark images of my father, Oscar Winslow, puncture through my cache of suppressed memories and imprint themselves on my heart: wavy brown hair tumbling into eyes as deep as wells; broad shoulders and back, which his job as a stonemason have formed into an immovable boulder; large hands as hard and dry as the mortar he mixed. He used to dare my brother, Benny, and me to prick his scaly palms with sewing needles and swear—with tears in his eyes—that he couldn't feel a thing.

Every few years, the manual labor would pinch his wedding band around his finger like a vise, and Benny or I would be enlisted to smear his fingers with Crisco to try and work the ring free. But as soon we did, our father would go to Crescent Jewelers in La Crosse and replace it with a new one. Otherwise, he never took the ring off— even though his high-powered equipment could have snagged that dull gold band and stripped his finger right down to the bone.

I ask, steeling myself for the worst, "How is he?"

"Fine," says Looper. I close my eyes in relief. "I mean,

he can't get 'round as fast as he used to. But he's still as ornery as they come. Goes into the American Café for his paper and coffee every morning, and then heads out to the job site to work like a man half his age."

"And Benny? Married? Kids?"

"Two," Looper says. "Kids, that is. Only one wife."

I smile. My only sibling, my brother, shall forevermore be Benny—the twelve-year-old with a farmer's tan, buck-teeth, and tousled brown hair sticking out from beneath a baseball cap, which is exactly how he looked when I left him. I cannot picture him capable of becoming the parent I have always wanted to be and yet—having birthed two children—could never attain.

Is it because he was too young to remember our mother's abandonment, while I am still living in the ruins of her devastation?

Swallowing hard, I ask, "Has anybody heard from my mom?" The title of the woman who birthed me, but who stopped being my mother the day she drove out that dusty farm lane, tastes like corroded metal on my tongue. The barrier between us will not allow me to read Looper's eyes. However, in the answering silence, I know that this time my mother has not just been located, but that something has happened. And that all hope of reconciliation is truly gone. How could I have believed that the energy sustaining my thirty-year-old anger would have kept my mother alive? How can I now mourn her passing when, for years, I ached for her return so much that I wished for some kind of abso-lution, even if that meant her death?

"When?" The word scrapes up my throat.

"A little over a year ago . . . around Christmas," Looper replies, as if afraid to hurt me. He should know that—like my father's calloused hand—I cannot feel the hot needle of his revelation poking into my flesh. I do not let myself feel anything. I *can't* let myself feel anything, just as I can't let anyone in. Tightening my jaw, I remind myself that there's no need to mourn my mother's passing because my mother became dead to me when she left. The alternative—believing she had simply chosen to stay away—was too heartrending to bear.

"Ya know, Beth, your mom never gave up on finding you," Looper adds. For comfort, I suppose. And I wonder if he's lying. "She wanted me to tell you that. She made me promise that I'd always keep looking, that I would find you for her—though even before she died, she kept thinking you'd come walking right in to say your good-byes."

"She's the one who walked out first," I snap, the pain flaring from that old desertion as from a phantom limb. "And she *sure* didn't say good-bye then!"

Looper doesn't respond. The barn is silent except for the radio and his panting dogs.

Staring sullenly at the opposite side of the buggy, I envision the framed picture my father used to keep on the nightstand next to his alarm clock and watch. It captured my mother in a time when she was not my mother, Mrs. Winslow, but a high school student named Sarah Graybill. In the picture, as older pictures always go, my mother looked far more accomplished than I had felt at eighteen.

She wore a floral blouse with a sweetheart neckline and a glinting silver cross. Her brown hair was stiff and smooth like fondant icing. Her wine-colored lipstick contrasted perfectly with her pearly white teeth.

I had talked to that picture on the morning of my first period; on the day Mrs. Looper took me to get my first training bra at Sears; on the afternoon I saw Ernest Looper, who was in tenth grade with me, kiss Chelsea Robbins before saying, "Get in here, kid," and driving me home from school. When I was the same age as my mother in the picture, I had stood before it dressed in my prom gown with the uneven hem that I had stitched myself. I had asked the picture if I was pretty. My mother had just stared at me in silence. *She* was so beautiful and perfect, I felt that I could never measure up. Was this the reason she had left? Not knowing the answer, I then stretched myself across my parents' bed—that my mother was not there to make—and cried.

"Were Dad and Benny with her when she . . . passed?" I whisper.

"Yeah. They were there," he says. "Your dad actually let her come home, no questions asked. It was real touching to watch how things got healed between your parents, especially in the end. That's when Ben flew in with his wife—and kids. It was hard for him to see your mom like that. But I could tell he was glad he came."

Only now do I cry. My father and brother got the moment of closure for which my barren soul has always longed. Yet what would I have said to my mother, if given the chance? Would I have screamed at her? Sobbed on her lap like a child? Would I have lied and told her that I forgave her, just to let her rest in peace? No, I realize; I would have told the truth.

"I think it's best I wasn't there," I murmur.

Wiping tears from my face, I step out of the buggy and see Looper put a folded envelope back into his pocket. Looking up, his eyes bore into mine with anger and compassion and every word he seems to think but does not say: How much has changed since I've been gone. How hypocritical it is for me to judge my mother, when at twenty-three, I disappeared without a word just as she left us all those years ago.

But when I fled Boston with the Fitzpatricks' child in my womb, my mother's memory was the reason I could not return home. So I instead entered a strange land called Dry Hollow, knowing full well that I was hurting Ernest Looper and knifing open my father's old wounds while trying to avoid confronting and healing my own. I did this knowing I was leaving my little brother behind. Yet I told myself he would rather cling to a phantom mother, anyway, than to the flesh-and-blood sister who for five years before her own child's conception had raised him as her son.

4

Exhaustion escapes through the sieve of my lips. I pull
Terese's door so as not to awaken Luca. Passing through the
dining room on my way to the kitchen, I see a radius of
light cast by an oil lamp. Alice is seated at the table, hunkered over her own meal. From the way she pokes at the
venison roast on her plate, I sense that she is not eating.

She has been waiting here for me.

I ask, "How are you, Alice?"

She says, "We've received a donation."

"From whom?" Between monitoring Terese's blood pressure and worrying over Star's nicotine addiction, I have
almost forgotten about the Channel 2 News story and the
subsequent changes taking place.

Alice swallows a bite of food and grimaces. I decide to

bypass my stop at the kitchen and eat some of the tuna packs I hoard in my bedroom instead. "A crisis pregnancy clinic in Cookeville," she says. "They saw the news story."

I grit my teeth and then release my jaw in a sardonic smile. "I'm sure they did."

"Don't you even want to know what it is?" asks Alice. Not even *she* can modulate the frustration in her tone.

"Somehow I get the feeling that you're going to tell me."

Alice narrows her eyes. She takes a sip of water before saying, "It's an ultrasound machine. An older model, of course. But they said it's ours for the taking." She pauses. "I thought Wilbur could pick it up?"

My heart is a hard fist knocking inside my chest. "So far we've managed just fine without ultrasound machines."

"Fine?" Alice points a finger out through the doorway. Her gesture is ambiguous, but I know she means Terese and Luca's room. The only private quarters in Hopen Haus besides Uriah's attic, which Looper is occupying until Uriah returns, and the three of five upstairs bedrooms occupied by us midwives. Alice says, "I wouldn't say that Terese is 'just fine.'"

"An ultrasound machine couldn't prevent preeclampsia."

"No. An ultrasound machine couldn't. But if we were better equipped, we could be giving Terese steroid shots in case of preterm labor and monitoring her platelet count and liver funct—"

"It wouldn't matter if we were given every piece of modern equipment in the world; we'd have no electricity to run it!"

"Yes, it *would* matter! These girls need more than what

we're offering them. But you just want to keep hiding behind Mennonite ways, when they're not even yours to hide behind!"

"*Enough!*"

Alice drops into the seat as if my words grabbed her shoulders and shoved her down. The plate rattles; the water lists in the Mason jar. I was so blindsided by anger, I didn't even know until that abrupt movement that she had stood up.

I straighten my slumped back, humiliated by my roiling fury whose unseen source never dries up. I look down into Alice's eyes, which shine with intimidation.

I say, contrite, "I'll speak with Wilbur about it. You said the ultrasound machine's in Cookeville?"

She nods.

"That's on the way to Split Rock Community. Perhaps he can pick it up on a produce run."

"So—we're going to get electricity?" Alice doesn't look at me, but picks at the venison roast.

"I never said that."

She stands again, this time to take her plate to the kitchen. The antagonist in me cannot keep from saying to her retreating back, "I noticed Uriah's been spending too much time with Lydie Risser. When he comes home, I'd appreciate if you'd speak to him about it."

Alice stops walking but does not turn. "He's almost eighteen, Rhoda. I don't have that kind of say over him anymore."

"Then perhaps he should move out from beneath this roof."

Alice clutches the swinging door that leads into the kitchen. She looks back at me and sighs, "Is this really about Uriah?"

"I don't know." I scan Alice's face, trying to shift the attention away from me so I can conceal the jealousy I have always felt about her close relationship with her son. "Is there something else you'd like to talk about?"

Alice shakes her head. *Kapp* strings swat her softly in the face. She passes through the door. I watch the darkness of the kitchen swallow her whole before I turn and make my defeated way up the stairs. I yearn to open my heart to Alice and to Looper, and to this sheaf of hurting girls tucked in bunk beds beneath this roof. But I can't. My eyes have tainted love until my mind views it as synonymous with pain. From the day my mother left until the day my second child was taken, I have used anger and inhibition to ward off anybody who might try to love me—just to find out that I am wanting, and then leave.

Beth, 1996

Pressure stretched across my abdomen in a thin, taut band. When it snapped, I knew this was not Braxton Hicks or merely my round abdominal muscles trying to accommodate the expansion of my womb but a tidal-wave contraction threatening to pull me under. Letting the bowl float down into the water, I wiped the suds on the towel folded over the spigot. Straightening my back, I breathed out through my mouth, trying not to panic. I walked over to the chairs circled around the kitchen table, dragged one across the linoleum, and sat down.

I was only at seventeen weeks. I had just started to feel the tiny fluttering kicks of the baby. Besides the bimonthly checkups, I rarely allowed myself to think about this new life cradled inside my womb. For ten minutes, I remained seated on the chair. I watched the clock embedded in the stove, as I had taken my watch off to do the breakfast dishes. When another contraction struck at eight fifteen, I folded my curved stomach over my legs and touched my forehead to my knees in desperate supplication. I cried out for my roommate, Jillian, although I knew she was gone. I cried out for our neighbors—for *anyone*—but the small apartment just echoed with my own high-pitched keen of fear.

Sweating and nauseous, I stumbled into the living room with the beige walls and forest-green curtains that, in the ten years since the renovation, the sun had leeched to a dingy moss. I dug past the jumble of textbooks and paperback novels stacked under the coffee table and pulled my wallet out of my purse. I searched through the card section for the slip of paper Thom had given to me the day we heard the baby's heartbeat. Another band of pressure pulled across my abdomen. I returned to the kitchen and sat on the pine chair again. But then I stood—rocking back and forth, side to side—gouging my nails into the back of the chair and swearing beneath my breath as if afraid someone could overhear.

Hunching over, I staggered toward the TV stand and dialed the numbers on the old rotary telephone. It rang three times before he picked up. "Thom," I said. The *m* of his name was drawn out as another contraction hit.

A clipped female voice said, "This is not Thom. This is Meredith. Who is this?"

I turned my head and pressed my mouth into my shoulder, exhaling the pain through my nostrils. Meredith's voice rose as she said, "Hello? Who is this?"

I was too concentrated to answer her. When the wave passed, I said, "Meredith, it's Beth. I think I'm having pre-term contractions."

"Why don't you call the fertility clinic?"

"It's Saturday. They're closed."

For a moment, I thought I heard her sigh. "Right," she said. "Tell me what you need. Thom's not here; he's out of town."

"I can't drive to the hospital like this," I said.

Meredith paused. Then, "Where do you live?"

I gave her directions and hung up. Stuffing my backpack with a toothbrush, a change of clothes, and a night-gown in case I had to be kept overnight, I went to the bathroom to check if I was spotting. My legs trembled when I saw that I was not. Even though the debilitating pain was subsiding as quickly as it had hit, the fear of miscarriage saturated my eyes and turned my mouth dry. For four months, I had dissociated myself from this child. I knew this child would have to be given away, just as I had had to give my baby boy away, never to see his beautiful two-toned eyes again. But for this moment, this child was sheltered inside my body—*thriving* inside my body—that was giving forth life, even when I felt so barren.

Stroking my stomach, I tentatively began to sing the lullaby the Mennonite midwife Deborah Brubaker, who had helped birth my son, sang to me. Of course, I did not know how to speak Pennsylvania Dutch. But a few of the phrases had withstood the test of time, as had the memories I had tried to suppress, and yet still held so dear:

"Voo bisht un anna gay glay birdie? Voo bisht un anna gay glay birdie? Ich bin zu my bahm um gay. Ich bin zu my bahm um gay. Ich bin zu my bahm um gay. Glay madly. . . ."

As my voice warmed up, I felt the grip on my womb relaxing. The muscles of my jaw, which I had not known I had clenched, began to unwind.

"It's okay," I whispered, my voice shaking as tears of relief trickled from my eyes. "You're okay. Nothing's going to happen to you. I won't let it."

Someone knocked. Staggering to my feet, I left the bathroom and put my overnight bag on the recliner. "It's open," I called.

Meredith stepped over the threshold into the apartment. "How're you feeling?" she asked.

"Better," I said. "The contractions have stopped."

She smiled. "Braxton Hicks, then." Satisfied with her conclusion, Meredith turned and surveyed the apartment. Through her eyes, I saw the sagging Goodwill sofa, the rickety coffee table and bookshelf, and my roommate's juvenile cat posters taped haphazardly to the walls. All seemed to declare how small my work stipend actually was.

"You live here by yourself?" Meredith asked.

"No," I replied. "I have a roommate, but she's visiting friends."

"Do you ever leave? Visit friends?"

"Not often. I'm busy with my thesis."

"Yes. Your thesis." Meredith stared at me. "What're you doing it on again?"

My mind went blank. Finally, I just relied on my elevator speech and said, "Viewing the practice of traditional surrogacy as a form of open adoption, where the surrogate mother could still be involved in the child's life—" I swallowed. "This would help surrogates who experience remorse after giving the baby up, like with the Baby M case."

Meredith turned toward the door. "I guess it's good we did gestational surrogacy, then," she said. "So you have no biological rights to our child."

I opened my mouth, then closed it, deciding it was safer to say nothing.

"Well," Meredith continued, "I guess I'll be going—since you seem fine." She paused, hand on the knob. "Or do you still need to go to the hospital?"

"Yes," I said. "I'd like to go."

Meredith's eyes widened. This was not the answer she'd anticipated, nor was it the answer I had expected to give. But I could not risk this child's life for the sake of convenience. Even though it was her offspring that I carried, my maternal instinct had sprung up as I folded myself in that pine chair sitting on the scuffed linoleum floor. That pain was real, and I had studied enough to believe primal instincts needed to be followed more closely than we gave them credit. A small part of me also wanted to see if Meredith cared enough to reschedule one afternoon in her life when I had rescheduled a year of mine.

I picked my book bag up from the recliner.

"That's it?" she asked.

"That's it."

Meredith left, clearly expecting me to follow, which I did. Digging into her purse, she found her keys and unlocked the passenger door before going around and unlocking the driver's side. Swinging my book bag to the floor, I clambered into the butter-leather seat. Meredith shifted into drive and tapped the gas. I watched her from the corner of my left eye. Everything about her was polished, clipped, painted, or tanned. Looking at her was like looking at a cascading stream turned into a dam, forest turned into structure, sediment turned into oil. It was as if she had taken one source and turned it into another. It was more commanding, some might even say more beautiful. But I wondered what Meredith looked like before money became her power.

"You too hot?" she asked, turning a vent in the walnut dash toward me.

I was shocked by her thoughtfulness. Her hands clutched the steering wheel again, her layered gold rings clattering on her fingers. On her right hand a vintage, dime-sized cameo was trimmed in delicate filigree, which seemed out of place with the rest of the collection.

"Where did you get the cameo?" I asked.

She adjusted the ring with her thumb and cruised through a yellow light without braking. "Mrs. Fitzpatrick, Thom's mother," Meredith explained without looking at me. "The ring's been in the family forever. Someday I'm supposed to pass it down."

I remained quiet as I contemplated the fact that Meredith was sentimental enough to wear a rather gaudy heirloom that had been in Thom's family. How could I ever understand this woman, whose character was a shifting amalgam of warmth and reserve? Though rarely glimpsed, was the former side the reason Thom loved her?

Meredith interrupted my thoughts, as if she could read them. "You know Thom didn't want to be a research professor?" Her words lifted up at the end like a question, but she was giving me a statement. She was telling me the life history that only she, as his wife, knew. The life history that, as his student, I would never know.

"No," I said. "I didn't."

"He couldn't do it," she said. "I put Thom through four *years* of medical school, and he couldn't figure out until residency that he wasn't going to be an OB/GYN." Meredith shook her head and passed a white sedan, although it was a no-passing zone.

"Why didn't Thom—I mean, Dr. Fitzpatrick—want to be an OB/GYN?" I asked.

"You can call him Thom," Meredith said, smiling

at me, though her eyes were cold. "I'm sure you do at school." She smoothed her hands on the steering wheel and looked in the rearview mirror, then back to the road. "Thom *did* want to be an OB/GYN. But he wanted to be a father more. My career was taking off by that time, and Thom knew I didn't want to give it up to become a nanny. He also knew his hours would be sporadic as a doctor—making it difficult to spend time with our children—so he became a professor instead."

"But the two of you . . ." I paused, not knowing how to continue and wishing I had never begun.

"We never had children?" Meredith supplied.

I focused on the sprawling hospital buildings coming into view.

Meredith said, "Thom made the assumption that if he promised to stay home with the children, then I would promise to *have* children." Her laughter did not escape her lips. "He should not have assumed. I could not put everything on hold and go on a three-month maternity leave. My business was just starting up."

"So," I said, "the surrogacy kind of works in your favor? You can just go about your life without morning sickness or doctor's appointments and let Thom take it from there?" I no longer cared that I was teetering on the brink of rudeness. Meredith made this child I carried sound not like a miracle, but like an inconvenience. If not for Thom, I knew I could not give this child to such a driven woman, who had allowed her job to overtake her life.

Meredith maneuvered her car into a space wedged

between two vehicles and shifted into park. She flicked off the key. The classical music faded. "I do not think surrogacy works in anyone's favor," she snapped. Jerking the keys out of the ignition, she cracked open the door and grabbed her purse. Bending, she met my eyes. "Except, of course, maybe yours."

She slammed the car door and stalked off toward the hospital. Once again, I had no choice but to follow. As I did, I wondered if Thom had preceded me in Meredith's anger, and if this child in my womb would trail in my wake.

A Filipino man with salt-and-pepper hair in a shoulder-length braid came into the room. He carried a manila envelope I assumed held the paperwork I had completed in the hospital lobby. Sitting on the stool beside the examining table, his pristine sneakers squeaked as his heels propelled him across the tile.

"You've had an ultrasound before?" His teeth gleamed in his tanned face. The computer monitor was tilted just beyond my line of vision, but I saw his fingertips were poised above the keyboard.

"Not here, but yes."

"How many weeks are you?" he asked.

"Seventeen."

A pause as he typed it in.

"This your first child?" He looked up, waiting.

I cleared my throat that was blocked with emotions and replied, "No. I . . . I've carried a child to full term before."

When he finished typing, he came over and stood before me. I had tugged my sweatpants down below my hip bones and pulled up my T-shirt. He squirted some of the warmed ultrasound gel on my stomach and rolled the wand that looked like a deodorant stick.

"Have you felt the baby move?" he asked.

I nodded. "Not too often, though," I said. "Just started to feel her in the past two weeks."

He rolled the ultrasound wand lower. It seemed he was trying to manipulate the baby. He didn't know that I knew a little about the medical profession, and I didn't tell him. I wanted to be like any other patient, allowing him to reassure me when I was afraid that something was wrong.

Fear grew in the silence until it became a steel trap bracketing my chest. "I had some pain this morning," I whispered. "And I just wanted to make sure that every-thing's all right."

The ultrasound technician didn't look at me. He removed the wand and wiped the gel off my stomach with a wet cloth. He gave me a hand and boosted me into a sit-ting position. It was not the weight of the baby I carried, but the weight of my apprehension, that made me weak. "I'll be right back," he said, patting my knee.

The computer screen flooded the darkness with a square pool of light. I stared at it and wondered if we had come this far only to have lost the child I'd just allowed myself to love. The terror I'd tried to keep at bay made me want to reach out to my mother, whose absence hurt as much now as it had when she had left. I even wanted to call Meredith and tell her to come back to the hospital. After pacing in the lobby and chain-sipping Diet Cokes for half an hour, she'd said she could not wait any longer. She'd given me the number to her portable phone and then walked out through the automatic doors without asking if I would be okay.

Although she was the least maternal person I had ever known, I wanted a face that was familiar to me, and it only seemed fair that the mother of this child should also have to hear these words. That the mother should help me grieve—that she should grieve too.

The door the ultrasound tech had shut opened again. I felt like a caged animal, blinking in the crackling fluorescent lighting after an older gentleman flipped the switch. He had white hair receding in a horseshoe shape and dangling pink earlobes. His smile was kind, as were his eyes. Taking the swivel stool the technician had occupied, he hitched up the material of his dress pants and placed his large feet at forty-five-degree angles. His shins were bony and covered with socks made of heavy gray wool. The leg hair was white.

"Miss Winslow," he said. I raised my gaze. He did not even deliberate if I was married or not, as I must have seemed so alone, sitting there in my sweatpants with the university logo and my eyes huge in my unwashed face. "I'm Dr. Carmichael." He reached out his steady hand with long, tapering fingers that felt like chilled candlesticks.

Did he think the exchange of physical touch would make the words easier to bear?

"I'm sure you know that my being called in here is not a good sign," he continued, "so I'm not going to make it worse by beating around the bush." He smiled. For an irrational moment, I wanted to assault him for his joviality at such a serious time. "There's some residual swelling on the baby's brain, and one of the upper ventricles does not seem to be developing. These two things combined with the fact that there's not a good flow through the umbilical cord . . . well, it makes us worry that there might be something wrong with your child."

"It's not my child," I whispered, tears flooding my eyes. The second I uttered those words, I realized that Meredith did not have to know that something was wrong. In my opinion, she did not *deserve* to know, as she could not take a few hours out of her Saturday to sit in a darkened room with a scared woman who was contracted to bear her offspring. Because of her apparent apathy, I did not want to tell Meredith anything. But it was not only Meredith's child I carried. It was Thom's child too, and for him I asked, "What's the next step? And how long 'til we know something for certain?"

Dr. Carmichael slipped on the reading glasses hanging down across his lab coat from a chain. With his left hand tilted at an odd angle, he scrawled something across my file and said, "I would like to schedule you for an amniocentesis and an MSAFP, which is—"

"Maternal serum alpha-fetoprotein screening."

The doctor looked up from my file. The blue eyes peering above his bifocals brightened. "Actually, yes," he said. "We'll check your fetoprotein levels to make sure the fetus does not have a neural tube defect, such as spina bifida or anencephaly. High levels of AFP may also suggest esophageal defects or a failure of your baby's abdomen to close. However—" he glanced over his glasses and smiled again—"as you might know, the most common reason for elevated AFP levels is inaccurate dating of the pregnancy."

"That wouldn't be the case here, Dr. Carmichael," I said. "I am a gestational surrogate. I know the exact minute this child was conceived."

"Ah, I see," he muttered. He had not heard me the first time. "Low levels of AFP and abnormal levels of hCG and estriol may indicate that the developing baby has some type of chromosome abnormality. But these are all just precautions, so we can know for certain that your child—or *their* child—is fine."

I ran a hand over my stomach, which was as hard as an unripened fruit. The T-shirt covering it was still smeared with the gummy ultrasound gel. "Thank you for being honest," I said. "I'm sure they'll appreciate it."

"You're welcome." Dr. Carmichael looked over his glasses and paused a moment before saying, "But I know if I were the parent of a contracted baby, I'd also want the surrogate to be honest with me."

5

Rhoda, 2014

At the knock, I get out of bed and whisk the shawl off the back of my desk chair. Spooling it around my shoulders, I pull open the door. I see a pale girl with wet hair dripping across the front of her floor-length nightgown.

"Lydie?" I ask. "You all right?"

She shakes her head. "I think . . . I think Star's hurt."

I step back inside my bedroom. Holding the fiery stub of a match, I lift the oil lamp's glass and touch the flame to the wick before snuffing the match out. I adjust the wick and bring the lamp closer. "What happened?" I ask.

Turning from the light, Lydie shakes her head. "I don't

know. When I came back from my bath, Star had locked me out. But . . . I heard her moan."

Passing the oil lamp to Lydie, I grab the birthing satchel I keep beneath my desk. Then, without speaking, the two of us hurry down the hallway. The lamp sloshes light across the log-and-chink walls. Our matching white nightgowns float around our ankles.

I rap my knuckles on the door to the bedroom Lydie shares with Star. "It's Rhoda," I say sharply. "What's wrong?"

Silence.

I hang the satchel over Lydie's other arm and motion for her to move. Twisting the doorknob hard to the right, I shove my shoulder into the door, displacing the ancient hook lock along with my shawl. The tang of metal and sweat assaults my senses. My eyes struggle to see in the dim light. Once they do, years of experience are overtaken by uncertainty. But only for a moment. I reach for the lamp, and Lydie wordlessly passes it to me. I set the lamp on the floor, where it illumines the scene. Lydie gasps and clamps a hand over her mouth. I hear her nostrils pump in and out with fear.

Star is tucked into the space between the dresser and the window on the left-hand wall. Her knees are pulled up to her chest. Blood spreads from the seat of her pajama pants—soaking her multicolored slippers—and sheens on the hardwood floor. Even in the darkness, every color fades next to the garish spectrum of the girl's purple hair contrasted with that waxing flood of red spilling from her womb. I have seen enough miscarriages to recognize post-partum hemorrhaging. If I cannot stop the bleeding, we will lose Star too.

Lydie is so dazed, she is not even aware that I am asking her to give us space. I bracket her small shoulders and push her toward the door. As Lydie clings to the doorframe with her eyes wet and lips moving in silent prayer, I dig into my satchel for Pitocin. I insert the syringe's needle into the vial and push down on the plunger. I turn the vial—attached to the syringe—toward the ceiling like a gun and extract all ten milliunits. Removing the needle, I set the vial down before flicking the side of the syringe to make sure the liquid is void of bubbles.

I lean over Star and peel down the shoulder of her bathrobe. Lamplight casts shadows over the galaxy of tattoos and scars whittled into her right arm, which has always been hidden under long sleeves. Some of the scars have faded with time; some are as bright as if they were inflicted yesterday. Perhaps they were.

I use an alcohol wipe to clean a circle on Star's skin before jabbing her deltoid with the needle. Star's sore eyes flicker open. They close again. Her chin dips onto her chest.

"How long have you been cutting?" I ask, recapping the syringe and cleaning the area of the shot.

"Dunno," she replies.

"How long have you been bleeding?"

"Dunno," Star slurs again. "Awhile."

I trace the scars on Star's forearm. I turn the arm over

to expose the paler flesh lacerated with angry red stripes running parallel to the sunken purple veins. I say, "You're lucky you didn't nick one."

Star drops the back of her head against the bedroom wall and rolls her eyes to the ceiling. "Lucky?" she says. Gravity pulls tears down her face. "Lucky woulda been the other way around."

Once Star is stabilized, I leave the bedroom and take a right. I enter the holding cell of the walk-in linen closet, where I often trap myself until my tears of anger have fled. After my entire life was taken, except my chance to bring new life into the world, I could separate myself from the child I carried so that it did not remind me of the child I had lost. But the more time that lapses since my womb was full only to become barren once more, the more certain I am that I will never again have the chance to hold a child—*my* child—in my arms. And this makes it harder and harder to distance my heart when I feel a baby thrashing inside the cocoon of a womb, like a butterfly trying to strengthen its wings.

Often I can relinquish my desire to nurture that unseen being if I know the mother whose stomach stretches drum-taut beneath my hands also longs for the day her child unfurls into flight. But sometimes, as that child thrashes, the mother's body locks up as if every kick to her ribs is a personal assault. This is when I desire to take that child and raise him or her as my own. Yet my becoming a parent is a hopeless case, and not just because I am a single woman who works a nonprofit job. I know no court would ever allow a woman to adopt a child when, out of desperation, she once kidnapped one.

Someone knocks and then rattles the doorknob like she's trying to break in. I clear my throat and cull the tears from my cheeks with my palms. "Who is it?"

"Lydie."

I turn the lock and open the door partway, splitting the globe of light from the lamp the young woman carries. Her lashes fan against the scald of my stare. I blink as well and look over at the shelf; the checkered pattern on the sheets transforms into a watery fusion of remorse.

"You all right?" she asks. When I don't answer, Lydie brushes a lock of damp hair with a trembling hand and says, "It's Star." It takes seconds for me to remember what has happened and who I am now supposed to be: not an abductor on the run, but a midwife and mother in a home for unwed girls. "I'm not sure if she's asleep, or . . . if she's passed out again."

I suck stale air in and expel it through my mouth, trying to bring myself back to the present and finding it a fight. Pulling the closet door, I pivot on the grit beneath my heel and follow the beam cast by Lydie's lamp. As we draw closer to the bedroom, reality clamps its ragged teeth, and the venom of panic courses through my mind. Lydie gives me wide berth as we enter and holds out the lamp. Across the floor, I see evidence that Star's bleeding has resumed.

My heart throbs. I kneel down and press two fingers to

the side of Star's neck. Her pulse is weak. *Oh, God, what was I thinking by leaving her unattended, even for a moment?*

"Lydie," I say, "please wake Charlotte and Alice and tell them to come."

Her eyes waver in the lamplight before she nods. I hear her feet flit down the hall. Fervent knockings and harried whispers are exchanged. Seconds drag past like hours as Star's pulse beneath my fingertips slows to a crawl. Two sleep-creased faces appear in the doorway, the brass oil lamp in Alice's hand polishing the silver coronet of Charlotte's hair.

"How is she?" Charlotte asks.

"Not good. Her PPH won't stop even with Pit. I need help moving her downstairs."

Alice and Charlotte look down at Star; then they look at me. I know we are all thinking the same thing: Star's a large girl awake, but now that she is unconscious, her body somehow weighs more.

Alice says, "What about Looper?"

I look over my shoulder at Alice. I had forgotten that his reappearance in my life was not part of my dreams. "Yes. Looper. Get him." I flutter my hands at Alice, who bolts out the door.

Charlotte and I heave Star into a sitting position. Soon, Looper—his sandy waves matted, striped nightshirt askew—steps barefoot into the bedroom and squats before us.

"What's wrong?" he asks.

I repeat what happened, and Looper slips an arm around Star's shoulders. Her head lolls to the side, and

I support the prickly spears of her hair with my hand. With a grunt, Looper lifts Star's upper body while Alice and I support the legs. He walks backward out of the bedroom, careful not to trip on her soiled robe that sweeps the floor like a train. A slipper thwaps to the floor. Alice sidesteps it and looks over at me.

"You think . . . ?" Her mouth hedges over words.

I snap, "What?"

"Should we take her to the hospital?"

Charlotte bunches up the bathrobe and holds it with one hand while supporting Star's lower back with the other. She won't meet my eyes. I know she also fears that Star may need more medical attention than we can give her here.

"Looper," I say. He squints at me while adjusting Star's weight in his arms. "Can you drive?"

Looper stirs as I brace myself on the arms of the vinyl chair and lower my body into the seat. "What'd they say?" he asks, stretching out his right knee, frozen stiff from the football injury he received the same night as the '89 homecoming crown.

"If the D and C goes well," I say, "they'll release Star in a few hours."

"Will she come back to your place?" Looper asks.

"She has no choice."

"No family, you mean?"

I pause. "'Least none she's willing to call or talk about."

Looper scratches his hair. In the lull, he looks down the

curved length of chairs and whispers, pointing. "What's her story?"

In my sleep-deprived state, even tilting my head to the right is exhausting. But I do it. I see that Alice is curled beneath the sleeping bag Looper must have brought in from his truck while I was busy admitting Star to the emergency room. Even with her pink bow mouth open and her prayer *kapp* askew, Alice is exquisite. Her eyelids skate restlessly over dreams. Her lustrous skin is haloed with escaped blond curls. Looper's interest in her causes envy to take easy root in the acidic soil of my heart. I feel worn out, sour, and about a thousand years old.

"Her story's like most, I suspect." I wince at the superiority in my voice that I have not earned. "She got pregnant. The father didn't want anything to do with the child, so she came here, and the community took her in."

"Yes," Looper says, "she told me about Uriah."

"Hmm."

I watch the bustling nurses' station. Looper's eyes scan over me, trying to decipher the reason for my aloof response. For the first time since he came, I am grateful these challenging years have not allowed for womanly pampering. The emotions igniting my skin cannot escape through the suncoarsened layers.

"What's her story?" he again whispers.

I roll my head toward Looper and see that he is pointing at me—asking me for *my* story. I look away and close my lids down hard.

What he does not know is that this version of my story

for twenty-some years has never been told. That this story is not just *my* story but his story too.

"We were so young, Looper," I whisper. "Your dreams— I didn't want you to give them up by having to support a child."

Looper's eyes are again on my face, and this time no layers of sun-coarsened skin can prevent the heat of my vulnerability from seeping through. I can't look at him; I am too scared to see our life history displayed across his face. "You saying that . . . that . . . ?" His words cling to false starts and ellipses, but the tears coating his voice tell me that he has already guessed the answer to the question he won't allow himself to speak.

"Yes," I say. "I conceived that summer."

"Did you . . . ?"

"I had the baby, if that's what you're asking. But I didn't keep it. I couldn't."

Looper takes his bearded face in hard-skinned hands. His back begins to quake, but I do not reach out to him. I find comfort in the fact that finally someone can help shoulder the loss I have been carrying on my own. I dig into my birthing satchel for a Kleenex, but find only individually sealed alcohol wipes. Tearing the package, I pass one to him.

He shakes it open, wipes his face, and looks over. His eyes are raw. "Girl or . . . boy?"

In that briefest hesitation, I see what he would have hoped.

The soft syllable stings. "Boy."

I remember how my own father had confronted me about my pregnancy before I had even contemplated telling Looper, the father, about it.

"Your mother looked just the same with you," he'd said, almost sadly, taking off a work glove to brush his thumb against my cheek. "That's how I could tell."

I had flinched at his touch—and at his words, since I did not want to look like my mother. My father's eyebrows lowered. His dark eyes grew moist. "Beth," my father had continued, his voice hoarse, "keep the baby. I'll help you."

I knew this offering was meant to soften my mother's absence that, despite his best efforts, my father's stable presence could never really fill. But I was unable to reach for the offer of support he was extending like an olive branch—or even to feel that I was worthy to accept it. I still don't fully understand my reasoning at the time, but somehow my mother's desertion made me certain I had to give my own baby up for adoption. She had not loved me enough to be a part of my life, so how could I possibly love my own child enough to be the mother it would need? That, more than fear or inconvenience, was the reason I could not keep the baby.

This was the reason I didn't tell Looper about the child. This was the reason I packed that night and left for college the next morning, although I still had two weeks left until classes started. But as I drove out that dusty farm road, with the sun's rim nourishing the cornfield's stalks, I glanced over at the Loopers' red mailbox and wondered if I was making a mistake. I knew Looper would take care of me and the baby. But would that only be out of obligation, which would leave him feeling trapped in the end? The two of us had never discussed love or future plans despite the passion of that summer, and I feared if I demanded more from him, he would turn his heart away, leaving me as broken as when our romance began. And yet I yearned to know the truth: was I just one last high school fling to be discarded when Looper's adulthood loomed, or did he want me with him, always? I didn't know the answer that day I left, driven by the grief my mother's abandonment had started all those years before. To this day, I still don't know, and I wonder if I ever will.

"A boy," Looper says now.

I blink and look down at my calloused hands in the lap of my cape dress.

"I wish I'd known." Drawing his legs back, he hunches his shoulders around his body.

I can feel him retracting from me—from the mother who took his son—and I don't blame him. I know what it's like to lose someone you love. I have lost not only my family but the two children I birthed only to give away. I should have learned from when my mother left: you should never give your heart to someone who can never fully be yours.

6

Beth, 1996

The silence remained deafening, even as we listened to the water trickling over the fountain near the fertility clinic's reception desk, to the nonsensical chatter of a baby in his car seat. I reached up and massaged the tense muscles of my jaw. One after another, expecting mothers were called back. And then, finally: "Bethany Winslow?"

I nodded and stood. Thom and Meredith stood as well. An overweight female technician with a sleek ponytail and tinted glasses led us down the hall. In the ultrasound room, I lay back on the metal table. Everything then proceeded as it had before: the warm gel coating my stomach, the swivel of the ultrasound wand. I thought my own heart would stop beating until I heard the roar of the baby's heartbeat.

Meredith and Thom crowded around the computer monitor. Though I couldn't see the screen, I knew what the technician would be doing. She'd measure the amniotic fluid cushioning the child's expanding frame. She'd measure the circumference of the stomach, the length of the limbs, and the dimensions of the brain, the kidneys, and the four compartments of the heart.

During all of this, I remained silent, as did the technician. But inside, I felt like I was screaming—*dying*. I knew that as the technician measured, Thom was tallying everything up in his mind and finding that this child of my womb—but of his flesh—was wanting. Still, he did not say a word.

"See that?" the technician said. From the examination table, I watched the technician scribble the computer cursor across the pad. "It's a girl."

Meredith breathed, "A girl."

Thom put a hand on the back of Meredith's neck, where her curled blond hair brushed golden skin. I watched her lean toward him. My heart felt so hollow, it ached. I looked to the wall as longing pooled in my eyes.

The technician stood and moved back from the computer screen as Dr. Hancock, the reproductive endocrinologist, came into the room. At her appearance, a wash of adrenaline slid down my shins to course in my feet— making it difficult to remain still, making it difficult not to run. Dr. Hancock greeted us, working her fingers into a pair of sterile gloves. From the instrument tray covered with a blue plastic sheet, she removed a syringe, swabbed a cool circle on my stomach with an alcohol wipe, and injected my skin with a local anesthetic. The technician got on the other side of the table and maneuvered the ultrasound wand so Dr. Hancock could extract the fluid without harming the baby.

The anesthetic must not have deadened the area completely. I felt a dull prick and I closed my eyes. Orange bloomed across my vision like a warning flare. Everything inside of me wanted to protect this child from the risks surrounding the amniocentesis procedure, yet this child was not mine to protect.

Dr. Hancock must have felt how rigid my body was becoming. She placed a hand on my goose-bumped flesh. "You're doing great," she said.

She pulled back on the plunger that filled the syringe with clear, amber-colored amniotic fluid. Swabbing my stomach with iodine, she placed a Band-Aid over the invisible puncture.

"See?" She smiled, tapping the side of the syringe with a gloved finger. "It's really as simple as that."

———

I stopped outside Thom's office door, which was propped open with a dense, leather-bound book. Moving closer, I crouched and squinted at the symbols embossing the border: the rod of Asclepius, an hourglass, a beaker, an antiquated microscope, an apothecary's mortar and pestle.

Inside this, the cover read: *You can do nothing to bring the dead to life, but you can do much to save the living from death.* I cupped the swell of my womb. A forewarning?

Thom's chair creaked as he sensed my presence and turned. "Hello, Miss Beth," he said.

I stood, heart pounding, and the blood in my body sank to my feet. Pressing my temple, I was halfway to Thom when the room curtained to black. The first draft of my fifty-page thesis fluttered from my hand to carpet the office floor. I heard Thom bolt from the chair and stride across his office toward me.

"Miss Beth? Beth?" His voice seemed far away.

I was opening my mouth to reassure him when another surge of vertigo struck. Thom placed a hand on my lower back and guided me over to his chair. My weakened state made the foot in distance seem like the other side of the room. I sat and Thom knelt before me.

As he did, I was reminded of that late afternoon in the darkened office when I'd told Thom about my son. With my eyes clenched shut, I could see everything. And I knew it was not Dr. Thomas Fitzpatrick I'd fallen in love with that day. It was the fact of somebody finally hearing my story, and through its telling, the deepest, darkest parts of me finally being seen.

"What is it?" Thom asked, taking my cold hand in both of his. "What do you need?"

I opened my eyes and breathed through my mouth, waiting for the wave to recede. "It will pass," I promised. "It just takes time."

"You mean this—" He pointed to my folded-over stomach; the nausea that I'm sure cast an olive hue over my sallow complexion. "*This* has happened before and you didn't tell me?"

"You had enough to worry about already. Meredith thought—"

Thom stood. "My *wife* knows about this?"

Hiding my face, I murmured, "I had pains when you were gone. I needed help. Meredith took me to the hospital. She . . . she took care of me." It seemed like the smallest gift I could offer his wife, when I had taken so much from her already. For deep below her self-protecting armor, I imagined that Meredith Fitzpatrick was like any other woman, and therefore grieved over the loss of being able to bring new life into the world while I did so effortlessly.

I sat upright as the baby moved. Thinking the vertigo had returned, Thom knelt again. He scanned my face, and then my body. "What can I do?" he whispered.

I could see the worry wrinkling his brow, and that is why I took the hand he had not extended and placed it on the lower portion of my womb. "Right there," I commanded, pushing my hand down on top of his. "Wait."

We stared into each other's eyes without blinking or breathing. The baby moved again. She gently somersaulted in my stomach as if to reassure us that, whatever the test results that hung in the balance, she was going to be all right.

Thom said, "That was the baby?"

"Yes," I whispered. "That was your baby."

I reached out and placed a hand on his shoulder. He leaned forward and cupped his cheeks before resting his forehead on my lap.

Spring light slanted through the rectangular window. Dust motes sparkled and fell like stars. In that moment fraught with an intimacy I had desired yet did not deserve, the emotion I felt was not jealousy that he was Meredith's husband or anger that this child I carried was not mine. Instead, I just felt wonder that I had been gifted with this child at all. My gratitude for someone whom my body would usher into the world, but whose life I could never fully claim, let me understand the beautiful sacrifice of true maternal love.

The force of the office door opening flapped the papers scattered across the floor. Thom's wife stood in its gap, staring down at her husband and me embracing. Her blue eyes glimmered. Her lips were hard pressed like marble. She had enough dignity not to say anything, but before I could explain what she thought she had seen, Meredith pivoted on her heel and stalked out of the room. The door remained ajar. The misaligned papers became still. If not for the trail of her citrus perfume, I would have thought I had dreamed Meredith Fitzpatrick's startling presence.

I stood from the chair with my hand still holding my stomach.

Thom rested his hands on my shoulders and eased me back down. "Don't," he said. "Please—let me take care of this."

I didn't know how he would, though. As I stood staring

at Thom's shoeprints marring the papers of my thesis, I no longer believed the argument I had spent months backing up with primary and secondary sources. There was no ethical solution when a surrogate fell in love with the child a contract prevented her from claiming. There was no ethical solution because there really was no choice. The child was never the surrogate's, even if the surrogate's heart belonged entirely to the child.

⁂

I did not know where to go once I had signed into the fertility clinic, aware of Meredith Fitzpatrick's eyes burning into my back from her chair along the left-hand wall. I had not seen Meredith in the two weeks since she entered her husband's office and found Thom and me embracing. And I knew she did not want to see me. I knew that if she could extract this child without causing it harm, she would. But she couldn't, so she had no choice but to be civil, although I am sure everything inside her itched to paint her handprint across my face.

Thankfully, Dr. Hancock and the genetic counselor, Dr. Michaels, came into the room as soon as we were called back.

Dr. Hancock smiled before pulling up the swivel chair. Dr. Michaels remained standing with her back against the wall. Everything from Dr. Michaels's cardboard expression to her stoic voice seemed an attempt to observe us from the shadows or to become a shadow herself. I noticed this because I often made the same attempt.

"Why don't you all take a seat?" Dr. Hancock asked, indicating the three padded chairs she must have brought in specifically for our visit.

She continued to watch us long after we were settled. In that moment, I understood that she was not just being reticent; she was trying to calculate her words. "It seems . . . ," Dr. Hancock began, then paused to clear her throat. "There's something wrong with your child, Mr. and Mrs. Fitzpatrick. For the past two weeks since Dr. Michaels and I've been monitoring your surrogate, Beth—" Dr. Hancock nodded at me—"we've noted the high level of alpha-fetoprotein in her blood; the excess of amniotic fluid; the coarctation of the aorta—a narrowing of the exit vessel from the heart. Although the baby did fine during the stress tests, the traces of trisomy 18 and 21 convey to us that your daughter might have a chromosomal abnormality."

Meredith inhaled, as if extracting whatever oxygen there was left in the room. "Like Downs?" she asked.

"We're not sure," Dr. Hancock admitted. "Sometimes everything we look at can point to a certain condition, but when the child's born, everything is fine. Other times, we will monitor mother and child and only discover a chromosomal abnormality once that child's born."

"What do we do now?" Thom asked. With a PhD in obstetrics, he must've known the answer. But as a father, he was baffled . . . stunned.

Dr. Michaels stepped from the shadows. The fluorescent lighting glinted off her beige hair.

"In a few weeks, we could do another amniocentesis," she said. "To make sure we haven't made a mistake. If the results are the same, we could do a D and C, which is—"

"I know what a D and C is," Thom snapped. His face softened. "Sorry. You just don't have to explain."

Meredith turned to her husband. "I don't know. You might, but *I* don't." She faced the doctor again. "And I'd like to."

Dr. Hancock continued the conversation where Dr. Michaels had been cut off, and I imaged that this tag team was accustomed to dealing with parents whose underlying tensions erupted during stress. "D and C stands for dilation and curettage," she said. "It is the most invasive of the procedures, as it would completely remove the fetus from the uterine cavity—"

"Hold on," Thom interrupted, shaking his head as vehemently as Meredith was nodding hers. "This is a decision that will have to take time."

Meredith said, "Just like deciding to have this child took time?" I looked over. Her legs were crossed, arms folded. Her blue eyes shot ice.

"We will not discuss this now," Thom said.

Meredith turned back to Dr. Michaels. "We want another amniocentesis." She waved toward the calendar tacked to the wall. "Put us on your schedule or whatever you do."

Dr. Hancock looked between the parents and then over at me. "You all right?" she asked.

I nodded, but I could feel the sweat beading my top lip

as the vertigo returned—making me the axis from which
the rest of the room spun. I wanted to have a say in the
decision, but I knew that—without a biological connection to the child—I had no right. I was just a conduit for
life that had, with the casual flick of Meredith's wrist, been
transformed into a conduit for death. With every puncture to the uterine cavity, both my life and the baby's were
put at risk through the potential for preterm labor and
infection.

My rattled mind echoed with the words I had thought
in the beginning: *This is a business transaction; that is all.*
But it no longer *was* just a business transaction, and if I was
honest with myself, it never had been. I had been coerced
into this business transaction not by the promise of money,
but by the phantom promise of Dr. Thomas Fitzpatrick's
love. I realized—sitting there, cradling my womb beneath
protective hands—that love not for the father, but for the
child herself, was the reason I wanted to weep over the loss
that was sure to come.

"I'm not prepared to raise a child who isn't normal,"
Meredith said. "I'm just not. I was never really prepared
to . . . to raise a child at all.'"

Thom stripped off his glasses and pinched the bridge of
his nose. "So what do we do if the amniocentesis shows the
same results?"

"We only have one choice," Meredith said. "Don't we?"
She looked between the doctors and then her husband as
if the woman whose body actually sustained her child's life
were not in the room. "It will have to be aborted."

As tears dripped upon my clenched hands, I wondered if I was the only one who noted the shift from a daughter, a baby, a life, to *it*.

Thom turned at the sound of my bike tires rolling over the uneven boards of the dock. He wasn't wearing his glasses. His hair hadn't been combed. If it weren't for the faint gray fanning out from his temples, I would almost think him the same age as me—and that there really was hope for us. But there wasn't hope. There never had been.

He smiled as I drew closer. "You came."

"Did I have a choice?" I leaned my bike against the side of the dock and walked toward him. "You told me to." My tone was clipped. But I wasn't angry, just broken.

"We all have a choice."

"Meredith doesn't think we do," I said.

Thom winced. He looked out across the lake, where swans stirred the water with their brilliant white wings and then settled down again as if they had never moved. "No," he finally sighed. "Meredith doesn't."

"And what do you think?" I stepped closer.

Thom cupped his hands over his mouth and exhaled hard. "We both signed the contract, Beth. We both have a say."

"But don't *I* have a say?" I cried. "Doesn't it matter that *I* want to keep this child? That I don't care if she's handicapped or not?"

Thom placed his hands on the railing of the dock. For

the first time since I met him, the boyish traces faded away, and he just looked . . . old. "I know Meredith wouldn't allow you to adopt the child. She wouldn't. Not after—" He cast a hand over the still water with its floating net of feathers, but I knew he was recalling the afternoon Meredith saw the two of us embracing in his office. I then understood that though Thom had surely caught up with his wife that day, he had never been allowed to explain our relationship. Perhaps he didn't understand it himself.

I said, "But to sacrifice a child to preserve her pride? To . . . to punish us? What kind of mother would do that? Already . . ." I placed a hand on my stomach, and as if in response, she stirred inside my womb, leaving behind an undercurrent of life long after her movements had ceased. "Already I would give everything up for this child, and she's not even mine."

Shaking my head, I took a step away from Thom, back up the dock. "No. It's not natural what Meredith's feeling and what she's not. That is not the kind of mother I want my daughter—" My mouth convulsed. My vision swam as, for the first time, I uttered the possessiveness for this child that I innately felt. It did not matter that I would never be able to study her features for traces of my own. It did not matter that she would instead look like Meredith, the woman who had allowed her body to go through such physical duress without ever opening her heart. What mattered was that, for this moment, this child was mine to protect—to cherish—and I would not let anything harm her. Or anyone. Even the man I had thought I loved.

Thom picked up the scarred leather satchel beside his feet and moved down the dock toward me. "I always knew what was at risk," he said.

"Then why risk it?" My voice cracked. "If you knew your wife didn't want this child, why'd you place me between you? Why'd you place *us* between you?"

"Everything just seemed to make sense." He looked down. "Surrogacy was the only way to be a father, and I knew that you needed money for school and that you'd had a child before."

The implication that money was the reason I'd agreed to bear his child made acid creep up my throat. "It was never about the money."

Thom glanced up to meet my eyes. "I know." He held out his satchel and then, at my curious expression, pulled it open. Inside, I saw green bills bound with blue and pink bands. He reached out, as if to skim his fingers across my stomach's surface. Dropping his hand, he swallowed deeply and said, "If we agree to terminate the pregnancy, I know . . . I know money can't offset your pain, but I want you to know that we . . . appreciate your sacrifice."

"*Sacrifice?*" I gasped, and the reality burned. "Are you paying me to abort your child?"

Thom turned and stared at the lake. His unfocused eyes gleamed with tears. I knew then that this choice was breaking his heart too.

I took a deep breath and reached out to touch his arm—beseeching him to reason, to care. "But isn't there a chance the baby's normal?" I asked. "Why don't you just cancel the second amniocentesis and hope for the best?"

Thom dragged a sleeve hard across his face. His voice was so carefully devoid of emotion, he might have been quoting from a textbook as he said, "An amniocentesis is 99.4 percent accurate, Beth. You know that."

Taking his hand from where it rested on the dock rail, I forced it against my womb. "You felt her move, Thom. You cried when you heard her heartbeat. Do *not* throw your percentages at me; you know very well that, normal or not, your daughter is as much a person as you or I!"

Thom withdrew his hand and folded his arms. I glimpsed his steel will girding his passive facade and knew he would not change his mind. To hide my fear, I stared out at the swans that were as exquisite as decoys. I saw a single Canada goose gliding through the water. She was beside them, but not among. Her tan-and-black wings were strengthened from numerous flights, while the swans' immense beauty had been clipped to stay. Had I always felt so isolated from my peers because I had never been meant to live a normal life? Had my trials toughened me, so I would now have the strength to take flight and save this child?

My mind reeled. If I fled, I would not only be leaving behind my unfinished degree—my future prospects—but I would also be leaving Thom, my only friend. This was the second time in my life I had been given a gift that came with an enormous price.

Tears filled my eyes. I looked over at Thom. "I'm sorry," I said. "I'm just . . . tired."

He bridged the distance between us and patted my shoulder. In that touch, I felt what I had never allowed myself to see: Thom had never seen me as a potential lover, but as the daughter that, before me, he'd never been able to have.

"I will take your money," I whispered, not meeting his eyes, "and if the amniocentesis results are the same, we will terminate the pregnancy."

Thom nodded and again swallowed deeply. The silence between us was broken only by the fowl's pulsating wings as she prepared for flight. As Thom embraced me for the final time, I could tell he thought that I had accepted his viewpoint. The truth was, however, I was just beginning to understand my own.

7

"Deborah?" I said after the Mennonite midwife mumbled a greeting into the phone. "I'm sorry to wake you. I found your number through the operator. My name's Beth— Bethany Winslow. You . . . you delivered my son five years ago at La Crosse Regional on February 3, 1991. . . . I'd just turned eighteen." Cradling the phone against my shoulder, I turned to the side and waited until I could continue speaking. "It was on the second anniversary of the court ruling of the *In re Baby M* case. I was watching it on TV . . . after I gave my son up."

I could hear Deborah Brubaker sitting up, the soft rustle of sheets peeling back. I could imagine her husband mouthing questions and Deborah using the same hand that had soothed my mourning to bat him away.

"I remember you," she said. "What do you need?" Her lilting Pennsylvania Dutch accent seemed diminished, but then I wondered if her tongue was still heavy with sleep.

"I'm pregnant. Again." My jaw tightened around the words. My ears burned with the implication. For some reason, I did not want this Mennonite midwife who had taken care of me five years ago to think I was an immoral girl who slept with every guy around. And for once, I wanted to tell someone—*anyone*—the truth.

"I'm a gestational surrogate for a wealthy couple," I explained. "But they don't want the child anymore—because of a defect. I need somewhere to stay until she's born. I don't have much money. And I need to leave right away. Do you know of any place?"

I would not know Deborah was still on the line except for the uneven pitch of her breathing. I sensed that she was deliberating whether this girl she'd helped so long ago was worth the risk of losing her job. The air conditioner kicked on in my apartment. The toilet flushed in the bathroom between my bedroom and my roommate's. I rubbed my forehead. Despite the coolness of the room, my fingers came back dampened with sweat. I looked at my watch. If I was going to leave unnoticed, I did not have much time.

Finally, Deborah said, "I know someone. We were trained by the same midwife back home, in Lancaster."

I sat on the corner of my unmade bed and closed my eyes. "Thank you." My voice quavered. "What's her number?"

"Oh, my," Deborah said, "Fannie doesn't have a phone.

Not even in the barn. She's still Old Order Mennonite. The only way you can reach her is by mail."

"By mail?" I repeated. "I can't write a letter. I have no time."

"You could drive there," Deborah said. "Fannie can't turn anybody away. It makes it difficult for her since the community doesn't always agree, but it'd work in your favor now."

"Where's she located?" I asked.

"Tennessee," Deborah replied. "Dry Hollow, Tennessee."

"Is it remote?"

"Remote? You can't get more remote than Dry Hollow. Henry and I traveled down there after Fannie opened Hopen Haus in '89, and we were driving dirt roads for miles. That's one of the reasons the community bought the place. It's so far from everything."

We were both silent. Then I cleared my throat. "I called too," I said, "because I never got the chance to . . . thank you. I don't think you'll ever know what you did for me that day."

"You're welcome," Deborah said. "But I didn't remember you because of the *Baby M* case."

"You didn't?"

"No," said Deborah. "Though it did help me put you in a timeline, of sorts. I remembered you because I'd never seen a girl your age go through what you did alone. You were really brave that day. I hope you know that."

Tears trickled from my eyes. At twenty-three, I was as alone as I'd been at eighteen. Would my entire life be spent in solitude? Would my entire life be a reminder of the familial intimacy I'd lost? Saying good-bye, I dabbed my face and padded into the hall. Resting my hip against the doorframe separating the bedrooms from the living room, I touched my stomach rising beneath my cotton shirt.

"I'll be brave," I whispered.

As if celebrating her resurrection, the child leaped within me.

<hr/>

I finished packing my car at dawn, not that I had much to pack. I had winnowed both my family's and my possessions when I left Wisconsin at seventeen. Since then, I had purposefully not met anyone or gotten anything that could not be left behind. I slammed the hatch and climbed behind the wheel.

I heard the sound of Jillian, my roommate, practicing her flute in the tiny apartment. Her daily routine usually set my teeth on edge, but knowing this would be the last time I would hear it made me wistful for the relationship I'd never allowed myself to cultivate. The high, sweet notes drifted out of my roommate's open bedroom window and caught in the crape myrtle dancing in the morning June breeze. I kept my own car window down so the music could serenade me as I drove out of Simms University's brick-and-mortar entrance, with its massive wrought-iron gates under an enormous golden letter *S*.

I cruised past the awakening estates called White Swan, where the Fitzpatricks lived and which hemmed in my

storybook campus. My mind conjured forth images of
Thom throughout the two years I'd known him: his cups
of milk tea that he never finished, his messy notes that I
could never decipher, his jewel-toned stacks of out-of-print
books, his lazy British accent, his ruddy hair and smudged
spectacles. . . . I had memorized everything about him
as one does with a celebrity or role model. But I realized
in that moment that I did not truly know him, nor did
he know me. In fact, if I had not become his surrogate, I
was certain that in time, Thom would have forgotten me.
Instead, he had asked me to carry their child, and in leaving a mark on my life, I had been forced to leave a mark
on his. Slowing my car, I looked out at the lake where I
had met Thom the previous morning. The black water was
still. Cherry blossoms clung to the limber willow branches
trailing along the pebbled bank. The swans were clustered
there, long necks tucked under magnificent white wings.

"Good-bye, Thom," I whispered, my tone heavy with all
I had not said. But I had to leave him because of the child
I'd been given that, this time, I refused to lose.

One day had passed since I left Massachusetts, three hours
since I'd exited the interstate that branched off onto a narrow two-lane and then a series of potholed country roads.
I was prepared for the rugged terrain, but I was still surprised at how the geography shifted as I drew closer to the
destination I'd circled on a gas station map. On one side of
the road and across the fields, fencerows lined acres of lush

grass where a colorful menagerie of cattle grazed. On the other side, grasshoppers sprang up from knee-high wheat with the whir of tiny machines. A dilapidated cabin with a tin roof eaten with rust perched on a hillside overlooking the valley.

I wondered if this was part of the Dry Hollow Community, but I doubted it was. There was nothing to let me know that the Old Order Mennonite community even existed, except for the address that Deborah Brubaker had given me. I felt vulnerable, surrounded by such open terrain. If my car broke down, it appeared I would have to walk for miles before coming upon any form of life— discounting the cattle and a few soaring hawks that cast shadows upon the green.

Sipping lukewarm Coke, I screwed on the lid and continued driving. In the distance, I saw what could only be members of the Dry Hollow Community toiling in the far end of the field, and suddenly it was as if I had driven back through time. A Clydesdale stallion towed some sort of antiquated farming implement down the center of the tilled strip of earth. A bearded rider sat aloft, holding tightly to the reins while a funnel of dust rose behind him. Along the road, several women—all with young children in tow—passed me, carrying baskets draped with cloths and what looked like large glass jars of sun tea.

A few of the women turned to stare at my vehicle with an inquisitive expression made further uniform by their long dresses and netted white *kapps*. I touched the gas pedal and made my way to the top of the hill. I parked in front of an old-fashioned hitching post, where two horses encumbered with buggies were tied. As I stepped out, I locked the vehicle out of habit before closing the door. A sorrel gelding turned his head at the noise and twitched his silken tail to ward off the flies alighting on his back, but he could not see me for his blinders.

Taking a deep breath, I walked toward the front door on trembling legs. The house was tall and rectangular except for a lath-and-plaster addition, which jutted off the log-and-chink structure like the bottom half of the letter *L*. The roof was patchworked with shiny and dull tin, marking the different repairs. From this, two brick chimneys jutted, their old gray mortar crumbling from age. Below the ten oblong windows, flower boxes spilled blue and pink morning glory blooms. A volley of hummingbirds darted and chirped. They were fighting over the glass feeders that hung from the three porch fascias skirting the house.

I mounted the steps and knocked on the door. Twisting my hands, I wondered if I had made a mistake. I did not have a plan for being here. I certainly did not want to join the church or take up the Mennonites' Plain lifestyle. I just knew that I needed a place to remain in safety and seclusion until my child could be born. Hopen Haus was the only option on such short notice. I was just about to knock again when the door opened. A thin, small-boned woman with a strapless white apron tacked to a dark dress stood in a square of light beaming in from a window beside the door. Her eyes infused with the same inner kindness as

Deborah's, she looked me over—pausing on my stomach that no baggy T-shirt could hide. She smiled.

I asked, "Are you Fannie?"

"*Jah*, child," she said.

If she had greeted me in any other way, I would not have responded with the heaving sobs that startled the midwife and stole my breath. Fannie stepped out onto the porch and pulled the door behind her. Without a word, she held me—her starched apron crackling like parchment against my chest—and patted my back. I leaned my lanky body on Fannie's short frame. I am sure our embrace looked awkward to anyone watching. But I did not care. Six years had passed since I'd been anyone's child, and it had been even longer since I had actually felt taken care of; after my mother left when I was twelve, I had tried to fill her grown-up shoes.

"*Ach*, now," Fannie said. She reached out that small hand with its clipped nails and calloused creases and rested it on my womb. "You need somewhere to stay?"

I nodded and sank back into her arms. She patted my back again and didn't say another word, just let me cry.

part

TWO

8

Rhoda, 2014

Star is asleep by the time I return with the requested cup of
tea and extra feather pillow that I've pulled from beneath
the covers on my own bed. Setting the pillow on the cane-
backed chair, I balance the saucer in my hand and look
around the mudroom. Charlotte had the forethought to
revamp it into Star's living quarters, so she would be able to
recuperate from the D and C without having to go up and
down the stairs.

Washtubs of laundry have been removed, and on a
small, round table an oil lamp glows, filling the dingy
space with cheerful light. The warped wooden floor—the
worst in the house due to a century's worth of damp shoes

and dirt—is softened with one of Charlotte's bright hook rugs. When a girl is laboring, I often come into the birthing room to find Charlotte rocking in the chair beside the four-poster bed. Her peaceful presence and rhythmic movements allow the girl to relax. Charlotte possesses a keen maternal instinct that lets her know exactly what these girls need before I can even guess that their needs haven't been met. Preparing Star's room is a perfect example of Charlotte's unique gifting that I have never possessed, and today—as always—it is a gifting I wish I had.

Looking at Star asleep on the birthing bed, I imagine her mother staring down at her as I am staring now—seeing the shadows rimming her closed eyes and veins branching across her forehead. Only through those eyes am I able to let go of my anger and discern the tender girl lurking underneath Star's bristling hairstyle and piercings.

I cross the floor, set the teacup on the table beside her bed, and place a hand across Star's forehead the same way Deborah Brubaker did for me—the same way Charlotte would surely do if she were here. At my touch, Star's eyes flicker open. She flinches as if anticipating the stinging lash of judgment I filleted her with last night, although my mouth never said a word. I retract the hand that I have placed and the words of compassion I have readied on my tongue. It is too much for her at this time. And honestly, it would be too much for me to say the things that need to be said, but which I am not yet sure I mean.

Clouded by pain medication and grief, Star will not remember opening her eyes and seeing the midwife whom

everyone fears crouching over her while burdened with
the yoke of sorrow she's been silently carrying these past
eighteen years. Lifting Star's head, with hair that has transformed from spikes into strange purple fuzz, I slide my
feather pillow beneath it. I bring her new slippers over
and set them beside her bed in case she needs them in the
night.

The next morning, it is bittersweet, watching unnoticed
from the kitchen doorway as Terese and Desiree open
cardboard boxes and hold up bags of bagels and trays of
sweet rolls swirled with cream cheese. Knocking their hips
together, they let out whoops and grin. Relief floods my
eyes as I stare at these Hopen Haus girls whose stomachs
will be not only filled this morning, but satisfied. I know
Terese and Desiree could not be celebrating such delica-
cies if the Lord had heeded my supplication and kept the
Channel 2 News story from being aired.

I don't know how to thank him or the bakery for
this bounty. Hopen Haus is used to receiving donations,
though they are often just as ill-kept and broken as the girls
who seek lodging beneath our roof. The "day-old" baked
goods the Split Rock Bakery just sent with Wilbur Byler,
however, are still so fresh that the plastic bags sheathing the
bagels are filmed with moisture. The cream cheese on the
sweet rolls is soft and smeared from trapped vestiges of the
oven's heat.

It is almost impossible to recall the time when such

treats were commonplace. Or how, after every meal, we'd pass down the table three or four deep-dish *abbel* crumb or shoofly pies topped with homemade whipped cream from the spoiled Guernsey, Mirabelle. But even if we had money to purchase the ingredients—and Mirabelle hadn't been sold at the Dry Hollow auction—we would never use our limited time for such a frivolous thing as baking desserts.

Someone taps my shoulder. Turning, I see Lydie Risser, who is also from Split Rock Community, where the baked goods just came from. Lydie's petite frame nearly topples with the weight of her womb. "A girl's outside needing to speak with you," she says, lacing arms over her middle, out of protection or still out of shame; I cannot tell which. "Says it's about some story she read?"

I haven't completely recuperated from the night Star miscarried, as her loss brought back the full magnitude of my own. The last thing I want is to share my story with a stranger who yearns to see my heartache in print. "Whoever it is," I intone, "please inform her that I do not wish to speak with any more reporters."

Lydie looks down. "She says she isn't a reporter."

I push on the door my back was leaning against and stride down the side of the house. A slender young woman stands below the east porch steps, bending at the waist to stretch out her back, the languid movements turning her hip-length hair into an auburn flame. She spots me coming around the corner and smiles. I do not smile in return. I've seen enough over the years.

"Are you Rhoda, the head midwife?" she asks.

"Yes. And your name is . . . ?"

"Amelia. I read your article."

"Sorry. Didn't write it, so it's not my article."

I make no apology for my abruptness. I still wonder if Amelia's a reporter, flashing her million-dollar smile while trying to get the true story behind my reason to stay in a community that is close to abandoned. I point over her right shoulder to a BMW whose windshield is splattered with bugs and dust. "That yours?" I ask.

"Yes," she says. "I'm not from around here."

"I can hear that."

Amelia looks down. "I was wondering . . ." She toes a sandal through the grass the goats have nibbled almost bald. Then she splays a hand across her stomach that's as flat as a piece of notebook paper. "Would your place have room for me?" She pauses, keeps her eyes on the ground. "I'm . . . pregnant."

It takes considerable effort to conceal my surprise. I've never had a girl of Amelia's economic level request to stay here. "Yes, we've got some bunks open," I say. "Room and board's free, but we expect every girl to pull her load. Health permitting, of course."

Amelia's eyes widen. She sinks both fists deep into her pockets, as if hiding hands never marred by one hard day's work. "How soon you want me to start?"

I scan her white jeans and silk camisole. "Soon as you can get changed." I about-face and march up the porch steps, already speculating about the story behind our new arrival.

"Sounds like a plan," she calls.

The slight tremor underscoring Amelia's confident voice stops me in my tracks. Turning from the screen door, I squint against the sun, trying to decipher whether the insecurity lurking behind her hazel eyes is authentic, or if this is just an audition and she is already playing her part.

Amelia, 2014

One of the pregnant girls named Lydie Risser pinches the skirt of her prairie dress and lets me step past her into the house.

She follows me, her weird black boots tapping. "This is where we eat," Lydie says, her eyes darting around the dining room like they're chasing a fly.

I stare up at the high ceiling's splatters of mold and then down at the wood floor covered with footprints. I touch the top of the table scarred with two sets of initials a bored boarder probably carved with a butter knife. I wonder if vandalism's the only proof of the love some boy claimed would never die. Whoever she is, I know how she feels.

"They have good food here?" I ask Lydie.

Probably paid to keep her mouth shut, the prairie girl doesn't answer, but instead leads me through the dining room and into the kitchen. Two boarders, introduced as Desiree Jones and Terese Cullum, share the butcher block, dicing onions and peppers for supper.

Desiree's watering brown eyes shrink to slits. Clenching her hip with one hand, she waves the knife at me like a pointer. "Where you from?"

"Connecticut."

"That's a long ways off."

Tell me about it.

I peer around the kitchen just to keep away from Desiree's eyes. The plain white walls are decorated with nail pegs above pencil tracings of different-sized frying pans. The wooden counters are scarred but clean. Huge old jars are labeled: sugar, rice, flour, oatmeal, coffee grounds, and raspberry leaf tea. An old-fashioned stove—trimmed in, like, chrome or something—crouches against the back wall. The stove's black legs make it look like an insect.

"There's no electricity?" I ask, trying to sound casual.

Terese and Lydie shake their heads. Desiree smirks.

"Oh, my gosh," I breathe. "Why'd you all come?"

Using her forearm to brush dreadlocked bangs out of her eyes, Terese squishes hamburger, eggs, and crackers into a mash and smiles. "Same as you, I'm guessing, sweetheart. We had no other choice."

Caught off guard by her words, I have to look away until I'm sure I'm not going to cry. What Terese and the rest of these girls don't know is that I *do* have choices. Too many of them, in fact. I had to come the whole way down here to the middle of nowhere just to find out who I am and, without my parents' pressure, what my choice would really be.

I've been slaving in the garden for hours, and Terese's five-year-old son, Luca, is *still* squatting barefoot in the dirt beside me—all of his sweaty blond hair making him smell a little like a wet dog. Weaving stubby fingers through the carrot tassels, he plucks out weeds that are taking over this garden as much as the insects buzzing around my head. But every other second, Luca has to look over and stare. He seems to find my annoyance with farm life as entertaining as most city kids would find reality TV.

Slapping a mosquito, I flick it off my leg and snap, "What?"

"Nothin'," Luca says, dropping eyes and knees to the ground. He begins to weed like his sixth year depends on it. Smart kid.

We weed a row in silence—well, except for my grumbling. Then I slap another mosquito and ask, "Your mom just lets you run around like this?"

"Yeah'um." Luca smears his forehead with dirt, which doesn't stand out since he's already so covered with dust and grime. "She be on kitchen duty." He shrugs a bony shoulder at the back of the house, covered by a straggly line of cedars. "And she can't catch me nohow. My brother or sister's making her toes all swelled up."

"Well—" I rock back on my sandaled heels and try to think of something smart to tell him—"You should be careful."

Taking a carrot from his pocket, Luca crunches it in half.

"What're you doing!" I scold. "That's not washed!"

Luca's sweaty hair swishes like a fringe. His jaws snap shut.

"Spit. It. *Out*," I command.

This time, Luca doesn't even bother shaking his head.

"Whatever, kid. It's *your* stomach." But leaning across the row, I brush carrot pieces off his chest anyway.

"What're you doing?"

Luca and I both jump at the sound of the deep voice. We step back from each other and turn toward the garden's gate.

This tall guy, in bare feet and black pants folded up to muscly shins, steps forward. The shadow cast by the brim of his straw hat hides most of his face, but I can see his lips are turned into a frown. "Luca," he says, snapping his fingers. *"Kumm esse."*

I brush my dirty hands off on my shorts. "He's okay. Really."

"No." The hat brim's shadow shifts, revealing his features, and I watch his dark gaze bounce off my legs and refocus on his feet. "You'll come now, Luca."

I've not been, like, patient with the kid myself, but his tone gets to me. "What's it to you?"

The guy lifts his eyes and stares like he's looking right through me. Then he snaps his fingers again. Five-year-old Luca throws me a grin before running after the arrogant stranger, who doesn't even look over his shoulder to see if the boy is following.

Rhoda, 2014

At the basin, I start to wash my hands. "I'd say you're about eight weeks. That sound about right?" There's no response. Wiping my hands, I glance over my shoulder. A blush has crept into Amelia's cheeks. She sits higher on the examining table and tightens the sheet around her waist. Then she nods.

"Are you eighteen?"

"Yes." Amelia pauses. "Had my birthday last month."

"Congratulations," I say drily. I can always tell when my boarders are lying.

I go over to the cabinet and extract Amelia's file from the Ws for her last name, Walker. Amelia hops off the examining table—dragging her sheet like a toga—and gets dressed behind the screen. I take a seat at the desk and flip open the file. Uncapping a pen, I fill in the information I've already gathered. "And do your parents know where you are?"

"Yes," she says. There's a tinny ring as a belt buckle strikes the floor. A rustle of material sliding over legs, followed by a light hop and the rasp of a zipper. As funny as it sounds, the familiar melody make me miss wearing jeans. "Well," she adds, "my dad does."

I wince. When I left Wisconsin, I did not know the scale of what I was doing until my own child was taken from me and *I* was the parent who was left behind. "Believe it or not, Amelia," I say, my voice firm, "just because you're eighteen doesn't mean that your mom doesn't deserve to know where you are."

"Believe me—" Amelia comes out from behind the screen, all sass and cranberry hair, the sheet bundled against her chest—"she's better off *not* knowing."

I tilt my head and stare at this striking girl, trying to understand the true meaning behind her words. "How did you hear about us?" I ask.

"I told you, read an article."

"The article that was posted online? 'Abandoned Mennonite Community Becomes Home for Unwed Mothers'?"

Amelia fingers an earring and sighs, "That's the one."

I recap the pen and drum it on the desk. Amelia crosses her arms and jiggles her bare foot. I look down at it and am taken aback. Her toes are mangled: the polished nails curl downward; the arches are calloused knots. Those tough dancer's feet look strange, compared to Amelia's soft, manicured hands. And instead of judging Amelia for her apparent wealth and obvious beauty—thinking the combination gives her a life of ease—I find myself remembering the insecurity I felt when I first arrived at Hopen Haus.

I say, still tapping the pen, "You're really brave, Amelia."

The girl tightens her arms. "You shouldn't say that yet," she says, staring at the wall.

For the first time in so many cases similar to this, I allow myself to feel Amelia Walker's pain. My chest positively *aches* with it. I want to tell Amelia that she is indeed brave, that many girls in her situation wouldn't even contemplate continuing the pregnancy.

And yet I say nothing. I simply close Amelia's file and

rise to my feet. Pulling open the cabinet drawer, I stow it among hundreds of others that conceal the information of girls and their babies long gone from here. I run my fingers over the tops—catching glimpses of crisp white pages tucked among the yellowish-brown folders. I know the girls' constant arrivals and departures are why I cannot let myself feel. I have already loved and lost enough.

When I turn back to the examining table, Amelia herself has left. So intent on my memories, I didn't even hear her close the door. The sheet she used rests on the table. In her wake trails a familiar perfume, and I find myself staring at the place she just exited through, wondering who she's running from . . . wondering who she is.

Standing in the doorway of the barn, I scan the stalls for Uriah Rippentoe, who has barely come into Hopen Haus since he and Wilbur Byler, our driver, returned from their trip. I had encouraged Alice to let Uriah go to Canada with Wilbur, as I had thought the manly camaraderie might alleviate some of Uriah's tension that washes over everything like a malignant tide. But Uriah's sullen disposition and avoidance make him now seem even worse. I fear that Uriah is angry with me for allowing Ernest Looper to share his attic room. It should not matter—because it would not matter if the girls did not care for their roommates.

I would like to speak with Uriah about this, mainly for an excuse to see how he is doing, yet I cannot find him. The Rhode Island Red hens are clucking from their enclosure. The loosened Nubian goats are nibbling on the crabgrass sprouting alongside the perimeter of the barn, their bells jangling as they shake rain from their ears. But Uriah, their master, is not in the barn or in the yard. The clothed figures suddenly flashing through the tack room slats blur my eyes with confusion. What are people doing, congregated in the barn? And what are they talking about? I have no answers, but what I *do* know is that they would not be hiding here if they wanted me, the head midwife, to know the topics being discussed.

I stride across the floor, sawdust clumping to my muddy boot heels. The barn door that I have released thwacks shut behind me. At the sound, a man's voice grows silent. I yank open the door to the tack room. I choke on the must the abrupt movement conjures and on the disbelief at those I see. Ernest Looper is among the group, along with Alice Rippentoe and Wilbur Byler. Alice's cheeks glow red. Looper stares at the floor, tangled with bridles and bits and crusted cans of saddle soap that are all as senseless as a buggy with no horsepower to pull it.

Pushing aside a hank of brown hair, Wilbur folds his arms. "We think it's high time you got electricity here," he says. So, though I am one of his employers, Wilbur is to be the defiant spokesperson of the group. But I suspect Alice is the one who initiated the meeting. The one who has taken advantage of the fact that Star's near-death experience two nights ago has underscored her belief that Hopen Haus must accept change to thrive.

I stare past Wilbur's posturing stance to Looper's

lowered head. I am hurt that I have opened my home to him and, in exchange, he has taken their side without hearing mine. As if sensing this, Looper lifts his eyes. In those two-toned orbs, I see no culpability or pleading. Only a firm reminder that, at eighteen years old, I once made the heedlessly life-altering decision to give our son up without giving the child's father a chance to express his feelings on the matter. And that now, we should not choose sides, but pay heed to the vantage points of each. This decision—to accept electricity or reject it—will not just affect those currently sheltered beneath Hopen Haus's roof.

It will affect the lives of every girl who will ever come.

"What would it take to—to get electricity?" I stammer, wondering if compromising will make it easier for Looper to forgive me. "Structurally, I mean."

Alice peers over her shoulder. Her face is still bright with embarrassment, but I know that she is shocked that I have given in so easily. Though I understand guilt is my main motivation, I am as shocked as she.

"It wouldn't be too hard," Looper says, each word well chosen, but he avoids my eyes. "I could wire everything in a day or two, and it wouldn't take that much renovation . . . or money."

"We'd have to talk to David Graber, I'm sure," Alice adds, naming Fannie Graber's son, the only deacon and ballast of authority Dry Hollow Community has left. "And then he'd probably have to go before the bishops in Indiana. If they don't want us to have electricity, or allow us to drive cars, we might have to secede from the community."

"We will secede from nothing," I say, my voice hard. "This is not the Civil War."

Wilbur Byler clears his throat and looks at the wall, where a yoke garlanded in cobwebs is hung. "Pardon me, Rhoda . . . Alice," he says, "but you might not have a community left to secede from. Uriah and I stopped by the community in Indiana on our way down here, and they're splitting off right and left. The conservatives are moving back to Lancaster, and the progressives are remaining behind."

Alice looks at me. Panic ignites her pale-green eyes. We have been receiving financial support from the community in Indiana: a predetermined agreement, since both those going and those staying knew Hopen Haus could not keep functioning if the majority of Dry Hollow left us behind. We have not been receiving a lot of support, obviously, but enough to cover the cost of dry goods and medical supplies. If their community implodes, Hopen Haus—like a child whose umbilical cord is severed—will not survive.

9

Amelia, 2014

Rain drips off the front of the arrogant stranger's hat, the owner of which I now know is named Uriah, the midwife's son. He takes the hat off, wipes it back and forth across his leg, and stomps his boots on the entrance rug. I glance across the breakfast table and see that Lydie's watching him too. Every girl in this place is probably watching him. Jealousy shoots down my spine like a lightning bolt, which is pretty ridiculous. We're all pregnant and couldn't get Uriah's attention if we wanted it. Not that I'm interested in him or anything. I'm just saying. But of course, prairie-girl Lydie is clueless to my feelings. The poor girl probably doesn't even know what jealousy is. She just smiles at me, takes a sip of apple juice, and wipes her mouth with the back of her hand.

"How long 'til you fell asleep last night?" she asks. "I heard you *rutsching*."

"I don't know—'round two?" I stab my fork into the sunny-side up egg and watch the yolk ooze yellow into my oatmeal. Pushing my plate away, I turn my head and ask, "What's *rutsching* mean, anyway?"

"Moving a lot; it's Pennsylvania Dutch." Lydie reaches into the pocket of her apron. (Yes, an apron. I'm telling you, this girl is strange.) "Here." She places a Baggie filled with dried green leaves on the cloth napkin beside my plate. "This always makes me feel better."

I look down. My bleary eyes grow wide. "Didn't think you were the type."

Tin plates drop onto the table and a chair scrapes back across the floor. "It's meadow tea, not marijuana." I peek through my fingers and watch Uriah hook his hat over the left spike of the chair. His dark curls are wet and his cheeks red, though the sun's barely up in the sky. Sane people aren't awake at this hour. I just want to be back home, asleep in my queen-size bed.

"Does Lydie look like a pothead to you?" he asks.

I glance over at my roommate. Her head—with its bobbing braids—is bowed and her hands folded as she prays over her meal, though none of the midwives are here to enforce the silent blessing. The girl could be one of Grandma Sarah's Norman Rockwell paintings brought to life. I look back at Uriah. I'm surprised to see that he's smiling. "Well, no," I admit.

Taking a seat, Uriah dusts his eggs with salt and pepper and cuts the slippery whites with his fork. "*Mamm* says you're from Connecticut?"

My face warms at the thought that he's been asking about me. Then I realize that blushing's not the way a pregnant seventeen-year-old should react, so I reply, "Yeah," as if I could care less. You'd think you wouldn't want attention from boys when you're pregnant, but you do. I guess wanting that attention's what got me into this mess in the first place.

"Man . . ." Uriah shakes his head and uses buttered toast to scoop up the eggs. "Wish I could live somewhere like that."

"The quiet's nice too," I say, thinking, *If you count goat-petting as entertainment.*

Lydie shifts on the bench. I look away from Uriah and follow the path of Lydie's eyes. Ernest Looper—who's, like, the Hopen Haus handyman—has come into the dining room. Beside him is this younger, huskier-looking guy with a pink face and a bunch of chopped brown hair. The two of them sit at the far end of the table. Looper takes the head; the man takes the left-hand side. The oatmeal and eggs polished off by us hungry preggo girls, Terese and Desiree bring out plates piled with hash browns made from last night's potatoes. The men lean back as the plates are set before them, thank the girls, and start eating.

To my surprise—and, yes, jealousy!—Uriah reaches

across the table and touches the top of Lydie's hand. He says something in a foreign language I guess is Pennsylvania Dutch. Lydie nods in reply, but her eyes are on the Mason jar. Uriah removes his hand and wraps it around his coffee mug. He takes a sip but keeps looking at the man who's been watching Uriah with Lydie. The man raises his coffee mug toward Uriah in some kind of toast. Uriah does the same, but he doesn't look happy.

Not able to stand it any longer, I ask, "Who's that?"

Uriah says, "Wilbur Byler."

"Lydie," I say, "you know him too?"

Lydie blinks and looks up from her plate. "I'm going to lie down," she whispers. "Will you wake me before chores?"

I nod and watch her go. Lydie's apron sash is hanging loose, and her left foot drags as if she has a limp, though she walked just fine when we came downstairs.

"What's with all the code language?" I ask Uriah.

He says, "It's not code if you understand."

"Well, fill me in, 007. What were you and Lydie talking about?"

Smiling, Uriah stretches across the table to stab a bite of Lydie's eggs. "Why, you jealous?" His dark eyes latch onto mine, refusing to let go.

"Don't flatter yourself," I snap, just to make up for the blush sweeping across my face.

───※───

I drop our plates off at the kitchen and go upstairs to find Lydie facedown on the bottom bunk. Closing the door quietly, I stare at the bare white line between Lydie's thick, dishwater-colored braids. I wonder if she's okay, but remembering all the times my mom would go into the master bedroom and I would stand in the open door—staring at her and waiting to be invited in—once again, I discover that I'm too afraid to ask.

So I tiptoe across the floor and pull open the bottom drawer of the cheap dresser we share. The stuff inside rattles and Lydie turns onto her side. Taking out a bottle of lotion, I squirt a line down my right palm that's blistered from pulling weeds. My hands are sore and I've lost two fake nails already, but none of this bothers me as much as I thought it would.

"You sick?" I whisper.

Lydie shakes her head. One braid flaps to the side. "Just homesick," she sniffs.

"For your family?"

She nods.

"Any brothers or sisters?"

Wiping her eyes on her skirt, Lydie sits up. "Five, counting me."

She looks so terrible that I have to tease. "That's a basketball team!"

Lydie says, "That's not that big of a *familye*. Our *nochberen* have nine *kinner*, and she's expecting again."

"Where do people like you live?"

"Split Rock," says Lydie, my sarcasm lost on her.

"Never heard of it."

"I would think not many *Englischers* have."

"Is that what I am, an *'Englischer'*?"

Lydie smiles at my attempt to mimic her accent. "Just means you're not part of the community."

"That," I laugh, "I'm most certainly not."

I toss the lotion back into my shower caddy, but there are no showers here, just this Stone Age tub we're only allowed to use on alternating days. (I've thought about bribing Lydie for one of hers.) Pulling back the curtain over the window, I hold a compact mirror out with one hand and try to spruce up my appearance. Crimping my eyelashes, I can almost picture that first ballet recital when my mom used her fancy makeup kit to prepare me for the stage. I was six years old, and since that night, I've learned it's better to hide behind a mask than show your true feelings to people who just don't care.

"What's it like?" murmurs Lydie. "Being *Englisch*, I mean."

Swiping gloss across my lips, I drive away thoughts of my mom and blot the leftover gloss on a tissue. "Hard to say. I've never known anything different." I point the tube at her. "Why don't you tell me what it's like being Mennonite?"

"I've never known anything different either." Lydie pulls at a thread on her dress. "But it's like everyone's watching, and you—you still can't be seen."

Smiling, I swagger over and toss my gold makeup bag into Lydie's lap. "Put some of that stuff on. It'll getcha noticed." I don't tell her that, while putting on that mask will get her noticed, the true, broken parts of her still won't be understood.

Lydie pulls the tassel that unzips the bag. She holds the tube of lip gloss up to the light coming in through a gap in the curtained window behind our bunk. For a while, she watches the oily bubble slip back and forth. "I already know what it's like to be noticed," she whispers.

I stop brushing my hair. Through the compact mirror sitting on top of the dresser, I stare at Lydie. She doesn't know she's being watched, so she lets sadness rise up beneath her clear brown eyes. Is Prairie-girl wearing a mask even harder to see through than mine?

Setting my brush on the dresser, I turn. "I'm not trying to be mean or anything, Lydie, but what are you doing here? You don't belong . . . not with the rest of us."

Lydie sets the tube of lip gloss in her palm and curls her fingers around it. "No, I don't belong," she says. "But I can't go back to Split Rock. Not now."

Beth, 1996

For many weeks after I arrived at Hopen Haus, whenever Wilbur Byler's truck drove up the lane, I would run to the springhouse or the barn and wait for him to leave, my arms laced over my womb and my heart thudding beneath my ribs. Wilbur was the only one in the community with access to the outside world. The only one with access to newspapers, television, radio, and whatever other media the Fitzpatricks might have employed to search for me and their kidnapped daughter. But weeks turned into months and nothing ever happened. Instead of running away when Wilbur came, I just started avoiding his eyes. For some reason, this made him more intent to meet mine. But when our gazes locked—across the yard or over the table at mealtimes—he never said a word. Fannie teased me, saying I had an admirer. I feared there was more to it than that. Did he know the truth?

However, as I entered my last trimester, the adrenaline that had accelerated by escape ebbed. The hearty food, manual labor, and fresh air started to lace my worried frame with muscle and brought out the rose hue in my cheeks. This is what I remember from those twenty-two weeks before my daughter's birth: lamplight polishing the spartan dining room table as the other girls and I savored a meal our hands had harvested from the earth, washed, diced, and cooked. The scent of lavender and lye as we stirred clothing in a large copper basin, suspended and steaming over a roaring outdoor fire. After rinsing, we'd spread towels on the side porch outside the mudroom. Placing clothing on half of each towel, we'd cover the clothing with the other half and twist the towel between us. Warm water would stream from the fabric, hitting the ground and splattering our bare feet. We'd talk and we'd laugh as suds shimmered on the breeze.

I remember the summer nights my roommates Hannah, Karen, Mari, and I draped our foreheads and necks with damp rags we'd cooled in a bucket in the springhouse. Beneath the white cotton sheets, our different-sized bellies bloomed before us like phases of the moon: waxing crescent, first quarter, waxing gibbous, full. In the darkness flecked with starshine that filtered through the curtained windows, we talked about the bonds we'd made before coming to Hopen Haus and those we'd severed by choosing to stay. Though I listened more than spoke, I knew that this crumbling, Civil War–era house had provided me with sisters and with the camaraderie for which I'd always longed.

Because of this, it was only natural that I would accept everything about the community so that they would, without question, fully accept me. I folded up the jeans, T-shirts, and sweatshirts I'd brought and started wearing tights and secondhand cape dresses printed with a smattering of pin-sized flowers. I parted my hair and twined the dark locks into a bun. I did not wear a *kapp*, since I was not baptized into the church.

During the bimonthly fellowship services—where the community sat in Hopen Haus's dining room that was converted into a sanctuary, with two sets of long wooden benches on which the women sat on one side and the men on the other—I could not sing the hymns in the *Ausbund* or understand the recited text or sermons, which the bishop and deacons all read in German. So I stared at the heads of the women seated in front of me, and then stared at the heads who were behind me when we turned and knelt in front of the benches to pray. I wanted their *kapp*. I wanted that exquisite symbol of belonging, more than I wanted to know what that symbol actually meant.

Also, I knew that casting off the apparel of my previous life would make it far easier to disappear.

Head midwife Fannie Graber accepted my interest in church baptism as she accepted everything else: without smiling or frowning. But somehow I knew that she was well pleased. Most of the Hopen Haus girls, upon delivery of their child, would begin itching to return to their former lifestyles, filled with the technology the community had shunned. Bishop Leon Yoder, however, took my baptism more seriously than Fannie did. After a week of discussion among the deacons, I was deemed suitable for baptism. But there was one stipulation: Fannie would first have to teach me the Mennonites' core doctrine.

I was excited to hear this news. Nonetheless, I cannot say that, at this point, I truly understood the motivations of my heart. I just knew that I wanted my daughter to be born into the safety of a *familye*. Though I'd become an orphan by choice, I wanted my child never to suffer from the loneliness that I'd felt growing up. My proving period—a requirement before entering the Mennonite church—lasted until the week before my daughter was born, which was pretty lenient, considering that proving times can take up to three years.

The Hopen Haus girls and I would finish taking turns bathing our awkward, beautiful bodies in the vintage claw-foot tub that had been deemed too worldly, so its gilded feet had been hacked off and replaced with halved cinder blocks. Then we brushed each other's hair, which clung to our skulls in long, damp skeins that pregnancy hormones had made thick and sleek. I watched the rest of them trundle off to bed with the languid strides and hooded eyes of adult children who rested in the fact that—for the time being, at least—they were cared for and loved.

Night after night, I would then pad downstairs in my braided hair and full-length gown I'd ordered from Lehman's catalog. I would find Fannie Graber in the living room, rocking in a cane-backed chair so close to the open woodstove, I feared an ember would pop and she would get burned. Her arthritic fingers would be clutching a treat: a burlap bag of *schnitzappels* left over from a pie or two fragrant mugs of meadow tea, whose steam curled toward the rafters like smoke. She would pass me half of whatever she had, and the two of us would savor the rare quiet, interrupted solely by the crackling logs or the brays of the donkeys corralled in the barn.

I looked forward to those evenings more than anything all day. In Fannie's presence, I was no longer cognizant of my faults, but confident and reassured. I felt much like I had felt when Thomas Fitzpatrick asked me to bear his child. My mother's abandonment had skewed my perception to the point where I equated the interest and attention with love, and I would have done anything—said anything—to ensure that it continued. I am not saying that Thomas Fitzpatrick abused this power. Nor did Fannie.

She did not make me memorize passages from tattered books whose titles I could not pronounce. She did not make me repent of everything I had ever done before I could spotlessly join the church, and fearing our intimacy

would wane if she knew the truth, I did not tell her.
Instead, with the soft smile and faraway eyes of a wizened
storyteller, she told me about the Mennonite church's
beliefs and practices, which had originated when Dutch
Mennonite leaders met in Dordrecht, the Netherlands,
on April 21, 1632.

The Dordrecht Confession of Faith stressed belief in
Christ, the saved status of children, the importance of pro-
claiming God's Word and "making disciples" (one of the
reasons, Fannie confided, that she and Elmer had founded
Hopen Haus), baptism of believers, absolute love, non-
resistance rather than retaliation as one's personal response
to injustice and maltreatment, and the church as a non-
hierarchical community.

Sometimes Fannie's eyes would close even as her mouth
continued speaking, and then her head would bob until
her *kapp* strings draped her gently rising and falling chest.
I often looked over and saw, by the firelight, the smile lines
crinkling the skin around Fannie's closed eyes; the coarse
gray hair unraveling around her temples; the knots on the
old, veined hands that had ushered so many children into
the world without losing a single one.

I was in awe of this woman, and of her servant's heart,
which went above and beyond to reach out to me—a way-
ward orphan who had found a family where no one was her
kin. In that moment, even more than my desire to escape
my past, I knew that I would have happily given up my
Englischer world just to step into that hallowed realm of
Fannie Graber's love.

Despite the idyllic nature of our community, even back then it was evident just how shorthanded the midwives were. Fannie and her younger sister, Charlotte—who wasn't young at all, and so revealed just how old Fannie was—and Sadie Gingrich took care of two dozen women, who'd all give birth within the next thirty-three weeks. Because of this, we were often brought into the examining room in pairs. We were taught how to measure our womb's growth and to watch our ankles and faces for signs of water retention, and encouraged to eat whole foods and exercise daily so our bodies would be prepared for labor—the most arduous task of our lives.

Although I did learn more about holistic remedies for prenatal and postpartum care—blessed thistle herb, raspberry leaf tea, evening primrose oil—this was my second child. What I had not learned in my first year of graduate school, I had learned from my previous birth.

Thus, my clipped answers to Fannie's questions during class revealed both my medical background and my mounting boredom.

One morning at breakfast, Charlotte told me I was exempt from that afternoon's class and that my next prenatal appointment would be scheduled alone. Maybe it was the awkward silence as Fannie examined me, or the weight of secrets that I could no longer shoulder along with the increasing weight of my womb. But just as I had once confided in Thom, I threw caution to the wind and told

Fannie the truth. I told her no specifics, only that I had kidnapped the very child I was about to birth. She—whose rheumy eyes had seen just about everything and could imagine the rest—did not falter. She just nodded, snapped off one glove that clung to the swollen knuckles of her right hand, and reached across the table to help me sit up.

"Beth," she said, "Hopen Haus has its name for a reason. It was founded so that you and others like you can find hope to begin again." She paused. "Now if you'd taken a child off the street, it would be another matter entirely. But the fact that the child's inside your womb makes me think an intelligent girl like you must've had a reason to run."

"They didn't want her," I whispered. "They decided they didn't want her anymore, and I . . ." I touched the stunning sphere housing my unseen baby, who was already in the transverse position in preparation to descend. Tears dripped on the sheet spooled around the lower half of my body, as in horror I imagined what could have been done. "And you see, I wanted her so badly . . ."

Fannie went over to the standing basin she called a *weschbohl.* She scrubbed her hands and forearms with a nail brush lathered with the harsh lye soap we used on our clothes. Looking over her shoulder, she smiled, though her eyes remained opaque. "For the sake of yourself and the child," she said, "you can't live in fear. . . . You must let yourself live."

After this conversation, I was excused from laundry duty and asked to assist Fannie in standard checkups. I tried to explain that a majority of my learning had been acquired through bioethics classes and not through first-hand experience, but she did not seem concerned. She did not seem concerned about anything, really. And I would have doubted Fannie's ability to manage Hopen Haus if I hadn't seen, beneath her dimpled smile and kind blue eyes, a woman who—like some New Testament miracle—could feed a houseful of pregnant women with venison and a few loaves of bread.

Amelia, 2014

I'm on my way to the springhouse for ham and cheese when that guy named Wilbur Byler comes charging out of the springhouse, his head down and gorilla hands balled at his sides. For some reason I freak out and hide behind a tree. I peek around it like a little kid and watch Wilbur dart across the yard faster than you'd think he could, judging by his appearance, which isn't helped at all by his grungy, bad-fitting clothes. He's almost to the fence that goes around Hopen Haus when he stops and turns, looking around the yard. Apparently not seeing anything worth his time, Wilbur opens the gate and jerks the bill of his baseball cap low over his eyes.

I keep standing there, barely breathing, and don't even know why I feel so scared. Soon I hear Wilbur's diesel passenger van start up, and I step out from behind the tree and push on the springhouse door. Wilbur didn't latch it, and it creaks as it opens, reminding me of every horror movie I've ever seen. And there have been a bunch. It's hard to see through the gloominess, since there are only two tiny windows, and they're covered with wooden blinds. My sweat turns cold and I start shivering. Is my body scrambling to keep up with the temperature change, or is there something creepy in here that I can't see?

Mold, sucking up the muddy water pooling on the dirt floor, runs along the bottom half of the white stone walls. Huge hams and slabs of mystery meat are hooked to the rafters holding up the roof. Big wooden barrels with lids store apples with labels like *Golden Delicious*, *Red Delicious*, *McIntosh*, and *Granny Smith*. Next to the apple barrels are tightly sealed ceramic crocks that hold rounds of cheese wrapped in wax paper. Shiny metal pitchers filled with buttermilk are dulled with cold. Another crock holds the goat cheese that Uriah pasteurizes on the stove all the time. I can't even stand to sniff the stuff without barfing.

Never a fan of the dark, I use the crock closest to the entrance to prop open the springhouse door. I walk back inside and stare up at the ceiling. The hams are still out of reach, even when I stand on my tippy toes. Somehow, when Lydie told me to "fetch the ham and cheese," I'd imagined my world back home: this gigantic, stainless-steel refrigerator with a deli section of sandwich stuff kept under plastic. Not this eerie cave where anything might be hiding.

I go over to the nearest apple barrel, thinking of using it like a step stool so I can pull down the ham. Taking hold of the top, I begin to drag it. From behind the barrel, someone stands up. I scream bloody murder and scramble backward.

"Be quiet!" Uriah yells.

I gasp, hands on knees as I catch my breath. Then I yell back, "You're the one yelling! What's going on, Uriah? What just happened with you and Wilbur?"

He shrugs. "I was supposed to go on a drive with him and help him load furniture, and . . . now I'm not."

"You go driving with him often?"

"Sometimes," he says. "If Wilbur needs help loading a piece of furniture that the Mennonites sell to the *Englisch*."

I think of Lydie's question about how it felt to be *Englisch* and ask, "You like it here?"

Tucking the tail of his shirt into his pants, Uriah leans against an apple barrel. "Did you know there used to be two hundred and fifty people living on this farm?" he asks, and I shake my head. "Back then," he says, "I didn't have to work so hard. This place wasn't so run-down. It was really—I don't know—nice." Uriah cocks his head at me. "What about you?"

I look past him, out through the open doorway, to the light. Suddenly not liking how the tables have turned, I say, "I'm just here to—to find out some things before I make a decision."

Uriah takes off his straw hat again and plucks at the strands. "What kind of decision?"

I cup a hand over my stomach. Closing my eyes, my pulse thumps in my ears. I remember that awful night, during supper, when I told my parents about my pregnancy, and my mom told me she could fix it—like this baby was just another one of my mistakes.

I say, swallowing hard, "I left because I wasn't sure I wanted to—keep an appointment."

Uriah says, "And you're here to see if you do?"

I nod. My eyes sting.

"What if you don't find what you're looking for?"

I look over at the spring in the dirt floor, bubbling up from some unseen place. What courage those pioneers must have had, to settle here trusting that the spring would never run dry. "Guess if I don't get my answer," I say, "then that will be an answer in itself." I walk out of the springhouse. Despite last week's rain, dust swirls around my feet.

10

Beth, 1996

The September morning I was baptized into the Old Order
Mennonite church, fog swaddled the valley below Hopen
Haus like cotton bunting. The trees had turned since the
premature frost. Their branches now resembled paintbrushes
whose tassels had been dipped in pots of yellow, red, and
gold. I had asked to be baptized in the wash-out creek running down the mountain behind Jonah and Miriam Fisher's
haus. Submersion seemed more definite than standard sprin-
kling, and I hoped that when Bishop Yoder drew me out of
the water, the part of my spirit that had dried up after my
mother's departure would be replenished and whole.

I walked through the woods, flanked by the rest of the

community, on a pathway that had been made by wild turkeys scratching the decaying foliage with their claws. I looked down and touched the fabric of the cape dress Fannie had stitched in hours she did not have to spare. Tears blurred my steps. It was the first cape dress I'd worn that had not been passed down from other women in the Dry Hollow Community. This, and the delicate *kapp* that I would don after my baptism, were the first articles of clothing someone had made for me with their own two hands.

During the past twenty-two weeks, ensconced in Fannie Graber's unconditional love, I learned that I had been trying to patch my mother's absence with things and with people who were never meant to fill me up. Ernest Looper had let me down by not keeping in touch when I purposely walked out of his life, humiliation curling my shoulders and my stomach concealing our unborn son. Although I never should have pursued Thomas Fitzpatrick's affections, he had let me down by agreeing that destroying his child was the best possible choice, therefore toppling off a pedestal I should have never placed him on. I had tried to fill my mother's void by gathering proof of my intelligence: being valedictorian of my high school class—granted, we only had a hundred students—pursuing a master's degree right after my bachelor's, and planning on acquiring a PhD right after that. And yet it had all failed me. Every single person and thing.

I knew better than to place Fannie Graber in a limelight whose malignant power was as transmuting as a black hole. However, plodding toward the creek, I did pray to the Savior Fannie Graber spoke of so intimately. I prayed that he would forgive my sins and wash me in the water, making me clean, so that the donning of my new name, Rhoda Mummau, and *kapp* would not be the only alterations. That the submersion would be a sign that I was leaving the bitterness toward my mother behind and could now be the kind of mother for which I'd always longed.

I stepped closer to the creek. Swollen from the previous night's rain, the water rose over its embankment, the chocolate froth polishing the tips of the community's shoes. The men, women, and children harmonized a cappella hymns led by Abner Zook, whose baritone was as commanding as his brow. Fannie and I approached the creek edge hand in hand. The sodden ground was surely placing her back in jeopardy; it had just begun to heal since the last time it gave out. But I knew Fannie wanted to lead me down to the water so that, through her uneven stance and arthritic hand, I could find the strength to stand on my own two feet.

Bishop Yoder, who was already in the creek, assisted Fannie as she minced down the muddy embankment. Her nostrils pinched and lips whitened as the water lapped up to her breastbone. The water was direct mountain runoff and therefore colder than it would have been cradled for hours against the earth. Bishop Yoder did not offer me his hand, but waded back toward the center of the creek and waited for me to follow.

A flock of crows cawed, dissonant with the community's lilting hymns. The water made my nerves tingle. The material of my dress swirled behind me and then sank as I walked deeper into the creek, resisting the urge to gasp from shock. Sound seemed heightened; colors appeared sharper. My daughter shifted languidly in my womb, as if the water had awakened her senses too. Fannie took my hand. Her fingers clutched for mine, seeking their warmth.

The singing ceased as abruptly as it had started. The silence somehow made me feel exposed, almost ridiculous for demanding that I be submerged in a cold, wash-out creek when we could have sprinkled my lowered head in shelter and in warmth. I glanced up to see the three deacons standing on the creek bank, their arms folded. They wore black pants and black coats with the collars pulled up around their ears. Some of the women—Esther Glick, Anna Miller, and Ruth Erb—wore black bonnets with the regulatory pleated two-inch brims. This helped to conceal their eyes. But their lips appeared so dour, I wondered if they would truly welcome me into their cloistered community with a dip in water and a few well-placed words.

Fannie squeezed my hand. I squeezed back and smiled, although my features trembled with fear. I shifted my gaze from the community rimming the bank to Bishop Yoder, who had begun to speak in Pennsylvania Dutch. At first, Fannie tried to interpret for him, but I shook my head, letting her know it was all right to stop. I wanted to immerse myself in the words of another language, in the customs of this antiquated world, where I prayed all of my troubles and sins could truly be forgotten, giving my daughter and me hope to begin again.

Bishop Yoder finished speaking. Water sloshed around him as he moved toward me. Fannie touched my forearm and then stepped back, trying to find her footing amid the slippery rocks. The bishop put his arm around my back and motioned for me to cover my nose. I did and looked to the sky, watching the crows' black bodies cyclone upward.

"Auf deinen Glauben den du bekennt hast vor Gott and viele Zeugen wirst du getauft im Namen des Vaters, des Sohnes und des Heiligen Geistes, Amen," Bishop Yoder said.

Then he dipped me backward. The movement was as graceful as a dancer's, although Bishop Yoder had never danced and, other than that starlit waltz with Ernest Looper, neither had I. The cold crested over my head, blocking all insecurity and sound. I felt my baby ripple inside my womb. It was difficult to tell where the torrent buffeting my body ended and her movements began. When the bishop brought me to the surface, warmth flowed out of my loins, starkly contrasting with the frigid creek. I was too diverted to recognize it at the time, but the moment I was brought gasping from water to air like a woman reborn was the moment that my bag of waters broke. It was the first step in ushering my daughter into the world. It was the first step that would lead to her being taken from me, just as I had taken her from her parents.

Amelia, 2014

I come in from the springhouse, where I've been talking with Uriah, and look around to see if Lydie's still in the kitchen. But Lydie's not in the kitchen, nor in the dining room. I go up to our bedroom and find my roommate sitting on the bottom bunk. She's writing so hard and fast, the pencil pokes through the paper on her lap, tearing the letter.

"What're you doing?" I ask.

Lydie jumps and uses her elbow to block the page. A blush covers her face like a stain. "Just let me finish," she says, "and I'll help you."

Is she writing to Uriah? The idea bothers me more than I'd like to admit. If Uriah and Lydie had showed up at my high school last August, I know I would've thought they'd just walked out of the twilight zone. But somehow here, nothing's really the same. My closest friend is a sixteen-year-old girl who still wears her hair in pigtails. The boy who holds my attention is one who I'd normally never give a second look.

Testing Lydie, I point to the window, watching her out of the corner of my eye. "Guess who I just saw out in the springhouse?" Of course she doesn't play along, just keeps looking down at her lap, so I say, "Uriah. He was talking to Wilbur Byler."

The pencil slips from Lydie's fingers and rolls across the wood floor. The two circles of pink drain from her cheeks. "Were you able to . . . understand?"

Picking up the pencil, I sit next to Lydie and duck my head so my hair won't tangle on the springs beneath the top bunk. "No. But Uriah seemed pretty shaken up."

Lydie looks down again but doesn't say a peep. Then she

crumples the page and hurls the letter onto the quilt on her bed. "I'm going downstairs," she says, smoothing out her dress.

After Lydie leaves, I last about two seconds before my nosiness gets the best of me, which is pretty two-faced, considering my mom's snooping through my diary to find out the things I'd never tell her is part of what drove us apart. I lean back and grab the letter my roommate's thrown. I glance down at the scribbled sentences. But even with a class in introductory German, I can't figure out a word. I know this is why Lydie didn't keep hiding the letter when she saw that I'd come in our room, or why she didn't mind leaving it out in the open when she went downstairs. But the name on the letter is easy enough to understand, even without knowing their foreign tongue. It's a name that's beginning to make my spine tingle: *Uriah.*

Narrowing my eyes, I mash the letter up again and pitch it back onto the bed. I'm annoyed with myself and with my roommate, who must have a real flirtatious streak beneath her sweet *Little House on the Prairie* costume. Suddenly, everything makes sense: that time at breakfast when Uriah reached across the table to touch the top of Lydie's hand; how Lydie cries herself to sleep almost every night; the way Uriah stalks around here like he's carrying the world on his shoulders.

I can picture Lydie downstairs in the kitchen, her big eyes—almost cowlike, now that I think about it—and spaghetti wrists as she chops up a vegetable to go with supper. Without the tranquilizer of Uriah's attention and Lydie's friendship (for I'm starting to wonder if she ever wanted to be my friend), I find that my numbness wears off and I just feel . . . sad.

It's always been like this: whenever I keep myself busy—flitting from project to project or from boy to boy with no time to think—I can forget about my mom's ongoing disappointment, along with this hole in my heart that no amount of attention from the opposite sex can fill. But when life slows down like it has now . . . well, all of the pain surrounding my mom's frustration floats to the surface. Even so, my loneliness makes me miss her so much that I'd rather face her anger than remain here in Hopen Haus, where I have no one but a baby in my belly to remind me of the trust that's been lost in me and, if I keep this baby against my mom's wishes, I will never get back again.

Beth, 1996

I had been Fannie's assistant for two weeks when she asked if I would help her sister Charlotte if any labors took place after sundown. Charlotte was the Hopen Haus dorm *mudder*, since Charlotte was single and both Sadie and Fannie had husbands and families to go home and tend to every night. When a boarder drew close to delivery, it was necessary for Charlotte to have an assistant until another boarder could ride over to Fannie's and bring her back. Fannie and Elmer's house was only a mile from Hopen Haus, as the

crow flies, but the switchbacks on the potholed road and
steep incline made the distance seem farther. At times,
a girl would be in labor, and there would be no way of
contacting Fannie. Unlike most Old Order Mennonite
communities, no one in Dry Hollow even had a telephone
installed in their barn. They had to rely on farmer Walt
Hollis's phone line if there was an emergency.

Seeing the need, I agreed to Fannie's request and became
Charlotte's stand-in midwife, though I would soon need
her birthing assistance myself. Those first few times, my
heart would race as I changed sheets on the bed in the
birthing room—which is the examining room now—or
stuffed the firebox with split wood and set a pot of water
on the stove to boil, sure that before Fannie's arrival, a baby
would be born. But Fannie somehow always made it in
time.

The Sabbath evening I went into labor, Charlotte confided in me that we were supposed to try to give Fannie the
night off. Fannie's arthritis was swollen from standing in
the frigid creek during my baptism earlier that day, which
made me feel guilty for wanting the unprecedented immer-
sion. But at that moment, when Charlotte and I were
speaking, I did not realize I was already in active labor. I
had not yet correlated the breaking of my waters with the
warm flood when I was brought to the surface of the creek.
I knew my uterus was contracting, yet I assumed it was
Braxton Hicks because my contractions were not increasing in frequency or duration, and I could talk through each
one without pausing for breath.

My son's delivery had taken twenty-four hours. I had such excruciating back labor that Deborah Brubaker had been forced to hold my shoulders and press her knee into the small of my back, or else I would writhe and howl in pain. Unbeknownst to me, this time I slept through some of my harder contractions. It was morning but still pitch dark when I awoke and realized I was truly in labor. At my gasp, my roommate Hannah sat up, one hand supporting her womb. Her ruffled bangs and the bent collar of her pajama top were outlined by the moonlight splintering through the curtains.

"You okay?" she asked.

I nodded and told her to go back to sleep. Labor was quickly losing its excitement for all of us because we were starting to feel like watched pots the midwives were waiting to see boil. A Hopen Haus girl was giving birth every other week, and the sounds from the birthing room kept many of us awake through the night as we clutched our stomachs and imagined ourselves going through that exact same pain. But even as I reassured Hannah, my voice shook.

Aware that I couldn't hide my labor for long, I went out into the hallway. My pace slowed as another contraction hit me. I leaned against the wall and panted through my mouth, my breath stolen by fear of the unknown as much as the pain.

Pulling my nightgown taut, I stared down at my stomach. Though the rest of my body had stayed thin, my abdomen had distended to a size I could not have imagined possible had I not seen it before with my son.

After much prayer and deliberation, I had chosen not to tell Fannie about the chromosomal abnormalities Dr. Hancock and Dr. Michaels anticipated my child to have. I knew I could not give birth at the hospital, where I would be required to fill out paperwork that would lead the authorities to the only home I had left, consequently taking it and the baby from me. Placing this unborn child's life in jeopardy just so I could claim her as my own seemed like the worst kind of selfishness. This caused me to wonder if—like many of the inherent character flaws we abhor and still somehow manifest—my mother's selfishness swam through my veins. And yet I did not know what other option I had.

For an hour or more, I continued to pace down the Hopen Haus hallway and breathe as my body prepared to give birth.

However, soon I could no longer focus on the wonder of the process, as much as surrender to the pain the process created. I hobbled over to Charlotte's room and knocked on her door. She answered immediately. Hopen Haus's most stalwart midwife has not changed much in the past eighteen years. Charlotte's hair was only highlighted with silver then, and perhaps her hips were not as wide. But she was the same gentle woman who opened her arms to whoever needed their soft embrace and never asked why.

"*Ach,*" Charlotte said, rubbing the back of her neck and searching my face as another contraction struck. "Gwen's in labor too." She pushed the door open with her foot. Once the pain had subsided, I looked inside. The room was dimly lit by beeswax candlesticks in brass holders, positioned on either side of the bed. The cosseted warmth exacerbated the sweet odor my laboring body was also exuding. Twenty-year-old Gwen Roberts was clutching the sheets of Charlotte's double bed. Thrashing from side to side, her head left a deep, sweat-soaked indentation in the white pillowcase. Her dark eyes rolled up and tears flowed down, sticking her frazzled brown hair to her cheeks.

"What should we do?" I asked.

"Don't know," Charlotte said. "How far along are you?"

"Not sure," I replied. "'Least beyond the latent stage."

Charlotte twisted her pudgy hands. Behind her, Gwen bucked and bit her teeth into the pillow, stifling her moan. Glancing down the hallway, Charlotte turned to me and said, "I think her labor's stalled. If you were not in labor, too, I would send you for Fannie right away."

Gwen groaned again. My womb contracted, as if sympathizing with hers. I leaned on the doorframe and forced my mouth into an O like Fannie taught, which was supposed to help our bodies stay relaxed as well. Charlotte rubbed her hand up and down my spine, which I couldn't stand. There are few times in my life I actually like to be touched. Labor is not one of them.

"I still have time," I said, stepping beyond her reach. "I'll go over to Fannie's and bring her back. Maybe Elmer can ride over and get Sadie, too." I glanced at Gwen. "Have you tried getting her out of bed? Making her do lunges or walk?"

Charlotte whispered, "I tried. She thinks moving will make it hurt worse."

I rolled my eyes. "It's better to hurt than to have failure to progress."

With these words, my teeth stopped chattering. My fear was giving way to a plan. I didn't even go back into my bedroom, in case I would further disturb my roommates, but grabbed a gray woolen shawl that was hanging on the coat peg next to the front door. I headed down the porch steps barefoot and bareheaded—just wearing the floor-length nightdress that I had purchased through Lehman's. The cold, damp grass numbed my feet as I hurried to the barn. I pried the wooden bar up and opened one side of the double doors. The scent of dust mixed with animal sweat and manure filled my nostrils, making me sneeze. Opening my eyes, I let the light from the full moon guide me across the cedar-chipped floor.

The handsome roan, Sampson, nickered as I approached. I lifted the largest bridle, reins, and bit from one of the hooks in the tack room and entered his stall, wishing I had taken time to put on my shoes. I called to the gelding softly, ran my hand along his neck, and slipped the bridle over his ears. I worked the metal bit carefully into his mouth, framed with square teeth the size of domino pieces. He munched on it until he found the right fit and then relaxed his left kneecap and snorted twin gusts of warm air, letting me know that he felt perfectly fine.

I was parallel with the ladder leading to the haymow when another contraction struck, forcing me to rest my forehead against Sampson's side. He continued to just stand there—shaking his shaggy mane adorned with the bridle—until the contraction had ebbed and I was ready to move again. Leading him over to the corral, I climbed up on the bottom rung, wrapped the reins around my hand, and hoisted myself onto his broad back. He did not shift until I was settled. Even then, I had to prod his sides and click my tongue to ease him into a canter. We took the lane that wound past Hopen Haus. The windows were all darkened except for the tallow light shining from Charlotte's room. Bowing my head, I said a prayer on Gwen's behalf.

Moonlight transformed the lane, turning the crusher run gravel into a skein of silver unfurled. The wind whistled down the mountain, bending the spruce trees' nimble spines that were planted on either side of the road. As if genuflecting to each other, their elongated tips touched. Another contraction hit. I hunkered low on Sampson's lunging back and wove my hands through his tangled mane. I clenched my eyes. Perhaps because of my position, the pressure of the contraction increased. I gasped, but Sampson did not flinch. His steps did not falter. For such a large horse, his strides were easy and smooth.

Then the pain released as abruptly as it had descended. I sat up and saw the sleeping, saltbox homes of the Dry Hollow Community, with their plain fronts, identical porches, and pitched roofs sheathed in corrugated tin. Barns, painted to match, loomed over these modest dwellings. Their shadows eclipsed the houses and yards until the darkness was countered by the brightness on the road. I urged Sampson with a mild prod of my bare heels. His

feathered hooves dug into the gravel. In the distance,
a coyote let loose a lonesome howl.

Fannie and her husband lived on the same twenty-acre
plot as their eldest son, David, who combed the mountain
for game and enjoyed seclusion to the point of a hermit.
Until they died or David got married, Fannie and Elmer
had no intentions to move. Everyone assumed that David
would always remain a bachelor. And so Dry Hollow
Community knew the Grabers were as deeply rooted
in their land as the twin black walnut trees on the knoll
behind their home.

I felt self-conscious as Sampson cantered up the
Grabers' lane. After all the strain Fannie had gone through
for my baptism, the very least I could do was let her recuperate with an uninterrupted night's sleep. But as another
contraction hit, I had to grind my teeth to keep from
crying aloud. Suddenly I no longer cared if I was inconve-
niencing anybody. I just knew that I wanted this baby out.

Sampson's hooves clattered over the cobblestones that
were nestled in the grass leading to the cottage. Easing
myself off his back, I knotted the reins to the Grabers'
porch and hurried up the steps. I used the knocker to tap
on the door. I heard nothing. I was lifting my hand to
knock again when the door opened. Holding on to the
door frame, Elmer Graber stuck his head out. Coarse white
hair sprouted from every angle. His beard trailed down his
nightshirt to the waistband of his pants.

Pushing his glasses up with one finger, he squinted at
me. "Rhoda?" he rasped.

By the moonlight, I looked beyond the glass lenses into Elmer's tired eyes. It was the first time someone had said my new name in passing, and I was surprised by how much it affected me. I thought this must be a sign that my prayers had been answered and my past life as Bethany Winslow had been washed clean when Bishop Yoder dipped me into the creek. My eyes stung even as another contraction hit. I looked over Elmer's shoulder and focused on breathing. My mind was fighting my body's primal urge to bear down.

Elmer said nothing at first, just stared. Then he said, "I'll get Fannie." I continued focusing on nothing. My distracted gaze watched his white shirt disappear into the gloom.

Before the surge had ebbed, Fannie came to the door. I could not concentrate long enough to drag my eyes up to her face. Wrapping an arm around my back, she led me through the maze of her kitchen. *Die kich,* I thought, nonsensically reciting the Pennsylvania Dutch nouns she'd taught me: *weschbohl, kochoffe, haffe, messer.* . . . Fannie struck a match on the corner of the table. She touched the wick of a lamp. The flame ate the oil-soaked material, flaring it to life. She tried helping me into a chair, but as soon as my backside touched the wood, I cried out and resumed standing. Clutching the back of the chair, I rocked from side to side and growled deep in my throat. Even in my haze of pain, I could feel the pressure and knew the baby was descending fast.

"Fannie!" I screamed.

"I'm here," Fannie said. "Rhoda, I'm here. Just keep breathing. You're doing great, *meedel*." Then she called over her shoulder, "Elmer. Elmer, bring me some hot water in a bucket and my birthing satchel. I'm going to need towels, too."

The old Mennonite midwife led me like a sleepwalking child over to her and Elmer's bed. It became hard to move my feet, but I knew that I could not sit or lie down. I crouched low beside the bed and cried out in anguish. I held the bed post, the ornate wood carvings imprinting my palms. My body knew exactly what to do, yet I knew nothing. Still, Fannie did not touch me. She must have sensed that I could not have stood the pressure of her little finger when it felt my entire body was being torn apart. I gingerly reached down and felt the downy globe of the baby's head, crowning.

My strength renewed, I groaned and bore down until my face filled with blood, and I had to bite my lip to redirect the pain. I gave the sum of my energy into that one deep push. Fannie knelt and caught the baby, whose womb-waxed body slipped out as swiftly as my son's had. I clutched the bedpost with my arms because my jellied legs could no longer support me. I closed my eyes and prayed—thanking God for the baby's safe delivery and promising that I would cherish her every cell, regardless of how many chromosomes she had.

"Rhoda," Fannie said, gently nudging my side. "Stand up, my *meedel*. Look at your child."

I did as she suggested, and my eyes filled afresh. The

baby's ears were whorled like the most intricate shell. Her ten toes were plump and pink, her ten fingers delicate and long. Her head—mottled with that dark, wet hair—showed no signs of the force that had expelled her into our world. I brushed a fingertip down her chest, watching gooseflesh arise on her dappled skin and her rib cage expand and deflate with breath. She opened her eyes and looked at me. She *looked* at me. She had the same clouded blue irises as most newborns, yet in them I saw reassurance that I was her mother. That though we shared no DNA, during the past forty weeks, the rhythm of my heart had become synced with hers.

With a clean dish towel, Fannie dabbed the baby's scalp, then swaddled her in another towel. She passed the child to me—still connected by the limp umbilical cord—and even with the baby breathing easily, eyes wide open, she did not let out a cry. Fannie tucked her into my shaky arms. I leaned my face down to hers. Bathing her in the brine of my sweat and tears, I held her close.

"What are you going to name her?" Fannie asked.

I looked down and touched my daughter's cheek, watching her instinctively root for my breast. I smiled and thought that, in all my life, I'd never known such love.

"Hope," I replied.

11

Amelia, 2014

The bedsprings squeak as I throw my legs over the side of the top bunk and jump to the floor. Peeling loose the shirt that's stuck to my spine with sweat, I look in at Lydie. Her huge stomach rises and falls with each of her breaths. I have to say, it's pretty annoying that someone thirty-nine weeks pregnant can sleep in this suffocating heat when I've been tossing and turning for hours. But I guess it's because Lydie's never lived with air-conditioning anyway.

I tiptoe downstairs and turn the doorknob to the bathroom that smells like some cut-rate porta-john since the plumbing's about the same as in a third-world country. Somebody's in there. Of *course* somebody's in there when

we've got four preggo girls beneath one roof, whose blad-
ders have shrunk to, like, the size of lima beans. Sighing,
I make sure the floor's clear of bugs and sink down against
the wall. It's cooler down here by about ten degrees. But
I stop enjoying my break when I hear whimpering.

I scramble to my bare feet and knock.

"Go away!" this small, scared voice says.

I ask, "What's wrong?"

Nothing.

"Can you hear me?"

A bunch of sniffling, then, "Yeah'um."

I smile. "That you, Luca?"

"Who *you* first?"

"Amelia. You helped pick weeds with me in the garden.
You want to come out here and tell me what's wrong?"

"I'm stuck," he says.

"Stuck?"

He rattles the doorknob. "I shut it. . . . Then it stuck."

I grip the doorknob and twist. It's not locked, but
jammed. "Move over there near the bathtub, Luca. I don't
want you hit."

He calls out, "Okay." I twist the doorknob hard to the
right. Stepping back, I put my weight against the door.
It whips open. The knob smacks into the wall, scattering
white plaster stuff like powder. Freed, Luca claps his hands
and moves into the hallway. His small outline—with all
this messy hair and a long nightshirt and white socks pulled
up skinny-kid calves—makes my chest hurt. Is this how my
baby would look?

Luca takes my hand though I haven't offered it. I stiffen at first because I'm not used to little kids, but then I loosen up, and Luca swings our linked arms. He grins up at me like I'm some kind of hero or something, when I just opened a bathroom door. I feel like I'm going to cry for a second. This kid's so trusting and has no idea that the people he looks up to now will eventually let him down—or at least that's how it was with me. I was about Luca's age the night I realized that who I was could never be enough. So at six years old, I closed down my heart and just stopped trying.

Using my other hand to wipe my eyes, I say, "Sorry you were scared."

"I weren't scared, just stuck."

I now try to hide my smile along with my tears. Luca might be a kid, but he still doesn't like anyone thinking he's not a man. "Stuck, it is," I say. "Where's your mom?"

"Sleepin'." He says it as if that was a stupid question.

"Then let's take you back to your room."

"Nummies first?" Luca scrubs the end of his nose and starts walking down the hall without me. "*Grossmammi* Charlotte, she be keeping nummies for me in a jar," he says.

Nummies? What in the world's he talking about? I catch up, and Luca again reaches for my hand. He's just wiped his nose and, having come out of the bathroom, who knows what else. But I let him take it, and we walk down the hallway into the kitchen.

"Up 'ere." Luca points to the glass jars lining the back wall of the countertop.

I hook my hands beneath his armpits and, in one motion, set him on the countertop, like he's—I don't know—more air than boy or something. He swings his legs and twists at the waist, reaching toward the jar.

"Wait." I get out one gingersnap and pass it to Luca. He takes a bite and smacks his lips, not even caring that these cookies were donated to Hopen Haus because they're stale. I fluff Luca's messy hair and swallow hard, knowing I don't have much time until a choice has to be made. I've been rebelling against my mom for years, so you'd think it wouldn't be that hard. But my entire future's never been hanging on one decision: go through with the appointment or give my baby up for adoption. Either way, my arms will be empty, a thought that doesn't relieve me like it would have a month ago.

I take a big breath. "You'll be able to sleep now?" I ask. "Since you've had a snack?"

Luca nods. Sugary crumbs dot the cotton shirt stretched across his lap. The kitchen slowly brightens, but this place has no dimmer switch. I turn and see the head midwife, Rhoda, carrying a lamp. She looks exhausted.

Remembering how angry Uriah was when he saw me and Luca together, I step back from the kid like I've done something wrong. But the head midwife just says, "Thought I heard someone down here." Crossing the kitchen, Rhoda sets the lantern on the island. Light pools around the globe. "May I have one too?" she asks, motioning to the cookie jar.

I pass a gingersnap to Rhoda and keep one for myself.

Luca reaches for another one and sticks out his bottom lip in a pout. I raise an eyebrow and Rhoda smiles. I give him another one. Then the three of us nibble in silence . . . well, except for the sound of the cookies crumbling between our teeth. To avoid meeting Rhoda's eyes, I stare at the copper pots nested on the countertop that Lydie treated with some kind of oil until the cracked wood looked almost good as new. While the spiced wafer melts on my tongue, the night my mom let me down floats up through the layers of my mind. I wish it were a memory that I could forget.

When I was Luca's age—and gullible enough to think every goal could be reached—I tried to do better than my mom's expectations. I tried to be the perfect ballerina, the perfect kindergarten student, the perfect daughter, the perfect friend. This determination stopped the Christmas I was six. The dance studio I attended was putting on *The Nutcracker*. My beginner class made up the mice army, and we'd been practicing our small part since Halloween. My mom came backstage seconds before the curtains were supposed to part. She found me bunched together with my class. We were pulling each other's costume tails, swiping cheese and nuts from the refreshment table, and doing other things typical of mice.

My mom shook her head and plucked the piece of cheese out of my foam paw. Without working fingers I'd had a pretty hard time getting hold of it. Tossing the cheese into the trash can, my mom brushed invisible flecks from my shoulders. Then she leaned down and whispered, low enough so no one else could hear, "Now, when you're up there, sweetheart, don't forget to suck your tummy in." She kissed my forehead and left the stage, leaving a trail of nervousness mixed with her perfume.

During the opening act, I remembered to keep my shoulders straight and my belly button sucked in toward my backbone as I chittered and demi-plié-ed across the stage. Then I saw my teacher, the gorgeous Miss Vivienne, in the wings of the stage, pointing to my cheeks to remind me to smile. I smiled and my tummy poofed out. My shoulders sank. My smile disappeared. I peered into the glare of the stage lights, trying to see if my mom had seen. But I couldn't see my mom, dad, or Grandma Sarah. I couldn't see anyone. Sweat trickled beneath my costume. My headband, where my velveteen ears were attached, started to itch.

The distraction was just for a second. But a second was all it took. I looked down at the black X marks taped to the stage, trying to remember how to begin again. The sugar plum fairy, Cynthia Greenwood, was from the advanced class. Beautiful and slim in her white leotard and sparkly skirt tipped with feathers, Cynthia came onto the stage, smiling and leaping en pointe like her ankles were suspended from a puppet's string. So, captivated by an audience she couldn't see, Cynthia did not see the confused mouse from Act I, who was still crouched beside the third X with her pink tail trailing across the ground.

Cynthia stretched out her toned arms. The swan feather in her headdress fluttered in the wind of her own twirl. She was halfway through her pirouette when she tripped over

me and landed—heavily, *loudly*—on her rump. Cynthia
had dreams of dancing with a company. They would've
never come true, anyway; she was too tall for lifts. But
to this day, Cynthia's mother blames me for her daughter's settling for an English lit teaching job at Concord
Community College. If it weren't for me, Mrs. Greenwood
could have shared with the country club that her daughter
was dancing on Juilliard's stage.

That night, after the sugar plum fairy's gawky topple,
was the first night my mom didn't come into my bedroom
to tuck me in. Huddled in my canopy bed beside the picture window, I could not sleep. A lump of dread settled in
my stomach, as heavy as a stone. This was the first time
I'd failed my mom. Getting up on my knees, I crossed the
eiderdown and traced the frost spreading across the black
windowpanes.

I tried not to cry. Minutes passed that felt like hours.

I kept myself awake by pressing my face and fingers to
the glass and staring out at the clear December night—
waiting, hoping for my mom to come. My fingertips were
growing cold and the glass was fogged with breath when
my dad came in with a Care Bear TV tray gripped between
his hands. He set it on the low table where my nanny,
Grandma Sarah, and I had tea parties (and sometimes even
my mom, if she was off work). My dad's sheepskin slippers
whispered as he shuffled over to my bureau and switched
on the carousel lamp.

By its glow, I looked at the glass of milk, gingersnaps
Grandma Sarah had baked, and a tangerine my father had

peeled and divided into wedges, the way I liked it. I tried to smile. But the lump in my stomach left no room for appetite, and I didn't know how I was going to speak, not to mention swallow, around the sense of failure that I felt, the sense of horrible dread.

"You feeling okay?" my dad asked, leaning across the bed to plant a kiss on my hair, still sticky with spray from the recital. Neither of my parents had even checked to see if I had brushed my hair or teeth.

"Yes," I said. But my voice trembled. I sat up and rubbed my watering left eye with my fist. I already knew that my mom didn't like to see me cry. I knew that my dad always blamed himself whenever I did.

My dad walked back to the tiny table and pulled out the chair. He sat down with the table at shin level and his knees bunched up toward his chest. He looked like a giant. Knowing this, he played it up by scrunching his face into a mighty Hulk grimace. This time I smiled. He patted the seat next to him. "Won't you come sit?" he asked. "I can't eat these biscuits all by myself."

"I'm not hungry," I said.

He frowned. "C'mon, honey. You've earned it. I'm sure you can eat just one bite."

So I climbed off the canopy bed and took the chair next to my dad. He reached across the distance and placed his arm around my back. I leaned toward him, as I usually did. Pulling me into his lap, my dad curled his chin over my head, protective. For some reason, the comforting thump of his heart made me want to sob. How many times had my dad held me like this? How many times had he also come to tuck me in? And yet, the night I failed to meet my mom's expectations, I found that I only wanted her.

"You happy, 'Melia?" he asked.

I nodded against the flannel material of his pajama shirt.

"I mean it." He moved me farther up his knee—the playhouse chair creaking with the weight—and searched my eyes. "Are you *really* happy?"

I stared up at him and wrinkled my brow. "Does Mommy love me?" I spread a hand across my chest. The tiny fingernails my mom had painted translucent pink that very day glinted in the carousel's light. "Me?" I repeated, as if there might be some other girl hiding in the window seat or in the Victorian dollhouse, with miniature china displayed inside a cupboard with real cherry doors (the china plates that I later, after another fight, broke on purpose). "Or does she want a different girl?" I looked down and scraped the paint off my nails with my teeth. "One who doesn't forget her steps?"

My dad gently took my fingers out of my mouth. Then he clutched me so hard, I thought he would not release me long enough to let me breathe. The mint of his toothpaste and the herbal shampoo he'd used in the shower—his hair still wet and curled over his pajama collar—was a scent as all-surrounding as his embrace. For a moment—just one— I did not worry about how I would ever be able to please my mom or if my steps would ever match the metronome of her demands.

Instead, I just clung to my dad, and when he told me that I was loved—so *very, very* loved—I tried to believe him.

Rhoda, 2014

Standing in the kitchen, the lamplight pouring out like a flood, I sense Amelia's discomfort. It saddens me for a reason I cannot express. Things are usually awkward between me and the residents of Hopen Haus. But then, things are usually awkward between me and anyone. Since Hope's loss, I have learned to keep everyone at a comfortable distance: Fannie when she was still alive, my fellow midwives, the members of Dry Hollow Community. Even God. The fledgling steps I had taken to opening my heart to him were halted the winter day life, as I knew it, ended. The resulting lack of intimacy has never bothered me. To be honest, I actually prefer it.

The wall around my heart makes it easier to perceive these Hopen Haus girls as residents or patients rather than as additional daughters I will lose. But now, I regret the wall between me and this resident, Amelia. I regret not having taken time to get to know this girl when I sensed, two weeks ago, the insecurities lurking beneath her confidence.

To keep the backs of his bare legs from getting splinters, Luca scoots across the countertop by supporting his upper body with his knuckles, like the limber monkey he is. He rests his head on Amelia's shoulder. She dusts off her hands and wraps an arm around his waist.

I watch the two of them and know from the burning sensation behind my eyes that I am about to cry. I glance away from the odd, fine-looking pair and wipe my face. "You'll make a wonderful mother," I whisper, mourning all the opportunities I had to be a mother to these girls and instead chose to protect myself.

The moment I say this, it is as if the warm room constricts. The muscles of Amelia's shoulders bunch high around her neck. The knuckle above her ring stands out as she clenches the countertop. She retracts her arm from around the child and helps him to the floor. Sweeping some minuscule crumbs from the counter, she brushes them into the sink.

"Did I say something wrong?"

Amelia about-faces and folds her arms. "No." Looking down at the countertop, the young woman trails her ragged nail along a crack Lydie's numerous coatings of mineral oil cannot heal. "It's just that . . . I'm not sure I'm *ready* to be a mother."

I look at Amelia a long moment, as my mind's eye replays the terror I felt when I realized I was carrying my son. I can feel the protective hedges coming down and my heart opening up to her like a bloom. I cross the space between the island where I stand and the countertop against which Amelia leans. As I do, holding the lamp, I know I am in the midst of crossing so much more. I, Rhoda Mummau—head midwife, yet wife and mother to none—am crossing an emotional divide I have never been able to traverse since the winter afternoon my daughter was taken.

"My *meedel*," I say, using Fannie's Pennsylvania Dutch endearment. I reach out to place my hand over Amelia's small, pale hand clenching the countertop. "You're a mother already."

※

The next morning, the duet of Looper's bass and Alice's soprano laughter streams out of the open windows of his truck. The resonant sound chokes me as much as the dust the truck tires have churned. In my pride, I refused Looper's offer to drive Alice and me to Deacon Graber's. The two of us have not spoken since the altercation in the barn, and I did not want to ride along as the unwanted third wheel. However, suddenly, I am not a forty-two-year-old woman, but a lonely teenager watching Ernest Looper drive down the dirt road running past our farmhouses with another beautiful girl seated beside him. Another beautiful girl who will never be me.

I fold my arms and breathe deep, trying not to feel hurt. Looper has been avoiding me these past two weeks—not because of the altercation in the barn, but because I told him about the child we conceived together, the child I gave away without his awareness or consent. I know I deserve his anger; I would be angry too. But I am not ready to face it . . . or him. Therefore, a part of me wants to keep walking past the Grabers' old homestead that is now their son's, past Fannie and Elmer's simple gravestone embedded in the knoll beneath the black walnut trees. I want to keep walking for miles, leaving behind this place and the people in it, all of whom I love so much and seem bound to lose.

If I'd kept our son, Looper, I find myself asking, staring at the jolting flatbed of his truck, *would everything have changed?*

I remember how much courage it took to put on the dress whose uneven hem I'd stitched myself. To pin my hair into curls and darken my eyelids with shadow. To spray my neck with the Shalimar perfume my mother had left behind and stare at myself in the mirror, seeing her face reflected back, and yet not knowing where she was.

"Don't you look nice?" my father had said when I'd come downstairs after finally drying my tears and smoothing my parents' bed, on which I had been crying. He even looked away from the TV to admire me.

I winced at his words, though everything I did was a silent plea for his spoken approval. But at that time, I was filled with so much anger that I inadvertently deflected it toward my father, despising him almost as much as the person—my mother—who had abandoned us both.

My father set the remote on the threadbare couch cushion he and my little brother shared and rose. "Is Ernest picking you up?" he'd asked, walking across the living room.

I shook my head. "I'm meeting him there." Another lie. I had told him Looper was my prom date. I could not bear the thought of him feeling bad for me, knowing I was attending the most canonized event of high school completely alone.

My father paused in front of me, then reached out as if to touch the fabric of my puffed sleeve. "Are you . . . are you wearing your mother's perfume?" he'd said, his voice hoarse. I stepped back. His fingertips brushed air. I could tell he was not angry, but unsettled by the scent of his wife, who had left without telling him where she was going or whom she was going with. And yet he *still* kept her high school picture on his nightstand; her battered robe hanging from a hook at the back of their shared closet; the wedding ring on his hand, though she had been requesting a divorce for years. Couldn't he see it was impossible to make our home a shrine to a woman who was not only fallible, but selfish?

The clock ticked on the mantel ledge. On TV, *Full House*'s theme song played. My little brother, Benny, happily ate popcorn—one flared kernel at a time—from a large cherry bowl resting on his jeans. *Benny doesn't even care,* I thought, and immediately felt guilty. I should be glad he wasn't haunted by a phantom memory; I should be glad he was too young to remember the nights he had awoken from a nightmare and cried himself to sleep in my arms, wishing that his real comforter would return. He was too young to remember how hard I had cried too.

I swallowed and said, "I guess I'll . . . be going."

My father nodded, looking down. His jaw knotted. Before he could ask to take my picture, which I knew would cause me to break down in front of him, I went out to my car and climbed behind the wheel, being careful not to catch my dress and crinoline in the door. By the time I arrived at the gymnasium where the banquet was held, tears had washed the makeup from my face. Walking up to the double doors trailing pink and white ribbons, I dried my cheeks and felt like Cinderella stripped of her splendor before the ball had even begun.

The tense exchange with my father replayed in my mind as the music pulsed and I remained in the shadows, watching "my date," Ernest Looper, dance with the girl on whose wrist he'd slid a carnation corsage. Three hours later, I followed everyone to the after-prom party at Ted Benson's house simply because it was my senior prom night and I did not want to go home. New location, fewer crepe flowers, and less confetti, but the cliques were still the same: geeks, jocks, preppies, and hicks. I did not belong to any of them and so was accepted by none.

I leaned against the fridge and sipped a warm rum and Coke from a Dixie cup. Looper, in a rented tuxedo and white crew socks, moonwalked across the linoleum and took two more girls' hearts by storm. Appalled at myself even more than him, I slipped off to the bathroom and poured the beverage down the sink but ate the fruit cocktail gummed along the bottom. I left the bathroom and sat in a dimly lit closet office, passing time flipping through Mr. Benson's Rolodex and doodling on his yellow legal pad. After an hour, I stopped telling myself I wasn't waiting for Looper to find me. I knew that's exactly what I wanted and why I stayed.

When I finally awoke and fled the office, the house felt like the end of the world had taken place. The entire first floor was empty, but the lights were on and somewhere music still played. I passed through the den, squinting through the haze of leftover smoke. Dixie cups littered the coffee table. Beer cans were crushed to metallic disks. Cigarette butts were clustered on an ashtray the color of root beer. Over the hypnotic melody on the cassette player, I heard the sound of open-throat snoring. I glanced around. It seemed to be coming from a person seated in the recliner whose triangular back was facing me.

I crept around to the front—afraid to walk into a cruel classmate's trick—and found my dear Casanova neighbor, Looper. His head was tilted back. His lips fluttered. His gelled hair fell over one eye as he surrendered wholeheart-edly to the snore. He was not even aware that everyone else, including his corsaged prom date, had left. He was not aware of anything. I patted his cheeks, which were scented with booze and Brut cologne, and helped him to his feet. He leaned heavily on me. My arm was around his lean waist, with his jacketed arm slung around my neck. This was not quite how I had imagined it.

"What I do widout you?" he'd slurred, stumbling over the garden hose coiled in the front yard.

I dumped him in the passenger seat of my car like a sack of silage and drove with the windows down. I thought it would help Looper sober up and keep me from feeling nostalgic for how we used to be, until our social circles made us orbit in two different worlds. By the time I turned onto our empty stretch of road hemmed in with freshly sown acres of corn, I could tell Looper was fully awake because he became quiet. The stars were bright. The moon appeared as crumbly and thin as a paring of wax.

I could have dropped Looper off. I could have acted like everything was the same as it had always been. I should have done this, I know. Yet I couldn't, because it wasn't the same. I was leaving. We were *both* leaving—maybe not next week, maybe not in a month. But soon everything was going to change, and we were going to change right along with it. Perhaps my urgency was accelerated by the infinitesimal alcohol that had soaked into the fruit cocktail at the bottom of my rum and Coke; by my shimmering, off-one-shoulder dress that made me feel like I actually had confidence to match my clothespin curves. Perhaps by the way the stars dappled the stubble lining Looper's strong jaw. Perhaps it was simply my heart wanting to feel the warmth of the spotlight when I'd spent seventeen and a half years clinging to cold stone walls.

I circled behind the barn and stared at the red slats whose creases were illuminated by my high beams. Taking a deep breath, I shut off the headlights. Darkness. I heard Looper's mouth click as he prepared to ask a question, but I asked him one first.

"Will you kiss me?" My breath and courage faltered, transforming my bold request into a whisper. "Just once?"

Looper shifted, stared out at the fields . . . adjusted his seat-belt strap. But then he grinned and said, "Jeepers creepers, Beth. Thought you'd never ask." His tone was playful, his smile mildly patronizing in a way that made me want to either recant my request or slap him. My cheeks seared with embarrassment.

I was about to turn to hide this when Looper caught my jaw and brought his face closer. He peered into my eyes, and I watched the look in his change as if a curtain had been dropped. His pupils absorbed the gold-green of his irises. His breathing shifted from its relaxed pattern. His rough cheek brushed against my previously tear-stained one, and then he ran a thumb down my jawline before tangling his fingers in the loosened pin curls at the nape of my neck.

He touched his lips to mine. I expected him to taste of liquor, but he tasted inexplicably sweet. I expected him to pull back after one brush of lip upon lip and tell me that we should go home. But he didn't. Instead, he popped open the passenger's-side door and came over to my side. Opening it, he swallowed my hand in his and pulled me out of my car. He then pressed me close and whispered, asking if I would like to take a walk with him through a cornfield alight with Wisconsin stars.

12

Wilbur, Looper, and Alice are already seated around Fannie Graber's old kitchen table when I knock once and come in the door. The front of my cape dress is blanched with dust from my walk down Dry Hollow Road, which led me to memory lane. Thus my face stings with the heat of that decades-old summer, and it is difficult to meet Looper's eyes. I look around the room instead.

It pains me to see the bachelor flotsam drifting in corners. The tin dishes crusted with food next to the sink. The light struggling through the clouded windowpanes, making the once-sunny house seem more like a cave. Even at the end, when Fannie's arthritis was so bad Elmer had to spoon-feed her like a child, she never let it get like this. But the one concession I can give hermit David Graber is that he tends his parents' grave like a garden: trimming grass, planting flowers, and never letting one weed take root.

Seated at the head of the table, Deacon David Graber points to the chair across from Looper. Alice sits on his other side and Wilbur at the end, though he is only our driver and it seems odd to have him here for such an important discussion. I guess Alice just wants to keep him close because he supports her viewpoint. I take the seat and square my shoulders, as if preparing for a fight. Alice pours a glass of water from the carafe and places it before me. "Thank you," I murmur. But I do not touch the glass.

I break eye contact with Looper—the first time we have looked at each other all week—and glance down the table. David's salt-and-pepper beard brushes the top of the letter he holds. At sixty-five, David is the same age his father was when I first arrived at Hopen Haus. He looks so much like Elmer, but in his pale gaze I see Fannie's calm spirit reflected too.

Readying his voice, David says, "I've asked you to come today because I want to tell you firsthand what the bishops in Indiana have ruled. They've decided to let Hopen Haus have electricity and a telephone."

Alice claps her hands to her chest. I turn away, toward the door, trying to stifle the panic backing up my throat.

"But—" David raises a finger.

Wilbur interrupts, rolling his eyes. "What's the hitch now?"

"Let him speak!" I snap.

"But," David continues, undeterred, "the electricity can only be used in the examining room, for the use of ultrasound machines and such. The telephone will be installed in the barn."

Alice's hands lower back to the table. She clenches the edge and leans past Looper to look at David. "Only one room? But . . . but we need lighting. We need air-conditioning . . . hot water."

"We've survived thus far without air-conditioning and hot water," I retort. "I dare think we will continue."

Looper reaches across the table and touches my hand. Of course, this is not an affectionate gesture, but a warning to guard my tongue. I do not take it well. I rise to my feet, and Looper scrapes his chair back from the table to stand as well. "Is that all you have for us, David?" I ask. When he nods, I move toward the door and lift the latch. "Then I guess—"

"Rhoda," Alice calls. "*Please.* Let's talk about this."

I pause with my hand on the door. Looking over my shoulder, I meet her pleading gaze. Between us, in the dim room, tension crackles as if our palms are placed on opposite sides of a plasma globe. But deep down, I know the true reason for this tension—the true reason I am jealous of Alice—and it goes far back before the noxious promise of telephones and electricity that hold the power to reveal my past, or even before Looper came here and Alice took notice of him. And—if I am to be honest with myself—he took notice of her. I have been jealous of Alice Rippentoe since that winter morning Uriah's newborn cry cracked through the log-and-chink walls of Hopen Haus, and in it I heard the echo of my absent son.

I drop my eyes and say, "I'll meet you all back at the house."

Closing the door, I step off the porch and retrace the chalky lane that I have just walked. Heat scorches my throat, but I continue walking down Dry Hollow Lane. I take a left at the old logging trail and glance behind me. The July sun has slaked its thirst on any moisture the rain has left behind. My boots stamp prints in the dirt.

I am trespassing on property the community sold to Walt Hollis when it heeded the siren call of better jobs and larger parcels of land in Indiana. But I have traversed it so often, it still feels like somewhere I belong.

My body is a scythe cutting through the field studded with milkweed pods and thistles topped with soft purple down. I keep going until I come upon, not Fannie Graber's grave, where I considered going first, but the Ashinhurst plantation graveyard, whose gothic beauty is encircled by a modern chain-link fence. The graves are covered with ancient charcoal stones that shield the remains of those who defended their property against drought, termites, fire, Union troops trying to claim the land, and Confederate bushwhackers marauding after the land was conquered. These people—the Ashinhursts—lived, loved, and died beneath Hopen Haus's roof. They had sorrows just like we do; they wept just like we do.

I chose to come here because I want to pay homage to the ones who have kept Hopen Haus whole through so many hardships, and to apologize for now not being able to keep it the same. Most of the names and dates on the graves have been smoothed by weather and time, and even if I wanted to enter to try and read them, I can't. The gate is locked, the bolt fused with disuse. When I first arrived at Dry Hollow Community and did not know the church had selected a grave plot of its own, I had hoped to be buried in this cemetery where the Ashinhurst family had found a final place of rest. But at that time I had a family, even if it was composed of just my unborn daughter and me. Since I am alone, I do not want to become a few specks of dust scattered across the bottom of a cedar-lined box, buried in the backwoods of nowhere.

Midwifery has been fulfilling in so many ways, and I know that I should be grateful for what I have. Nevertheless, suddenly, I'm not even sure what I want, or *who* I want, or why it feels that I am lacking. I just know that right now I cannot imagine remaining here, at Hopen Haus, where my job is to bring other women's children into the world while never having a child or a family to call my own. Maybe Ernest Looper's arrival has made me see just how much time has gone by, and that I am no longer the fractured young woman who threw caution to the wind so she could glimpse her entirety reflected in another person's eyes.

Covering my face, I blink hard and straighten, peering through the rusty diamonds of the fence. I stare at the graves, the reminder of mortality making me feel both anchored and weightless, and then turn to head back up the logging trail that meets the whitened lane. But as I do, my peripheral vision catches movement. I squint against the sun and perceive that Ernest Looper has followed me. The German shepherds are positioned on either side of him. Despite their aging forms and arthritic hips, their black-and-tan shoulders slinking through the waist-high grasses remind me of lions. Crossing the distance, Looper comes to stand before me. The dogs sit beside him, panting, but their tails lash the ground.

"You all right, Rhoda?" Looper says. His face is devoid of a smile.

My head is still swirling with memories of that starlit Wisconsin night. I step back. "How'd you find me?"

"Shoe prints." Looper wipes the sweat dripping past his temple.

I search my mind for a topic less combustive than the one we discussed at Deacon Graber's or the one we discussed that night at the hospital when we last allowed ourselves to speak. "How's the remodeling coming?" I point beyond the field to Hopen Haus, where the roof's new tin patches glimmer through the trees.

The sun skulks out from behind a cloud. Looper shields his eyes, but not before I can feel their blistering hurt. "Going well," he says. He clears his throat. "Now that I know what you want, I can probably be out of your hair in two weeks."

This time *I* am the one who averts my gaze. I don't know what I want; I don't know anything. I rip a hank of grasses out by the roots. The sweet, green chlorophyll oozes out of the long blades and stains the creases of my fist. Looking down at my ragged nails and cracked skin, I wonder if there is anything left in me that is womanly and fragile. Anything left in me that will truly let someone in. I open my hand and watch the yellow seeds scatter on the breeze.

"And who's to say that I want you to leave?" I swallow hard, knowing that with vulnerability, there is also great risk.

Looper hangs his head. "I don't know what you want from me, Beth. I just know that you don't want me here."

I turn my back to him and cross my arms over my chest. "Rhoda . . . now Beth?" My voice shakes. "Why do you keep switching names?"

Looper is quiet for such a long time, I have to force myself not to look over my shoulder at him. Then he says, "'Cause sometimes I can see that little girl—that Beth—inside you, still feeling guilty for something she hasn't done. When I see her, that's when I know . . ."

He clasps my hand and turns my body toward his. "That's when I know that I have to forgive you for giving away our son because you're already blaming yourself for something you couldn't have changed."

With one finger, Looper lifts my downcast face. The movement is gentle, but I can feel the smoldering frustration that I know he is trying to quench. "Your mom's leaving had nothing to do with you, Beth." He holds my eyes. "She made me promise to tell you that."

My throat tightens. Looper wraps his arms around my

back, drawing me into his exhibition of forgiveness. This is the closest we have been since he arrived. The closest we have been in decades. He smells of sweat and pine and something akin to sadness. But my own grief dulls any age-old magnetism, and I am only aware of the comfort of his familiar embrace.

"If it wasn't my fault," I say, "then why'd she leave?"

Beneath my hands, Looper's muscles grow taut. He looks over my head, and then stares down at me. "Your mother . . ." Looper scratches one hand across his beard and swallows. "Your mother tried to stay for you and Benny, Beth, but she and your dad had grown apart. He wouldn't give her a divorce, so she just . . . left."

Surprise stings my eyes as the revolving door of my mind entraps one thought: *She didn't leave because of me.*

Looper holds me against him, and I remember how my father used to hold my mother, as if his arms could repel the force field of my anger toward her. At twelve years old, I could sense my mother's discontent and resented her for stripping away my security at the cusp of my teenage years when I needed her support the most. But perhaps my father wasn't trying to protect my mother from me; perhaps he also sensed my mother's unrest lurking beneath her serene smile and was trying to keep her close to prevent her from breaking our family apart. Not knowing that, in five years, his daughter would follow in her mother's footsteps by heeding the urge to flee rather than remaining and taking the risk of getting hurt.

Moving out of Looper's embrace, I can feel

self-preservation erecting its barricade around my heart. If Looper didn't love me when I was seventeen and our lives were so connected, he surely does not love me now, when I am just a husk of the person he once knew. I now understand why he sought me out here, at Hopen Haus. He came to unburden an old friend by telling me it wasn't my fault that my mother had left. Nothing more, nothing less.

I step away from him and take the desolate trail, which will lead back to the lane that, eighteen years ago this summer, brought me to Hopen Haus. In the background, dogs bark. Looper calls out, asking if I'm all right. He calls my name—my *given* name—Beth, Beth, Beth. But I am crying too hard to stop. I begin to run, my cape dress fluttering with the breeze. For now I know it is time to let go of the past. It is time to let go of the bitterness toward my mother, but also of the hope that I did not know I was holding on to until I was certain it was already gone. The hope that a barren midwife could have a husband and a child of her own. The hope that there would ever be a future left for Looper and me, a future left for us.

Amelia, 2014

I crouch toward a hen that spreads her wings and hunkers low, guarding her eggs like treasure. I dart my hand beneath the feathers and feel a hard orb. The hen rises on her claws and squawks. Beating her wings, she fills the coop with swirls of hay and darts her head out of the shoe-box cubicle to peck my hand. Jerking back, I scream and crack the shell against the side of the coop. Two weeks ago I would've cursed or at least made a scene. But now I just wipe my fingers off on my shirt, toss the egg into the basket, and go down to the next hen. (Maybe prairie-girl Lydie's having more of an influence on me than I thought.)

This time, I make vague "shoo shoo" motions, trying to get the hen off the nest. The hen remains. Her yellow eyes and hooked beak wink in the barn's dingy light. Rubbing the puncture on top of my hand, I try to be more aggressive in my shooing—a little closer this time, but still out of pecking reach. The hen stretches its beak into a yawn. Out of options and running low on time, I bend my arms into wings, cluck my own tongue, and stamp my feet. Despite my two-hundred-dollar jeans and my pointe skills, I look like a performer at one of those old-fashioned hoedowns, doing the chicken dance.

Then something or somebody blocks the sunlight coming in through the barn's open doorway. A shadow falls across the coop. My jig for the bored red hen stops. Groaning inside, I turn. Uriah Rippentoe is standing there. His arms are folded. His mouth is straight, but the tilted corners make me think he's trying not to smile. "How difficult is it to gather eggs?" he says, swaggering into the barn and glancing at the straw bale, where my basket's sitting empty, except for the single cracked egg. "You've been down here, like, what? An hour?"

"The chickens don't like me."

"Don't like you?" He laughs. "You just need the right touch."

Without hesitating, Uriah reaches under the hen that pecked me and takes out two smooth brown eggs, as easy as a fox. He passes them to me and moves down to the next hen. His hand reaches in and out so fast, the hen doesn't even know he's been there until she resettles her feathers over the nest and feels that her eggs are gone. He continues passing eggs to me, which I tuck into the cloth-lined basket.

"You build this?" I gesture toward the chicken coop.

Uriah nods.

The cubicles are painted white and stuffed with fresh straw; the outside is black. I wonder if I should, like, comment on it somehow, but I don't know the terms. So I settle for a solid knock against the wood and say, "You want to be an architect or something?"

This time Uriah doesn't even try to hide his smile. But then his eyes drift away from mine. "Our school only went to eighth grade."

Without thinking, I reach out and place a hand on his back. "I'm sorry," I say, removing my hand. I can feel the tips of my fingertips growing warm along with my ears. "It must be hard for you here."

Uriah says, "It's not so bad now." Then he turns so quickly I have no time to even blink or breathe. Taking the basket of eggs from me, he sets it on the ground and brings that hand up to touch the layers of my hair, which are frizzing like crazy from the heat. I look up. His head leans down toward mine. My eyes close. Then they spring wide as I remember Prairie-girl.

"What're you doing!" I hold my hand up like a traffic director. "What about Lydie?"

The current between us snaps to nothing. Uriah goes over to the bin. Using a scoop, he refills the chicken feeder with cracked corn. The leftovers sift over the ground in flakes. Sticking the scoop back in the bin, Uriah clangs the lid on top. A dark flush creeps up from the neck of his shirt. He rests his arm on the side of the chicken coop and looks at me without saying anything. A vein pulses on Uriah's high forehead, with its stripe of white skin where his ugly straw hat blocks the sun. "I've never touched Lydie," he says. "Not like that. I just feel responsible for her, I guess."

I roll my eyes. "Responsible? But you never touched her. Right."

"I don't feel responsible for her pregnancy, Amelia." And I can tell he's ticked. "I feel responsible because I could have *saved* her."

With this, Uriah Rippentoe pushes past me. I hear his footsteps as he leaves the barn, slamming the doors behind him. Hay drifts from the loft and spins through the air like those helicopter leaves Grandma Sarah and I used to collect at the park when I was a kid. Staring up at them in the semidarkness, I remember how we'd take the leaves and helicopters home, shave red, orange, and brown crayon over them, and iron everything between two pieces of the parchment paper Grandma Sarah kept in the pantry for baking. It was one of my favorite projects in the fall until I realized it wasn't cool to do craft time with my nanny.

Catching one of the pieces of hay, I hold it against my chest, which is suddenly tight with this frustration that I can't even understand. Maybe it's because I know a summer fling with Uriah would sidetrack me enough that I wouldn't have to feel much of anything at all. But now that he's gone—and angry with me on top of it—I have no buffers left to stand between me and my own pain.

I wait until I can hear Uriah calling for the goats down at the pond. Then I slowly sink to the ground beside my basket piled with brown eggs, hold my face in my hands, and—for one of the first times in over a year—let myself cry over the loss of Grandma Sarah, who was more like a mother to me than my own mom.

Beth, 1996

Fannie was asleep in the cane-backed chair before the fire; her thin chest rose and fell, her chin sank beneath her top lip, and her prayer *kapp* sloped forward. At noon, Fannie and I had driven her buggy up into the mountains to deliver Mary Hoover's tenth child. Though Mary's delivery was as fast as we'd expected, the mother had started hemorrhaging afterward. Fannie knew just what to do to save the mother's life, including climbing up onto the feather-tick bed and kneading Mary's abdomen with arthritic fingers until the afterbirth had been safely expelled.

We returned to Hopen Haus before bedtime. Charlotte took newborn Hope from me—she had spent the majority of Mary's labor asleep in a wrap against my chest—and told us that Alice Rippentoe's quickening had started less than an hour ago. But we knew her first labor could last long past dawn. The fact that Sadie Gingrich had been in Lancaster visiting family for two weeks—therefore handing even more responsibility off to Fannie—made me determined not to disturb Fannie's much-needed rest. Once Charlotte offered to watch Hope, I told her I would try to deliver Alice's child on my own.

Eight hours later, in the birthing room, I stared at Alice's file, illuminated by two kerosene lamps suspended from hooks embedded in the beam dissecting the ten-foot ceiling. Alice's complication-free prenatal appointments were documented by Charlotte's looping cursive and Fannie's precise script. There were no issues that might portend a difficult delivery. So what was stalling Alice's labor? Alice stayed quiet except for panicked breathing through her contractions. I had witnessed women screaming and spitting before true labor had even begun, so I had to admire her silence.

I could see fear in the flush of Alice's cheeks and the watery gleam in her wide green eyes as she suddenly breathed, "Something's wrong; something's wrong," like a chant.

I did not say it, but I was fearful as well. I glanced at

the watch I kept hidden under the elbow-length sleeve of my cape dress, as we were not supposed to wear jewelry. It was now 6:35 a.m. Alice had been in labor for over eleven hours, and there had been little to no progress. Fannie believed that letting nature take its course—with our guidance, in case something went wrong, as it had with Mary Hoover—was the best application of midwifery. I admired Fannie's standard of minimal interference, yet it was essential that Alice give birth before seven o'clock tonight. We had a twenty-four hour window from the time her water broke before mother and baby were at great risk for infection.

I would soon have to notify Fannie of Alice Rippentoe's failure to progress. With our labor window cut in half and nothing left to lose, I tried an experiment. After a careful examination, I smiled encouragingly. "You're almost to six," I said. "Over halfway there."

At this point, the hours of withstanding contractions with nothing to show for them were chipping away at Alice's strength. She needed something—even a lie—to buoy her up.

Alice blinked back tears. "I *am*?"

I nodded and helped her off the table. "Now let's put you to work."

The damp terror left Alice's eyes and determination took its place. I knotted a sheet to the bedpost, twined the fabric around Alice's hips, and pulled and pulled on my knotted end, like a strange game of tug-of-war. The "double hip squeeze" maneuver usually requires two midwives. But the bedpost—for the most part—served as the other arm. Alice sighed and closed her eyes. I felt such satisfaction, knowing this had relieved the pressure on her lower back.

Alice's breathing grew harder as her contractions increased.

I held her hand as she breathed through each one. Another contraction bore down before the previous one had abated. She groaned and whittled her nails into the sides of the lacquered wood.

My heart pounded with each of the guttural sounds Alice made. I wanted to run and get Fannie; I wanted to tell Charlotte to leave Hope for a moment and come. *Come quick!* But there was no longer time. Suddenly, Alice's bellow reverberated through the small room, and her child was born.

I suctioned the crying baby's nose with the bulb syringe and cradled him close. Tears filled my eyes as those almond-shaped eyes opened and looked around the room. He was breathing perfectly, his color was golden, but—just like my daughter—he did not utter one more cry. His dark irises seemed to deflect every ray of sun spilling through the curtains. He stretched his tiny fingers toward it, as if to cradle the cosmic star in his palm.

"Uriah," Alice whispered. "I'll call him Uriah—'God is light.'"

Blinking free of my stupor, I helped Alice gingerly sit down on the bed. Her teeth were chattering. I placed her son in her arms and went over to the cupboard to get another quilt. I wrapped the heavy, wedding-ring pattern around her shoulders. She reached out and clasped my hand.

"Thank you," she said, "for bringing my son into the world."

I nodded but continued looking out the window, where the sun had fully tipped over the mountains and poured its rays across the valley. In the wash of Alice's child's birth, I had felt more cleansed than at my own baptism. Yet before the amniotic fluid had dried on my palms, my heart clenched with jealousy. Turning, I watched them together. Alice's face was still bright with exertion. The rim of her blond hair was darkened with sweat. Her lips were red and swollen from so many hours of biting through the pain of fruitless contractions.

As the halo of light spread to ensconce them both, I saw how she held her child. I saw how she cradled him close, not needing to be aware of time, since no one was waiting in the wings. She would not have to stop suckling him or swaddling him or nuzzling his fragrant skin to sign papers that would let the child who was bone of her bone and flesh of her flesh be taken away.

Tears slipped down Alice's cheeks, dampening the faint curls covering Uriah's head. He rested peacefully against her breast. Watching them, my own breast ached with longing. For a moment, just one, I yearned to snatch that beautiful boy-child from her arms and claim him as mine—just so Alice would know what it felt like to lose someone so dear to you as effortlessly as pearls slipping off a broken string.

I withdrew from Alice Rippentoe at that moment. Like her intuitive response to labor, my recoiling from the pain she and Uriah evoked felt like the only way to survive. I am not sure it would have been easier if she had given birth to a girl. But I know that her giving birth to a boy only increased the vividness of my own loss.

As I clamped off the umbilical cord and severed it with the sanitized scissors, I found it ironic that *I* was the one to separate this mother from her child, when I had suffered from that separation one way or another since I was twelve years old.

When I knew from my blocked throat that my soul was a wellspring about to be wrung dry, I awoke Charlotte in my bedroom and asked her to finish checking Alice and the baby.

I then ran to the linen closet and shut the door. In the darkness, sobbing, I buried my face in the folded stacks of towels. I breathed in the icy fresh scent and forced the image of my own newborn son away. Though my soul rejoiced in the presence of my eight-week-old daughter— a rosy-cheeked cherub tucked in the Moses basket beside my bed, a gift—she could never fill the hole he had left behind.

As another baby boy was born into the world, my grief was birthed anew.

13

Lowering my face into the wrap, I kissed Hope's forehead and hugged her warm body against my chest. Right there—standing in the kitchen, stark sun streaming through spotless windows, donated apples gleaming crimson in the wooden bowl—I vowed I would never wish for my son when I had my daughter right here. Not the way I had wished for my son when I helped birth Alice Rippentoe's child last night.

The kitchen door leading to the back porch swung open before I had even finished the thought. An arctic gust caught it and smacked the door against the clapboard siding, again and again, until I thought the door would slam shut in slivers. Wind swooped into the kitchen, rattling the copper pots hanging overhead, making them clang like chimes. I clutched Hope, hoping to shield her from the draft. She remained asleep in the wrap, yet I shivered with equal parts premonition and cold.

"Please close the door," I called. "We're not heating the outside."

It was not one of our Hopen Haus girls who entered, but the driver, Wilbur Byler. Stomping mud from his boots, he came into the kitchen. "Sorry," he said. Wilbur blew hard on his hands. "The door got away from me."

I nodded, picked up the knife, and continued paring apples in quick, clean strokes. The juice ran down my chilled fingers. The countertop was festooned with teardrop-shaped seeds and long tendrils of skin. My actions were relaxed. But deliberately so. Between my shoulder blades, tension sunk like an ax. I could never shake the unease I felt whenever Wilbur Byler came around. I had no reason to doubt his character; everyone in Dry Hollow trusted Wilbur without question, granting him access to their finances, their families, their homes. In my six months at Hopen Haus, he had not singled me out or asked one question. However, the covert way he watched me made me wonder if he knew more than he let on.

"Is there hot water in there?" Wilbur pointed to the cast-iron pot on the stove. "I'd like some coffee 'fore I hit the road."

"No. But I can make some."

Wilbur shook his head. "You've got your hands full. I'll do it."

I gritted my teeth, eager to have him leave, but continued peeling. I heard Wilbur lift the heavy cast-iron cover over the burner and wedge pieces of kindling down into the box. Still, I felt his eyes scanning my back, as if willing me to turn. My hands shook as the blade separated fruit from skin. The paring knife slipped and gouged the pad of my left palm, just below the thumb. I cried out. Startled, Hope began to cry as well. Blood welled in the cut and dripped down my hand, plopping onto the fresh, off-white fruit.

"You cut yourself?" Wilbur called over the din of Hope's sobbing.

I nodded and tried to calm my daughter with my uninjured hand.

The heavy stove lid clanked into place. The kitchen floor absorbed Wilbur's heavy tread as he crossed the kitchen toward me. "Here," he said. "Wrap this around it." He held out a tea towel. I bound it around the wound and curled my fingers into a fist.

I thanked him and shifted from side to side, trying to rock Hope back to sleep. But she would not be soothed. Her face reddened. Her desperate cries seemed to ricochet across every metal surface in the kitchen. My chest heaved against her heaving chest. I knew Hope was not only reacting to being awoken from her nap, but also from the nerves wracking my body.

Wilbur held out his arms. "Let me take her," he said.

"No." The word was a growl, as emphatic as a curse. My heart pounded. Blood throbbed in my hand. I looked

down and saw red blooming through the floral tea towel, as bright as a poppy. I pressed Hope's head harder to my breast. She cried and thrashed, trying to escape the person who was trying to keep her safe.

Wilbur stepped back. "You okay?"

I looked up. His square hands were raised in a defensive gesture, as if he feared I was going to attack him with the knife. But this gesture did not hold my attention as much as the connotation undergirding his words.

Let him think I'm crazy, I thought. *That'll make him leave us alone.*

I did not nod or break eye contact, daring him to look away first. "Not sure," I said.

The sun glinted off the blade I had just picked up. Hands shaking, I lowered the knife. My eyes burned with a primal protectiveness unlike anything I had ever known. "You'd better not hang around here too long, Wilbur, or somebody might get hurt."

Two days before Farmer's Market Saturday, Fannie Graber claimed that I was the best choice for overseeing Dry Hollow's booth: I spoke perfect English for the paying customers, plus she had taught me enough snippets of Pennsylvania Dutch to have me be considered genuine Old Order Mennonite. When pressed, Fannie also revealed that she thought Wilbur still harbored a crush for me that would work itself out if the two of us were given enough alone time. She was even more interested in providing

Hope with a *dawdy* than she was in providing me with a husband. It did not seem to matter that I was not attracted to Wilbur in the least, or that my knife-wielding incident a month and a half ago had left him in no hurry to interact with me. But for Fannie Graber, I would do anything.

Consequently, Farmer's Market Saturday arrived and there I was, sitting in Wilbur's idling truck as panic flared inside my chest, making it difficult to breathe. I glanced beyond the fingerprints marring the passenger's-side window. Crowds were flocking toward the pavilion that some men from Dry Hollow Community had been hired to build. I could see similarities between it and our own dwellings in the pavilion's stout, rough-hewn cedar beams and corrugated tin roof. On the last Saturday before Christmas, the farmer's market reopened, and vendors from across the county gathered to sell their wares with more intensity than normal, as the money must hold them over through the sluggish winter months.

Even from inside the cab, I could see many of the booths were set up with displays of earth-toned pottery, beaded jewelry, wool purses and hats dyed in a kaleido-scope of color, glass-bottled lotions, and baked goods taste-fully packed in white paper boxes stacked on overlapping red and green tablecloths. But none of the vendors were Mennonite or Amish.

Business ventures were never openly discussed in Dry Hollow Community because Bishop Yoder believed that money—and anything associated with it—was the root of all evil. Yet that morning, as Fannie handed me a lunch, she said that my *kapp* and cape dress and the bits of Pennsylvania Dutch vocabulary I had learned were crucial for sales. *Englischers* believed they were getting a better product if it came from a Plain community, where morality supposedly held the "Gentle People" to a higher standard than the rest. And sales were necessary, far more than even Fannie Graber let on. Hopen Haus relied on food and funds hoarded over spring and summer when Dry Hollow better resembled the Promised Land. But Fannie said they were sometimes scraping the bottom of the barrel before the next harvest season came around—which was why, having gone through our own orchard's supply, we were baking with donated apples.

Watching the people now milling beneath the pavilion, I understood to what extent the community had sheltered me, how they had offered me refuge when I had nowhere else to turn. Though I was grateful to them, I was slowly realizing that the Dry Hollow Community was no utopia as the *Englischers* thought. I was baptized into the Mennonite church, but despite my cape dress and *kapp*, I was still perceived as *Englisch* as when I'd come. I was *still* a woman with a daughter and no husband: a toxic blend the Dry Hollow families did not want encroaching upon their well-ordered lives. Nonetheless, in seven months I had never stepped across the border of the property. I suppose it felt like hallowed ground upon which no ill-intentioned footsteps could trod. But looking out at that crowd, I felt vulnerable—my exposure to the public reawakening my fear of getting caught.

I looked over at Hope, nestled in the car seat beside me with her cheeks round and bright against the trailing strings of her knit hat. Then I looked over at Wilbur. He smiled and stroked the top of her hand. I had to ball my fingers into fists to keep from striking him away. Hope was not frightened, though. She just looked at Wilbur with those large hazel eyes framed with light lashes that seemed to see through a person's mask and still love what was beneath. Cooing, Hope held on to one of his proffered fingers.

"Such a sweet-natured thing," Wilbur said.

The bumper-to-bumper traffic bottlenecked around the square started to flow again. Wilbur shifted out of neutral and drove a few feet, parking his truck in the slanted white lines outside the Scottsburough Emporium. Wilbur got out. Sound poured into the vehicle, like a submerged port-hole undone. My hands shook as I unfastened the straps of Hope's car seat.

The passenger door creaked open. "Here," Wilbur said, "I'll take her."

I'll take her. The simple sentence ripped through my ears, but I reminded myself of Wilbur's and my last alter-cation and the type of attention-seizing behavior that I did not want to repeat. "All right." My acknowledgement was barely audible, but I could clearly hear my fear. I held Hope out, and Wilbur took her from me. Settling her against his shoulder, he patted her back with the heel of his hand. She pushed off his chest and tried to look up. Laughing, Wilbur took his hat off and hooked it over the hat already on her head. Hope wobbled from side to side, knowing something was different but not knowing what or how to take the hat off.

I slid off the bench seat and reclaimed my daughter, wrapping my coat lapels around her body and pressing her to my chest. Since Wilbur could not get the truck any closer to our booth, he stayed behind to unload the boxes. I felt insecure, knowing that I would be parting the masses all by myself, and was then amazed that the man I felt threatened by was also someone who—when faced with countless strangers—brought me comfort.

Keeping my head down, I wove among *Englischers* for the first time since Hope's birth. The air was crisp, but sweat dripped down the small of my back. I felt, rather than saw, the stares of the people as they realized a Plain woman was in their midst. My entire life, I had been over-looked. But now that I craved anonymity, the *kapp* and cape dress—the very articles intended to keep me from view—seemed to propel me into everyone's sight.

I pulled the lapels of my coat tighter until they obscured Hope's face. She arched her back and cried out, struggling to break the hold of my arms. Again, I knew she was sens-ing my tension; I had to relax. Breathing deep, I smelled popcorn and funnel cakes and recalled unspooling cotton candy on the Ferris wheel at the La Crosse County Fair with Looper when we were children.

In the street, children laughed and ran pell-mell through the crowd. Silver helium balloons floated high above them, tied with ribbon to their small wrists—airborne buoys that let the parents know where they were. Centered under a doorway, a volunteer rang a bell for the Salvation Army bucket. Cameras flashed. Vendors hawked wares. Car horns honked as vehicles struggled to find parking spaces where there were none left.

After seven months without even the electrical buzz of power lines to dispel the quiet, this cacophony made me want to clap my hands over my ears. I pondered afresh Fannie's motivations for requiring me to oversee Dry Hollow's booth. Surely she knew there were women in the community far more capable than I. Although I had never told her the fears I battled, she could probably deduce from my avoidance of Wilbur and refusal to leave the community that my past haunted me still. I stood motionless, the din swirling around me, and recalled what Fannie had said when I told her why I'd taken Hope and run: "For the sake of yourself and the child, you can't live in fear. . . . You must let yourself live."

My courage renewed, I locked my gaze on the pavilion and parted the crowd.

Wilbur grabbed a stack of old newspapers off a folding chair and dropped it on the table of the booth. "Brought these to wrap the candles and jams," he said. "Be careful not to pop the tops." Ducking low, he grabbed a box of plastic T-shirt bags and set it beside the newspapers. He put his hands on his hips and surveyed the booth. "Well, I guess that's it."

"You going somewhere?" I asked.

He nodded. "But I'll stick around until you're comfortable, then come back to help load everything up."

"Thank you," I said, purposely meeting his eyes.

Wilbur avoided them and looked at the ground. "You're welcome."

My first customer came within seconds. She was a stout, middle-aged woman with sun-dried skin and high cheekbones offset by short, peppery hair. I wrapped her oatmeal-and-lavender bar and "Home Sweet Home" candle in newspaper, then slid them into the bag.

As I passed it to the woman, she reached out and clenched my hand. "You one of those girls?" she asked. Native American earrings trembled in her lobes. I could not have looked away from her gray eyes if I'd wanted to. She pressed my fingers and clarified, "The ones at that home for unwed mothers?"

Hope chose that moment to coo from the basket tucked against the table, giving me away. My face filled with so much heat, I was sure it would glow right through my skin.

"Jah," I said, retracting my hand from the woman's grasp. Sweat moistened my palms. Below the table, I wiped them on my skirt. When would a simple exchange with a stranger stop feeling like a threat?

I tucked the woman's twenty-dollar bill beneath the change compartment and crouched to check on Hope. She had fallen asleep—one arm over her head, fingers unfolded—and had found her thumb on the other hand without my assistance. Her cheeks were red; her mouth looked dry. I wondered if she was hot. I pulled the hat off her head and covered her ears with the blanket. Someone cleared his throat. I stood up and smiled.

"I'd like to buy this, please." A tall, older gentleman—bundled in a finely cut navy wool coat—slid across the table a jar of blackberry preserves.

"Yes, sir," I said. "Let me wrap it."

"It's not a gift."

"No, I just don't want it broken."

He nodded, curt.

Setting the jam on its side, I wrapped it and crunched the paper around the gilded lid and then wrapped the jar in another layer. I was about to wrap it a third time when he said, "I think that's enough."

My movements froze, but not because the impatient man had stopped me. A single word in the newspaper article had caught my eye; the tiny font magnified by the glass jar and then obscured by the dark purple jam inside it. The jar rolled as I slid the newspaper pinned beneath. The feather-light section A and B of the *Tennessean* flapped like wings, even though I seized the edges with trembling hands. I could barely read the words through my panic, yet the collage of them—*surrogate, graduate student, Simms University, Dr. Fitzpatrick, alleged kidnapping*—told me that a nightmare had resumed.

"What's wrong with you?" the man gruffed. "Here—take the money."

But I could not look up from the newspaper. I heard him slap the bill on the table and stomp away. The article, "Search Continues for Missing Surrogate," was dated August 13, 1996—a month and a half after I fled. If a newspaper in another state had carried the story weeks after my disappearance, how much coverage had it received in Boston?

My mouth filled with saliva. Acid backed up my throat. Dropping the newspaper, I clamped a hand over my mouth. I searched the booth for a trash can. Nothing. I retched into an empty cardboard box. Looking up and dabbing my mouth, I saw Wilbur watching me. His satisfied expression seemed out of place, almost like a mime who had forgotten what face to display at different parts of the show. But when he noticed that I was looking at him, he frowned, stood, and came running over.

"My word . . . Rhoda? You okay?" Wilbur helped me into a chair and passed me a clean napkin from his jacket pocket. "What happened?" he asked. "Do you feel bad?"

I wiped my face and tearing eyes, buying time. I could not let him know what I had discovered.

I blinked hard, willing myself to appear strong, and stared right into Wilbur's eyes for the second time since I met him. It was like looking in a dim pool; they didn't reveal anything. Could he have seen the article? Could he have planted it there for me to find?

I shook my head, willing away the fears my paranoia had birthed.

"I'll be fine," I lied.

⸺◆⸺

The afternoon after I discovered the article and the contents of my Pandora's box unfurled, I took Hope upstairs and nursed her in bed. I awoke a few hours later, sweat-soaked and screaming. Clutching Hope, I sat up and panted. Footsteps pounded up the staircase. The knob to my bedroom door turned. It did not budge. I had wedged the back of the rocking chair beneath the knob. "Open the door, Rhoda," Fannie called, rapping knuckles on the solid wood. "Rhoda. Open the door."

Shivering as my sweaty body cooled, I kept Hope close, who somehow remained sleeping. I removed the rocking chair from the door with one hand but held the chair in front of my body, blocking the entrance. Fannie had one crooked finger wedged in a brass candle stand. The candle's faltering light etched furrows in her face. I saw the wiry gray hair that had escaped her *kapp*, the slump of her shoulders, the responsibility of so many lives dulling her eyes. At almost seventy, Fannie Graber was tired—and far too old for this.

"Come on, Rhoda." The head midwife sighed and pushed two fingers against her right temple. "You've got to let me in." I knew Fannie was not just speaking of physical passage, but of emotional trust. I had let Fannie assist me in labor—the most intimate act beyond conception. Nonetheless, terrified of being hurt, I continued to safeguard my heart—letting Fannie see bits and pieces and yet never its whole, bruised entirety.

I hated that this had stifled our bond, for I loved Fannie. She was the closest thing to a mother that I had known in years, and yet drawing close to her made me feel like I was being disloyal to the mother who was only mine in memory, the woman who wore a crisp white apron over my father's worn bib overalls, her only adornment a checked handkerchief tied over her brunette waves and a lavish brand of department store perfume. I recalled the diamond crumb in her engagement band glinting as she sifted cocoa and confectioner's sugar into a bowl that filled the morning kitchen with a decadent chocolate haze and the promise of an afternoon treat. I recalled peeking over the countertop and my mother passing me the glistening brown beaters, which I licked until my cheeks became an abstract canvas stamped with a wide white smile.

This was the mother I loved and remembered. However, I now had to make a choice as my little brother, Benny, had been forced to make so long ago: cling to a phantom memory or to the flesh-and-blood woman standing before me. The woman who had never abandoned me. The woman who loved me too. I exhaled and pulled open the door. Stepping to the side, I let Fannie pass. I touched the damp hanks framing my face. Jiggling Hope with one arm, I covered my mouth and began to weep.

Fannie set the candle stand on the seat of the chair, stepped toward me, and placed two papery hands on my cheeks. My tears dripped over her fingers. With one hand, I reached up and clasped hers, tilting my head toward her touch like a blossom toward life-giving sun. "You can't live in fear, Rhoda," she whispered, searching my eyes. "That's no life at all."

Fannie removed her hands from my face and ran a finger over the skin pulsing over the delicate fontanel of my daughter's head. I drew Hope to my chest and turned away, using my body to shield her own. Fannie stroked my forearm as if I were a runaway child or horse.

"It's all right," she soothed. "I won't hurt her."

Reluctant, I released my daughter into Fannie's waiting arms. The old midwife looked up and smiled, cradling Hope against her. Joy roused her careworn eyes. The years slipped away like a shed skin, and I saw that though Fannie loved us Hopen Haus girls, our babies were why she remained.

"She's perfect, Rhoda." Fannie's voice was hushed with reverence. She traced the spread fingers and tiny, matching nails of my daughter's dimpled hand. "So incredibly perfect."

I started sobbing then, sobbing so hard I clenched my sides, trying to keep my body from breaking apart. I did not open my eyes but felt Fannie wrap an arm around my back. She led me, blind and keening, over to the bed.

"My *meedel*," Fannie said. *"Vas es letz?"*

I could not reply. I could barely breathe. I heard water pour from the pitcher on the nightstand beside my bed. The mug touched my fevered lips. "Drink," she commanded.

I drank the mug's entirety and used the neck of my nightgown to wipe my face. Fannie took the mug. I opened my eyes and looked down at my sleeping daughter. "I know it's wrong," I said, "but I wish . . . I wish Hope *weren't* perfect. If she weren't perfect, I could keep her. But now that she is, I know she'll get taken away."

I reached for my child. Fannie leaned down and settled

her in my arms. The return of my familiar scent awakened Hope. Clutching the cotton fabric, she rooted groggily against my chest. I undid the two top buttons of my nightgown and let the babe suckle. I traced Hope's button nose pressed into my pale flesh; the side of her rosebud lips perched in drinking; her heart-shaped face and pointed chin; her long lashes and fine, russet-colored eyebrows.

Even by the nebulous light of Fannie's candle nub, and even taking into account how much infant features can change, I could see how closely Hope resembled her father, how closely she resembled her mother. If anyone ever doubted the credibility of my story, they only had to see Thomas and Meredith Fitzpatrick to know that it was true: the child I had given birth to was in no way mine.

"We're not safe anywhere," I said. It was both a grievance and a fact. I'd given up safety the morning I fled Boston. What amazed me most was that I knew I would do it all again.

Fannie shook her head and ran a hand over my cheek. "You know," she said, sitting down on the mattress, which bowed beneath her slight weight, "Elmer and I did not always live in community. We did not always live in safety."

"You didn't?" I could not imagine Elmer and Fannie Graber living anywhere besides their tiny gray cottage with its cobblestone walkway and navy tin roof.

"No," Fannie said, gathering the material of her dress. "When my eldest three children were just knee-high, Elmer and I went down to Paraguay as missionaries. Everyone— my *familye*, his—told us that what we were doing was foolish, that we were risking so much to bring light to that dark world, but I knew those women needed me. And Elmer . . . Elmer wanted to share the gospel with them." She swallowed hard and sat up straighter on the bed. "I knew it was dangerous. We *all* knew it was dangerous, but we went anyway. We knew that all could be lost—our lives, our children's lives—but we felt called, and so we knew we had to go."

Pausing, Fannie sighed. "We were there a year when our youngest, Lois, caught dysentery because she drank from an abandoned well. I tried everything to take care of her—broth, poultices from the village. But without a hospital, I knew that it was soon going to be to no avail. It was not a pretty death, as most deaths aren't, and for two days after she passed, I kept holding on to Lois because I felt if they took her dead body from my arms, that was the moment she would really stop living."

I drew Hope close, recoiling at the mention of death when my own living, breathing child was in my arms. But out of respect, I said nothing, just allowed Fannie to continue her story.

"Elmer was finally the one who came and took Lois from me," Fannie continued. "The monsoon season had come, and I just sat in our hut on the side of that rain-swept mountain—knowing Elmer, right then, was trying to dig our daughter's grave in mud—and I wanted the rains to wash me over the cliff. I wanted to drink the tainted water and feel life ebbing away from me, too. But I couldn't. For the sake of David and Levi and Elmer, for the sake of our ministry, I couldn't. I had to go on."

I opened my mouth to tell Fannie how sorry I was. Still shocked, no words would come. I just stared at the old midwife, not understanding how she could take care of daughters and bring daughters into the world when it seemed every one would be a reminder of the one daughter she had lost. "But . . . how'd you continue once your greatest fear came true?" I asked.

Fannie Graber leaned down. Her fingers shook as she touched Hope's head. "Faith," she whispered. "Faith got me through. Faith that one day he will 'give unto them beauty for ashes, the oil of joy for mourning, the garment of praise for the spirit of heaviness.'"

Getting to her feet, the midwife picked the candle stand up from the rocking chair and turned. The flame wavered with the movement. Fannie met my eyes. "Even if the worst comes true—and I'm not saying it will—you will get through it, Rhoda. The same as I did. You just must let faith overcome fear one minute, one hour, one day at a time."

Fannie left my room but kept the door open. I watched the glow of her candle flame slowly vanish down the stairs. I closed the door and lay Hope on the bed. I knelt as if in prayer and leaned in. My daughter's warm, sweet breath mingled with mine. I watched her chest rise and fall, rise and fall, rise and fall. . . . It was like watching a bonfire's first kindle or the rolling ocean tide at dawn: the view was both miraculous and mesmerizing.

Tears pricked my eyes. In the quiet of my moonlit room in the corner of an ancient house, I let them slide down my neck without my mouth emitting a sound. Hope did not stir as I continued to weep, and I kept blinking—refusing to lose one glimpse of her face. Kneeling there, that braided rug transmuting my knees with its pattern, I could see how God had already turned the hardships of my life for good. If I had not lost my son, I would have never confided to Dr. Fitzpatrick about the child whom I had been forced to give up. If I had not told him this, he would have never considered asking me to become a surrogate for his and Meredith's child. If Meredith had not needed a hysterectomy and had conceived that child naturally, or if another surrogate besides me had carried that child, this beautiful gem shielded inside these quilts and dreaming so peacefully might have been lost.

Wiping the grateful sorrow from my face, I clambered into bed. I slid one hand beneath Hope's diapered bottom and nestled her closer. She pressed her feet into my stomach like small, hot stones. I turned my head on the feather pillow and watched the moonlight splashing in through the curtains and trickling across the hardwood floor.

Remember this; remember this; remember this, I thought as our hearts beat as one.

14

Amelia, 2014

In Hopen Haus, I roll two dozen of the eggs I gathered from the barn in a bath of diluted bleach water and pat them dry with a cloth. The other two dozen eggs I don't clean. Lydie said that the gross, waxy coating from the hen helps keep the eggs fresh, like a seal, and we should just store the unwashed eggs in the springhouse until we need them.

I shudder, swearing to myself that I'll never eat an embryo again, and tuck the eggs into cartons, marking each one with a date the way I was trained to do when I took over the egg duty position from Terese. Recapping the marker, I stack the eggs next to the sink since I don't know where the cleaned ones should go. I'm about to leave the kitchen when Star comes in through the swinging door leading to the dining room. Shadows rim her eyes like smeared liner. They're the same bruised color as her hair, which looks flat and depressed, devoid of its gluey gel.

"You on kitchen duty this week?" I ask.

Star rolls her eyes. "Least they let me off for a month." Looping an apron over her neck, she crosses the apron strings behind her back and ties them in front. My eyes are drawn to the magnet of her stomach, as I remember Lydie's story about the night Star miscarried her baby. I wonder how she must feel, knowing her body doesn't carry life anymore. Does she miss the baby, although she never met him? I know I would miss my baby if I lost him.

I can feel Star's eyes on me and look down to see that my arms are wrapped around my middle. A pause stretches between us, just long enough to feel awkward. Removing my hands, I fold my arms high above my waist.

"How're you feeling?" I ask.

Star studies the menu, with the step-by-step instructions that Alice Rippentoe writes out according to whatever food's been gathered, shot, or donated that week.

"Like I been hit by a truck," Star says. But the words are followed by a smile. Even with her tattoos and piercings, that smile makes Star look as if life's been as easy for her as it's been for me. Guiltily, I stare at my feet and twirl the ancient cameo ring my parents gave to me on my sixteenth birthday, which my, like, great-great-great grandmother wore when she met the queen. That was the same night they also gave me keys to my very first car: a baby blue BMW roadster with white leather seats and convertible top, which was the envy of my entire junior class, but left me feeling dull.

I knew the gift was supposed to make me feel special . . . loved . . . but I'd rather have spent a week's vacation with my mom than drive a car she'd spent half a year working to buy.

Still, I know Star's here not because she's pregnant like the rest of us but because no one cares enough to pick her up, and that makes me feel stupid for wanting more from my life when I have a mom and dad who love me like crazy—though with strange ways of showing it—and every gadget a girl of my techy generation could want.

I hear a pop of suction and glance up. Star's twisting a lid off a Mason jar containing canned tomato sauce and then three more jars containing canned mystery meat (I hope it's beef or venison) ground into burger. She measures everything and dumps them all into one large cast-iron pot. Then Star adds a big squirt of mustard and cubes of onion and some bright-green sweet pickles that are lined on the kitchen windowsill in clear glass jars.

I'm not on kitchen duty this week but don't like the idea of leaving Star alone—because, well, I know how it feels to be lonely. So I gather the knives, forks, and spoons from the drawer beside the sink, Mason jars for glasses, and cloth napkins that are tattered along the edges from too many washings by hand. The kitchen is quiet except for the clinking of the empty jars that Star puts in a cardboard box, along with the lids and seals that can later be reused for canning. (I'm surprised they don't reuse toothpicks.) Star knocks this thing called an ash catch into a bucket beside the stove and refills the box in the stove with wood.

Soon the water tank is hissing as the fire inside the stove gets stronger. Star takes a long wooden spoon from the crock and stirs the meat and sauce before setting the pot on the stove to heat. I set the tray on the island, gobsmacked by the image of a pretty terrifying Goth girl doing such old-fashioned chores without thinking twice. I then remember how good I felt whenever I watched Grandma Sarah chop peppers and onions on the cutting board next to the sink, and then scrape the colorful squares with a knife so they would tumble into the sauté pan and sizzle in the oil. The memory makes the back of my throat burn. I swallow hard, telling myself not to cry in front of Star, who has so much more to be sad about than I do.

"Did your mom teach you to cook?" I ask. The words are out before I can think to change them. Or maybe just not say them at all.

The tops of Star's ears look red against the limp purple petals of her hair. "What do *you* think?" she snaps. Her eyes narrow, and I know that whatever bond we've made is lost.

Layering the napkins on the tray, I place the silverware in a jar and set this on the tray as well, making it easier to carry everything into the dining room in one trip. I keep my eyes focused on the forks, knives, and spoons and real-ize that—with our disconnected mothers—Star and I have more in common than she would ever guess.

"I think from the time we're born, we miss our mothers. . . ." I pause, gathering nerve until I can meet Star's angry gaze. "Even when we become mothers ourselves."

The setting sun angles through the kitchen windows, shining off each of the panes.

"You know nothing about it," Star finally spits from between her teeth. The silver bauble pierced through her tongue gives Star an odd lisp that makes her sound like a scared schoolgirl, when she's really trying to intimidate me.

I busy myself by turning and drying off the rest of the lunch dishes. I curl my shoulders in toward my chest and rub the plate so hard with the towel, the china squeaks. But the whole time, I can feel Star's mean stare and wonder who's hurt her to the point that she feels like she has to keep everyone at arm's length.

Rhoda, 2014

I close the ledger revealing Hopen Haus's imminent financial ruin and leave my room. Halfway down the stairs, I see Ernest Looper standing on a ladder in the foyer, with a bandanna tied around his silvering blond hair. He runs calloused hands over the drywall cracks that make the ceiling better resemble the parched Death Valley floor. The old German shepherds are curled up head to tail, like yin and yang symbols, under the ladder. It is endearing to see how they trust Looper not to tread upon their limbs.

"Hey, Looper," I call.

He first looks down and then turns and glances over his shoulder to see me paused on the staircase. "Hey, yourself," he says.

I tighten my lips. "Can we talk a minute?"

Lowering his arms, Looper claps his left shoulder and rolls the bone, trying to work out a knot. "Sure," he says. He clambers off the ladder. The dogs awaken at the sound and rise to their feet, shaking their coats and making their tagged collars jangle. A few stray canine hairs float in the sunlight streaming through the windows. Among the first things I'm going to purchase after we get electricity in the examining room are a vacuum and an extension cord.

Looper folds the ladder and slants it against the wall. "I've actually been meaning to talk to you about something," he says. Turning, he pats the crumbling chink filling in the gaps between the logs. A few pebbles of plaster roll into his hand. I wince, embarrassed by how derelict Hopen Haus has become. "Beth," he continues, "I really don't think it's smart to run electricity in a house waiting for one stiff wind to knock it down. It'd be hard to remodel 'cause nothing in this place is plumb. Even if I *could* remodel, I don't know what I'd find if I tore out drywall and replaced logs. We're not just talking termites and dry rot, either. There could even be black mold from the roof having leaked so long."

I descend the rest of the staircase and glance through the foyer into the dining room. It is empty, and though I can hear voices in the kitchen, I cannot distinguish words.

I hope they cannot distinguish mine. "We can't afford much of anything anyway, Looper," I intone. "I just went over the books, and we barely have enough money to buy wire for electricity. There's no way we can afford logs and drywall as well."

Looper looks up at the cracked ceiling and clicks his tongue, assessing unseen damage. "I can't just putty over the cracks in the ceiling—not when it's this bad."

I look around Hopen Haus and see, suddenly, a metaphor for my own life. Ever since my daughter was taken, I have been trying to prevent more pain by not letting myself feel. But I *have* been feeling all along, even when I did not want to. Now that Looper's here—his presence ushering back the pain of the past—the fractures splinter through the putty of my self-preservation, letting me know that they have always been here, just biding their time.

Sensing my pensiveness, Looper reaches out and touches my arm. I draw back and beckon him to follow. I leave the foyer and walk out onto the porch. But even this does not feel private enough. I go down the steps and march toward the barn. The dogs run after me, panting. Looper trails at a measured pace. We do not speak before we reach the corral to the left of the barn's entrance. To calm my drumming heart, I rest my back against the warmed corral bars and focus on the cicadas' vibrating contralto and the tall white oaks bordering the lane that remind me of the peeling, papery birches back home in Wisconsin.

"Remember when I called you from that phone booth years ago?"

Looper says nothing. From my peripheral vision, I watch him untie his bandanna and wipe the sweat gathering at his temples. But I know he remembers. I know my phone call that dark day left him as bereft as it left me. After a moment, he nods.

"Well," I continue, "I'd just left my daughter behind. I was a gestational surrogate, and the people who'd hired me to carry the child did not want the child when they realized she might be handicapped."

Looper looks at me; his eyes remain guarded.

"The child wasn't handicapped." I smile. "She wasn't. She was a perfect baby girl. Though I would've thought so, regardless. She was almost eight pounds at birth, with this pointy chin and a mop of dark hair. I named her Hope, and for so long, no one questioned that she was mine. How could they? The entire Dry Hollow Community had seen that I was pregnant, and they'd seen me after I had birthed the child—wouldn't that make her mine?

"But then time passed—five months—and the parents who'd wanted to have the child aborted somehow found out I was hiding here, and they came and took her back."

I choke down a sob and turn from Looper, facing the corral instead. I gouge my fingernails into the rust sleeving the corral bars—the same corral I'd held when I clambered onto Sampson's broad back and rode to Fannie Graber's the night Hope was born.

"They took her away from me," I murmur. "Legally, I had no right to the child. I had kidnapped her in my womb, and I had run. But I knew that Meredith, the

biological mother, did not love the child. She was just trying to reclaim what she felt was rightfully hers. It hurt me
to see that. And it made me angry . . . possessive.

"When I knew Hope was lost to me forever, I prayed
that there would always be enmity between the child and
her biological mother. I prayed that they would not have
a good relationship because I didn't want my child to have
that kind of relationship with anyone if she couldn't have
it with me."

When Looper realizes that I'm finished speaking, he
opens his mouth, then reaches a hand into his pocket, as if
searching for the right words among the peppermint wrappers and loose change. "You don't got that kind of power,
Beth," he says after a while. "You really don't. God can sift
through prayers spoken out of selfishness or hurt. If that
girl has a bad relationship with her parents, it's not because
of something you did."

I wipe my tears on my palms. "But don't you see? If I
really loved that little girl—if I was really a good mother—
I would've wanted her to have a good relationship with the
woman who'd taken her from me. I wouldn't have punished
her because I wanted to punish her mother. I wouldn't have
wanted her to be lonely like I was. Like I *am*. I would've
wanted her to be loved."

I rest my arms on top of the corral fence and lower my
face. I feel the heat of Looper's proximity before he places
one arm around my back. I pivot and bury my face in his
chest, not caring who in Hopen Haus might see. The walls
of my world are crumbling, and I pray that if I remain in

Looper's capable arms long enough, I can find the strength to build again. This time, though, instead of building a smokescreen of self-preservation first, I will have to restore my soul from the inside out.

15

Beth, 1997

In the weeks following my discovery of the article among Wilbur Byler's old newspapers, a debilitating fear would sometimes give me the urge to run, to take this child who'd so captured my heart and leave everyone I loved but her. However, when Wilbur returned to Hopen Haus after traveling among the Plain communities in Kentucky and Tennessee, it was like he was trying to reassure me that everything was all right. He'd bring Hope a beaded teething ring. Or a woolen bonnet and sweater set that one of the younger Mennonite girls had crocheted for the accumulation of pocket money. Once, he overheard me complaining that I had nothing to read. The next time he came to Hopen Haus, he handed me a box filled with a year's worth of *Reader's Digest* condensed books.

I could have cried, handling those hardback covers. I was beginning to understand snippets of Pennsylvania Dutch. Nonetheless, residing in a secluded community where my first language was the rest of the community's second felt, at times, like I was living in a foreign land. When Wilbur saw how much I enjoyed the books, he began bringing me smaller gifts: a treasure box of candy or a coil of brightly colored yarn. At first, these gifts from Wilbur flattered me. I was never the type to garner admirers. Then I noticed that he was watching me open the gifts, as if waiting for compensation. When I next saw Wilbur's truck barreling up Dry Hollow's steep lane—which the men continued to rake and level despite the gullies continually formed by the rain—I found that my stomach clenched.

It was time to tell Wilbur that his gifts were no longer welcome.

Hope squirmed in my arms. I wrapped my shawl around her to block the wind and tried to smile as Wilbur clomped up the icy porch steps, hugging to his chest a basket of cellophane-wrapped bounty. I stared at the flamboyant summer fruit popping up from the basket like the first clump of daffodils after a long winter: pineapple, mango, grapefruit, kiwis, pears. . . . Since coming to Hopen Haus, I had feasted on new tastes such as rice pudding, Yorkshire pudding, Dutch apple bread, ham loaf, parsnip fritters, chicken soup with rivvels, pickled okra, beets, baby corn, and chowchow, along with numerous other homemade concoctions that crowded the supper table yet were somehow always consumed before an array of desserts. But in all my time there, I had not eaten any imported fruit—even bananas. My mouth watered.

I stared over at Wilbur. I did not know how to best broach the subject, so I just came out and asked, "Why're you doing this?"

"Doing what?" he said.

I pointed to the basket he'd set on the porch. Hope looked down too, as if to inspect.

Wilbur shrugged. "Just trying to help you out, is all."

"You don't know me."

"But I want to. I want to know you both."

I watched him a moment, trying to gauge his motivations. Alice Rippentoe was beautiful beyond reason, but Wilbur paid her no attention. And then I began to understand: Wilbur knew he had no chance of securing the affections of someone like Alice, but an unremarkable woman such as me would not be trailing around a host of men. With me, a bachelor who drove Old Order Mennonites and Amish around for a living would actually stand a chance.

Or so Wilbur thought.

"I'm sorry," I said, holding Hope's head. She was beginning to thrash, ready for her afternoon feeding. "You've been so kind. Really. I'm just . . . just not ready for any kind of relationship right now. I'm not sure I'm ever going to be."

Wilbur plucked off his orange hunter's hat and scratched at his scalp. Returning it to his head, he said, "Why, sure, Beth Winslow . . . I understand." Then he turned and walked down the pathway without pinching Hope's cheek or commenting on how big she was getting, as he usually did.

It wasn't until I watched his truck drive away that I realized he'd called me by my real name.

Though I was of non-Mennonite background, Fannie Graber's taking me on as her midwife-in-training helped the community accept me and my daughter. They really had no other choice if they wanted birthing assistance. But this wasn't the only reason. When I stopped regarding the Gentle People with suspicion, they began to trust me. Soon I could embrace their beautiful families without feeling a whiplash of pain.

I remember how I would sit on the front porch with the butter churn pinned between my legs. Stirring the stick through the cream slowly, so as not to leave lumps, I would watch a mother in a long cape dress and *kapp* walk down the lane past Hopen Haus with a line of bundled, stair-step children waddling behind her like ducklings. At Elam Glick's barn raising, after his barn roof collapsed from the weight of snow, I would arrange the hot casseroles on the food table and admire the tenacity of the young boys— tongues pinched between teeth, cheeks ruddy with the novelty of handling grown-up tools—as they hammered nails alongside their fathers' gloved hands. I could watch them, admire them, and not think of my son.

I even allowed Fannie to teach me things my mother never had: how to knit with Wilbur's gift of yarn—which I could accept by telling myself I had imagined him uttering my real name—sprinkle potato starch before pressing laundry with an iron, French-braid hair, sew a straight hem, and bake a shoofly pie from scratch.

The rare occasions Fannie spent the night at Hopen Haus, she and Charlotte and I would pull rocking chairs close to the hearth. Hope, in my arms, would be lulled by the fire's crackling melody. She would curl her fingers around her nose and suck her thumb, watching the sisters with serious eyes until she nodded off against my chest. And the sisters were worth watching. With their white nightgowns and crowns of silver hair, the contrast of Fannie's thin figure and Charlotte's plump one made them resemble mismatched twins. Their stiff fingers would slip thread through beeswax before inserting the needle into the vibrant fabric warming all our laps.

What a peaceful time that was. I am glad we did not know the measures being taken to draw it to an end.

One month after I stood on the front porch and told Wilbur Byler the two of us could never be anything other than friends, I had cabin fever and wanted a reprieve from motherhood and midwifing. Hope was in my bedroom taking a nap. I was walking down the lane—my boots

punching through the sleeted crust—when the smell of
death arose in the clearing of the pines. I shielded my eyes
against the sun and watched the orbiting bodies of vultures
sail down to land on their carcass—a yearling, I surmised
from the glimpse of tawny hide in between the dark, fluttering wings.

I had no sense that life as I knew it was about to change,
no sense that it was time to hold my child—to take my
child and run—even though I was as bound to the earth
as the vultures' deceased prey. I felt nothing except the
sun's rays penetrating the ash-gray clouds and warming my
face—and the sweat limning my body due to my unneces-
sary layers beneath a buttoned boiled-wool coat.

Something flashed down in the valley. I squinted
through the snow-covered trees. A dark-green Land Rover
crawled down the lane around the old cattle chute, its
hubcaps glimmering like mirrors. I was curious who would
be traveling these icy back roads when the main ones were
scraped. I continued walking and covered my mouth to
block the scent of death that grew more potent as the wind
shifted direction, blowing a snowdrift of glitter across the
land.

The Land Rover shifted into four-wheel drive and
ground up the hill. The windows were tinted; the golden
sides were splattered with road salt and snow. Though
interaction with outsiders wasn't encouraged, I lifted my
gloved hand and waved. The vehicle passed without braking. I turned and looked at the plates: Davidson County,
Tennessee. It was a bad day for travel. But sometimes

tourists visited Dry Hollow Community after seeing our address stamped on soaps or canned goods displayed in an Amish store located near Nashville.

The *Englischers* didn't often bother us. The bolder ones might lean out of their car windows and take pictures. The quieter ones would just drive slowly by, taking everything in with the same curiosity that I had the first day I came. Now that I was part of the community, this curiosity made me feel like a rare species trapped in a nature preserve. But Fannie Graber didn't mind. She said, with her usual forbearance, that the *Englischers* were merely trying to capture the simplicity their own lives lacked.

I continued walking until I reached the old cattle chute. Swatting the snowflakes mounded on the post, I stared across the land, remembering the summer afternoon I'd first come to Dry Hollow. How I'd watched the Clydesdale horse chip his hooves into the dirt, the bearded rider holding the reins with everything he had. That time seemed so far removed from me now, but not the sense that I would do whatever it took to ensure my child—not a child of my body, but a child of my heart—had a fighting chance.

For a moment, the earth stood still; the snowflakes froze in the midst of their descent.

Though I was yards away from the deer carcass, its odor clung to my nostrils like a harbinger. I gripped the fence post as images superimposed themselves over each other, creating a dire collage: the article about the missing surrogate, Hope asleep in the house, the Land Rover crawling up the hill, the vultures orbiting in the charcoal sky.

I splayed fingers across my chest, unable to breathe, and yet I forced myself to run. The wind peeled back my bonnet. The *kapp* beneath it wobbled with the intensity of my stride. My boots scrambled to find purchase on the sheets of ice. Chunks loosened and slid down the sloped lane. Extending my hands to keep myself from falling, I cried out and lifted my head. Pieces of hair hung in my face. My vision was blurred with panic and pain.

Blinking, I looked to the left and saw sated vultures hunched on the peak of the barn. Their oily feathers were extended across the thawing tin roof; their warty heads were as red as blood. The barn edges were fanged with icicles that cracked in the wind and punctured the snow. The sound sent the vultures scuttling into the air. Wiping my eyes with my sleeve, I took a deep breath and continued running—hoping that my intuition was wrong. That the Fitzpatricks had not found us, that I was not already too late.

The Land Rover was parked outside of Hopen Haus, the engine left running. Exhaust silently streamed from the twin mufflers, twisting into the air like breath. The property was quiet. Not a bird twittered in the white oak bedecked with feeders filled with black sunflower seeds; none of the tree's bare branches stirred the cauldron of the wind. For a moment, I wondered if I had mistaken everything—if the Land Rover's owners were parents of one of the residents and not the Fitzpatricks like I feared. Then I heard someone lock the vehicle doors.

I paused in the yard and turned to peer through the Land Rover's tinted windows. I stared at the silhouette of the person seated in the backseat, but I could not distinguish enough to tell if it was a woman or a man. Apprehension curdled my stomach. My mouth tasted bitter, but I didn't have enough moisture to swallow. Who was here? And what did they want? Plodding up the front porch on heavy legs, I opened the front door.

The staircase creaked. I looked up. Fannie was descending the steps as if the nodules of her spine could not withstand more pressure.

I pushed against my chest, forcing words to exit my windpipe that terror had sealed shut but for a rind's width of breath. "What is it?"

Fannie paused. The old midwife looked down at me. Tears filled her eyes and then the grooves on her face, water in an ancient riverbed. "I'm sorry, Rhoda," she rasped, pressing a knuckle to her mouth. Fannie descended the steps and reached across the landing to take my hand. "I'm so very, very sorry."

I wrenched my fingers free and gripped my upper arms, shaking. "What happened?"

"Hope's parents are here." Fannie glanced behind her, up at the steps.

I reared back as if I'd been struck by those cruel words—wasn't *I* her parent?—then I hurled my body forward.

Fannie blocked my path, her weak body fortified by a stronger will. "We must be rational here, Rhoda." The midwife seized my shoulders, and her eyes bored into mine.

"They have papers. They have a lawyer. They told us they won't press charges if you let Hope go quietly."

I felt such an acute sense of betrayal, my cheek stung with a Judas kiss. Since the evening I had allowed Fannie to cross the barrier around my heart, I had confessed everything. Everything about my childhood when I'd been forced to take the place of the mother who had abandoned us; about the child I had conceived out of wedlock with my longtime friend, and how—in a way—I had left both him and our son; about my infatuation with my married graduate school professor and the tainted reasons for which I'd agreed to bear his child; about running away because I loved the child, but also because I was weary of being alone.

I had said all of this in the hope that pouring my darkest self out to Fannie might absolve the magnitude of my guilt and, in compensation, keep Hope from getting taken away. But now, all of that was gone. My Hope, my faith in the Creator whom I'd just started to believe in, my trust that life could be good again, my trust in my adopted family, my trust that this remote place could become my sanctuary where—if I never stepped beyond its boundary—nothing could ever go wrong.

I heard a murmuring sound. Turning, I expected to see the Fitzpatricks. Instead, I saw Alice Rippentoe leaning against the dining room wall, her infant son nestled against her chest. Her eyes were closed, but her lips moved in prayer. Breaking Fannie's hold, I marched toward Alice. My entire body tingled and hummed with an energy that could kill, kidnap, or maim to protect my daughter, whom the courts would never grant as mine.

"Don't you dare," I seethed. "Don't you *dare* pray for me and my child when your child's still in your arms."

Alice opened her eyes and shielded her son, Uriah, from my fury. Disgusted, I pivoted and maneuvered around Fannie Graber without meeting her saddened gaze. I charged up the stairs and flung open my bedroom door.

Meredith and Thomas Fitzpatrick and an older man in a pin-striped suit looked up at my entrance. My eyes frantically scanned the room. Thom was standing behind the rocking chair, his face white. Meredith was beside the bed. A suitcase was on the mattress, its dark mouth gaping. The well-dressed stranger was standing in the center of the room—his shoulders hunched, his raked steel-gray hair flush with the dried lavender hanging from a beam on the ceiling.

But Hope was not there.

I walked into the room. The tautness was as palpable as trip wire.

With a jerk, Meredith zipped the suitcase closed and strode over to her husband. The dresser top revealed what she had taken. The missing objects were now just cutout shapes in the dust: a circle for the small container of grape-seed salve I massaged into Hope's skin after her baths; a rectangle for the mother-of-pearl comb I used to brush Hope's fledgling hair; a square for the stack of laundered cloth diapers piled with shiny, tangled pins.

The stranger stepped forward, acting as a barrier

between the Fitzpatricks and me. His height only added to his imposing appearance, making him seem larger than life, an otherworldly judge. A detective, I thought—or the Fitzpatricks' lawyer. Neither was good.

"I'd advise you not to interfere today," he said. "The Fitzpatrick family has every right to press charges, and if you fight back, that's exactly what we'll do."

My heartbeat was a sharp staccato against my ribs. "Where is she?" I whispered. Stumbling over to the bed, I unspooled Hope's yellow blanket from the quilt. It floated in the air like a contrail of sun. I pressed my face against it, breathing in her scent. "Tell me where she is!"

No one spoke.

My legs buckled, kneecaps ramming the hardwood floor. Clutching the blanket, I lifted my gaze and traced my eyes over the indentations in the mattress where my daughter and I slept. Someone crossed the room. The floorboards groaned as the person knelt beside me.

"Get up, Thom." Meredith's strident voice cut the room. "She's making enough of a spectacle as it is."

Thom began to rise. I pivoted and threw my body over his feet. "Please!" I stared up at him. His features were made indistinct by my horror. "*Please*—don't take her from me!"

Startled, Thom tried to move. "McClintock, Meredith—help me here."

Solid hands gripped my shoulders. Meredith tried peeling my fingers off her husband. The face of her cameo ring winked at me like an eye. "Let go," she commanded.

I wondered if she wanted my daughter or if she was punishing me for having wanted Thom.

Spent, I released him. He staggered backward and I collapsed. I heard the suitcase handle click. The wheels rolling
across the floor. A volley of heels. Footsteps made a reluctant report.

"Come, Thom," Meredith said. "Leave her."

"I'm sorry," he murmured.

The door closed.

I spread my hands over the icy floor, seeking my daughter's lost warmth, and wept.

⁘

Hopen Haus had long settled with the sounds of sleep.
But I continued staring up at the ceiling, my eyes burning into the darkness like coals. I had braced the door shut
with my rocking chair, and Fannie had stopped knocking
at midnight, finally surrendering to the fact that this time
I would not let her—or anyone—in. My milk let down
again; each release was more painful than the last. It was
ten minutes after Hope's two-o'clock feeding. The sixth one
she'd missed. The concept that Meredith would be the one
meeting Hope's needs did not devastate me as much as the
fear that Hope's needs would not be met. Was my daughter hungry? Was she crying, wondering why I would not
come—wondering why I had abandoned her the same way
my mother had abandoned me?

I knew the contracts I'd so thoughtlessly signed the previous fall abolished all legal rights to Hope, who was then

just someone else's child and the means to the completion of my degree. Plus, I remembered in the *In re Baby M* surrogacy case that the only reason Mary Beth Whitehead was granted visitation rights by the New Jersey Family Court was because Baby M was, genetically, half Mary Beth's. Hope was entirely the Fitzpatricks' in kinship and on paper. And on paper was the only thing that mattered—regardless of the way I had carried, birthed, and sustained the child for the past fourteen months through my own flesh and blood.

I took the rocker from beneath the doorknob and went downstairs. Fannie was seated at the head of the dining room table. A mug was clamped between her hands. In the candlelight, her Plain dress and wizened features made the old midwife appear like a person of history carved in stone. Fannie looked up. Her eyes were as raw as mine. "Saved some *esse* for you," she murmured. "It's cold, but it might still taste *gut*."

The nonchalance of her words penetrated me to the core. I did not know how to discuss food when my child was gone, due at least in part to my own lack of diligence. But for Fannie's sake, I walked over to the sideboard and picked up the utensils and white ceramic plate. I sat across from her and flicked the cloth napkin open on my lap. The table was cleared and spread with a crisp tablecloth. The centerpiece was a quart jar filled with berried holly branches. I was facing the kitchen, and though it was dark, above the swinging doors the suspended copper pots gleamed. Hopen Haus was oddly quiet for the mass of girls inhabiting it. The lack of noise was almost disturbing—as though Fannie and I had awoken from a nightmare only to find ourselves the lone survivors after a plague.

Fannie took a sip of tea. I knew it was cold. "Would you like to go somewhere for a while?" she asked. "Have some space?"

I speared pasta with my fork but looked at the bite with repulsion. "I don't need *space*," I said. "I need my daughter."

Fannie reached across the table, placing her hand on top of my own. "Of course," she said, and then looked down. "I know how you feel."

The fork clattered to my plate. "No," I snapped, withdrawing my hand. "You don't *know* how I feel. You lost a daughter, but she wasn't taken from you. There's a difference."

Fannie's tender eyes felt like the harshest rebuke. A tear rolled down her cheek and splashed onto the black waistband of her dress, darkening it like ink. It was probably three o'clock in the morning, and she hadn't changed her clothes. I doubted she had taken time to go home since Hope was taken. For a moment, I wanted to go over and rest my head against Fannie's bosom. I wanted to become that daughter who had died so young; I wanted her to become the mother I'd never really had. How could I compare the pain of our respective losses as if it were a competition? The far more important truth was that through our mutual loss, we had gained each other.

I hung my head and pushed the plate away. Wiping my

fingers on the napkin, I reached across the scarred kitchen table to take Fannie's hand again. "I'm sorry," I said. "It doesn't matter how you lost your daughter; she's still not here."

The old midwife nodded but said nothing.

"Is Wilbur in town?" I asked after a moment. "I need a driver."

Fannie's eyes clouded with confusion, then worry. "*Ach*, Rhoda," she said. "You must remember that fighting back is not our way."

"So you want me just to turn the other cheek? I'm sorry, but I have no more daughters to give!" I swallowed hard, trying to quell my emotions. But it was no use. At the mention of my child, my breasts stung. I picked up the cloth napkin and pressed it against my chest with both hands. My tears began to stream as my milk continued to let down. "I cannot," I sobbed. "I cannot just *wait* here while my daughter's being raised by someone who didn't even want her to survive!"

Fannie nodded and reached across the table. "I know you can't, *meedel*," she said, pressing my hand with her parchment fingers. "I don't think I could respect you if you could."

part

THREE

16

Amelia, 2014

I push through the swinging door after talking to Star and almost smack right into my roommate, Lydie. "Excuse me," she says, arms crossed over her stomach. "May I speak with you?" I nod and slide the tray onto the dining table. Turning, I see that Lydie's holding out a letter. Curious, I take it from her, but the two pages are written in German, the same language she used to write that letter to Uriah Rippentoe. Annoyed because I still don't know what's going on between the two of them, I try to hand the letter back. But Lydie's now staring at the bows on her funny lace-up boots. Her braided pigtails bob as she seems to search for words.

"My *dawdy*'s sick," she says. "*Mamm* said it's time to come home and make amends." Lydie's voice sounds like she's about to lose it. But when she glances up, her eyes are dry.

243

"Thought you were shunned or something." This comes out nastier than I mean it to. Of course, Lydie doesn't notice. She just refolds the letter and slips it into her apron pocket.

"Mennonites don't shun," she says. "But I was too afraid to go back . . . before." Moving closer, she takes my hand. "Will you go with me? I . . . I can't go alone."

I take my hand from hers and fold my arms. I haven't come to this hillbilly village to spend time with a sixteen-year-old Mennonite girl who sometimes seems like my grandma and sometimes like my kid. I have come to Hopen Haus to have room to breathe and—without my mom constantly breathing down my neck—to find out who I am. But even if Lydie's backward ways drive me up the wall, what can it hurt to go on a trip for a few days? It's not like I could put my baby in danger by going someplace else, and a break from Hopen Haus might be nice, though I don't know how fun it's going to be to stay at a Mennonite community. Plus, it'd be good to avoid Uriah, who I'm becoming obsessed with, now that he's making a point to avoid me.

"When you want to leave?"

"Wilbur Byler's already here. The letter was written two days ago. For all I know—" Lydie takes a breath—"my *dawdy* could already be dead."

"Let me pack a few things first." I squeeze her hand to make up for my snarky comment earlier. "Then I'll come right down."

I cross the dining room to climb the steps. The head midwife and I meet in the middle of the staircase. Rhoda Mummau doesn't say a word, and for some reason, I feel so uncomfortable that it's all I can do to hold her stare. "I'm sorry, Amelia," she says, balling her hand at her waist. "It's just that—" She looks away. Then she looks back at me and asks, "How are you?"

"Fine, thanks," I say quickly and pass, thankful to escape her. At the top of the steps, I grip the railing and look down. Rhoda Mummau is still watching me. Sadness tugs at her features. Meeting my eyes again, the midwife turns and goes down the stairs.

Opening the door to our bedroom, I see sun beaming in through the window, as straight as a spotlight. It exposes the rusty bunk beds covered in these ancient ragbag quilts that are beginning to smell like Grandma Sarah's perfume that I sprayed over everything to make it smell like her, my home. Stuffing my overnight bag with a change of clothes and a tank top and shorts, I sling it over my shoulder and hurry toward the door. Then I remember where I'm going. A Mennonite community probably wouldn't care for my skimpy tank top and pound's worth of jewelry. Peeling off my rings, I stride across the room and spill them across the dresser. I grab a sweater and go back downstairs to meet Lydie, waiting by the door.

Beth, 1997

The morning after Hope was taken, Wilbur Byler parallel parked between the lawyer's office and the emporium. He shut off the truck engine, tapped the steering wheel with his thumbs, and opened his mouth. But then he closed it. Taking his cap from the dusty dashboard, he pulled it on. "I'll be at the diner," he said.

I nodded but had to wait five minutes before I found the willpower to get out of the truck. The wind painted the cape dress to my quivering legs as I walked down the sidewalk toward the lawyer's office. Outside, a sign reading *Williams, Attorney at Law* swung and screeched from two lengths of weathered chain. I pushed open the door and a bell chimed above it. I knew hiring a lawyer to argue on my behalf would only be wasting what little money and time I had. But logical or not, I could never forgive myself if I did not try.

Behind a desk, the secretary's Timex swished around her wrist as she continued stamping checks resembling Monopoly money and tapping them into a pile. Then she glanced over her glasses—giving my Plain garb a thorough once-over.

"Can I help you?" she asked.

I forced a smile. "Yes. I'd like to speak to Mr. Williams. Do I need an appointment?"

"My word—no," she said, and then rolled her chair out from beneath the desk and stood. "Just let me tell him you're here."

I nodded and went to stand in the waiting area. The coffee table in the center was crowded with dusty, dog-eared magazines that were at least three years old.

"Mr. Williams said to come on back," the secretary called.

In a trance, I walked to the end of the hall. A nightlight glowed shell-pink inside an opened bathroom on the right. Breathing hard, I knocked on the office door.

"Come in," a voice said.

I opened the door and saw a barrel-chested man sitting behind a desk that took up three-fourths of the room. He pointed to the chair across from it. "Have a seat," he said.

I sat.

Mr. Williams loosened his tie and interlaced his short fingers. He leaned his shoulders forward. "Yes?" he prodded.

I pressed my kneecaps to keep my legs from jumping; Mr. Williams must not be allowed to realize how near hysterics I was. "Last year," I began, "I was hired as a wealthy family's gestational surrogate, but when an amniocentesis showed the possibility of the child having a chromosomal abnormality, the family wanted to do one more test and then—if it came back with the same result—abort the child. I had already fallen in love with the little girl, so before they did the second test, I fled down here to a Mennonite community in Tennessee. But I suppose the Fitzpatricks—that's the name of the family who has her now—got wind of the fact that the child was healthy, so yesterday they came down here with their lawyer and took her back."

Mr. Williams winced. "Let me make sure I'm following you," he said. "You kidnapped a child who has *no* biological connection to you?"

"There's more to it than that."

"There'd have to be. If I understand correctly, you're lucky they just took the child and didn't throw you in jail."

"What if the biological mother never wanted the child?" I shrilled. "What if she's just using the child as a way . . . a way of punishing me?"

"Punishing you for what?" Mr. Williams said gently. "Was everything aboveboard?"

"Yes," I murmured, looking down. "There were plenty of contracts."

"I'm sorry, Miss . . ." He paused as he waited for me to provide a name, but I did not know which one to give.

"Rhoda," I said after a pause. "Rhoda Mummau."

"I'm sorry, Rhoda, but I'm just going to tell it like it is." Mr. Williams patted the pocket of his dress shirt and tugged out a pack of cigarettes. Tapping a stick, he looked at me. "You mind?" I shook my head. He continued. "I've dealt with a lot of custody cases—" the cigarette nodded between his lips—"and I've seen them drag on for years and years." Flicking out his tongue, he picked off a piece of tobacco lint. Then he lit the cigarette and took a long draw, expelling a wreath of smoke toward the ceiling. "By the end," he said, "the child's old enough to understand what's going on, and regardless of the verdict, he—" Mr. William pointed the cigarette at me—"or *she* feels guilty because she doesn't know who she's supposed to belong to. Or who she's even supposed to be."

He tilted his head, a curled coxcomb of hair dangling over his left eye. He brushed it impatiently aside. "You read your Bible?" he asked, then stopped and smiled at my *kapp*.

"Of course you read your Bible. Believe it or not," Mr. Williams said, "even lawyers crack their Bibles from time to time, and I often thought these custody battles remind me of the quandary with King Solomon. You know, where those two women claim the same child, and the one who's really the mother gives her rights up so the child can survive?"

I nodded and thought of the title of my master's thesis: "Solomon's Choice: Finding an Ethical Solution for Remorseful Surrogates." I realize now, having felt the full cleave of maternal separation, that I'd had no idea what I was talking about back then.

"Rhoda, the question I want you to ask yourself is—" Mr. Williams rested his cigarette on the ashtray without scrubbing out the butt—"are you the kind of mother who would hurt her child just to retain her rights?"

Looking down, I clenched my hands in my lap. The pattern on my cape dress blurred. My throat thick with emotion, again I just shook my head.

"I didn't think you were," he said. "But please, Rhoda, if you ever need anything . . ." Mr. Williams patted the pocket of his shirt as if searching for a card, but I just heard the crinkle of the cellophane wrapping his cigarettes.

I stood from the chair and pulled my dress free from a cut in the vinyl. "Thank you for your time," I rasped, knowing that I had to leave now or cry in front of him.

It wasn't until I was standing on the cracked sidewalk with the lawyer's sign creaking in the wind that I knew I could never take the Fitzpatricks to court.

But neither could I walk away. Not yet. I would push against every door, legal or otherwise, until I knew that nothing else could possibly be done—even if that meant entering back into the *Englischer* world I'd sworn I would leave behind.

Amelia, 2014

I open my eyes and see a circle of my foundation smeared across the van's tinted glass. I glance over at Lydie to see if she's slept too. But she's just staring at Wilbur's head, with its wiry brown hair sticking through the back of his baseball cap. "What's wrong?" I ask.

"Nothing," Lydie whispers.

The diesel passenger van chugs up the road winding through what Lydie told me is the Cumberland Mountains. This bluish mist covers the vehicle, making it almost impossible to see farther than the low lights. I look at the floorboard scattered with hamburger wrappers and at the windows smudged with fingerprints from hundreds of passengers who've ridden in here before us. I thought I'd like getting away from Hopen Haus, where nothing seems to happen besides the midwives' OCD baby monitoring and this ton of mind-numbing chores. But it didn't occur to me that Lydie and I were leaving a place of safety until we'd already gotten past Hopen Haus's boundary walls. Now I'm not sure it was such a good idea.

The van shoots through the rest of the mist. Wilbur switches his low lights to bright and says, "Must feel strange, Lydie. You heading back home." These are the first words he's said since we climbed in the vehicle, which seems funny, since I've seen him chat it up with Looper and Rhoda. Not to mention that friendly heart-to-heart with Uriah out in the springhouse. In the rearview mirror, I watch Wilbur search my roommate's face. Lydie nods, but her eyes stay on her lap. She twists her fingers together before reaching over and grabbing mine.

Her small palm is sticky with sweat. At first, I feel awkward, but then I remember that Lydie's as innocent as a kindergartner and should be treated like one. So I let her hold my fingers. As I do, I wonder what it would be like to have a family member—a mom, a sister—who was as close to my heart as the reach of a hand.

I mean, when I was growing up, Grandma Sarah insisted that I hold her hand whenever we were at the playground, the mall, or the zoo, and there were all these strangers around. She also hugged me so hard whenever she came and left for the day that my back would pop, and she would say, "I love you so much; I could just squeeze the puddings out of you!"—which was kind of a weird thing to say, if you think about it. I could tell from this, and from all these cookies she baked and these awful scarf and glove sets she knitted, that Grandma Sarah tried her very best to make me feel like her real grandchild and not just her babysitting charge, even insisting that I call her "Grandma" and not Miss Sarah like my mom wanted. And though I knew Grandma

Sarah from the time I was born, she *was* getting paid to take care of me.

Clearing my throat, I say mostly just to fill up the quiet, "I had this project in preschool. We . . . we were supposed to bring in something from when we were babies: hair from our first cut, the outfit I wore home from the hospital, a picture of my mom pregnant. But she had none of this. Not a thing. My mom seemed really mad when I asked her too. Like it was *my* fault or something that she didn't have this stuff around."

Lydie whispers, staring out the window, "I don't have any pictures from when I was a *bobbel*, either."

"But you all don't believe in taking pictures," I say. "It's different with the *Englisch*. If I was, like, the fifth kid or something, it would've been different—it would've made sense that my mom was too busy to keep up with such things. But I was their first kid. Their *only* kid. I guess my mom just didn't care enough to record anything. Or maybe she just didn't care, period."

"*Ach*, Amelia," Lydie says. "I'm sure she does."

I shrug with the same I-don't-care attitude that drove my parents nuts when I lived at home, which is only a cover-up for the fact that I take everything really hard. All of a sudden, I want to put my head on Lydie's knees and bawl my head off over this feeling of abandonment I've struggled with for as long as I can remember. Then the hair on my neck stands up, and I blink away tears and look up into the rearview mirror, aware that Lydie's not the only one listening. Wilbur's doughy hands are still throttling the steering wheel. His diesel passenger van is still zooming along ten over the speed limit. But under the curled brim of his red cap, his flat eyes are watching me. And I know he's seen everything, heard every word I said.

Wilbur Byler breaks eye contact and flicks his right blinker before turning down a road that is as flat as a Fruit by the Foot and goes for miles. Right when I'm thinking we're never going to get there, the van's headlights reflect off a large white sign jammed in the ground. It reads, *Welcome to Split Rock Mennonite Community*.

Lydie claps one hand over her mouth, struggling out of her seat.

I scream, "Stop the van!"

Wilbur slams the brakes. An empty soda can rolls to the front.

Lydie claws her way out of the seat and yanks the latch. Doubling over, she spews all over the road. My own stomach shudders, watching her barf with her hands on her knees. But I don't know if Lydie needs space or comfort. I realize that my mom would give her space, so I do the opposite. I get out of the vehicle and gather Lydie's braids. Holding them to the side, I rub her back in small circles until Lydie straightens and wipes her mouth. I am comforting her the same way Grandma Sarah used to comfort me when I was sick. I am comforting her the way my mom has never done.

"I'm fine," Lydie whispers, but her face is pinched. "I'm fine."

I wrap my arm around my little friend's waist and lead

her back to the van. Again, Wilbur Byler doesn't say anything. The two of us just climb inside, and he shifts into
drive, crackling over the gravel lane. Wilbur takes another
right and continues driving until the van lights sweep
across a tall, clapboard-sided house. He wrenches the steering wheel and parks. No one speaks. The engine ticks.
Black pants and floral cape dresses flap on the line strung
between the house and the matching gray barn. A tiger
tomcat cleans his paws next to a rosebush blooming in the
mulch-lined flowerbeds leading to the house.

"It's . . ." I pause, continuing to take it all in while com-
paring it to my parents' brick-and-mortar McMansion and
ruler-perfect hedges. "It's magical," I say.

"I know," Lydie replies. "It's home."

After Wilbur Byler unloads our overnight bags and drives
off, Lydie and I stand in the yard for some time, catching our breath and listening to the windmill creak in the
breeze. Then Lydie touches my hand and we walk down
the pathway to her parents' house. Stepping inside, my
eyes adjust to the light of the kerosene lamp hanging in the
kitchen, dispelling the outer darkness. By its glow, I see the
hardwood floor that is shiny with what smells like lemon
polish and the windows that sparkle even against the backdrop of night. I look over at the couch draped in a knitted
throw that somehow appears even prettier because everything else is so plain.

A number of bare feet patter halfway down the staircase.

I glance up. Lydie's four siblings are peering over the railing at me. Sandy bangs hang over the little boys' curious blue eyes. The preteen girl's braids, and her younger sister's, dangle over the tiger wood; their long patterned dresses can be seen through the slats.

Lydie's mom, who Lydie told me is named Rebecca Risser, comes out of the door closest to the woodstove. She closes it behind her and looks up. Lydie walks toward her mother. Rebecca does not speak. She just moves her eldest daughter over toward the kitchen table so she can see her better by the light. Holding Lydie out by the shoulders, she stares down at her daughter's stomach swelled beneath her apron. Rebecca then cups Lydie's cheeks and whispers something only Lydie can hear. The two hug, looking more like sisters than mom and daughter, with their petite builds and blonde hair. Rebecca takes Lydie's hand and leads her over to the door she just exited. She turns the knob and pushes the door open. Choking down a sob, Lydie lowers her head and follows. Inside, I guess, is where Rebecca's husband—Lydie's dad—lies dying of kidney failure at forty-two years old. He is younger than my own dad was when I was born. Understanding my parents aren't going to be around forever makes tears come to my eyes. For the first time since I left Boston, I would give anything just to hug them both.

"What is your surname?" someone asks. I look away from the door and back at the staircase. The older boy comes down the steps with his arms crossed.

"Walker," I say, wondering who's called it a surname

in the last century. "Amelia Walker." I've said it so many times, the lie no longer sounds so strange.

"My first name is Henry," he says.

"Nice to meet you, Henry."

"You as well," he replies, like we're having high tea.

With an encouraging lift of Henry's chin, the three other Risser kids come down the steps, one by one, and introduce themselves. There's Ruth at twelve, Mary at ten, and Benjamin, five. Benjamin clatters down the staircase and looks at me. With one hand, he flattens the cowlick on the back of his head.

"My *dat sterbt*," he says.

"What did he say?" I ask Ruth.

The kids look at each other, and then they look down at the floor.

"Our *vadder* is dying," Henry finally says.

"I'm sorry." I pull on the hem of my shorts—because I feel so indecent and because I have no idea what to do with my hands.

The bedroom door opens. Rebecca and Lydie come out. Lydie takes a hand away from her stomach to wipe her tears. She walks over to her brothers and sisters, who are still standing in front of me like a receiving line at a wedding. Lydie carefully kneels around the bulk of her unborn baby and opens her arms. The Risser kids hug her without hesitating. Benjamin even rests his head on her belly. Lydie glances up and meets my eyes, her own spilling over. The Rissers are holding each other up, even as they lean on each other for support through the pain that is ahead. I know, as I stare at this show of unconditional love, that I would never have been able to leave such a priceless support system behind.

Beth, 1997

Wilbur asked, "How'd it go?" but kept looking through his truck windshield at the *Williams, Attorney at Law* sign.

I swallowed. "He said I have no case. I'm lucky the Fitzpatricks didn't throw me in jail."

Wilbur stayed quiet, and then he turned the ignition. The cab rattled as the V-8 flared to life. I pressed back against the seat as he shifted into reverse, orbiting the square with the mammoth courthouse as its keystone. The state and national flags cracked in the stiff winter gust, and I knew I would never willfully darken the courthouse doors. The law would never give me back my child, so I would not do anything according to the law.

My thoughts began to reel with absurd possibilities. Adrenaline slipped through my veins, the heady concoction blurring the lines of my perception, making me wonder if anything was truly black and white, or merely transmutations of gray. Was it possible that I could go up to Boston and kidnap my child a second time—not because I was trying to preserve her life, but because, this time, I was trying to preserve mine?

I hedged, though my mind was already made up.

"Maybe . . . ," I said, "if you talked to the Fitzpatricks, they'd let me come up to Boston and hold Hope one more time."

Wilbur did not take his eyes off the road. "Maybe," he said. I heard the dry click of his throat snapping open and shut. "I could drive you," he added.

Fifteen minutes later, Wilbur gunned up the washout lane toward Hopen Haus. The pressure between us was as potent as the silence. Each of us stared straight ahead. I had written the Fitzpatricks' home number on a paper napkin and slid it across the bench seat toward him. If the Fitzpatricks agreed to let me come, Wilbur would drive me to Boston. There I would hold my child again, and then try to run with her, though I knew an escape was senseless. But I was at a dangerous crossroads. I had already lost everyone I loved; therefore, I had nothing left to lose.

Fannie Graber entered my bedroom without the formality of rapping on the half-open door. She crossed the floor faster than I would have thought her able. Clutching my upper arm, she forced me to drop Hope's clothes and meet her gaze. My eyes were stark reflections of the anger I felt. I broke her hold and placed the infant sweater set in the suitcase, belligerent about my lie and not caring if—looking at the items I was packing—she understood the truth: I was not going up to Boston to say good-bye; I was going up to Boston to take my daughter back.

I straightened the only regular clothing I hadn't given

to the other boarders who, in the process of keeping their children, had lost almost as much as I. Shaking out a gray Simms University sweatshirt that had seen better years, I doubled it against my chest and tucked it back in the suitcase. Fannie didn't say anything, but I felt her eyes tracing my disheveled hair and salt-stained face, which I hadn't bothered wiping the last few times I cried.

"Wilbur drove up to the diner and called the Fitzpatricks," she said. "And they . . . they said they will let you come say good-bye." Fannie reached around my extended arms and touched my bound chest that was as hard and knotted as my heart. "I want you to have that closure, Rhoda," she said, holding my gaze. "I want you to stare into Hope's face and remember all the things you did together. And then you can leave. But as long as you have breath left in your body, you'll not really have to let Hope go."

"But she's not *dead*, Fannie," I spat, anger oiling my tongue. "And I'm not going up there just to let her *go*." My voice grew with fury until it felt too large for the cramped room. I didn't care whom I destroyed or used in the process of getting Hope back. Even if that meant hurting the midwife who had become more like a mother to me, even if that meant temporarily hurting the daughter I was trying to reclaim.

The midwife's face fell. She clasped her ancient hands in front of her and bowed her head. "All right," she said. Her thin voice wavered, and I knew she was afraid for me. "Just know I'll be here, waiting for you, if you need to come back."

Restraining my own tears, I focused on checking the accessory compartment where I'd stowed Thomas Fitzpatrick's bundled hundred-dollar bills that I hadn't touched in all this time. They were all there—every last one a paper promise I hoped to make tangible. I snapped the suitcase closed and looked at Fannie. Heartbreak trickled from her crystal blue eyes.

"Why do you love me after I've been so cruel?" I asked.

The old midwife looked up and smiled sadly, cupping my cheek. "Because, *Liebe*, that's what a mother does."

17

I could not sleep on the drive to Boston. Part of it was due
to the pain surrounding my departure from Hopen Haus
and the anxiety regarding my destination. Part of it was
because of the milk that kept surging in my chest, a relent-
less reminder that I had no baby to swill the sustenance
her birth had taught me to make. I stared at the flakes that
swept back toward the windshield and then were immediately replaced with another batch, like cotton pieces shaken
free from a continuous factory loom. Wilbur kept driving
until the gas meter again sunk into red. Then he pulled
over and refilled the tank as I went inside to express milk
while leaning over the toilet, and then reapply Fannie's
parting gift of comfrey salve.

At the gas station, I looked into a mirror for the first time since I had left Boston—as Hopen Haus was devoid of such vanity—and was startled to see the reflection of a woman far older than her twenty-four years. A few stray hairs at my temples were coarsened with silver. How had they gone unnoticed? I rubbed the fogged glass with my elbow and recalled that severe pain can drain pigment from hair follicles. I wondered if my own accelerated aging had happened in the past twenty-four hours. It seemed improbable, but if I had been put under the knife without an anesthetic, my body could not be under any more stress.

Outside, Wilbur was in the driver's seat of his truck, unwrapping a piece of tinfoil that glinted in the lights of the gas station pavilion. I climbed in the passenger's side, and Wilbur passed me an identical foil-wrapped sandwich.

"Thank you," I said.

The intimacy of the cab increased with the outside snowfall spattered across the ink-black night. I shivered and heard the engine fan kick on as Wilbur turned up the heat. Though he spoke not a word, I knew he was attuned to my every movement, my every breath, as if this observance could also attune him to my thoughts. This unsettled me, but I tried not to act like it did. Regardless of my misgivings, I needed him to think he was taking me up to Boston to say good-bye and not to take my daughter back.

I must have nodded off, for when I awoke, the sun was a bauble suspended above the purpling horizon. I rested the back of my throbbing skull against the seat. Bobby pins, embedded in my *kapp*, speared my scalp. It seemed ridiculous to keep up such a facade, but I found that the mantle of Plain life gave me strength to face the weight of this uncertain world. And I did not want to make Wilbur suspect my impending need to blend in by changing into *Englischer* clothes.

Wilbur asked, "You nervous?"

"Yes," I whispered. He had no idea how much.

The truck entered the track-lit tunnel that was a vein leading to the fisted heart of the city. A vehicle behind us topped with the strapped luggage of tourists honked, the high-pitched sound clanging off the stone dome. Exiting the portal, we were only miles from Simms University and the Fitzpatricks' elite neighborhood, White Swan Estates. The closer we drew, the harder it became to breathe. Wilbur did not ask me any more questions. He simply folded the map, stowed it in the glove box, and pulled up to the tollbooth, refusing my paltry offering of change. The tollbooth bar lifted. Unaccustomed to city driving, Wilbur white-knuckled the steering wheel as traffic zipped past us on all sides. Sweat stained the temples of his shaggy brown hair. He exhaled through his nose, but hardly sped up.

Somehow we made it to the fringes of Boston, where the elite Simms University was set like a multifaceted jewel. As we passed the campus, I stared out the rear window at the foot-tall letters glinting on the brick entrance accented by its curlicued wrought-iron arch. Less than a year since I'd fled those university gates. Yet already, I felt so fully removed from that person who'd climbed behind the steering wheel and let her roommate's trilling flute serenade her reckless departure from all her long-cultivated dreams but the one nurtured inside her womb.

I took a deep breath and pointed through the spider-web crack branching across the windshield. "Park there, Wilbur," I intoned. "Their house is just over that rise."

He nodded and circled the wheel, parallel parking his rust bucket between a Jaguar and a Mercedes Benz whose sleek, low-slung roofs were capped with snow. I creaked open the passenger door to cycle in some fresh air. I closed my eyes and tried to pray for direction, but I was still too angry to converse. Just as I knew I would not relinquish my daughter to the courts, I knew I would never again place her life in God's incapable hands.

"Want me to go with you?" Wilbur asked.

I shook my head and took the satchel containing my money, but left my suitcase under the seat so Wilbur wouldn't guess that I was about to run with my daughter. Binding the woolen shawl around my shoulders, I clambered out of the cab and wondered if I was making the right decision. But I was out of realistic options, so I had to follow my gut instincts. I looked up. Extinguished streetlights stretched their nimble, dinosaurian necks over either side of the cobbled road. Ice crunched beneath my pilgrim shoes as I crossed the salted curb and minced down the sidewalk. I felt self-conscious as I looked down, as I touched the pleated back of my black bonnet hooked over my netted *kapp*. It was too early to be ogled by passersby, but the garments that had once made me feel protected now made me feel vulnerable, exposed.

From the street, the Fitzpatrick dwelling resembled more of a citadel than a home. Brick, cantilevered stories trimmed in enameled molding rose to a central point that was crowned with a cupola similar to those adorning the buildings on Simms University's campus. Numerous windows gleamed with the dawn, moisture beading down the thawing glass. In the yard, a marble statue of a woman sensuously draped in a toga looked as if she should be balancing the scales of justice. Instead, her extended hands cupped decaying autumn leaves.

Looking at her, I had to resist the urge to flee and instead keep moving forward, up the paved path toward the front door. I don't know what kind of security I'd been expecting around the Fitzpatrick residence—police surveillance, perhaps—but there was nothing. Or at least nothing that I could see. My shoes slid on the ice; I held on to the gate's wrought-iron spires for support. Lifting the latch, I slipped inside. I continued walking past the yard's entire, frozen splendor and stepped closer and closer to the front door.

"Beth?"

My entire body bolted with shock. I pivoted and saw Dr. Thomas Fitzpatrick walking out of the garage toward me. Thom stopped two yards away and folded his arms. He looked different than I remembered. In yesterday's panic, I had not noticed that everything about him had been manipulated by the nondiscriminatory seamstress of aging. His jaw and abs were loosened; his hairline taken in. Stitches of anxiety were sewn around his eyes and mouth.

Perhaps he actually regretted his willingness to cast away the child he thought was defective. But looking at the determined set of his mouth, I knew that he was now making up for lost time.

"Meredith doesn't know you're here," he said. "So you have to make this quick."

I gripped my elbows, acid burning my throat. "Meredith's not here?" I asked. "Is she at work? Are you telling me you took Hope yesterday, and Meredith's already back to putting her job before my daughter's life?"

"She's *not* your daughter," Thom snapped, all mercy gone. "You need to get that straight. I let you come, but you are not welcome. You will *never* be welcome. And if you show up again . . ." Thom pinched his hands beneath his arms and looked up. The green flecks in his eyes blazed with wrath, revulsion. "If you come back here again, I swear . . . we'll get a restraining order."

I didn't know how to respond. I'd thought Thomas Fitzpatrick was a docile man browbeaten by his wife. But he wasn't. His charming, absent-minded professor persona was as much of a subterfuge as my alias and Plain clothes. Now he wanted to discard me when I had provided him with his final pawn and all the pieces of his chess game were back in one place. I looked down at the driveway piebald with my footsteps and comprehended that I would be retracing the pattern with my arms as empty as when I'd come. Perhaps I'd know this all along. Tears glittered in my periphery, but I was too defeated to cry. "Can I at least see her like you promised?"

Thom didn't say anything, and then acquiesced. "Just a second," he said. "Wait here."

Snowflakes drifted up behind his shoes as he plodded up the front steps and entered through the doorway. How had I ended up like this, starved for any breadcrumbs Thom would throw my way? How had *we* ended up like this? In him, I saw no traces of the man whose kindness had garnered my affection. Or had motherhood changed me—my rebirth giving me new eyes in which to judge people's character and understand their true forms?

I looked up when someone rapped sharply on the window. Heart thudding, I inched closer to the glowing panels of sunroom glass until the light shifted and I could see inside. All the blinds were pulled down except for one. Thom was standing in its view with Hope bunched against his chest. Her knees were drawn up, thumb corked, diapered bottom jutting in the air. She didn't even know I was gone. This revelation brought both relief and a frantic ache.

With one hand, Thom awkwardly clicked the latches on top of the window and slid it up. Then he removed the screen. "I don't want to take her out in the cold," he explained. But I knew from the possessive way Thom held Hope that he could see the desperation in my eyes.

I stepped up to the ledge and breached an invisible barrier to stroke my daughter's hand for what could be the very last time. I had won the fight for Hope's life. But the battle I wanted to wage for custody of her now was lost before it could even begin. How could I possibly let her go?

How could a few months of memories sustain a lifetime otherwise spent in regret?

My wind-chapped face burned as tears dripped and melted the snow beneath my feet. And even then, I knew the grains of this child's ephemeral infant life were slipping through both mine and the Fitzpatricks' hands. I closed my eyes as revelation struck: if no one had ever uncovered what I'd done and my life with Hope continued undisturbed, I would have still raised her, loved her, only to be forced to let her go and live her own life once she was grown.

Oh, the exquisite ache of adoring someone you cannot fully have.

I leaned forward and pressed Hope's hand to my chest, trying to brand my heart with the weight and scent and warmth of her being. Closing my eyes, I tried memorizing her scent that would soon be replaced with theirs. Stifling a sob, I held my daughter. But then . . . gradually I opened my hands.

"I know you won't . . . tell her about me," I said to Thom, though my words were halted with sobs. "But will you at least . . . tell her that she was wanted, always?"

In the beat before his reply, I heard a dog bark somewhere in the neighborhood. Then Thom murmured, "I will."

Dashing tears from my eyes, I stared at Hope's sleeping form once more and then turned, stumbling down the icy drive. When I looked back, the window was shut, the blind already closed tight against me. Though my daughter was only a few yards away in proximity, in my heart I knew that she was truly gone. Taking all hope of redemption with her.

Amelia, 2014

My stomach queasy, I rest my forehead on the table and listen to the two youngest Risser kids, Mary and Benjamin, slurp cheese sandwiches they first made soggy by soaking them in beef rice soup and covering them with apple sauce sprinkled with cinnamon. I haven't touched one bite. I dare to look up only after everything's quiet except for in the bedroom, where Alvin's death rattle has slowed to one nerve-racking gasp. The older Risser kids—Lydie, Henry, and Ruth—remain at the table with their backs straight and light supper not eaten. Henry and Ruth stare at their hands; Lydie stares at the farming calendar on the opposite wall.

Then Rebecca Risser comes out of the bedroom and stands before her family. She smiles, but her hazel eyes are wet with tears. *"Kumm, kinner,"* she murmurs. "It's time." Mary scrambles off the bench seat and buries her face in the skirt of her mom's dress, clinging to the gathers without even crying. "You come too," Rebecca says to me, like she knows I'm not sure what I should do. "This is no time to be alone."

So from oldest to youngest, Alvin's kids quietly circle their dad's sickbed. Even five-year-old Benjamin doesn't flinch. Having never seen even Grandma Sarah's death, I remain near the door, knowing that I am out of place but not wanting to seem rude by turning away. Somehow, the news about Alvin must spread because the whole first floor begins filling up with members of Split Rock Old Order Mennonite Community. Moms carry babies, whose chubby legs are pretzeled around their mothers' hips. Toddlers nod off while sitting on top of their dads' shoulders. Two sulky teenage boys stand near a corner, making it obvious that they don't like this reminder of death when their lives are just starting. They remind me of the selfish girl I was just two months ago and who I hope to leave behind when I leave here. After everyone's settled, the families stand in groups and begin to harmonize lyrics that touch my heart, though they are sung in a language I can't understand.

I glance across the mattress and see Lydie Risser, haloed by an oil lamp burning on a nightstand beside the bed. My sixteen-year-old friend sits on the edge of the quilt, an old Bible perched on her low, round belly. The book's titled spine glints in the darkness, and I see that it's written in German. Lydie catches me looking at it. Her smile cuts through the darkness, revealing a strength I don't think I could have if I were in her shoes. Lydie wipes tears as she looks down at her dad, who is swollen and yellow with jaundice. Seconds pass without the breath everyone strains to hear. Lydie's uncle Titus takes out a pocket watch and cracks the dull gold case, tracking time with a device his brother-in-law will soon no longer need.

And then Alvin inhales again, the rattle jolting us as much as the silence.

Lydie takes her dad's hand. "Go, *Dawdy*," she says, kissing his knuckles. "Go with *Gott*." Alvin's spirit seems to listen, though his body has long shut down. The breath shudders through his body and then stops as effortlessly as I imagine it began.

The Risser girls' bedroom door opens. I sit up on the mattress and see Lydie's outline stretching across the floor, lit up by the oil lamp she carries. From where I sit, you would never guess that she's about to give birth.

"You okay?" I ask.

Lydie draws the lamp up to her chest, the globe tucked beneath her chin. The flame haunts her glance at Mary and Ruth, asleep in a double bed right next to mine. But Lydie's young sisters are curled together like those Russian dolls—their long blonde and brunette hair covering the decorated pillowcase, their bodies adjusting to each other's movements even in sleep. Lydie turns the lamp's wick down and walks over to the dresser along the left-hand wall. I can smell her homemade verbena shampoo. Her wet feet leave prints in the lamplight.

Careful, Lydie pulls out a drawer and pleats the fabric of another dress before smoothing it again. "*Mamm* and I just finished preparing my *vadder*," she whispers. "I took a bath to help me sleep . . . , but I don't think I can." Closing the drawer, Lydie holds the knob. Her lips grow thin. She closes her eyes, and then breathes out. "Will you come outside with me?" she asks, and reaches out a hand.

I can't say no.

Downstairs, Uncle Titus sits in a kitchen chair beside the simple pine casket, like a guard. He greets us with a stiff tip of his chin but keeps his arms crossed over his coarse black beard that trails down his shirtfront. His booted feet are like tree roots planted in the seams of the hardwood floor. The casket lid is off, and I can see the careful fold of Alvin Risser's large, lifeless hands that are the same size as his brother Titus's. Lydie touches my elbow. Holding back a shiver, I follow her outside. Lydie pulls her damp hair over one shoulder and sinks onto the concrete slab of the porch. She draws her knees up as far as her stomach will allow. I sit beside her. A damp summer breeze sweeps over the lawn. A bird cries in the distance.

"A loon?" I ask.

But Lydie doesn't answer. She instead lifts her face to the night sky clouded with stars and says, "When my *vadder* was first ill, he would go to a clinic in Knoxville. My *mudder* would go with him, but sometimes she couldn't if one of the *kinner* was sick. So I was sent in her place. I had already finished eighth grade, and I was expected to help the *familye*. I did not mind. I liked getting away and seeing the city. While *Dawdy* went through dialysis, I would sit and read to him. Or we'd play Dutch Blitz. I really enjoyed that time.

"I did not go often, but whenever I did, I began looking forward to the jokes the driver would tell during the trip, the way he would always bring crossword puzzles to keep me occupied. I was young." Lydie sighs, as if sixteen is old. "I was so young. I smiled at the driver, and I laughed. I guess I shouldn't have, but I just didn't know better. . . ."

Lydie pauses, swallows hard before continuing. "The first time he touched me, he just took my hand. We were crossing the street to McDonald's while my *vadder* was finishing dialysis. I didn't even flinch. His hand in mine felt like the most natural thing in the world. I remember the chill in the air, how my fingers felt so small compared to his; a helicopter hovering overhead that was getting ready to land on the hospital roof.

"I felt so guilty afterward—even for just letting him hold my hand. But I still looked forward to those outings to Knoxville because secretly I hoped that something like that would happen again. And it did. Somehow it always did. He would give me a hug, or tug on my braids, or smile in a way that made me scared and excited all at the same time. He began to come to Split Rock more often. He would always pick up produce or jams or baked goods or quilts and peddle everything around to the Nashville and Knoxville farmer's markets. But no matter what, he would always stop and see me. *Only* me. My heart thrilled whenever he would come around. So you see . . . you see, he was not the only one in the wrong."

My mind scrambles to slide the puzzle pieces of Lydie's life into place. Then she looks at me and continues speaking, and I know that I can't use this time to uncover the mystery, but just listen to the pain behind her words.

"Around this time, the driver told my *mudder* that he could no longer take my *vadder* to dialysis. That she had to hire this woman in Blackbrier to do it, and so my *mudder* did. She called the number that the driver provided and told the woman the situation. And so, while my parents were in Knoxville trying to keep my *dawdy* alive, the driver would park behind the bakery and walk through the cornfield over to our house. It happened slowly, gradually. He still brought me gifts; he still complimented me and told me I . . . I was beautiful. I was only fifteen, Amelia," Lydie murmurs, her voice thick. "Nobody had ever really seen me before. Nobody had ever told me I was beautiful. The words were like magic, making me forget everything but the hunger to hear them again."

"And so, when Henry, Ruth, and Mary were off at school and Benjamin was down for a nap, the driver would come to our house and for a handful of compliments or a beaded bracelet, I would let him do with me whatever he wanted."

For a second, Lydie cradles her cheeks, but then drops her hands and straightens her spine. She again lifts her face up to the stars, like she's seeking wisdom or forgiveness. "I did not understand, Amelia. I didn't. I was naive, trusting. I had been around a farm all my life but . . . but didn't know the ways between a woman and a man. I found out I was pregnant because my monthly flow stopped. I didn't understand what was happening, but the driver suspected. He told me he knew of a place where I could go and stay until after the *bobbel's* birth. He said that if my parents found out what had happened, they would be so—" she looks down—"ashamed."

"So I did what he told me to do. I . . . I packed up a small cloth bag with everything I could take, and one afternoon the driver picked me up and brought me to Hopen Haus. I don't know how my parents found out where I was; I don't know how they knew enough to send me that letter. But somehow they did, and now it is too late to tell

my *vadder* what happened. Too late to explain that I was
as trusting as a child, and so I had become pregnant with
a child myself."

Far off, the strange bird continues its cry. Lydie presses a
hand over her mouth and jackknifes her body to keep from
making noise. I reach out and pause, my fingers flexed
with uncertainty, and then place that hand on Lydie's back.
Turning, she puts her head on my lap—just as I had wished
to rest on hers—and sobs. I look up at the overturned
bowl of sky. Tears stream down my cheeks as I pray for my
friend. And though the communion is as new to me as
the hymns the congregation sang while Alvin Risser's soul
passed from the earth, I can sense that somewhere a Father
sees our orphan state—and is listening.

I plod up the church steps in my sandals and enter the left
side of the two side-by-side doors—trying to stoop slightly
so the cape dress Lydie let me borrow hits below my knees.
If the church members are shocked by an *Englischer* attending an Old Order Mennonite funeral, they don't show it
by turning around to look. Or maybe they're too focused
on pregnant Lydie, who's sitting up front with the rest of
the Risser family. I take a seat in the back and look at the
pine casket displayed on the scarred pine floor next to the
podium. The family's already finished viewing Alvin, so the
coffin lid is nailed closed. Morning light pours in through
the four windows, bleaching the community's dreary ward-
robe of black, off-white, and gray.

As kids from another family file into the pew next to me, Uncle Titus rises and takes out a shiny little flute. The congregation, in perfect unison, frees books from the back slats of pews and stands. I grab one just for show, since I can't read the hymnal's words, but remain seated. Thousands of musty pages flutter as dust fills the warm, sunlit air. Uncle Titus selects the key on the flute, and the harmony begins. The song sounds similar to one sung at Alvin's deathbed last night.

While they sing, I peer across the aisle toward the men. In the second-to-last pew, I spot Wilbur Byler, who's also sitting but whose brick-red work coat stands out like a kinged checker piece against the backdrop of plain black suits. Wilbur's hair is combed, and his unhealthy jowls glisten with aftershave. I have a hard time dragging my eyes away, even after Wilbur meets my gaze. Nervousness shoots down my spine. I face the casket again, my cheeks burning and my pulse slamming in my ears. I remember the depression that assaulted Lydie after Wilbur visited Hopen Haus. I remember the argument that Uriah and Wilbur had out in the springhouse. Was Wilbur so mad because Uriah had told him that he knew the truth? Do I know the truth as well? I want to shriek out my accusation over the community's harmony. And yet I can't. This is the Rissers' time of mourning, and I must respect that. But now that I suspect who fathered Lydie's child, it's time to make things right. I am not some naive country girl Wilbur Byler can also take advantage of. He is going to confess to me what he's done and then pay the consequences for his actions.

18

Rhoda, 2014

One day before Terese Cullum's pregnancy is declared full-term, and her blood pressure's nearly perfect. Her swelling has abated to the point she can wear her chunky turquoise rings and braided ankle bracelets without the threat of them cutting off her circulation. The pH strip in the urine sample she left after today's prenatal appointment shows only a trace amount of protein. If these positive signs continue, Terese should be able to give birth at Hopen Haus without us midwives having to worry about the preeclampsia symptoms she had less than a month ago.

I fill out Terese's OB record card, so giddy with relief

that I have to battle the inclination to doodle a heart over the three letter *i*'s: *Visit date 8/1; WT 138; BP 124/82; Urine PG tr/-; FH 36; FH 156; EGA 36 wks, 6 days.*

I tuck the small pink card into Terese's folder and pull open the middle drawer of the cabinet. Filing it in the back next to Marie Warren's folder, whose Hopen Haus daughter must be in kindergarten by now, I hear a knock. I roll the drawer closed and cross the examining room. Uriah Rippentoe is standing on the other side of the door with his battered straw hat in his hands, pulling out loose strands and dropping them mindlessly at his feet.

"Uriah?"

He looks up. His bead-dark eyes glint at me from a tanned face cut with angles like razor blades. Again I find myself wondering what Uriah's father must have looked like to genetically counter Alice's delicate features and blonde curls. Backing away from the door, I usher Uriah inside. He peers with such curiosity at the table, filing cabinet, and privacy screen, it makes me realize that he has not been in here for years. But why should he have been? I walk over to the table and begin folding sheets overflowing from a wicker basket. The buttery-yellow cotton is scented with sun. I am doing this task to keep Uriah from feeling cornered; though, strangely enough, he is the one who sought me out.

"You know Wilbur Byler?" Uriah studies the conduit, which holds the electrical wires running along the plaster wall. All my patients have started gravitating toward this, Hopen Haus's first contemporary addition, whenever they feel awkward during an examination and don't know where else to look.

"Of course I know Wilbur."

Uriah's head dips forward in acknowledgment, but he continues facing away from me. I cannot help but notice how rapidly he is transforming into a man. With his long, loose black hair brushing broad shoulders, ropey forearms, and hard waist, he reminds me of Absalom. He reminds me of someone who cannot properly remain in a household full of young, impressionable girls—pregnant or not. But, oh, how I shall miss him when he leaves.

"D'ya know Lydie and Amelia are with him right now?" he asks.

"Yes," I reply. "Lydie's father's very ill. He is not expected to live."

Uriah turns. The intensity in his gaze is disquieting. "You remember last summer when I'd go with Wilbur on drives?"

Snapping the sheet, I fold it in half and nod.

"This one time he told me to wait in the van while he gathered produce from the farms. I thought that was strange since he'd brought me along to help. But I didn't say anything. After a while I started wondering if Wilbur had forgotten about me, so I got out of the van and walked down the lane. Right then is when I saw him leave the Rissers' house and cross the field."

"What do you mean?" I place another squared sheet on the pile.

"Lydie's parents weren't home," he says. "Her father,

Alvin, had to go to dialysis every week in Knoxville, and after I saw Wilbur walk across the cornfield beside her house, I started paying attention. He had me load produce and wares from every farm but the ones in Split Rock. And every time we went to Split Rock matched the times Lydie's parents were gone."

I stare at Uriah's downcast face as he picks at a scab grafted over his knuckle. My mind races to keep up with the words careering through my ears. Taking a deep breath, I stammer, "You—you're saying you think Wilbur Byler was visiting Lydie?" *Visiting* is too euphonious a term for the rendezvous I infer from Uriah's story. But I cannot verbalize such a vile accusation without hearing Lydie's side first. I cannot imagine that docile child opening the door of her parents' house and ushering a man twenty years her senior into bed. And what about Wilbur? After eighteen years, during which my initial suspicions of him went unconfirmed, I ascribed my misgivings to new-parenting paranoia. Was I wrong in this? Was the taciturn bachelor who frequented Hopen Haus truly wicked enough to commit statutory rape? "You're trying to protect Lydie, aren't you?" I ask.

Uriah's temples hollow out as his jaw throbs. "I'm trying to protect . . . everyone," he says, his voice choked. "But I . . . I just don't know how to anymore. I told Wilbur I knew what was going on, and he threatened me. Said that if I told anybody about him and Lydie, he'd go to the police first."

It takes conscious effort to focus on Uriah's face. "Go to the police with what?"

Uriah lifts his gaze. His cheekbones darken with embarrassment and worry. "Wilbur told me he'd tell them what you did."

Beth, 1997

I sobbed as Wilbur Byler's battered truck traversed Tennessee lines. Leaving my daughter behind no longer felt selfless; I felt I was making the most cataclysmic mistake in the world. For a moment, my tears wetting the passenger window glass as fast as the rain was falling outside it, I wanted to tell Wilbur to turn the truck around. I wanted to tell him that I did not care if my daughter's childhood was spent in courtrooms if only, inside those courtrooms, our paths could sometimes cross. I instead said nothing. My throat was siphoned off with the reality that the Fitzpatricks would teach Hope to hate me for disturbing their lives.

It was better, then, that she not know me at all.

Wilbur pulled over at a gas station tucked miles inside the state line. Pinching some quarters out of the ashtray, he set them in a neat pile between us. The coins clinked together, like poker chips. "You got somebody to call?" He stared straight ahead, as if my sorrow was obscene.

I didn't respond, just slid the quarters off the seat into my hand. I was drenched in the seconds it took to sprint from the truck cab to the telephone booth. Water

splattered my calves, soaking through the tights and pooling in my lace-up shoes. Shivering, I pulled the thin glass
door behind me. I fed quarters into the slot with damp,
shaking hands. I didn't allow myself to think as I dialed
Looper's parents' home number . . . by heart.

The phone rang and rang. Just when I was about to give
up, someone answered. "Hello?"

My pulse leaped. It was him. The one person in the
world I wanted to tell, but this was the first time we'd
spoken since that regretful summer, and I could not put
together the words.

Into the silence, Looper said, "This some kinda joke?"

"No—" I covered the mouthpiece and swallowed.
I forced syllables through my trembling lips. "It's me,
Looper. It's Beth."

"Beth?" Looper breathed my name, apparently stunned
to be conversing with a person who was as dead to him
as our past. I could picture him as he'd been six years ago:
rangy and fun-loving, with his hands calloused from farm
work, his mop of brown hair tipped with summer blond.
But this was not the Looper I'd left, for I wasn't the same
either. "Why'd you call?" he asked.

The poor connection magnified the distance in his
voice. But I could not explain why I had called now or why
I had left him then. I also could not explain why I wanted
to come home and borrow from his reservoir of strength
when I had left him parched.

The operator requested another quarter, and though
my apron pocket was still heavy with Wilbur's change,

I murmured, "I'm sorry; I shouldn't have called," and clanked the phone in its cradle. I was so numb, I couldn't feel the deluge needling my skin as I crossed the parking lot toward the idling truck. And as Wilbur navigated toward the interstate that would lead us to Hopen Haus—where midwifery devoid of a husband and child was waiting—I wondered how many times in my life I would have to turn my back on those I loved.

Rhoda, 2014

I leave the examining room after Uriah's revelation and mount the steps, hoping to find among Lydie's things the letter from her mother that might reveal their home address. Wilbur Byler would obviously know where Lydie's family lives. But at this point, I am not sure it is wise to let Wilbur know we're aware of his alleged affair with a sixteen-year-old girl. I would rather hear everything directly from Lydie before taking any legal measures against a man whose motivations have always been as enigmatic as he is.

I push open Lydie and Amelia's bedroom door. The gridlocked hinges squeak as the door swings wide. The space smells of talcum powder and that mystical fragrance that causes chills to scatter across my skin, even though the upstairs is sweltering. Other than the scent, there is nothing too noticeable about the small room. On the bunk beds, threadbare quilts cover tangled sheets that look like the underground pathway of moles. The dresser is crowded with the standard female debris, most of which is Amelia's: bobby pins, a lipstick capsule, an eye-shadow case with squares of glittering, earth-toned hues, a brush nested with long red hairs, jewelry. . . .

My breathing stops. My booted feet click across the floorboards faster than my mind can process the need to walk. I blink and, heart racing, pluck a white-gold cameo ring from amid the cheap costume pieces. I stand motionless, staring, knowing that I've seen it before. Then I cradle the delicate treasure in my two trembling hands.

"Where did you get the cameo?" I asked.

"Mrs. Fitzpatrick, Thom's mother," Meredith explained without looking at me. "The ring's been in the family forever. Someday I'm supposed to pass it down."

I inhale sharply, but my lungs struggle to inflate. Amelia told me her last name was Walker. And she wasn't born in September. But even as I think this, I know Amelia's not the first Hopen Haus boarder to lie about her name and age.

I look back at the dresser and pick up the hairbrush. I hold it in the light filtered through the curtains and watch the sun kindle the strands. Surely I would've known. Surely some part of me would have guessed that the tall, self-assured woman—living in the house I'd paid for with money stolen from her father—was the daughter I lost as an infant.

But then I remember. I remember that hot day Amelia arrived at Hopen Haus and how I'd stared at her, thinking I was taken aback by the dichotomy of her wealth in our underprivileged world, when my soul was spellbound by the fact that she was actually here. I remember wanting to weep in the examining room after Amelia told me about the child in her womb that she felt she had to give up. And how, that night in the kitchen, I felt such an urgency to reach out to her—to trespass the boundaries of my heart— when I had never allowed myself to connect with a boarder before. Just yesterday, didn't we pass each other on the staircase, and I was so captivated by her strange familiarity that I wanted to force her to pause so I could memorize every nuance of her face?

I glimpse Amelia's purse strap peeking from under the bunk beds, and the brush clatters from my hand. Crouching, I drag the purse out and stand, digging in the main compartment until I feel the wallet. I apologize to Amelia for this intrusion, but I have to know. Hands shaking, I pop the snap on the leather wallet and look at the window for the driver's license. *Massachusetts*, it reads at the top. *Not* Connecticut. I never even thought to check her license plates after Amelia parked her car behind the barn. I look back down. *DOB: 09/14/96. HGT: 5'7" Eyes: GR.* Then, at the very bottom: *Fitzpatrick, Amelia Janelle. 314 White Swan Road, Boston, MA 54763.*

The Fitzpatricks must have known I wasn't a serious threat, for all this time they've been living in that same house in White Swan Estates. Amelia's birth date is only two days off. I never filled out a birth certificate, so Meredith and Thom must've used the date of the IVF to approximate the day of her birth.

The day of her birth.

Everything—all the loss and the love—I remember just as clearly as I remember the first time I held my daughter. And my son. Oh, my children . . . my child.

My legs collapse, knees striking the hardwood floor just as hard as the day my Hope was taken. But I do not feel the blood ballooning beneath my kneecaps, as I had not felt it then. This time, joy rather than pain sets every synapse in my body afire because I know—after eighteen years of deferred dreaming—the impossible is true. Holding the tiny picture on the driver's license to my lips, tears stream from my eyes. I lift them to the ceiling and marvel at the forbearance of God that let, through the return of my daughter, his own prodigal daughter again be found.

Although my worst fear came true and my Hope was taken from me, I have to remember that she was never mine to begin with. Nor was she really the Fitzpatricks'. Hope has always belonged first and foremost to her Creator—the one who, that day I left my daughter behind in Boston, I'd vowed was incapable of taking care of my child . . . his child. For he is the one who formed her cranberry hair and rosebud mouth; he is the one who knew exactly how many chromosomes her body would carry and the battle that would rage for her life. He is the one who possibly even gave me that heedless inclination to run.

Still kneeling, I pray that whatever happens in the future, I will rest in the truth that his ways are greater and that, though I may not understand it, he has a plan.

Amelia, 2014

The whole Split Rock Community is invited back to the Risser house after Alvin's funeral, but I can tell from Rebecca's dazed expression that she's in no state of mind to prepare the food. Because of this—and maybe because Lydie is nowhere to be found—the neighbor women roll up their sleeves and begin to help.

One heavyset woman in a wide cape dress chatters at Henry in Pennsylvania Dutch, and he goes down to the basement, resurfacing with his arms filled with ham, rounds of cheese, and two quart jars of canned peaches. The woman then squints at Wilbur Byler, who is leaning against one of the Rissers' kitchen cupboards. He looks like a dog just waiting around to be fed.

"Wilbur," the woman says, her accent as stout as the forearms pressing against the sleeves of her dress. In response, his heels practically click as his body skids to attention. She begins rattling off instructions in Pennsylvania Dutch. He nods and then nods again. I watch this exchange while hidden by the bookshelf next to the couch. I want to help, but I'm too terrified of being asked to do something I wouldn't have the first clue how to begin. I've learned a lot since coming to Hopen Haus (how to pull weeds, for example, or to bake an apple pie as long as someone else makes the crust, or to polish copper pots, or—thanks to Uriah—gather eggs from an angry hen), but working next to these Mennonite women would be intimidating as can be.

I've also been waiting around for a chance to speak to Wilbur, to interrogate him about him and Lydie and find out the truth from what he won't say to me. So when Wilbur leaves the Rissers' home—to do that woman's bidding—I get up from the couch and slip out the door behind him.

He's just opened the driver's side of his diesel van when I work up enough courage to call across the yard, "Can I ride along?"

Wilbur doesn't even turn to see who's spoken. Shrugging, he says, "I'm just going up the road," before climbing into the vehicle. I scurry down the sidewalk, my sandals slapping, and pull the handle to the sliding door, suddenly not sure if I'll have the nerve to cross-examine him or not. I sit back, and Wilbur maneuvers the van around the black buggies clustered in front of the house. The horses strapped to them don't spook as the engine starts up. They just shake their bridles and shift their weight to their other mud-splattered legs.

Nervous, I rip off a hunk of the yellow stuffing popping up through a tear in the seat. I drop bits in my lap, which stick to the fibers of Lydie's worn-out cape dress. I rack my brain, trying to think of a way to get Wilbur to talk since he barely spoke to Lydie and me on the trip up here. We haven't yet passed the Rissers' square mailbox when I decide that I don't know where he's going, and so I'm just going to come out with it.

But right then Wilbur says, "Don't you remember getting kidnapped?"

I close my mouth, trying to understand what he's just said. Finally, I murmur, "I don't know what you're talking about."

Wilbur doesn't say anything else. He just takes a right back toward the main road and the entrance sign. *I can run faster than this,* I think, and suddenly I *want* to run. I want to escape from this man who's watching me through the rearview mirror as he says, "I didn't know it was you 'til I heard you talking on the way up here."

"You don't know me," I say. "I . . . I've never seen you before Hopen Haus."

"You just don't remember 'cause you were a baby."

I sink my fingers into the sponge padding of the seat, grappling for something to hold on to. I speak between shallow breaths, "How . . . how do you know me?"

For a while, Wilbur says nothing. Then his face twitches in a smile that is scarier than anything I've ever seen. "I haven't been in touch with Meredith or Thom since they came to take you back to Boston," he says, "but I *do* know your birth mother."

Confused and terrified, I gape at the back of Wilbur's head. The thought of a birth mother is so weird, I couldn't be any more surprised if Wilbur had started speaking pig Latin. How can I possibly understand—or believe—such crazy words? But how does he know my parents' names? And where we live? And deep down, haven't I wondered why I've always felt like my parents were in this play that I could watch from the outside and never participate in or belong to?

Throat tightening, I face the window. My eyes sting with tears as the entire Old Order Mennonite community shrinks to the size of a telescope lens. I can picture the men who were at Alvin's service working these fields tomorrow, the disks of their wide-brimmed straw hats turned up toward the sun and their sweated, watercolor shirts tucked into the black pants with the black suspenders crisscrossing the broad Vs of their backs.

The peace of this Plain ground collides with my rising panic. And I discover that I'm no longer Lydie Risser's street-smart protector, but a stupid girl who thought she could trap a lion in its den and come out unharmed. My nerves intensify the canned air, stinking with a mixture of old hamburger wrappers and body odor. I push a fist against my mouth, trying to keep back my nausea. The white sign for Split Rock Community blurs as the van engine picks up speed. Tires spit gravel as Wilbur Byler pulls out onto the main road.

"Hey—" I smack my fist against the glass. "Where're you going?"

I ask this question at the same moment he locks the doors.

Rhoda, 2014

Chunks of mildewed clapboard break free of Hopen Haus's fascia and clatter across the grass, like a poor man's game of matchsticks. Even from where I stand near the garden fence post, I can see termites infesting the old logs that clapboard once kept from view. Every hidden place is being revealed, and it's obvious that it's time.

"Looper?" I call; my voice trembles.

Ernest Looper shifts his body, although he is straddling the top of a twenty-foot ladder. Old salt stains tie-dye his red shirt with white. He grins down at me and hooks the hammer over one shoulder. "Know it looks bad now," he says, "but—"

"I'm not here for that." I pick my way through the debris and wrap my fingers around the ladder's base— steadying it, steadying myself.

Looper holds on to the shiny lip of the new roof, whose old gutters are still clotted with pine needles and leaves. Making sure I'm out of harm's way, he drops the hammer to the ground. His steel-toed boots clang against the aluminum rungs as he climbs down the ladder. He wipes his forehead with the hem of his shirt and stoops, seizing a glass of tea sitting on a cedar stump drifted with splinters from his ax. I imagine that Alice brought this refreshment to Looper. Picturing the two of them talking as the two of us are talking now, an old sense of propriety looms. But I cannot focus on such piffle when my daughter's life may be hanging in the balance. And I cannot drag into my misfortune this man who has obviously come here for charity alone. My mind whirling, stomach clenched, I begin to turn away.

Looper clutches my arm. "What's wrong?"

I cannot meet his eyes. If there is compassion in their familiar gold-green depths, memories will spill over the compartments of my life, causing me to remember how wonderful it was to rely on someone besides myself. How wonderful it was to rely on him.

"I think . . . I've found my daughter." I have to breathe around the amazement and the sad understanding that she has been here for weeks. "Amelia," I add. "The redhead."

For a while, Looper says nothing, and I wonder why he will not rejoice with me or at least ask for proof. Instead, he just touches my left hand clenching my right arm and interlaces our fingers. "What will you do?" he asks.

"Do?" I step away from him. But he keeps holding my hand. "What *can* I do?" I snap. "I'm going to see her, Looper. After all this time, I'm going to bring her back."

"From Split Rock?"

"From everything."

"And what if she doesn't want to come?"

I look up at him and withdraw my hand. "What do you mean by that?"

Seeing the hurt filling the corners of my eyes, he sighs and stares out over the garden's rows that are becoming indistinguishable as the harvest season draws to a close and the weeds reclaim the untilled earth. "Just don't set yourself up for heartbreak, Beth."

"You can't break something that's already broken."

Looper says, "Maybe you can't." I hear him move toward me, his truck keys already jangling in his hand. "But you can sure make it harder to mend."

19

Amelia, 2014

I fold my arms to stop their shaking, though it's so hot outside. The leaves on the trees—the trunks stick-pinned to the long grass lining either side of the road—are limp in the humidity that's only gotten worse since the early-morning rain. Wilbur Byler flicks the blinker and takes a right again. He's slowed way down since we left the Mennonite community, but the child-safety locks are still on. The automatic controls are shielded by the pudgy flat of his left hand. I look up at him through the rearview mirror. A bead of sweat traces my spine.

"Where . . . where are you taking me?" I whisper.

His dull eyes meet mine in the rearview mirror. "Sure can't take you back to the Rissers'," he drawls, "and have you shaking the family up by spreading rumors about Lydie and me. I seen how the two of you been talking."

I twist the fabric of my borrowed cape dress. I have no money with me, no cell phone, no driver's license, no jewelry to pawn. I don't even own the clothes on my back. My identity has been stripped. After years of taking my parents for granted, even resenting their smothering support, I realize just how well they've protected me all these years. "I won't tell anybody about you and Lydie," I say, my words rushed. "My parents will pay—"

"Quiet!"

Startled, I point my frightened gaze back to the road.

"I always knew there was something off about your birth mother," Wilbur continues, though his voice is so distracted he might as well be talking to himself. "She was too eager to become Mennonite. Too eager to change her identity, her name. Seemed to me she was running from something—or somebody—so when I seen this article in the *Tennessean* with her old name in it, saying she'd kidnapped a child, I kept it for a while and watched. I watched her with you. I watched her with others. She was so jumpy that I just knew she was the same one that article was talking about."

Wilbur speeds up, as if to add to the tension. Not sure what to believe, I can't decide if I want to hang on his every word or cover my ears. "To test my little theory," he says, "I slid that article in a pile of newspapers when I knew she would probably see it. And see it, she did. You were only a little thing then, and when she read that article, she got sick in a box right next to where you were sleeping. But I knew that if I let on that I was onto her, she'd run. So I just bided my time. For two weeks I waited, and then I called the number in the article and said I thought I knew where that woman who'd kidnapped the child was. That she was hiding in a Mennonite community, in this place called Dry Hollow, Tennessee."

I squeeze my hands between my legs and fold my body over them. Only in this position can I breathe. I don't know which scares me more—the thought of this man being insane, or the possibility that he's telling the truth. Wilbur says, "It took longer than I expected. About three weeks or so. But then the phone call came. The investigator said they'd found evidence that my claim was correct, and the parents would be coming down the following week with a lawyer and papers and stuff. I was supposed to keep everything quiet. Even the newspaper wasn't allowed to let anybody know what was going on."

I sit up. My arms wrap my waist. Isn't the kidnap victim supposed to keep her captor talking—bonding—and then the captor feels so bad, he lets her go? "Didn't it bother you to see a mom separated from her kid?" I ask, trying to separate myself from the kid in the story.

"She hurt enough people over the years; I figured it was time she paid her dues." Wilbur nods, pleased with himself. "Anyways . . . I don't even know how it all went down. I wasn't there 'cause I couldn't just wait around, and the

Fitzpatricks wouldn't tell me when they were coming. They wired half of the reward money beforehand, and they said they'd wire the other half if I agreed to keep quiet and keep out of their way. I didn't tell *nobody* what I knew. I acted just as shocked when you were gone as everyone else did."

The question I have been afraid to ask forces itself through my lips. "Who . . . who was my birth mother?"

"Rhoda's the one that birthed you." Wilbur's eyes narrow beneath his drooping hair. "But she was just the sarogate. Like an incubator for your parents."

And thank you for that science lecture, I think. Laughter bubbles up from inside my chest, and I know that I'm in shock. But then the seriousness of this changed universe crashes in, making me press the heels of my hand into the socket of each watering eye. My vision spirals out of the blackness with waving yellow fronds, like I've stared too long at the sun. Rhoda, the cranky head midwife, a kidnapper? *My* kidnapper? Or stranger still, my birth mother? Can Wilbur be serious? But why *does* Rhoda always look at me like I'm someone she's seen before, yet can't remember my name? More than this, why did my dad send me down here, to the middle of nowhere, if there wasn't a connection made before now?

Opening my eyes, I replay the night my escape was set into motion; the same night I told my parents I was pregnant over supper.

My dad shuffled into my room only after my mom had gone to bed with a sleep aid and a glass of wine. The leaf of paper he held out to me was flimsy, but his fingers

shook as I took it from him and flattened it on my desk.
The ceiling fan blades cast shadows on the typed words,
and for a moment I wanted to do anything but read them.
Because, following my greatest letdown, I knew they'd have
to change everything.

"Read it to me," I whispered. "I don't think . . . I can."

He reached past my laptop and ran his thumb over my
hand. Picking up the page, he unhooked his glasses from
the pocket of his robe and used his index finger to push
them on his nose. "'Abandoned Mennonite Community
Becomes Home for Unwed Mothers,'" he said.

As my dad kept reading about a small Old Order
Mennonite community located in Dry Hollow, Tennessee,
that was abandoned when the group of two hundred and
fifty members decided to move north, panic dried my mouth.
Blood swam through my ears. Was he *really* going to ask me
to go there? Was he *really* going to ask me to give up my life?

My dad paused—waiting for me to refocus—before he
read, "Rather than joining this exodus, Rhoda Mummau,
one of the community members and head midwife for a
home for unwed mothers called Hopen Haus, purchased
from the community forty acres along with the farm's Civil
War–era homestead so the unwed mothers residing inside it
did not have to leave when the surrounding property went
up for sale."

He finished the article and rattled off the list describing
Hopen Haus's financial and physical needs. Even though
I was looking at the paper clutched in my dad's hands, I
was not listening to what he said. Instead, I was staring at

the dark box printed on the left-hand corner, where a black and white image showed a middle-aged woman in a funny *kapp* covering half of her face with one hand.

"Dry Hollow," I whispered.

"Yes," my dad said, folding the paper and laying it on my desk. "Go to Dry Hollow, Amelia. Go . . . and find yourself there." He leaned down and squeezed my fingers. For the first time in years, I responded by wrapping them tight around his hand. "When you return," he said, "we'll talk."

I glanced down at the article, not wanting to spend the last summer before my senior year in Tennessee. But what options did I have? My mom claimed that I had no life, that I had already wasted it the night I got pregnant and would never get it back unless I kept tomorrow morning's appointment. An appointment where a counselor would act like she was giving me choices, when she was really getting paid to tell me what to do. That's when I made my decision. "Okay," I said. "I'll go. But . . . what about Mom?"

My dad looked at me. The ceiling fan whirred and the computer's screen saver kicked on before he folded his arms and sighed. "I'll take care of her. I already put Dry Hollow into your GPS, and I'll give you some money to hold you over while you're gone."

I turned in my chair to face the closet, feeling both thankful for my dad's kindness and overwhelmed by my choice to leave this life behind.

My dad touched my arm. "Just look for Rhoda Mummau," he said. "The head midwife. Tell her you read this article and that you're pregnant. But don't tell her your birth date or your last name or any information like that—you don't want to get in trouble for being under-age. . . . She'll take you in."

"Why are you doing this?" I asked.

"Because, Amelia," my dad said, and then he looked away too, "it's the right thing."

Wilbur Byler now flicks on his blinker and takes exit 42. After the van barrels down the ramp and turns left, directly ahead I spot the cage of the retired Scottsburough County fire tower. My throbbing pulse steadies at the sight of a landmark after miles of unfamiliar land.

"You're . . . you're taking me to Hopen Haus?" I ask.

"Got to," Wilbur says. "Called your mom and dad last night. They're coming down here."

Though the van is cruising past the courthouse, my head snaps back, whiplashed as my changed universe tumbles out of orbit. If Wilbur Byler has contact with my parents, he's not crazy but actually telling the truth: my parents are my parents, but my mom's not the one who birthed me. I was kidnapped in the womb and then, like a piece of missing luggage, reclaimed. And as I accept this truth, I feel like my entire life has been a lie.

Rhoda, 2014

Looper turns in at the house whose mailbox number matches the one on the envelope Rebecca Risser mailed when writing Lydie about the impending loss of her father. We are forced to park halfway up the lane, as the yard is crowded with every horse and buggy in the community and, if they rode through the night, the communities beyond.

Two blond children—a boy and a girl—wearing their Sabbath best come running out of the house. The girl holds a spool of string while the boy caresses a homemade kite that is wider than his chest. They pause when they see us getting out of the truck. Their milk-white smiles and flushed cheeks let me know that they are Lydie's siblings. Then they take off running again. The boy releases the kite. The diamond shape bounces against the earth until the boy's momentum increases and the girl slackens the string. The kite sails toward the sun, and the newly fatherless children let out a whoop of exultation. The two of them sprint into the flower garden. Weightless, the kite continues fluttering through the air, anchored to this terrestrial ball by an angel-hair string.

The children's joy even on the day of their *dawdy*'s funeral tells me they do not fully understand the death that has just assaulted them. In this, they remind me of myself as I waved at my mother's station wagon as it crackled down the lane—thinking she was on the way to the library or the grocery store, not knowing she was leaving us. My heart hurts for the Risser children. Reality will soon come hurtling in as surely as that kite will buckle in the wind and plummet to the earth. Though impossible, I find myself wishing I could do something to keep them buoyant, to suspend their oblivion to pain.

Looper waits for me on the mulched path that leads to the porch. I pass him, mount the steps, and knock on the door. It is opened by a slender woman with dark eyes and an apron overlaying a cape dress cut from an equally muted cloth. "May I help you?" she asks. I glimpse a dimple when she speaks.

"I'm looking for Lydie Risser."

"*Jah.* Hold on, please." The young woman closes the storm door. Though I am dressed Plain, I notice that she does not invite me in. Perhaps it's because I've asked for Lydie.

Waiting, I look out at the pasture bordering the house, where a herd of doe-eyed Guernseys grazes in a clover field. The waning daylight shimmers across the velvet expanse of their smooth, buff hides. A few of the posts in the fence encircling the herd are made from ancient cedars; in places, the wires braiding the fence spear the rust-colored bark protecting the trunks. I am sure those trees were here when this strip of mountain land was just a patch of woods waiting to be cleared. It is all I can do not to walk over and curl beneath the trees' extended boughs that screen this mind-numbing heat. I have not felt this elated and this tired since Hope—Amelia—was born.

I hear a noise. Turning, I see Lydie Risser, holding on to the screen door for support. "Lydie?" I ask. "Are you all right?"

Lydie looks over her shoulder. Pulling the door behind her, she steps out onto the concrete porch. "What are you doing here?" Her tone is not accusing, just curious.

I glance around the grounds, as if expecting my

daughter to appear from behind the dogwood tree or rho-dodendron bushes. I realize, though it is inconceivable, that I expect her to be as unchanged by time as is my love for her. "Is Amelia with you?"

Lydie shakes her head.

My stomach drops. I search her face. "She's not?"

"Someone said she went for a walk."

"How long has she been gone?"

"Not sure. I was upstairs, lying down."

I look at Looper. He shakes his head, just as perplexed as I.

Lydie says, "There's something else. . . ." I face the girl again. She stares down at her boots and hugs her belly. "Wilbur's missing too."

The maternal alarm I feel gives my words intensity. "I'm going after her."

Lydie's pale cheeks bloom, causing her freckles to dis-appear. And as the suspicions Uriah Rippentoe roused are confirmed, my urgency alerts Lydie to the fact that I am aware that Wilbur Byler is her child's father.

Lydie sways and grapples for the back of a wicker rock-ing chair. Steadying herself, she clamps both hands on the outside of her womb and bites her bottom lip. Blood lipsticks her mouth. "I don't think you should leave," she breathes. "I've been having pains."

I point to the rocking chair, and Looper helps Lydie into it as if she is a baby herself. I kneel on the porch beside her and check her pulse. One hundred beats per minute. "How long have you been having contractions?" I ask.

"Since last night. I . . ." Lydie pauses and flicks her eyes at Looper. He turns his head respectfully away. "I had bloody show," she whispers.

"But your water's not broken?"

She shakes her head, and her two plaits—furred in the humidity—swat her gently in the face. "I don't think so," she says. But the poor girl seems unsure.

"Have you been timing your contractions?" I ask.

She makes a wavelike motion with her hands. "They're still too *doppish*."

Irregular, she means. Must be early first stage of labor. This is good. I was in such a hurry to leave and find my daughter that for one of the rare times in my years as a midwife, I forgot my birthing satchel. Plus, I am so exhausted, it would be safer to minister to Lydie alongside Alice Rippentoe's capable hands. Having taken such pride in being an island unto myself, needing someone else is not easy to admit. Especially needing Alice.

I ask Lydie, "You think you can make the drive back to Hopen Haus?"

She nods and then grips the arms of the rocking chair. Her nostrils flare as she breathes through the contraction. Less than five minutes have passed since the last one, and already they are increasing in intensity, not allowing Lydie to speak. My stomach roils as I comprehend that she might be further along in labor than I thought. I am really not prepared to deliver a sixteen-year-old's baby in a truck parked on the side of the road.

"Can my *mamm* come?" Lydie says.

From experience, I know that a woman craves her mother's presence the most when faced with birth or death. This poor child is being faced with both within one twenty-four-hour period. I want to grant her request, but we have no time to lose—nor do we have room for Lydie's *mamm* in Looper's truck.

I look over at Looper. "Can you tell Mrs. Risser that we need to leave now?" I ask. "See if she's able to get a ride and follow us as soon as possible. And can you please use someone's phone to call Wilbur and ask him where Amelia is?"

"There's a phone in the barn," Lydie says. I am about to rattle off Wilbur's cell phone number when Lydie Risser stares right into my eyes and recites it. Looper nods and walks off the porch toward the barn.

Lydie chokes out, "I'm sorry." She bows her head.

I kneel on the porch and press the calloused pad of Lydie's small hand. Her body exudes the energy and the warmth that will propel her through childbirth and the trying months afterward, when she faces life as a single mother in a community filled with picture-perfect families. "It's all right, my *meedel*," I soothe, just as Fannie Graber once soothed me—a forgotten kindness restored. "None of that matters now. We just need to focus on bringing your baby into this world."

Rocking back on my heels, I stare into the yard. The foliage on the trees blurs as my eyes flood with memory. I may not have had the daughter who was taken from me, but I have been surrounded by these precious daughters who have all been as alone in the world as I. For eighteen years I have taken them for granted. Nonetheless, I vow to open my heart to them, and through that communion, become the kind of mother I have never had.

Amelia, 2014

Wilbur parks, and the fog I've been floating in, ever since his leak about my parents, evaporates. Uriah Rippentoe runs out of Hopen Haus like he's been waiting for us. His straw hat blows off in the yard and snags on a clump of dandelion weeds. His eyes scan me as I get out of the van. I'm relieved to see him, but as I turn toward him— my eyes swollen, my bones aching with shock—I'm also embarrassed by how strange I must look, wearing Lydie's too-small cape dress and with my hair finger-brushed into a messy bun. I know that Uriah's not checking out my appearance as much as he's making sure that I'm all right. However, faced with my parents' lie, I'm not sure I'll ever be all right again.

"What happened?" Uriah asks. Then he turns toward Wilbur without waiting for my answer. The two men stare at each other. Wilbur doesn't blink. The veins throb in Uriah's hands.

I move between them. "I'm fine," I say, though my voice is hoarse from crying. "Lydie's dad died. They buried him today." When neither speaks, I ask, "My parents been by?"

Uriah says, "Your parents?"

"Yes." I wrap a hand around my throat, watching Wilbur walk over to his van. "They're coming down here. They . . . they might be here soon."

"They're coming to take you back?"

I nod. My body trembles as I understand what *back* really means: a meeting with a counselor, a doctor's appointment, followed by a ton of Ivy League college applications. My mom has no doubt taken every step to make sure that my future is only rescheduled, not derailed. But is that what *I* want? I wrap my arms around my thick-ening waist, wanting to scream—to weep—yet somehow I remain standing. After living in Hopen Haus and see-ing cases like Desiree's and Star's, I know I'm lucky to have parents who are not only involved in my life, but so hands-on they'd drop everything just to come down here and guarantee my safety. But how can they guarantee my safety while my mom is asking me to harm my child, *her* grandchild?

I came down here to find myself, and instead I've never felt so lost. How can a baby be growing inside a body that doesn't even know its birth mother . . . its original name?

Covering my mouth, I begin to sob. Uriah crosses the short distance between us and folds me into his arms. I rest against him a second, absorbing power from a boy's touch as I've always done; then I close my eyes and picture the two of us hugging with this invisible child between us, a viewpoint that suddenly helps me see our flirtation for what it is. Every time I've been forced to face the darkest parts of myself, I have instead turned the opposite direction and faced someone else. I did this the night my baby was conceived; I am doing this now.

Breathing deep, I blink tears and step back from Uriah, not because I want to, but because my baby deserves a mother who is willing to break the cycle and try to become more than who she currently is. Then I see that Wilbur Byler is watching us. His body is slanted against the hood of his van, which is still ticking with the engine's trapped heat. His thick arms are crossed. Our eyes remain locked until Wilbur points to me, brings a finger to his lips that is as straight as the barrel of a gun, and shakes his head— a threat that is also the worldwide demand for silence. I continue watching him as he climbs into his van.

His brake lights flash once before he drives down the lane.

Rhoda, 2014

I give Looper a pointed glance, and he punches the gas pedal. The truck rattles as the engine accelerates us down Dry Hollow's coarse county road. Unsnapping her seat belt, Lydie writhes and turns, facing the truck bed. She digs nails into the seat and pants until the dusty rear window fogs with breath. *Not in the truck,* I think. *Please, Lydie. Don't give birth in this truck.* I delivered Henry and Arlene's nine-pound daughter in a buggy discreetly parked behind the ticket booth at the annual farm auction in Scottsville,

Kentucky, but I've never caught a baby in a speeding vehicle. Lydie's mother was hoping one of her *Englischer* neighbors who had come to pay their condolences could shuttle her to Hopen Haus in an hour or two, once the majority of the mourners had left for home. Looking at Lydie now, though, I am not sure Rebecca will make it before her grandchild's birth.

I wedge myself between Lydie's body and the dashboard, placing my left knee on the floorboard. Gently pushing on her shoulders with the flat of my hands, I press my other knee into the small of her back. She pushes against the seat, bracing against me. Tenderness swells in the forty-five-degree angle of my wrists, and a bottle cap is gouging my kneecap on the floorboard. But I continue administering counterpressure until Looper's hurtling Chevy dips into a gully in the washed-out lane leading to Hopen Haus.

I topple toward the floor, and my ribs chip against the gearshift. Clenching my eyes, I bite back a moan and can feel Looper's hand touch mine in sympathy. Lydie emits an unintelligible stream of Pennsylvania Dutch as another contraction assaults her, and no one is able to help her grapple with the pain.

Looper abruptly shifts into park and the truck lurches to a stop. He jumps out and runs around to help Lydie. Crawling out of the truck, I drag a bridal train of sawdust and ten-penny nails onto the flat-topped grass. I limp in Looper and Lydie's steady wake toward Hopen Haus, holding my right side. My ribs echo with the pulse of the heart beneath them. I try to straighten and wince. At least one of my ribs may be broken, if not more. My breathing is shallow. These physical limitations do not bode well for delivering a child. I am so focused on the agony of inhaling and exhaling, I am taken aback when I look up and see Amelia Fitzpatrick, in a cape dress and bun, standing on the front porch beside Uriah.

Her red hair is the eye of the vortex swirling around us. I want to dart up those steps and embrace her. I want to hold her against my chest and thank God that she is safe from Wilbur Byler and that she somehow came back to me, even after seventeen years. I want to whisper her birth name in her ear like a prayer. I want to mourn what we've lost and rejoice over what we have left, no matter how insignificant that might be.

But as Lydie's keening reverberates across the yard, I know this is not the time for the mother-daughter reunion for which I've always longed. Looper places one arm around Lydie's back and scoops the other beneath her legs. Her ramrod body loosens in this strangely matrimonial embrace. Tears drip across Lydie's temples and she bites down hard.

"Breathe through it, Lydie," I call, though breathless myself. "Don't fight. Just breathe."

Uriah scrambles over to the screen door and pulls it open. Looper plods up the steps and turns sideways before carrying Lydie past Uriah and into the darkness of the hall.

"She okay?" Amelia asks. Her fingers hover near her mouth. I can see the thin, pale circle where Meredith Fitzpatrick's cameo ring used to be. This is the first time

I've looked at Amelia as a mother viewing her child. My eyes burn with the intensity of the emotions I feel. I extend my hand to touch this phantom brought to life, this child turned woman. But I retract it at the last moment, fearing that Amelia would prefer not to know the truth.

"Rhoda?" Amelia says.

My scalp prickles as I understand that this young woman will never consider me her mom. I look down. "She'll be fine," I say, not knowing if I speak for Lydie or for myself. Then I stare at my daughter for one second more before entering Hopen Haus, knowing that, somewhere in its depths, another mother and her child are waiting to be born.

Fatigue is its own anesthesia, letting Lydie remain half-asleep through two lighter contractions. Alice stands to the right of the four-poster bed, listening to the baby's heart rate through Fannie's old fetoscope, its fluted mouth pressed against Lydie's stomach like a kiss. Alice moves the scope higher and then higher still. Her fair brows furrow. She looks over, and though she is obviously concerned, I am not able to interpret her expression. Straightening her back, she walks toward me.

I push up from the cane-backed chair and hobble over. I lift the edge of Lydie's sheet with my right hand—and even this movement is almost too much to bear. I turn to the side and wince, trying to keep from gasping aloud. But then Alice Rippentoe's gasp echoes what I have not uttered.

I look over at her, perturbed that a midwife has emitted a negative sound in the birthing room. A patient is never more attuned to her caregivers' verbal and nonverbal cues then when about to give birth.

Alice meets my eyes. I follow the trajectory of her pointing finger, and my jaw goes slack. Clutching my side, I shuffle closer. I try to breathe through the panic, as I have instructed Lydie to do. But I can't. One of the baby's feet has emerged. It's really as simple and as complicated as that. Though I assisted Fannie once in the delivery of a shoulder presentation, I have never seen a foot presentation before in my life. And I have most certainly never delivered one. Even if I wasn't incapacitated by my broken ribs, I wouldn't know how to begin. Why did I make the oldest mistake in midwifery and assume that the protuberance at the top of Lydie's womb was the bottom and not the head?

I've only delivered one breech baby since Fannie died, and I had Sadie Gingrich to assist me, who had once assisted Fannie and therefore knew what to do when I felt so inept. Everything must be done slowly and precisely— if the umbilical cord gets clamped during pushing and the head is still anchored in the womb, the baby will not receive oxygen through the mother's blood. The baby will then either be severely handicapped or asphyxiated before he's even drawn his first breath.

I turn my back on Lydie and gouge my nails into my palms, angry that I allowed her to go to Split Rock—for her *dawdy*'s funeral or not. It was too close to her due date. I should've known better. If Lydie had been in my care from the beginning of this complication—and if I had remembered my birthing satchel—I could have determined the baby's position from the location of the heartbeat. There would have been ways to relax the womb and try to manipulate the baby into the correct position for birth.

Now it's too late. Holding on to the edge of the bed, I reach out and stroke the bottom of the tiny, neonatal foot. My pulse thumps in my ears. I wonder if our intervention has come too late and the child's already dead. Then the foot moves. The five perfect toes with their five perfect nails unfurl. The movement is so infinitesimal that it is like watching a flower bloom, one petal at a time. And yet the child is alive.

"Praise be," Alice whispers. I look over and see her touching the back of her gloved hand to her lips, contaminating it without thinking. "Praise be," she repeats.

Lydie stirs from her exhausted half sleep. "My *bobbel* . . . my *bobbel* all right?" she asks.

I give Alice a sharp look of reproof and say, "Change your gloves." Then I soften my voice. "Yes, Lydie. Everything's all right. We just think you might've been in labor longer than we anticipated. You can't remember any time your waters might have broken?"

Charlotte moves to the front of the bed and brushes the hair back from Lydie's brow. She brings over a glass of raspberry leaf tea and bends the straw to allow the girl to drink.

Lydie swallows and sinks into the pillow. "I'm not sure," she rasps. "Might've happened in the bath—" Her word becomes a soft moan as another contraction hits. Grinding

her teeth, Lydie rises and scoots up the mattress, trying
to escape the pain. She breathes through it by mimicking
Alice's open-mouthed panting and then wrenches her body
sideways. Charlotte darts over with an old milk pail. Vomit
spews from between Lydie's fingers and pings against the
bottom of the tin.

"It's all right," Charlotte murmurs, rubbing Lydie's
convulsing back and holding the pail steady. "It's all right,
liebe."

The putrid scent is exacerbated by the heat trapped
inside the room. I stand and move around the bed to open
the window and then remember that I can't. I motion to
Alice, and she lifts the window for me. Flecks of paint
break free as her svelte arms heave and the old glass panes
clatter upward. The room swells with the sound of bullfrogs croaking down near the pond; the steady tappity-
tapping of a pileated woodpecker drilling for bugs; the
jangle of the Gypsy goat herd's bells.

Watching Lydie Risser in the center of the four-poster
bed, curling her body around the clenching fist of her
unborn baby, anger burns within me. How could Wilbur
Byler have been so calloused—so cruel—as to steal Lydie's
childhood by making her with child herself?

I yearn to strike out. I yearn to banish Wilbur from
Hopen Haus and from our lives forever, knowing the only
way to do so is to involve the law that I have been trying to evade for eighteen years. The same law that Wilbur
would use against me, by revealing how I kidnapped the
Fitzpatricks' daughter and hid in the very place meant to

keep others safe. I know bringing a suit against Wilbur for statutory rape is outside my jurisdiction, but would *he* know that? And would newly widowed Rebecca Risser be able to rise above her grief long enough to bring the suit against him that I cannot? Or would her pacifist beliefs force her to let him go? These questions have no ready answers, and so they are answers in themselves. I must notify the police of Wilbur's actions in the hope that they will put enough fear into him that he will not repeat such a travesty. I do not dread the repercussions of my heedless past brought to light. I would not want to do it over, but I would do it all again. What I fear is how Amelia Fitzpatrick would be affected if she found out that her own parents did not want her until they knew she was not malformed.

But I know I will do anything within my power to ensure that what happened to Lydie does not happen again. Even if that means hurting my own daughter by revealing the truth behind the lifetime lie. I hear the crunch of gravel beneath tires and turn toward the window, though I can only see the shaded garden. I imagine that Wilbur Byler has just arrived. That he's somehow learned of Lydie's labor and has returned to ensure the safety of the life his selfishness has risked.

"Alice . . . Charlotte," I say as I hear a vehicle door slam. "Will you be all right if I step outside a minute?"

Lydie is oblivious to anything but the compression of her womb. However, the two midwives look up. Sweat curls the silver strands that have come loose from Charlotte's *kapp*. Alice's cheeks are smudged with exertion.

Alice opens her mouth—to ask me to remain, I'm sure—but then she says, "Hurry."

Downstairs, I cut through the dining room to intercept Wilbur Byler. My left hand is on the screen door handle, about to pull it open, when a flurry of movement in the yard catches my eye. It's not Wilbur Byler's silver minivan that has just pulled up. A black luxury car is parked in the driveway. Meredith Fitzpatrick is striding across the lawn. Thom is following in her wake.

He looks much the same as he did when I left my daughter behind in Boston. I do not remain focused on him; Meredith's transformation requires more attention than that. Her khaki pants are rumpled. The collar of her shirt is flipped up into blonde hair that hangs as limp as curtain panels on either side of her face. The lines of Meredith's face and body are just as symmetrical, but everything is softened, as if the woman I once knew and feared was nothing but a lump of malleable wax set too long beneath the sun.

Suddenly, Amelia's back appears in my line of sight, her slim silhouette framed by the screen door, but she does not take one more step toward her mother.

My eyes dart to Meredith's face, which is fitted with a mask of immense relief and rage. The aim of Meredith's gaze does not take in Hopen Haus's dilapidated state. It does not take in the gleeful chickens pecking the dirt her quick steps have tilled. It does not take in the shadow of the woman who hides behind this screen door. The screen door separating the woman from the daughter she birthed—the woman who is now watching the woman who wanted to take her daughter's life claim her daughter again. No, Meredith's gaze is focused wholly on her daughter, as it should have been focused all along.

Meredith marches up the steps. She is so near, I can watch the abalone buttons glint on the front of her shirt. I can hear the chime of sterling bracelets on her wrists. Meredith is so close that I can see the anger give way and tears rise in her eyes.

"Amelia," she says. "Oh, sweetheart . . . I'm sorry."

Amelia says nothing. She *does* nothing, until the three of us—mother, daughter, mother—are breathing together as one. Then Amelia opens her arms. Meredith closes her eyes and holds her daughter close. She buries her face in the red twist of Amelia's hair, crosses her arms behind that long back, and cries. I watch the nodules of Amelia's spine release, and I know that she begins to cry then too. After a while, Meredith lifts her head. She dabs tears with her knuckle so as not to pinch the delicate skin around her eyes. That's when our eyes meet over her daughter and through my screen door. I press my fingertips to the dark mesh—feeling a knife in my side—and wonder if this is as close to a reunion with my daughter as I will ever come.

20

Amelia, 2014

My dad jogs up the porch steps, having given us some space. Standing behind my mom, he wraps his arms around her—and so holds me too.

The picture-perfect family, I think.

"We're willing to hear you, Amelia," my dad says through the thin filter of my mom's hair. "We talked, and we're willing to hear you out."

I let my parents hold me until I know I'm not going to break apart. Then I push free from them and search their faces, trying to see the strangers who could let their own daughter believe a lie. Wiping tears, my mom straightens her shirt collar. My dad reaches into his pocket and passes her one of the million ironed handkerchiefs he started keeping around when I was a kid, constantly running across the playground with a split lip or scraped knee that he'd clean and patch with a Band-Aid and a kiss. I can't remember my mom ever kissing anything but my forehead—an affectionate gesture that was as dry as her love seemed to be.

But now my mom takes the handkerchief and thanks my dad. She won't meet my eyes. I'm not sure if it's because she knows something's wrong, or if she's just embarrassed that I've finally seen her cry. It would've helped our relationship if she'd allowed me to see this softer side of her from the beginning.

"What is it?" my dad asks. I'm not sure who he's speaking to, until I look away from my mom and see that he's looking at me.

I say, "Wilbur Byler told."

The sentence sounds ridiculous, like I'm a toddler tattling on a friend. But the meaning's not lost on my mom. "Told you what?" she says. I notice that she doesn't try sidetracking me by asking who Wilbur Byler is, and that she tries to keep her expression blank. Still, I can feel the aftershock of my words rolling off her body in a wave.

"That you hired Rhoda Mummau to carry me," I say, "because you couldn't carry me yourself. That she kidnapped me, and you came down here to take me back."

Frowning, my mom turns and walks down the porch. Her gaze is fixed on the pond, but I have a feeling she's not seeing anything except the day she reclaimed me.

My dad moves forward, as always trying to patch the hole left by my mom's absence. He opens his mouth to speak. Then stops. He looks over my shoulder for a long time before saying, "Try to understand, Amelia. We kept saying we'd tell you when you were older. . . . But then we told ourselves you just didn't need to know."

My breastbone aches from the violent drumming of my heart. "So you just decided to send me down here?" I fling out an arm to take in the yard, with its ancient trees I had admired and now just see as paper and dust. "To see if I'd figure everything out?"

Placing his hands on my shoulders, my dad just stares at me. Our eyes mirror each other's rich green until his pupils expand and the color gleams with tears; I refuse to cry. "I'm sorry," he says. "We hurt you, Amelia. . . . We hurt you by trying to keep you safe." His fingers tighten on my shoulders. He stares at me for a moment before spinning my body away from his and facing it toward the door. My eyes flicker at being maneuvered like this. And then I see the outline of a tall woman standing behind the screen door in a cape dress and *kapp*. Rhoda Mummau, Hopen Haus midwife. My birth mother. My kidnapper. Her strong hands—that have been taking care of my baby and me for a month—are knotted against her chest. I can see how they shake every time she breathes.

Are my parents now just going to turn me over to her? Are they going to switch ownership like I'm really nothing more than a piece of luggage?

The head midwife doesn't push the screen door, and I

don't pull it open. Through the separation, I can see that I do not know her, and I don't even know myself. We're like unrelated family or acquainted strangers: a contradiction of terms. The hush of an entire buried lifetime is broken only by our breaths. Then the heavy air is cut in half by Lydie's animal-like cry. Rhoda turns toward the sound, and seeing her distraction, my body hums with the urge to flee.

Twisting out of my dad's hold, I bolt down the porch steps and lose a sandal. I kick the other one off and continue running. My parents call my name, again and again, but over this I can hear another name: "Hope! Hope!"

My ears ring. I stop and stand frozen on the lane. Turning, I squint against the coming night and can see the shape of my parents. Then I see Rhoda, standing alone, leaning on the porch post like it can keep her from falling. One hand is still pressed against her chest. The other hand's outstretched toward me.

"Hope!" she cries again.

My name was Hope. . . .

Swallowing tears, I turn and keep running down the lane.

Rhoda, 2014

The Fitzpatricks and I watch Amelia's red hair stream and her legs flash white beneath her dark cape dress. Then Meredith strides across the porch and clasps my arm. I look away from the lane and down at her hand, with its network of fine blue veins and bones.

"Go to her," she says. I look up and see desperation carving lines between Meredith's eyebrows and along the dour rim of her mouth. "Fix this."

I jerk my arm out of her grasp. Meredith Fitzpatrick is ordering me about just as she did when I was her gestational surrogate and Thom's graduate school pawn. I'm neither now, so she has no right to treat me this way.

Sensing my anger, Thom puts an arm around his wife's shoulders and pulls her back. "Beth," he says, not even faltering over the use of my pseudonym, "you heard us try to talk to Amelia. She won't listen to us. She needs someone from the outside. Someone who can tell her how much we need her with us."

Someone from the outside? Is the woman who felt Amelia leap inside her womb truly from the outside? Laughter spews from my mouth—a harsh, sarcastic sound. Thom winces. Meredith's eyes glint like lapis.

"You want me to tell your daughter that you have always wanted her, when you are the very ones who wanted to take her life?"

"That doesn't matter," Meredith hisses. "We want her now."

"It *does* matter," I snap, my chest heaving. "Despite the love I poured into Amelia—despite everything I tried to give her in those months before you separated us—she felt your rejection in my womb."

Meredith steps back, cowering in her husband's leashing

embrace. "I didn't know," she cries, her words muffled by the handkerchief pressed against her lips. "I didn't know I would love her in the end."

I stare at this beautiful, broken woman and can feel the specter of wrath leave my body—a specter that has possessed it since Amelia was taken from me. I would never have had a second chance at motherhood if Meredith Fitzpatrick had not wanted her child, so I should be grateful to this woman who has destroyed my life. I should be grateful for the time my daughter and I had together, even if it was shortened by Meredith's decision to take her back. And because I truly love my returned child-turned-woman, I do not want to punish her in an attempt to punish her mother. I don't want her to be lonely like I was. Like I am. I want her to know she's loved.

"That's where we're different," I rasp, but I reach out to touch Meredith's hand—an olive branch gesture, a bridge traversed. "You loved Amelia in the end, but I loved her from the start."

Amelia, 2014

My back stiffens as I hear someone coming down the lane. "I don't want to talk to you!" I scream. "*Neither* of you!" The footsteps stop. Curious, I turn from the fence post. Wiping my face, I murmur, though it's no apology, "Thought you were Mom or Dad."

The wind blows, shifting branches and covering Rhoda in the moonlight falling through the trees. Her head is bowed, her *kapp* glowing silver. Finally, she looks up. Her face is twisted with pain. "I used to be your mom too," she says.

Her words throttle me, making it difficult to breathe. I turn toward the fence post again. I don't know what to say or think. It was easier to do both when I knew nothing, and now I know why my parents hid the truth from me. It wasn't just because they didn't want me to know; it was also because they didn't know how to explain.

"I don't remember you," I say, but the honesty burns. "I don't even remember my name."

The midwife steps closer. I flinch, waiting for her hand on my back, but she doesn't touch me. Finally, she says, "I just wish you could remember how much you were loved."

"Is that why you took me?" I ask.

She says nothing for so long that I am forced to face her again. The midwife's eyes are closed, tears threading the strands of her lashes. Then she opens them. This time she does reach out. Her fingers are calloused, but her touch is featherlight against my cheek. "Yes," she says. "I took you with me because I loved you so very much."

On the hill, my mom calls my name. The midwife drops her hand from my cheek and peers into my eyes. "Your parents love you too, Amelia. Please try to listen to them. It will be easier for you both if you can hear each other out."

My mom's getting closer, her footsteps careful as she

picks her way down the path. "Amelia . . . ?" she says. I can hear the worry in her voice. We don't have a lot of time.

"But why'd you name me Hope?" My throat narrows around that simple word.

The midwife smiles and looks away. In her profile, I can almost see the woman beneath the sadness. And I let myself wonder how different my life would've been if she had raised me instead of my parents. The thought isn't as scary as it was at first.

"Because you were my hope," she whispers. "And you always will be."

I stare at the midwife, my mind struggling to understand that my entire life, I have been not only loved . . . but wanted and claimed. Even fought over. In the distance, on the hill, I hear someone striking the triangle that hangs on the porch of Hopen Haus. The midwife tilts her head toward its noise, listening. Then she turns to look at me before stepping into the shadows, allowing my mom to take her place once again.

Rhoda, 2014

When I crest the hill—my side aching—I see Thom and Looper out in the yard, pacing like anxious fathers awaiting news about the birth of their daughter or son. Behind them, Alice stands on the porch. An oil lamp is at her feet and her arm poised to clang the triangle again. I step out from behind the oak tree, and she murmurs, "Thank God." I know by the break in her voice that she has not said this in vain.

"How's Lydie?" I ask.

"Not good," she says. "The fetal heart rate keeps dipping."

"How low?"

Pausing, she says, "Sixty-five."

Through the dimness, I search for Dr. Thomas Fitzpatrick's eyes. He falters in his pacing, probably wondering if the woman who has despised him for so long actually wants whatever knowledge he has to give. "Any complications?" he asks, walking toward me.

"The baby's breech," I say. "A foot's already birthed."

Alice adds, "And the mother has a fever. Her water broke without her knowing, and we think she's been in labor for twenty hours . . . perhaps more."

I turn toward Alice. "How high's the fever?"

"A hundred and one."

"Infection," Thom says, and though I know it's true, I wish he hadn't voiced it aloud. "Did you give her penicillin?" he asks.

"Amoxicillin," Alice says. "Lydie's allergic to penicillin."

He asks, "How far's the hospital?"

Alice shakes her head. "She's progressing too fast. The baby will be birthed before an ambulance can come out."

Thom's already moving past me. "May I see her?" he says. Alice looks askance. "I studied to be an OB-GYN," he adds.

Alice's expression does not change. Then, resigned, she picks up the oil lamp at her feet. Her skirt swishes as she stands, the wick's flame illuminating the liquid length of her frock. Shielding the globe, Alice turns toward him. "Follow, please."

I am taken aback by Alice's authoritative manner, but I am feeling so poorly that I do not care. Thom goes inside but holds the screen door open. I walk toward him and, before I enter, glance down at Looper, still standing in the yard. "Don't let Wilbur Byler set one foot in this place," I say. "Get Uriah to help you. Call the police. . . . We must keep Lydie safe."

Looper stares at me before looking at the door. I can see his comprehension dawn. He glances at his boots and nods. "Tell her I'm praying," he says.

"I will." I turn toward Dr. Fitzpatrick. "I think we need all the prayer we can get."

<hr>

When Thom and I enter the room, Lydie is slumped on the edge of the bed, her small hands opened on either side of her body like wilted tulips. Charlotte takes a tin from her birthing satchel, twists the lid, and kneels before the girl. Propping Lydie's shoulder with one hand, Charlotte massages salve into Lydie's skin, and the pungent scent of willow bark oil permeates the room.

Lydie groans as another contraction crescendos. Though her forehead is a colorless marble, her cheeks are rouged with fever. I am alarmed by her lethargic manner, and when I look over at Thom, I can tell that he feels the same. A gust blows through the open window, and the kerosene light hooked from the beam overhead sputters and flares in its netted bulb.

Thom crosses the shadowed room and crouches beside Charlotte. "How much blood has she lost?" he asks.

"Far less than a pint," Charlotte replies softly. Thom's confident bearing and British accent are so quietly demanding that, unlike Alice, Charlotte doesn't question Thom's right to ask. "But her pressure's risen, as has her fever."

Charlotte finishes massaging Lydie, and Alice gently turns her body so that she is positioned toward the end of the bed. Thom scrubs his hands in the *weschbohl* and dips his forearms and elbows into the hot water with an efficiency not diminished by time.

I drag a stool in my awkward left hand and position it toward the end of the bed. "Here, Thom," I say. "Sit here."

Lydie is so tired, she doesn't even wince when Thom reaches careful, gloved fingers past the baby's foot to trace the rest of the body still lodged in Lydie's womb. "I'd say about seven and a half, eight pounds. Pretty large baby to deliver breech," he says.

"Do you think we should push her?" I whisper, looking down at Thom.

He shakes his head. Easing his hands back out, he looks up at us midwives clustered about him, waiting for orders. "Ever heard of a water birth?" he asks.

We nod, of course, but none of us has ever seen one

performed. Fannie feared allowing a woman to give birth in water, in case she or the baby had complications and we could not climb inside the claw-foot tub fast enough to get her out.

"Water birth's becoming more popular, especially in—" Thom motions to the oil lamp smoking on the nightstand—"more primitive circles." He continues, oblivious to my irritation at being categorized in such a way. "I think the water would relax Lydie's uterine muscles—perhaps removing the cervical lip—and take pressure off her perineum. Otherwise, she is bound to tear." He stands from the stool, pulls the sheet down over Lydie's legs, and snaps off his gloves. "Beth?" he says. Alice and Charlotte look confused until they see the direction of Thom's gaze and know that he is talking to me. "You all have a bathtub here?"

"It's very *primitive*," I murmur sharply. "But yes, we have one down the hall."

Thom says, "I need someone to scour it with bleach. I mean, *really* scrub it down. We'll need towels and a lot of hot water. I'll carry Lydie when we're ready."

Charlotte leaves to fetch the water she set to boiling on the stove when Lydie went into labor. Alice looks at me, silently asking if we're really going to allow Lydie to give birth in a tub. But considering I've never delivered a breech birth without a more experienced midwife present, I am relieved to rely on Thom's knowledge—even as unconventional as that knowledge might be. "We have no choice," I whisper.

Alice nods warily. She picks her oil lamp up again. Her cape dress rustles as she swishes out of the room. Lydie opens her eyes just wide enough to look at me. My heart aches at the sight of her *strubbly* braids and pale, freckled skin. She should be attending Saturday night hymn sings and sewing doilies for her cedar-lined hope chest, not giving birth to a child who was forced upon her by an older man who I am sure abused her trust.

Making sure Lydie's still focused on me, I point to Thom. "Lydie, this is Dr. Fitzpatrick, Amelia's father. He's going to help deliver your baby tonight. It's called a water birth."

Lydie offers a weak smile. Then her eyes close again.

When Alice appears to tell us the bathtub has been cleaned and filled, I motion to Thom. Tucking the sheet around her shoulders, he scoops her up, and the thin, floral material laps over his arms.

The bathroom was converted from a narrow closet, so it is only wide enough to fit the toilet, standing sink, and tub suspended on halved cinder block risers. Rendered useless by my broken ribs, I remain in the doorway but hold an oil lamp to help illuminate the room. Thom eases Lydie down on the closed toilet seat and tests the bath's temperature with the inside of his wrist. His action is so second-nature that it makes me wonder if it is one he did when Amelia was a child. The thought fills me with both unbearable envy and thankfulness that, though she was not raised by me, my daughter was cared for and loved.

Lydie is almost comatose with exhaustion, so Alice and

Charlotte link arms behind her back, maneuver her over to the tub, and lower her into the water. A wave sloshes over the edge, and her submerging nightgown billows like a sail. Lydie sighs and smiles.

"Lydie," Thom says, "we're going to let your body rest here a moment, and then we want you to push for us, okay?"

A ghost of a smile flickers around Lydie's mouth, and then her pale face contorts as another contraction comes. But I am relieved to see her roused enough to feel the pressure. In all my years of midwifery, I have never seen someone become so docile when faced with such excruciating pain.

"All right," I say, stepping into the bathroom. "You ready to push on the next one, Lydie?" She nods, weak. Alice positions Lydie's feet against the foot of the tub, so they can give her leverage. "Take hold of your calves, then," I say, standing behind Alice and holding the lamp high. "That's right. Now, when the next contraction comes, we're going to count from one to ten. At one, I want you to take a deep breath and curl your torso forward and then slowly let the breath out while push—" Lydie's face darkens in a grimace. "This is it," I say, then begin: "One, two, three . . ."

Alice plunges gloved arms into water and chants, "Push, push, push," over my counting.

Lydie's pushing slackens when I get to ten. Alice listens to the baby's heart rate through the fetoscope and holds up a thumb and smiles in relief. Lydie groans softly. Tears leak from the corners of her closed eyes. Maneuvering around the sink, Charlotte spoons cool raspberry tea into Lydie's panting mouth. Sweat and steam condense on her forehead. Charlotte wipes this tenderly away. Lydie's breathing quickens. She turns from Charlotte and writhes. The water becomes tinted with blood.

"Here we go, Lydie," I call. "Another one. Big breath." She sucks in air, and her nose sharpens as her nostrils pinch down. "Good. Here we go: one, two, three . . ."

Alice chants, "Push, push, push . . ."

"Four, five, six—"

Lydie cries out.

I say, "Don't, Lydie. Put that energy into your push! Seven, eight—"

Alice says, "The legs are out—it's a boy!"

"What about an episiotomy?" Thom whispers beside me.

"No!" I cry. "She's got this!" Then to Lydie: "Okay, *ten*!"

Lydie lets go of her calves and sinks back against the tub.

"All right, Lydie," I say. "You're doing great. This next time you're pushing, I want you to reach down and touch your baby's legs, his tiny feet, and know that you can hold him soon."

I can feel Alice and Charlotte studying me, both skeptical and curious. Each of us midwives has our role, and mine has certainly never been the mollycoddling nursemaid. But there is no time to analyze the rebirth taking place inside my heart, as I let the anger toward the

Fitzpatricks die. There is not even time to take a drink of water before Lydie grits her teeth, takes a breath, and begins pushing without any of us counting her down.

Alice rearranges the towel beneath her knees and leans over the tub again. The lamp light shines on Lydie's wet braids and on the skin of willow bark oil covering the surface of the water. Lydie presses her lips together and curls her torso forward until the sodden bodice of her nightgown is perched over her knees. She expels a fierce breath through her nostrils.

"Slow it down, Lydie," I say, as I glimpse her baby's torso. "I know it's hard, but this is the part where we want you to go slow and easy. Slow and easy. That's it. Just keep up a steady pressure."

"Good girl, Lydie," Alice says. "Little pushes . . . little pushes." Hooking her fingers around one of the baby's shoulders, Alice pops it free and the other slides out. She turns to us and grins. "The shoulders are birthed."

Lydie is so tired that, even during the heightened pain of childbirth, she is fending off sleep. Her eyes remain shuttered as she reaches down to touch the baby's small shoulders and chest. A smile spreads across Lydie's face. As often happens when a laboring mother feels her baby's body for the first time, Lydie finds a reservoir of strength she did not know she possessed. She bears down hard—her face red, her eyes bulging—and expels the child's head in one protracted push, although there is no longer breath left to sustain *her*.

The infant is discharged into the water like an oddly

exquisite tadpole. The life source of the umbilical cord is still intact, and though Lydie has lost some blood in the delivery, the water is clear enough to see the boy-child open and close his eyes, searching out this brave new world. Alice's first reaction is to withdraw the child from the water, but Thom reaches out to stop her. "It's all right," he says. "Just let him get used to his new surroundings. There's no meconium present, so it's safe."

A few seconds pass before Lydie stirs and extends her arms toward her son. Alice draws him out of the tub. Water sluices off his womb-waxed skin and beads across the fair hair insulating his thin, newborn frame like fur. Alice lays him on Lydie's chest. Staring down at him, Lydie holds one of his fingers, and then kisses the top of his fine, round head.

"He's perfect," she murmurs.

I look over at Thom and see his green eyes are brimful with tears. Feeling my gaze, he turns and smiles with such bittersweet remembrance, I know that I can forgive him everything.

Amelia, 2014

My mom and I and Uriah and Looper are sitting on kitchen chairs we dragged onto the front porch at midnight. We're drinking weak tea from jelly jars and waiting to hear how Lydie and her newborn are doing. Looper has just stood to find out what's going on when Wilbur Byler rattles up to Hopen Haus and gets out of his passenger van.

He fumbles with his keys and drops them to the ground. Picking them up, he squints, trying to see us as clearly as we can see him. "How is she?" he asks.

Before we can say anything, the screen door smashes open. We all turn to look. Dressed head to toe in black, the head midwife, Rhoda Mummau, stands in the screen door's black mouth. One hand wraps her ribs and her other arm is extended; her pointer finger like a weapon aimed right at Wilbur Byler's heart. "You'd better get off my property," she says and draws in a shallow breath. "Right now. Or I'm calling the police."

"What are you talking about?" Wilbur says, but he's not stupid. He takes one step back.

"You know full well what I'm talking about."

Wilbur turns his head. The headlights light up his profile, showing the fat beneath his chin and making the tips of his ears—peeking from beneath his chopped brown hair—glow red. Then he makes a huffing sound and pockets his keys. He faces us again. "Do these people know what you've done, Rhoda?" he says. "Or should I say, *Beth*?"

Looper, who has remained standing since Wilbur's arrival, says, "Watch it," real low.

"Or what?" Wilbur laughs.

"Just mind yourself," Looper says.

Wilbur moves closer to the porch. "I don't have to mind nothing." For the first time, I can hear the slur in his words and see the wobbliness of his feet. Wilbur Byler's been drinking. He might even be drunk. "Rhoda's the one that has to mind herself," he says. "I know stuff that can throw her in jail faster than—"

My mom bolts from the kitchen chair like it's taken all her willpower to stay in the seat. She marches past me to stand at the top of the porch. "Sir, before you start accusing others, I think you should know that you're facing accusations and being investigated yourself." Pausing, my mom tucks hanks of blonde hair behind her ears. I watch her diamond studs sparkle. "Were you going to tell Rhoda about the money you've been embezzling from the communities?" she says. "The money you've been pocketing from the donations Hopen Haus has received?"

Wilbur just stares at her. His round face looks comical, lengthened by his gaping mouth. "That's what I thought," she says. "Now, the best thing that can happen for you and for us is to return the money you've stolen, go up to your little Canadian commune, and—" my mom snaps her fingers—"just disappear."

I look at my mom with the same mixture of awe and intimidation that Wilbur—and, I suppose, everyone else on the porch—is displaying. I don't even know this woman who could find the kindness to defend the same person who took her kid. And for one of the first times in my life, I am proud to be Meredith Fitzpatrick's daughter.

"We . . . we have money?" Rhoda finally asks.

My mom turns from Wilbur and faces the midwife. "Yes," she says. "McClintock's son made some calls after Wilbur contacted us yesterday and tracked down a woman who claims she made a sizeable donation after reading your story online—one that you all seem to have never received. McClintock went from there and found that not only has Wilbur been embezzling donations, but he's been siphoning off money the Dry Hollow Community has allocated for Hopen Haus and funneling it into his own account."

Hearing this, Ernest Looper steps down off the porch. Wilbur Byler holds up his hands, fingers splayed wide, and backs up three paces to his van. Keeping one hand at hip level, Wilbur fishes keys out of his pants pocket and opens his door. He climbs in awkwardly, not removing his eyes from Looper, and cranks the ignition.

Before the vehicle's interior light fades, Looper, my mom, Rhoda, and Uriah stand in a straight line in front of Hopen Haus and watch Wilbur place his arm on the passenger's-side headrest and crank the steering wheel hard to the right before shifting into reverse. His knobby tires spit gravel as he slams the gearshift into drive. The passenger van rockets down the lane. This is the fastest, I imagine, that Wilbur Byler has ever gone.

21

Rhoda, 2014

I stare out at the predawn light inching over the horizon and know that today's the day my daughter leaves me again. She and the entire household are still sleeping, but I have not slept. I have instead sat on this front porch for hours, praying and reading through Lamentations by lamplight in an effort to find solace in the suffering that I am, once again, having to endure alone. I skim over passages until I come to these verses in chapter three:

I remember my affliction and my wandering,
the bitterness and the gall.

I well remember them,
and my soul is downcast within me.
Yet this I call to mind
and therefore I have hope:

Because of the LORD's great love we are not consumed,
for his compassions never fail.
They are new every morning;
great is your faithfulness.
I say to myself, "The LORD is my portion;
therefore I will wait for him."

I lower the wick of the lamp until the circle of light covering the porch boards is barely distinguishable from the waning darkness. I close the onionskin pages of Fannie Graber's worn leather Bible, which she willed to me before her death, and pull it close to my heart.

"Yet this I call to mind and therefore I have hope," I whisper, evoking the sound of those words being uttered from between the ailing midwife's cracked lips. I remember how, crying, I clasped her knotted hand, refusing to relinquish her, though she was only waiting to go home. After my daughter's loss, I had vowed not to let anyone near me again. But somehow Fannie's gentle nature had torn down my every fortification, except for my ability to trust in the Savior she loved. However, now that she is gone, I know that though she had provided me with a refuge, she was never meant to be my sanctuary. My hope is found in God alone, and I cannot get through today's trials or tomorrow's triumphs without his supernatural strength to guide me.

In the past month, since I started rebuilding my life from the inside out, I have started to realize that love is not about holding on to someone, but about allowing someone to grow and change and loving them through this never-ending metamorphosis of life that—in the process—sometimes changes us too. Still, at times, it seems unfair that my daughter should leave my life just after I found her, and yet I know I should be grateful that I have found her at all.

The truth is, the daughter I loved and lost is still missing. Hope is as distant from me now as the day she was taken. But this does not mean that I cherish her memory any less. It means that to love Amelia the way she deserves, I have to relinquish the phantom child who has haunted my life for nearly eighteen years and allow this beautiful young woman to take her place.

The screen door creaks open and then shuts. Blinking, I turn and see Ernest Looper standing on the front porch, staring over at me. Steam rises from the mug in his hands. "Want coffee?" he asks.

I clear my throat, averting my gaze as I set Fannie's Bible beside the lamp. "No."

He pauses. I hear him blow on the liquid before taking a sip. "I know you're hurting, Beth," he says. "I also know that nothing can really help how you feel, but I have something that might take some of the pain away." I look up at him. He sets down the mug and, from his back pocket, takes out an envelope. "I could never really find the right time to tell you that . . . well, I didn't just come here to help you out." He swallows. "I made a promise to your mom that I'd get this to you."

Looper passes the envelope to me. Across the front, in shaky script I almost cannot recognize as my mother's aging hand, is my name: Bethany. It is not sealed. I flip out the tucked portion, my fingertips tingling with equal parts anticipation and dread, and begin to read:

Dearest Bethany,

I know you do not understand how I could have left you and Benjamin, and the older I get, I do not understand it myself. I kept thinking that I had to find a life beyond my family, but now I know that you and your brother and your father were my life. Without you all, I had nothing. It didn't take me very long to learn this, but I thought it was still too late when I did.

So I lived in Iowa and worked for many years. Your father and I only divorced five days before our silver anniversary. Right afterward, I moved from my apartment to the suburbs of Boston. Your father told me you were attending college there, and I wanted to be near you. I was hoping that, with enough time, you would forgive me and I would forgive myself, and that we could rebuild a relationship . . . if you would let me. And yet, two years passed and a connection between us was never made. I had found a job working as a nanny to a family in the university. But even though I saw you once— hurrying to class, your head down against the wind—I could not get up the nerve to approach you. I knew you had made it clear that you did not want any contact with us. I do not blame you for this; I only blame myself.

Then, a few months later, I saw your name in the newspaper and the story about your gestational surrogacy. I read how you had kidnapped the Fitzpatrick child in your very womb and wondered if the way I had abandoned you made you now not want to give that child up.

I went back to your university and visited your department. I met Dr. Fitzpatrick there. In the months following your sudden departure, I got as close to him as I could. I guess by doing so, I was hoping that eventually I would find you again. I had told no one about our connection. I had reverted to my maiden name, so no one would have guessed that we were mother and daughter. When Thom asked if I knew of anyone who could provide child care in a rather difficult situation, I asked if he would explain the situation to me.

Thomas Fitzpatrick then told me that the child you, Beth Winslow, had carried and kidnapped had been found in a Mennonite community in eastern Tennessee. He told me that he and Meredith were leaving in a week to bring the child back home, but that they both had to return to work after Christmas break, and they needed someone who could watch the child full-time. I hadn't even resigned from my former position, but I told Thom I would gladly accept the job.

I could tell the Fitzpatricks were nervous about

*becoming parents overnight, and the fact that I had
been a mother of two and a nanny for years seemed to
reassure them. Do not doubt that I can see the hypocrisy
in this. The Fitzpatricks asked me to fly to Tennessee
with them and their lawyer. I know it might anger
you to learn that I was their accomplice in a way, but
I wanted a second chance, Beth. I wanted to do things
over with you, and when I knew I couldn't, I thought
maybe I could do things over with your daughter.
Though she was not genetically yours, knowing that
you had loved her enough to run let me know that her
heartbeat thrummed in your veins. Through loving her,
I could begin again. I could love her the way I should've
loved you.*

"You read this?" I ask Looper, my voice hoarse.

He looks away from the yard but keeps leaning against
the porch post, sipping coffee. "No," he says. "I didn't
think I had the right."

I look back down.

*I saw you that day we came to Tennessee to take
your daughter—and their daughter—back. The
Fitzpatricks carried the child out to the rental car and
placed her like a bundled heirloom in my arms. She
was half-asleep and fragrant from her nap, and she
yawned and cuddled right against my chest as if she had
always been there. Thom and Meredith went back
inside to gather the rest of her things, and that's when*

you crossed the yard and looked at the car—and it seemed that you were looking right at me.

I could feel your eyes boring through the tinted glass and seeing the woman who had abandoned you holding tight to your child. I wanted to go to you. I hope you know this. I wanted to ask your forgiveness. But I was still too afraid. I could barely recognize you beneath your Plain clothes, and I could see in your bearing that you were stronger than before.

What if you hated me? You had every right. It was better not to know.

So I remained silent; I remained a coward. I locked the doors and kissed the child's warm forehead. I pressed my back against the seat and breathed. I watched you walk up those porch steps like a lamb to the slaughter. Inside the house, I knew, you would learn that you would never see your daughter again. . . .

I've had to pause in my writing. My strength is not what it once was and this story is so very hard to recount. But I want you to know the truth, Beth, and I expect that this disease will claim me before I can see you again. The only thing I can say in closing is that I have loved and raised Amelia as if she were my own flesh and blood, my grandchild, and through this love, I hope you can find the strength to forgive me for leaving you.

My love always,
Your mother, Sarah Graybill

I look up to glimpse the sunrise: a citrus peel of orange arranged behind two indigo mountain peaks. Pine branches tinseled in blinding fool's gold. As I stare at it, I can feel the promise of light on my face. *"His compassions never fail. They are new every morning."*

"You okay?" Looper asks.

Folding the letter, I slip it back into the envelope. I turn it over and stare at my mother's handwriting. I smooth the crease between the *t* and the *h* of Bethany, my given name. I imagine my mother in the hospital bed—dying of a disease that I, her daughter, cannot even name. I imagine an IV tethered to her shrunken vein as she doggedly wrote out this last will and testament of her undying love.

I close my eyes to keep from crying, but sorrow streams down my face unchecked.

In one day, I have found my daughter and my mother only to lose them both again. In one day, I have been both restored and crushed. But more than anything, I have learned the truth in the adage that there are two sides to every story. My mother did the best that she could with what she'd been given. And Meredith and Thom have loved, as best as they could, the daughter they took from me.

Just as Looper was wise enough not to mention my tears, he is wise enough not to repeat his question or respond to my unspoken answer: *I will be okay, but I'm not okay now.* Instead, he sets his mug on the step. Then he crouches down before me. His calloused hand wraps my own. My lifeblood stirs as he uses his other hand to tip my chin up toward his face. The two of us are altered by loss and by time—but the gentleness in his eyes remains untouched.

"Beth," he says, and my true name sings on his lips. "I want to be here for you. . . ." He swallows hard, turns my hand over, and traces a square thumb across the soft inside of my wrist. "I want to be here for you if you want me to stay."

I lean in toward Ernest Looper and rest my forehead on his shoulder. Closing my eyes, I can picture our child—our nameless, ageless son—sprinting through a strawflower field. His fair hair glints in between the blood-red cox-combs and golden dahlias just like the Risser children's had. Weightless, a homemade kite flutters through the air high above him, buoyed by hope, but anchored to this terrestrial ball by an angel-hair string.

"Stay," I murmur. "I want you with me and my Hopen Haus daughters. I want us to begin again."

Again, Looper says nothing, just folds me into his arms.

A flush sweeps Amelia's neck and cheeks when she comes down the landing and sees me standing here in front of the screen door, holding Lydie's son. The dynamics of our relationship have literally shifted overnight. She does not know how to proceed on this new terrain, and—honestly—neither do I. Amelia comes down the rest of the steps and rolls her suitcase to the door. Tears that used to fall so sparingly now rush to my eyes. Facing the screen, I hold the infant a little closer, grateful that my arms are not empty when my daughter is about to leave.

"Thank you for letting me stay," Amelia says.

I nod, too choked to speak.

From the corner of my eye, I watch Amelia look up the staircase for her parents, who have returned from the hotel to help her pack. She places a hand on her stomach, which barely shows the hint of the baby growing inside it. "Will you come to Boston when it's time?" she asks. "When I give birth? I . . . I want you there."

I hear someone descending the steps, the wheels of another suitcase clattering down behind. Reaching out, I place my palm against Amelia's smooth face. I close my eyes. My fingertips braille her skin like a plea. I open my eyes and say, "Amelia, I'd be honored."

Her smile looks so much like her father's. Adjusting her bag on her arm, she picks the suitcase up and catches the door behind her, so it won't slap shut and disturb the newborn, Alvin, who has fallen asleep again. Through the screen, I watch Amelia stride out to her car and stow the suitcase in the opened trunk. I can feel the warmth of Meredith's presence before I pivot to see her staring at me . . . staring at her daughter.

In the harsh morning light, Meredith's eyes look tired but calm. She steps closer, and the two of us—our bodies outlined by the frame—stand side by side. For the time being, our past is forgotten, and all we can focus on is the radiance of this young woman who has joined our disparate lives in love.

Meredith leans in. She cups the newborn's head before smiling sadly and popping the handle to the suitcase. I hold the screen door open for her, and she rolls Amelia's items over the threshold: a peculiar parallel of a horrific day that shall never be forgotten but now, at least, doesn't hold the same amount of sting.

Dr. Thomas Fitzpatrick is the last to leave. He balances two stacked laundry baskets of clothing in his arms. Setting them on the porch, he hands me a check. "Meredith and I want to say thank you, Beth," he says. "We owe . . . We owe you our daughter's life."

I open the check, and my mouth goes dry. "You're welcome," I say. "Thank you."

Nodding, Thom gathers the laundry baskets and plods down the steps. He finishes loading everything and climbs behind the wheel. The sun glints off the windshield as he shifts Amelia's car into reverse and Meredith follows in their rental car out the long, rutted lane. Holding Lydie's child close, I then watch my daughter being taken away for the second time.

Opening the screen door, I slip into Hopen Haus. Looper is slanted against a ladder while rolling a paintbrush on the newly repaired ceiling that now mirrors the smoothness of the sheet protecting the hardwood floor. Flecks of white paint speckle his silvering hair, letting me imagine how he will look when we grow old together . . . side by side. Feeling my presence, Looper turns and smiles at the image of me holding the sleeping babe. Then he looks up at the ceiling and continues working, but I can hear him hum. Smiling myself, I walk down the length of hall where—at the end—a mother waits for the return of her child.

And this time, I will let her hold him for as long as she wants.

This time, through the growth of that child and the children to come, a barren midwife's soul can come to life again.

EPILOGUE

Amelia, 2019

Staring through the driver's-side window, I press the brake and let my car idle on the lane. The small boy in a straw hat and black pants folded up to skinny shins continues swatting two fat ponies with a bamboo shoot a head taller than he is. The ponies shake their bridles. They kick their miniature heels and toss their manes, and then meet like outlaws once they believe the tiresome boy is past.

But the boy eventually manages to grab the ponies' bridles and lead them through the gate and down to the pond. The ponies snuffle the reeds and cattails at the pond's edge before lowering their heads to the water and drinking their fill. The boy takes off his hat and runs a hand through his wild red hair. Glancing behind him, he sees my car. His hat is in one hand and the bamboo shoot is in the other, the arc of it hanging over him like a fishing cane.

The curls and the fronds hide part of his face, but even from this distance, I can recognize him from the color of his hair alone. He's my birth son, Thomas Looper, whom I haven't seen since my college graduation five months ago.

Thomas's eyes narrow as he studies my new car, and then he looks at me, seated in the driver's seat. His freckled face brightens in this straight-across grin. "'Melia!" he cries. Jamming the straw hat on his head, he tosses the bamboo shoot and starts running. I jolt my car into park and sling open the door. I scramble across the dirt and rocks and awkwardly scale the split-rail fence.

"Thomas!" I call. "Look at you!"

He continues running to me—his growing-boy arms pinwheeling—and then we meet in the center of the sloping field. He latches to my waist and burrows there a moment. I hold him tight, feeling his heart beat against my stomach—a distant echo from when I carried him.

"Does *Mamm* know you're here?" he asks.

I take off his hat and ruffle his hair. "Not yet," I murmur. "Should we surprise her?"

He looks up and smiles. "Yes!"

Dropping the hat back on top of his head, I take Thomas's hand and help him over the split-rail fence to my car. "Can I drive?" he asks, as he asks every time I come.

"Of course." I slide the seat back and Thomas plops on

my lap. Shifting into drive, I tap the gas and Thomas steers the wheel. In the windshield's reflection, I watch him pinch his tongue between his teeth. His pale brows crease. The tires dig in and climb the lane. To our left, the Goods and the Martins have a clothesline snapped between their twin gray houses. From it, dresses and shirts deflate and then fill, deflate and then fill, like wind socks meant to trap the warm fall breeze. To my right, the orchard's branches are bowed low with harvest. If I squint, I can see the bees landing on the Red Delicious apples already ornamenting the ground.

The bottom land's being worked by a dozen or so members of the community, who began to return after the farmer Walt Hollis died and the land he purchased from them went up for sale again. Each time I come, more horses and buggies are clattering down Dry Hollow Road, more houses are being refurbished, and more parcels of land are being turned into self-sustaining farms. I can see acres of Rox Orange sorghum, which Dry Hollow Community is becoming known for, ready to be reaped and cooked.

One line of men—with heavy beards and forearms—slices through the base of the cleaned sorghum cane with scythes that glint with continual, synchronized motion. Behind them, another line gathers and lays the cane bottom first, so the pieces won't jam up the mill. The women gather the cane into sheaves of five, and then tote them like wheat over to the horse-drawn mill that is a few yards from the cooker. The mill's lifted off the ground by a stout wooden base. The year I came to Hopen Haus on fall break and participated in Sorghum Day, Rhoda explained that the base is inspected before and after each squeezing, as the weight of the mill is immense and must withstand the force of the turning log, propelled by the horse that drives the connected pole around the mill.

"Let's go!" Thomas begs, pulling on the steering wheel. Sorghum Day does not hold the same excitement for Thomas as it does for me.

Laughing, I touch the gas, and we make our way to the top of the hill. I place my arms around Thomas's and guide him to a stop in front of the hitching post, next to two horses and buggies. Parking, Thomas and I get out. I almost lock the doors before remembering where I am. Smiling, I toss my keys on the seat and close the door. The horse with the blaze turns her head at the noise and twitches her silken tail, but she can't see me because of her blinders. I swat flies away and scratch her neck. I haven't been around farm animals since the summer after my junior year when Rhoda encouraged me to come and stay at Hopen Haus.

It was the summer I delayed an internship so I could spend time with my birth son, whom Rhoda and Looper had just officially adopted. It is bittersweet, recalling that time when love, for me, meant not holding on to someone but letting him go until I could find out who I was. And though I've since healed from the aftermath surrounding my unique beginning, I know allowing the Loopers to adopt Thomas was the right decision . . . for all of us.

Breathing deep, I take Thomas's hand and walk toward the front door of Hopen Haus. It is as if I'm on the set of a film I've already viewed. Even my movements mimic those I've already made—making me feel like I live in the skin of the girl who came here, to Dry Hollow, five years ago, and maybe every girl who has or will ever come. I'm amazed at the work Looper has put into the property. Two new brick chimneys jut from the tin roof. Below the ten windows, painted flower boxes spill yellow Mirabelle blooms. A shower of hummingbirds zigzags through the air. They are fighting over the glass feeders brimming nectar that hang near the replaced woodwork trimming the house. A treated split-rail fence hems in the grounds.

Still holding Thomas's hand, I climb Hopen Haus's steps and knock on the screen door. I rock on the sockets of my hips, wondering if I've made a mistake. I have no real plan for being here. I certainly don't want to join the church or take up the Mennonites' Plain lifestyle. I just know that Hopen Haus needs a new midwife since Charlotte's passing last year, and I can apprentice under Rhoda until I finish my nursing degree in Nashville. I'm just about to knock again when the door opens. A dark-haired woman with a strapless white apron tacked to a dark dress stands in a square of light beamed in from the window beside the door. Her eyes infused with kindness, she looks me over and smiles. "Hello, my *meedel*," she says.

"Hello, Rhoda."

The midwife steps out onto the porch and pulls the screen door behind her. Without a word, she wraps her arms around me—her starched apron crackling against my chest like parchment—and pats my back. I lean on her tall frame. I'm sure our embrace looks strange to anyone watching. But I don't care. Five months have passed since I've seen my birth mother, and I hope this hug can make up for lost time.

"Now," Rhoda says. She releases me but keeps holding my shoulders. With one hand, she touches my cheek. "You need somewhere to stay?"

Before I can answer, Thomas wiggles in the spot between our conjoined bodies, holding us together, keeping us from pulling apart. "Look!" he crows. "We make a circle!"

Yes, I think, smiling at the midwife, whose eyes are bottomless wells of love. *A circle by birth and blood.*

A NOTE FROM THE AUTHOR

I have always heard that the most heartfelt novels are those drawn from personal experience. My daughter was twelve weeks old when I began writing *The Midwife*. Staring at her perfect, delicate fingers wrapped around one of my own, I struggled with the need to protect her in our fallen world. I believed that overcoming fear with faith—by placing my trust in my daughter's Creator rather than in my abilities as her mother—was the real-life experience that I would have to learn, and therefore apply to my main character, Rhoda Mummau, as well.

Little did I know that, fifteen months later, my own faith would be tested as one of my worst fears came true: I miscarried a child. But I do not care for that term, *miscarried*. I was more than just a carrier, a means to an end. For those ten weeks of my too-short pregnancy, I became a mother of two. My firstborn, toddler-age daughter . . . and, I believe, a boy—my son. I imagined tall, bookend children with their father's straight-across grin and sparkling hazel eyes. Instead, on a black, drizzling night, my husband and I found ourselves burying our secondborn next to a cedar-rail fence.

The days after were hard—and yet, even in death, life goes on: laundry needed folding, diapers needed changing, tomatoes needed gathering from the garden before the incoming frost. I took long walks with my daughter and spread petals from the rosebush across my son's grave. After a harvest celebration, I kissed my infant nephew's cheek good-bye, and then continued cleaning up the detritus of our evening meal when suddenly I had to go lie down, realizing that kissing my nephew was the closest to kissing my son that I would ever come on earth.

My publisher kindly granted an extension on my editing deadline for *The Midwife*. But writing, for me, has often been more of a catharsis than a job. Therefore, in the mornings, I peeled back the covers, went out to the living room, and turned on the computer. As I stared through the French doors at the ember sun rising over the valley, I could suddenly see the midwife Rhoda's loss through another grieving mother's eyes. I wept with her as I reread scenes that my own fingers had typed, but that now felt like something God had devised as he portended my loss and knew that this story would bring healing to my own soul.

One week after we lost our baby, I was standing in church when the worship team began reading passages from the Bible. A few recited promises that I had long ago memorized at the urging of my parents or my teachers.

And then one man started reading from Lamentations, a book I had read but that had never spoken to me before: "I remember my affliction and my wandering; the bitterness and the gall. I well remember them, and my soul is downcast within me. Yet this I call to mind and therefore I have hope: Because of the Lord's great love we are not consumed, for his compassions never fail. They are new every morning; great is your faithfulness. I say to myself, 'The Lord is my portion; therefore I will wait for him.'" (Lamentations 3:19-24, NIV)

Hearing those words, I closed my eyes and felt the warmth of the sun slanting through the kaleidoscope of stained-glass windows. Tears began streaming down my face, unchecked. It may sound strange, but I knew those verses weren't only meant for me, but for the midwife Rhoda, as well, who feels as real to me as anyone I have ever known. Then I realized that those verses weren't only meant for us grieving mothers; they were also meant for my readers who have suffered loss. And haven't we *all* suffered loss, in one form or another?

And so I pray that the midwife's story will remind you—even in your darkest nights and most broken places—that whenever you call to mind the Lord's great love, you will find healing and hope.

Turn the page for an excerpt
from Jolina Petersheim's bestselling debut,

THE OUTCAST

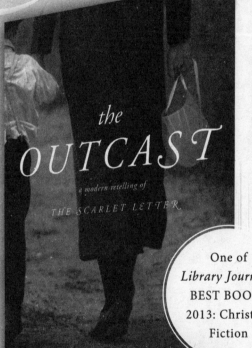

One of
Library Journal's
BEST BOOKS
2013: Christian
Fiction

1

My face burns with the heat of a hundred stares. No one
is looking down at Amos King's handmade casket because
they are all too busy looking at me. Even Tobias cannot
hide his disgust when he reaches out a hand, and then
realizes he has not extended it to his angelic wife, who
was too weak to come, but to her fallen twin. Drawing
the proffered hand back, Tobias buffs the knuckles against
his jacket as if to clean them and slips his hand beneath
the Bible. All the while his black eyes remain fixed on me
until Eli emits a whimper that awakens the new bishop to
consciousness. Clearing his throat, Tobias resumes reading
from the German Bible: "'Yea, though I walk through the
valley of the shadow of death . . .'"

I cannot help but listen to such a well-chosen verse,

despite the person reading it. I feel I am walking through the valley of death even as this new life, my child, yawns against my ribs. Slipping a hand beneath Eli's diapered bottom, I jiggle him so that his ribbon mouth slackens into a smile. I then glance across the earthen hole and up into Judah King's staring, honey-colored eyes. His are softer than his elder brother Tobias's: there is no judgment in them, only the slightest veiling of confusion not thick enough to hide the pain of his unrequited love, a love I have been denying since childhood.

Dropping my gaze, I recall how my braided pigtails would fly out behind me as I sprinted barefoot down the grassy hill toward ten-year-old Judah. I remember how he would scream, *"Springa! Springa!"* and instead of being caught by Leah or Eugene or whoever was doing the chasing, I would run right toward the safety of base and the safety of him. Afterward, the two of us would slink away from our unfinished chores and go sit in the milking barn with our sweat-soaked backs against the coolness of the storage tanks. Judah would pass milk to me from a jelly jar and I would take a sip, read a page of the Hardy Boys or the Boxcar Children, and then pass his contraband book and jelly jar back.

Because of those afternoons, Judah taught me how to speak, write, and read English far better and far earlier than our Old Order Mennonite teachers ever could have. As our playmates were busy speaking Pennsylvania Dutch, Judah and I had our own secret language, and sheathed in its safety, he would often confide how desperately he wanted to leave this world for the larger one beyond it. A world he had explored only through the books he would purchase at Root's Market when his father wasn't looking and read until the pages were sticky with the sweat of a thousand secret turnings.

Summer was slipping into fall by the time my *mamm*, Helen, discovered our hiding spot. Judah and I had just returned from making mud pies along the banks of the Kings' cow pond when she stepped out of the fierce sun into the barn's shaded doorway and found us sitting, once again, beside the milking tanks with the fifth book in the Boxcar Children series draped over our laps. Each of us was so covered in grime that the jelly jar from which we drank our milk was marred with a lipstick kiss of mud. But we were pristine up to the elbows, because Judah feared we would damage his book's precious pages if we did not redd up before reading them.

That afternoon, all my *mamm* had to do was stand in the doorway of the barn with one hand on her hip and wag the nubby index finger of her other hand (nubby since it had gotten caught in the corn grinder when she was a child), and I leaped to my feet with my face aflame.

For hours and hours afterward, my stomach churned. I thought that when *Dawdy* got home from the New Holland horse sales he would take me out to the barn and whip me. But he didn't.

To this day, I'm not even sure *Mamm* told him she'd caught Judah and me sitting very close together as we read from our *Englischer* books. I think she kept our meeting spot a secret because she did not want to root out the basis of our newly sprouted friendship, which she hoped would one day turn into fully grown love. Since my *mamm* was as private as a woman in such a small community could be, I never knew these were her thoughts until nine years later when I wrote to tell her I was with child.

She arrived, haggard and alone, two days after receiving my letter. When she disembarked from the van that had brought her on the twelve-hour journey from Pennsylvania to Tennessee, she walked with me into Leah and Tobias's white farmhouse, up the stairs into my bedroom, and asked in hurried Pennsylvania Dutch, "Is Judah the *vadder*?"

Shocked, I just looked at her a moment, then shook my head.

She took me by the shoulders and squeezed them until they ached. "If not him, who?"

"I cannot say."

"What do you mean, you cannot say? Rachel, I am your *mudder*. You can trust me, *jah*?"

"Some things go beyond trust," I whispered.

My *mamm*'s blue eyes narrowed as they bored into mine. I wanted to look away, but I couldn't. Although I was nineteen, I felt like I was a child all over again, like she still held the power to know when I had done something wrong and who I had done it with.

At last, she released me and dabbed her tears with the index nub of her left hand. "You're going to have a long row to hoe," she whispered.

"I know."

"You'll have to do it alone. Your *dawdy* won't let you come back . . . not like this."

"I know that, too."

"Did you tell Leah?"

Again, I shook my head.

My *mamm* pressed her hand against the melon of my stomach as if checking its ripeness. "She'll find out soon enough." She sighed. "What are you? Three months, four?"

"Three months." I couldn't meet her eyes.

"Hide it for two more. 'Til Leah and the baby are stronger. In the meantime, you'll have to find a place of your own. Tobias won't let you stay here."

"But where will I go? Who will take me in?" Even in my despondent state, I hated the panic that had crept into my voice.

My *mamm* must have hated it as well. Her nostrils flared as she snapped, "You should've thought of this before, Rachel! You have sinned in haste. Now you must repent at leisure!"

This exchange between my *mamm* and me took place eight months ago, but I still haven't found a place to stay. Although the Mennonites do not practice the shunning enforced by the Amish *Ordnung*, anyone who has joined the Old Order Mennonite church as I had and then falls outside its moral guidelines without repentance is still treated with the abhorrence of a leper. Therefore, once the swelling in my belly was obvious to all, the Copper Creek Community, who'd welcomed me with such open arms when I moved down to care for my bedridden sister, began to retreat until

I knew my child and I would be facing our uncertain future alone. Tobias, more easily swayed by the community than he lets on, surely would have cast me and my bastard child out onto the street if it weren't for his wife. Night after night I would overhear my sister in their bedroom next to mine, begging Tobias, like Esther beseeching the king, to forgive my sins and allow me to remain sheltered beneath their roof—at least until after my baby was born.

"Tobias, please," Leah would entreat in her soft, high-pitched voice, "if you don't want to do it for Rachel, then do it for *me*!"

Twisting in the quilts, I would burrow my head beneath the pillow and imagine my sister's face as she begged her husband: it would be as white as the cotton sheet on which I lay, her cheeks and temples hollowed at first by chronic morning sickness, then later—after Jonathan's excruciating birth—by the emergency C-section that forced her back into the prison bed from which she'd just been released.

Although I knew everything external about my twin, for in that way she and I were one and the same, lying there as Tobias and Leah argued, I could not understand the internal differences between us. She was selfless to her core—a trait I once took merciless advantage of. She would always take the drumstick of the chicken and give me the breast; she would always sleep on the outside of the bed despite feeling more secure against the wall; she would always let me wear her new dresses until a majority of the straight pins tacking them together had gone missing and they had frayed at the seams.

Then, the ultimate test: at eighteen Leah married Tobias King. Not out of love, as I would have required of a potential marriage, but out of duty. His wife had passed away five months after the birth of their daughter Sarah, and Tobias needed a *mudder* to care for the newborn along with her three siblings. Years ago, my family's home had neighbored the Kings'. I suppose when Tobias realized he needed a wife to replace the one he'd lost, he recalled my docile, sweet-spoken twin and wrote, asking if she would be willing to marry a man twelve years her senior and move away to a place that might as well have been a foreign land.

I often wonder if Leah said yes to widower Tobias King because her selfless nature would not allow her to say no. Whenever she imagined saying no and instead waiting for a union with someone she might actually love, she would probably envision those four motherless children down in Tennessee with the Kings' dark complexion and angular build, and her tender heart would swell with compassion and the determination to marry a complete stranger. I think, at least in the back of her mind, Leah also knew that an opportunity to escape our yellow house on Hilltop Road might not present itself again. I had never wanted for admirers, so I did not fear this fate, but then I had never trembled at the sight of a man other than my father, either. As far back as I can recall, Leah surely did, and I remember how I had to peel her hands from my forearms as the wedding day's festivities drew to a close, and *Mamm* and I finished preparing her for her and Tobias's final unifying ceremony.

"*Ach*, Rachel," she stammered, dark-blue eyes flooded with tears. "I—I can't."

"You goose," I replied, "*sure* you can! No one's died from their wedding night so far, and if all these children are a sign, I'd say most even like it!"

It was a joy to watch my sister's wan cheeks burn with embarrassment, and that night I suppose they burned with something entirely new. Two months later she wrote to say that she was with child—Tobias King's child—but there were some complications, and would I mind terribly much to move down until the baby's birth?

Now Tobias finishes reading from the Psalms, closes the heavy Bible, and bows his head. The community follows suit. For five whole minutes not a word is spoken, but each of us is supposed to remain in a state of silent prayer. I want to pray, but I find even the combined vocabulary of the English and Pennsylvania Dutch languages insufficient for the turbulent emotions I feel. Instead, I just close my eyes and listen to the wind brushing its fingertips through the autumnal tresses of the trees, to the trilling melody of snow geese migrating south, to the horses stomping in the churchyard, eager to be freed from their cumbersome buggies and returned to the comfort of the stall.

Although Tobias gives us no sign, the community becomes aware that the prayer time is over, and everyone lifts his or her head. The men then harness ropes around Amos's casket, slide out the boards that were bracing it over the hole, and begin to lower him into his grave.

I cannot account for the tears that form in my eyes as

that pine box begins its jerky descent into darkness. I did not know Amos well enough to mourn him, but I did know that he was a good man, a righteous man, who had extended his hand of mercy to me without asking questions. Now that his son has taken over as bishop of Copper Creek, I fear that hand will be retracted, and perhaps the tears are more for myself and my child than they are for the man who has just left this life behind.

ABOUT
THE AUTHOR

Jolina Petersheim is the bestselling author of *The Outcast*, which *Library Journal* gave a starred review and named one of the best books of 2013. *The Outcast* also became an ECPA, CBA, and Amazon bestseller and was featured in *Huffington Post*'s Fall Picks, *USA Today*, *Publishers Weekly*, and the *Tennessean*. Jolina's sophomore novel, *The Midwife*, also taps into her and her husband's unique Amish and Mennonite heritage that originated in Lancaster County, Pennsylvania. They now live in the mountains of Tennessee with their young daughter. Whenever she's not busy chasing this adorable toddler, Jolina is hard at work on her next novel. She blogs regularly at www.jolinapetersheim.com and www.southernbelleviewdaily.com.

THE MIDWIFE
Reading Group Guide

INTERVIEW
WITH THE AUTHOR

Did you always aspire to be a novelist, or did you have other options on your career shortlist?

Every kid goes through a spell of wanting to be a nurse, doctor, or veterinarian. I was certainly no different and yearned to deliver babies and/or mend hurt animals. With my mother's help, I raised a piglet, owls, turtles (snappers and painted), kittens, and a slew of abandoned baby birds that never survived the fledgling stage. Looking back, I think their immediate demise had something to do with the watered-down orange juice I fed to them through a dropper.

Then came the seismic shift in my future career: I entered third grade and started doing long division. My brain fizzled at the sight of so many numbers, which were all necessary for any kind of medical degree. I countered my arithmetic phobia with books—oodles and oodles of books. I fell in love with words even more after discovering my dislike, nay *hatred*, of numbers. In sixth grade, I used my journal with the tiny gold lock to record my first novella and—even during my brief stint in college, trying to become the next Katie Couric—have ever since been trying to perfect the novel form.

What was the most surprising thing that happened once your first novel was published?

One of the occupational hazards of working from home is that I am often in my bathrobe at eleven o'clock in the morning. That morning was no different. I knew I couldn't leave the nursery without being seen through the glass front door, but I didn't want the person to continue knocking and awaken my daughter who was drifting off to sleep. So I popped the collar of my bathrobe and walked right out.

The UPS man waved at me through the glass. I was relieved and promptly opened the door. I signed his clipboard, and he slid the box of books from my publisher across the hardwood floor. Then he asked if he could purchase an autographed copy for his wife's birthday. My jaw about dropped, but I just closed the door and sprinted upstairs to fetch a copy. I signed it on the lap of my bathrobe and passed the book to him. He passed me back the correct change, waved good-bye, and bounced down the lane in his big brown rig. That was certainly my most surprising experience!

Was the process of writing your second book any different from writing your first?

I'd just found out I was expecting when I started writing

The Outcast, my debut. I began writing *The Midwife* when our bouncing baby girl was twelve weeks old. So I went from writing for eight hours a day to writing whenever my daughter could be cajoled to sleep. Sometimes it felt nearly impossible to take care of her—my precious little insomniac—and the house, and still work on my novel.

The silver lining during that trying ten months of sleep deprivation is that it taught me to write whenever I got the chance. It didn't matter if I was feeling inspired or if there were crumbs on the floor and dishes in the sink. When my sweet child's eyes closed, it was time to grab my laptop and delve into Dry Hollow's world. Not only was writing *The Midwife* one of the most challenging things I've done, it was also one of the best. I am so glad I had that creative outlet to pour myself into. At the end of the year, I not only had a little girl who (mostly) slept through the night, but a completed novel. I will take that over a spit-cleaned house any day.

Where did you get the idea for this story? Do you usually start with a scene, with plot, or with characters?
My closest friend in college had a heart transplant when she was fifteen. Because of the antirejection medication she was taking, she knew that when she married her fiancé, she would be unable to carry his child and mentioned using a gestational surrogate when it was time to expand their family. I thought often about the complications of such an undertaking: What if the surrogate became attached to the baby she carried? What if something was wrong with the

child? What if, God forbid, one of the biological parents died?

I mulled over the concept of surrogacy for many years. But it wasn't until the birth of my own daughter that I knew that if she'd swum inside my womb and received sustenance from my body—even if she was of no genetic connection to me—she would indeed be my child. I would do *anything* for her, even if that meant going against the law. In the end, when I began writing *The Midwife*, the surrogacy thread became more of a tapestry of what it means to be a mother: genetics or love.

Is Fannie Graber based on anyone you've met? What about any of the other characters?

I researched both of my novels without realizing I was doing it. For *The Outcast*, I learned about a bone marrow transplant by watching my best friend receive her eight-year-old brother's bone marrow at Vanderbilt Medical Center in Nashville. For *The Midwife*, I read two books by Ina May Gaskin—a phenomenal midwife who was one of the forerunners of a hippie commune in Summertown, Tennessee. She is now in her early seventies and known throughout the world for her competency in the midwifery profession, even if some people disagree with her unorthodox methods.

I never got to meet Ina May, but Fannie Graber's gentle nature and physical characteristics are based on her. In writing some of the birthing scenes in *The Midwife*, I also drew on my experiences with the midwives at a birthing center where I'd hoped to have my daughter. Unfortunately, I ended up at the hospital, but even then the midwives stayed beside me. If we're blessed with another child, I would like to visit The Farm in Summertown, Tennessee, and see if it's a place I could give birth with Ina May Gaskin as my midwife. Who knows? Maybe she would even let me interview her in between contractions!

How has your Mennonite background shaped your writing? Did you always intend to write about Mennonite culture?
I never thought I would write about my Mennonite heritage because I was just too close to view it objectively. It wasn't until someone told me a true story about an affair that had rippling effects throughout an Old Order Mennonite community that I began to see a different spin on the quintessential "bonnet fiction" genre. I have witnessed firsthand that the Plain people are not a utopian society but struggle with the fallibility of man that affects the rest of us. I have combined this viewpoint with my experiences of living in a Christian community for eight years as an adolescent.

I am vastly intrigued by what pulls a community together and what tears it apart and how this convergence of separate belief systems affects the families locked within the community's confines. So far, I believe this combination has created its own niche, since I use a story to explore the intricacies of community rather than using a community merely as the setting for a story. I will write these narratives for as long as they come to me and aren't forced.

You have used somewhat unusual storytelling techniques in both of your novels. In The Outcast, *one of the POV characters is, in fact, dead; and in* The Midwife, *the chronology is fractured. Why did you choose this technique for* The Midwife *in particular?*

The Midwife is told through two perspectives: Beth Winslow and Rhoda Mummau. These two separate narratives help divide the timeline and add tension as the stories overlap and the reader understands where the action of both is headed. I like to begin my story by knowing the characters' destinations, but the journey is always fraught with its own twists and turns. Oftentimes, I am as surprised as the reader; this makes the novel very fun to write!

Are there certain themes you hope to weave into all of your stories?

I like to address topics that intrigue me in everyday life: What hidden strengths and weaknesses will erupt in a community when the families inside it are placed under physical or emotional duress? Then I take these families to the very brink of themselves and help them find healing and redemption through a deeper relationship with their Creator, which also leads to deeper, healthier relationships with each other.

What are you working on next?

A dystopian novel set in a community in Montana that addresses the Mennonite belief of pacifism, even when faced with losing one's life.

DISCUSSION QUESTIONS

1. One of *The Midwife*'s main themes is learning to trust God, even after our worst fears come true. How does Rhoda's spiritual journey progress throughout the story? At what point does it falter? Does this remind you of your own spiritual journey? Why or why not?

2. *The Midwife* is told mainly through two viewpoints: Beth's and Rhoda's. Though they are actually one and the same, what differences do you see in their responses to hardship? What caused the change?

3. Rhoda loves her estranged mother almost to the same extent that she despises her. Have you ever had a family member who incites this kind of response in your heart? If so, how do you work through those feelings?

4. Have you ever had a family member or friend pass away before significant issues between you could be reconciled? How would you feel if you received a letter from them like the one that Rhoda receives from her

deceased mother? Would you welcome such a letter
or not? Why?

5. Though Rhoda is a responsible head midwife, she
rejects any medical advancement because she fears that
modern technology, such as electricity, will illuminate
the secrets of her past. In what ways does your past
thwart your ability to move forward? Is there ever a
time when it's okay not to "move on"? If so, how can
you discern and identify such times?

6. Hopen Haus's derelict state could be seen as a symbol
of Rhoda's and Amelia's broken spirits: their facades
don't look as bad as their lives' crumbling foundations.
In what ways do we portray that we have everything
together? In what ways do cultural forms, such as social
media, encourage this facade?

7. *The Midwife* is filled with relationships between
mothers and daughters, both through birth and
through circumstance. In a way, the midwife Fannie
Graber is a surrogate mother to Beth, just as Beth
is a surrogate mother to Amelia. Who has been like
a mother to you? Do you feel like this relationship
adds or detracts from the one with your birth mother?
Why?

8. Could you see yourself serving as a gestational
surrogate like Beth (no genetic connection), or a
traditional surrogate like Mary Beth Whitehead (the
child genetically half yours)? How do you think the

challenges—physical, emotional, and otherwise—would be different for surrogates in each of these methods?

9. Do you think that surrogacy should be legal? If so, do you think a surrogate should get paid for her services? Why or why not?

10. If you were a gestational surrogate like Beth, and the parents were contemplating terminating the pregnancy, how would you respond? Would you also run with the child, or do you believe that the parents retain the rights since you have no genetic connection? What rights should a surrogate have in such a scenario?

11. Do you think it is morally wrong for Beth to accept Thomas Fitzpatrick's money when she knows she isn't going to keep her promise to terminate the pregnancy? Do two wrongs ever make a right? Why or why not?

12. Do you think it's safe for midwives to deliver babies at a facility like Hopen Haus without a doctor presiding over them? Why or why not? In "real life," do you think Hopen Haus would be shut down for its primitive conditions?

have you visited **tyndalefiction.com** *lately?*

YOU'LL FIND:

- ways to connect with your favorite authors
- first chapters
- discussion guides
- author videos and book trailers
- and much more!

PLUS, SCAN THE QR CODE OR VISIT **BOOKCLUBHUB.NET** TO

- download free discussion guides
- get great book club recommendations
- sign up for our book club and other e-newsletters

TYNDALE FICTION

Are you crazy for Tyndale fiction? Follow us on Twitter **@Crazy4Fiction** for daily updates on your favorite authors, free e-book promotions, contests, and much more. Let's get crazy!

CP0021

8-14